Chase

A novel of America in turmoil

By
William Allison

Copyright © 2006 by William Allison

ISBN 0-7414-3375-3

Published by:

PUBLISHING.COM

1094 New DeHaven Street, Suite 100
West Conshohocken, PA 19428-2713
Info@buybooksontheweb.com
www.buybooksontheweb.com
Toll-free (877) BUY BOOK
Local Phone (610) 941-9999
Fax (610) 941-9959

Printed in the United States of America

Printed on Recycled Paper

Published October 2006

To Penelope,
whose warm embrace nurtured book and author
through the long journey.

Acknowledgments

This novel is the product of research conducted with the support of many persons and institutions. The list includes:

- Maine: Calais Public Library, Calais Town Office, Downeast Heritage Center, St. Croix Historical Society, Washington County Court House Records Room and Probate Office, Maine State Archives, Maine Law and Legislative Library, Offices of the Maine Legislature, Camden Public Library, Camden Town Hall, North Haven Historical Society, Maine Historical Society.

- Washington D.C.: National Archives

- Hawaii: Lahaina Restoration Foundation, Lahainaluna School, Hawaiian Historical Society, Hawaii State Archives, Hawaiian Mission Children's Society, Lahaina Historical District.

- Massachusetts: New Bedford Whaling Museum, Kendall Institute, New Bedford Public Library, Captain Haskell's Octagon House.

- Family: Deepest thanks to my wife, Penelope Allison, who patiently listened to many chapters. Thanks to Helen Mitchell Spring, who knew the generation born from the generation who knew George and Harriet.

- Friends: To the Radnor Writers' Group who sustained interest in the project over three years, carrying me over the rough spots.

Foreword

Chase is historical fiction, based on the life and writings of George Monroe Chase (1806-1855) and Harriet Norwood Chase (1811-1893), whose love story carried them from Camden and Calais in Maine to Maui Island in Hawaii. Their lives embody the vast changes in American society before the Civil War.

The novel reflects the real deeds and thoughts of George and Harriet. Original sources include George Chase's speeches, discovered in a trunk, written in his own hand. Other traces of their lives are lifted from Maine newspapers, county records, and census reports.

Some public records left more personal information such as friends' testimony in State Department archives. Chase left a rich trove in official dispatches while consul on Maui Island, but those records comprise only the dry skeleton of the tale.

The story's vitality rises from private family legend, recorded in *These Were My People*; a family history by Helen Mitchell Spring, great-granddaughter of George and Harriet Chase.

The novel portrays several historical persons, including Salmon P. Chase, Ralph Waldo Emerson, Roger Taney, Frederick Douglas, Dwight Baldwin, David Malo, and Harriet Tubman. Fictional characters – a Hawaiian nobleman, a slave girl, an emancipated African-American, scoundrels, Quakers, priests, preachers, and whaling crews - round out a romantic epic of pre-Civil War America in turmoil.

Chapter One

"Man overboard!"

The pilot spun the wheel. The sail luffed, and the schooner slowed in the ocean trough.

"Where?" shouted crewmen, loosening the lifeboat.

"Off starboard," the pilot craned around to point. "The boom knocked over our passenger. See 'im anywheres?"

"Hold on there. Whataya doin'?" a crewman yelled.

A teenager, stripped of shirt and knickers, balanced atop the rail. He dove long to emerge ten yards on a rising swell. Heavy kicks, butterfly strokes, the swimmer disappeared beyond wave crests.

"Get that boat off," skipper ordered. "Follow the boy, afore I lose 'em both."

Crewmen scrambled to smack the lifeboat on the marbled-green surface. Six men pulled oars where the helmsman pointed.

"Damn slight chance the fool's alive," grumbled a rower. "Jest like a landsman ta' get drown on his maiden voyage."

The helmsman glimpsed the pair, an ashen face gripped by one mahogany arm, while the other arm stroked toward the boat.

"Pull to port," the helmsman called. "Harder, lads. Steady. Now, ship those oars. Henry, grab his jacket, and heave 'im aboard."

Sailors lifted a young man's limp body over the gunwale and onto the boat's floor, face up. His rescuer sprang into the lifeboat and shoved shipmates aside.

"Paul, fix 'em."

"No use, boy. He's a goner." They shrugged and slumped back.

The dark youth, robust body glistening with seawater, moved over the drenched passenger. He flipped the body and lifted to squeeze the man's chest with thick arms. Water drained from sodden mouth and nose. Satisfied, he propped the body face up against the boat's side and gripped the face.

"Hey, what's he doin'?"

The boy knelt and covered the man's mouth with full lips. His muscular chest heaved as he blew air down the inert lungs while hands pressed the rhythm of breath. The man sputtered and gagged. The rescuer released him to struggle alone.

"Spirit come back. Not need my breath. Paul cold. Take us to ship."

"Never saw nuthin' like it," the helmsman grunted. "To the oars, men. Quick, quick. Don't want our delicate passenger to catch his death of cold."

Skipper and crew lifted the man, clad in damp suit, aboard the two-masted vessel. His eyes swam loose, and his nose ran phlegm. They stretched him out on the deck.

"Best let the heathen see to him, capt'n. The boy's a fish in water, but no Christian ever used such unnatural practices ta' bring the dead back to life."

Crew carried the groggy passenger along passage-ways and flung the body onto the berth. The swarthy youth followed. He unbuttoned the man's trousers, jacket, and shirt, peeling off the soaked clothing, but, when he tried to remove underclothes, the man resisted.

"'No good wet. Be dry or be sick, boss."

Pushed away, the boy sat on the edge and looked around the cabin. Blankets lay atop a trunk. Removing one, he discovered a bottle of rum, partly drunk.

*   *   *

"Captain, I must register a complaint. I woke from a nap to find my berth damp, my clothes scattered wet upon the floor. Furthermore, someone's pilfered an object from my cabin. You have a thief aboard."

The schooner rolled and yawed as it ploughed through heavy seas. Chase braced against jolts and shutters, holding to a rail. The Captain's eyes never left the rigging, but his mouth formed a terse smile.

"Have ye no memory of yer misadventure, Mister Chase?"

"Misadventure?"

"The pilot believes the boom struck ye and pitched ye ass over tea kettle into the Gulf a' Maine. Ship's boy saved ye and conjured ye back to life. Do ye recall none a' this?" The Captain's head swung around, and his eyes trapped Chase.

"God in Christ, man. That accounts for my rasping throat and a taste of salt."

"Watch yer language, Mister Chase. I allow no blasphemin' aboard this God-fearin' ship. To the point, ye owe the lad a debt of gratitude. I'll call 'im up from the galley." He gestured to a crewman.

In moments, Chase saw a large figure bound up the companionway, shoulders touching the narrow passage. Closer, the figure became a man-sized youth with a reddish-brown complexion. Thick hair, straight and black, extended in a braid below the shoulders.

"Yes, Cap'n," he said, remaining a respectful distance below the two men.

"Paul, I've called ye ta meet Mister George Chase, the passenger ye saved."

"Paul hurt you? Most sorry. Fight 'tween water and life. Water angry, fight back, but life win." A bright set of teeth grinned at Chase.

"Yes, you and water had it out over my rib cage, sore as that is, young man. I suppose I owe you thanks for the heroic effort. My parents would have been distressed at my passing, and my future employer would have wondered at my absence. Paul, is it?"

"He okay?" Paul asked the skipper.

"Mister Chase, English ain't Paul's first language. Speak directly ta' the lad. Yes, Paul, he's okay."

3

"By the way, young man," Chase halted the departing boy. "Something disappeared from my cabin. You have it?"

"Bottle of rum? Paul take and throw into sea. Now boss not fall off ship."

Chapter Two

All afternoon, they passed a scatter of islands, some settled, some rookeries. To the west, coves and harbors dotted the headlands as the schooner turned north into Penobscot Bay. Chase watched the bow's wake, hoping to catch sight of schools of dolphins. He almost hated to see his first voyage end.

An island blocked the schooner's passage as the pilot headed the bow away from the Bay's shimmering reaches into a settlement. The island hovered over its harbor like a mother hen. As the vessel passed into the channel, the town of Camden opened like a bowl. Chase scanned the steep sides.

Hills rimmed the bowl's crest and peaked with a mountain that cast a shadow upon the water. On the slopes, porches and widow walks of stately homes faced the harbor. A jumble of shacks surrounded the docks.

The schooner slowed to land against town wharves. Moorings dotted the harbor with a mixture of watercraft. Three-masted vessels rigged with square sail vied with two-masted with fore-and-aft sail.

"Ships, sloops, schooners, barks, brigs..." Chase mumbled.

He hadn't a clue which was which and fewer words for the variety of small boats. Long and slender skiffs moved like water sprites, oar tips dipping. Others were so broad that men, dressed in slickers, labored on separate oars, rowing loads of fish and lobsters.

Beyond the bustle of the harbor were industries – sail making, rope walks to winding hemp into rigging, and warehouses. On town outskirts, ship carpenters labored on framed skeletons in great sheds.

The whole of Camden leaned to the sea.

"Need box carried, boss?"

Paul, the ship's boy, came up behind Chase.

"Yes, but I know not where. Carry the trunk. I'll carry the satchel of papers."

Chase and Paul dove down the companionway. While the youth wrestled the heavy trunk, the man stopped to check his appearance in the cabin's mirror.

Dark hair oiled down, he adjusted a beaver hat and brushed lint off the shoulders of his black wool suit. He checked the shine on his black boots and tugged the cravat's knot.

On the dock, the two threaded their way past cargo on the harbor's plank walkways. Townspeople stopped to watch the pair, a bear-sized barefoot youth and a gentleman in a business suit. One-handed, Paul balanced the trunk on his thick shoulder.

"I hope I am not taking you away from your duties," Chase offered.

"Paul tired of ship. Time for land job."

"You mean to abandon ship?" Chase turned.

"Okay with captain. Crew spooked by Paul. Where we go? Can't carry this all day, boss" He leaned the trunk against a brick wall.

Chase caught the attention of a young woman bearing a parasol.

"Miss, would you please be so kind as to direct us to the law office of Ezekiel Kent?" She pointed toward the town common. Paul shoved off the bricks and strode forward.

Chase hurried to catch up.

"What's your tribe, young man? Wampanoag, Narragansett?"

The youth turned to face him.

"No Indian. *Kanaka Maoli.* Hawaii; grandson of great King Kamehameha." He slapped his chest and continued walking. Chase followed.

"*Hawaii*," Chase tested the word. "In the South Seas, the Sandwich Islands, discovered by Captain Cook? Ah, yes, here's the office now."

Chase offered his hand. "Paul, you carry yourself like a gentleman. Just bring that thing inside and you're on your way." He reached for the knob.

*   *   *

Ezekiel Kent sat at his desk, back to the office windows. Ambient light over his shoulder shone on the ship contract. *"The said owners of the ship "Fortune" do commission Captain Wm Norwood....."*

As Kent read, it was his habit to stroke his shiny bald head, spectacles riding on the end of his nose, slouched in the office chair, papers held high to capture the natural light, small grunts rose from his throat at significant passages in the text.

Kent's office faced Elm Street. Light flowed onto the room's two desks and a long worktable. An oriental carpet covered wide planks. At the doorway, a rough hemp mat lay for the convenience of clients with muddy boots. At the back of the office, beyond the natural light, shelved books comprised the law library. A small fire flared in an iron stove.

A girl of fourteen studied at the table. Texts spread, she wrote carefully on a notebook's lines, eyes shifting between pages. A bright ribbon held her hair. A foot kicking within long skirts belied the studious pose.

The lawyer's little expressive grunts halted at the sound of the doorknob. Entering first was a pale young man, outfitted in professional business garb, shoes polished like a black mirror. He was followed by a swarthy youth in a mariner's outfit, bearing trunk and canvas bag.

The young man strode across the floor, hand extended.

"Good day. I am Mister George Monroe Chase, Esquire. May I assume you are Mister Ezekiel Kent?"

"Ah, yes, Mister Chase, welcome to Camden. You've arrived as expected." The elder shook with both hands.

Chase turned to include his companion.

"Allow me to introduce Paul. This young fellow saved my life by retrieving me from a cold watery tomb and saved you the trouble of hiring another junior partner."

Chase clapped the boy's shoulder, and Paul extended his hand.

"Interesting," said Kent, hand remaining at his side. "Have you tipped him?"

Chase opened the office door to usher Paul outside. "Excuse us for a moment."

"Friend want no tips." The boy's brown eyes glowered. "Good-bye."

"Wait, stop. You want a land job? Come back at six o'clock for supper. We talk about work and a berth," promised the young lawyer. Paul nodded and walked away.

Chase returned to the law office where Kent introduced the girl. She curtsied.

"My daughter, Penelope, is studying Greek in preparation for Portland Female Seminary. "

The girl's face flushed.

"What would you be translating, Miss Kent?"

"Plato's *Republic*," she answered.

"Allow me," said Chase, and he leaned over the text. "Do be careful when encountering *agape, philos, and eros*," he said. "We mistake to translate them all as "love." The Greeks had many words for our poor little, overworked word, *love*."

Penelope held her breath until the two resumed discussion about Mister Chase's position when she interrupted, "Father, may I walk home to help Mother?"

"Certainly, my child. Please tell her to plan for another person at supper, if Mister Chase will join us."

"May I postpone the visit until tomorrow evening? I best establish quarters before nightfall."

"Absolutely right, but now let us finalize our partnership contract."

Penelope darted off, but she had no intention of walking directly home. Tying bonnet and gathering up skirts, she sprinted down Elm Street, soon to arrive at the Norwood home.

She entered the front door without knocking.

"Harriet, Harriet," she called to her cousin.

"Whatever is it, child?" Aunt Deborah emerged from the kitchen.

"Oh, Auntie, tell me where Harriet is."

"Pen, up here." A voice called from the second floor balustrade.

Penelope mounted the stairs, two at a time, skirts aflutter. Deborah Norwood returned to the kitchen, shaking her head.

Harriet Norwood caught her cousin's hands and drew her into a bedroom. She sat on the canopy bed while Penelope took the loveseat. The girl glanced around at the young woman's exotic décor, souvenirs of her father's China trade. On one wall hung a tapestry of strange birds and on the floor lay a colorful carpet.

"Come to the office to meet Mister Chase, Father's new junior partner. You would like him right away. Just wait till you see his clothes, and he even knows all the words for *love* in Greek."

"Words of love in Greek? What kind of man is…never mind. You know I can't just appear. How would that look? Besides, I am already afflicted by too many young men. What is one more?" She waved a hand.

"This one is different, different from all boys on Penobscot Bay. You shall see."

          *   *   *

Ezekiel Kent and his young partner remained at the office until evening. Kent began the young lawyer's education with arcane details of maritime law and ship terms.

"You can't call them all 'ships', Mister Chase. That word applies only to ones with three masts – the fore, the main, and the mizzen, all rigged square. A bark has fore-and-aft sails on her mizzen, like a schooner. A brig has two masts, but when the mainmast has fore-and-aft sails, she's called a hermaphrodite brig."

Chase scribbled notes.

"Did you note the wide ones, rounded at the bow?" added Kent.

"Yes, they look filthy."

"Whalers are grimy with smoke and oil and stink up the town in an east wind. But, it's those vessels that light America." Reminded by the fading sun, he lifted a lamp's glass chimney, carried a taper from the fire, and lit an oil-soaked wick. Then, he reached for a book.

"Here's a manual. There are 131 terms to learn just for spars and rigging. Now you can see why mariners call their apprenticeship, 'learning the ropes'."

Turning to politics, Kent inquired, "I assume you are a 'Jackson' man?"

"Yes, I uphold the ideals of the Democratic party."

"Politics convivially received in Maine. We had enough of the Whigs when we were part of Massachusetts. May I suggest a means of introducing you to the community?"

"Say on."

"The selectmen asked me to give the main address at the Fourth of July; however, I am averse to public speeches. If you were to speak as the preeminent orator at the festivities, the public would have an opportunity to evaluate the new lawyer in town and you would relieve your senior partner of an odious duty," Ezekiel Kent smiled.

"Tell the selectmen I shall be prepared by July Fourth." George Chase replied.

Chapter Three

Above the door swung the tavern's sign; the familiar profile in silhouette – hawk-nose, firm jaw, and hair braided in a short queue. The General Washington Tavern catered to ship and harbor men with hearty fare for the weather-worn. A blast of tobacco smoke and steam met Chase as he pulled open the door.

"Follow me, lad." Calling back to Paul, he charged through the crowd, aiming for a distant table, but when he reached for a chair, he stood alone. His young companion remained at the entrance caught by a crowd.

"Hold on. What's the trouble?" Chase walked back.

"This here's a proper establishment, mister," the barkeep answered. "We serve white only, no savages. Ya haf to take that boy outta here."

The crowd muttered agreement.

"Where in Camden can a gentleman be served?" Chase argued.

"Gentleman? We got no objection 'gainst gentlemen," the barkeep explained.

"This young man is a prince in his own country, the grandson of a king in Hawaii, which is to say, a gentleman," Chase smiled at the barkeep.

"He kin pose as the king of Siam, fer all I care. He ain't ta be served in the Gen'ral Washin'ton, lessen he's some…"

"Some? Come on man, speak up," Chase demanded.

"Lessen he's servant to some gentleman 'sponsible fer his conduct."

Chase turned to the crowd. "I am George Chase. You and your employers will encounter me as the new partner of Ezekiel Kent, Esquire. Paul is my manservant. He goes where I go and where he's sent. I shall expect him well treated in Camden's streets and businesses. Come and sit, Paul."

Paul probed his milky chowder, lifting bits of onion, potato, and cod with a spoon.

"Manservant? What's this work, boss?" A cloud of steam rose from the bowls. Chase concentrated on the food, a tumbler of punch at his elbow.

"A figure of speech, my boy."

"Finger a' speak?" Paul's eyebrows squinted.

"A way to talk. Look around us," Chase leaned forward and lowered his voice. "You stand out in this town so we give you a place, 'manservant to a gentleman.' Not a stranger. Something these people can understand. By the way, what's your surname?"

"What's that?"

"Family name. You are Paul what?" Chase's hand made a rolling motion.

"I...Paul Kamehameha, grandson of the Great..."

"Yes, the Great Kamehameha, who did what exactly?"

"He George Washington of Hawaii. After *haole* come, he pull nation together."

"*Haole*?"

"You people, whites." He pointed. "Paul no servant. Paul *ali'i,* a chief."

"Then, you must have a job worthy of a chief. What work before the sloop?"

"First class seaman. The whaler *Saratoga.* Maui to New Bedford. We catch many baleen, fill barrels with oil." He slapped his broad chest.

"Good. I just learned that a whaler's being refitted all winter and signing up crewmen right here in Camden. Perhaps they need skilled labor. I say, you take up rooms with me until the whaler sails in spring."

The boy nodded.

Chase leaned back and hailed the barkeep. "Send over two rum punches, my man, to seal a bargain."

"Boss already drink two." Paul pointed at Chase's tumbler.

"The second one's for you, my lad, now that we're cordial companions." Chase stumbled to his feet, hand offered.

"Demon rum never pass Paul's lips. Paul pledge to missionary," he said, jaw set.

"Just my damned luck to sign on with a temperance man." Chase plopped back into his chair. "Ah, well, perhaps 'tis best. Who knows what Providence ordains for us both?"

*   *   *

Settled into the second desk, George Chase checked every jot and tittle of a shipping contract. The effects of the breakfast coffee worn off, his stomach growled. He welcomed interruption when Paul entered the office.

"Oh, boss, I come back when not busy." The boy backed up, his bulk filling the threshold.

"No, come right in, Paul. Sit a while." George shoved a cane-bottomed chair toward the tanned youth. "How's that whaling ship coming along?"

"That why I come, Mister Chase. She ready by spring. All hands getting orders, and I not like mine."

"So, you've come to a lawyer. Litigation between a captain and crew over your portion of the value of the oil, what's the correct term?"

"No, not the *lay*. On Maui, I sign on as *greenhand,* but make *seaman* before we reach New England. I'm good enough for *boatsteerer,* to harpoon whales. Maybe even good enough 4th *mate,* to be *officer.*"

"You're too young, Paul. Can youths rule over other seamen? What is your age?"

"Sixteen, I think, but I good enough." His raven queue wiggled as he shook his head.

"You may speak a native kind of English but can you read?" Chase leaned back and clasped hands behind his head...

"Give me newspaper. Listen: 'William Higgins, Printer, of Portland, reports a runaway apprentice. Irish boy, freckled, blond hair, blue eyes, answers to the name, Shamus O'Donnell. Two dollars reward for boy's return.'" Paul read woodenly. "I read six years at Lahainaluna Academy, English and Kanaka. I write, too."

"Show me your script. Copy that advertisement." Chase shoved pen and inkwell across the desk. The black pen disappeared into the boy's massive fist. Artistic loops emerged in a line across the page, 'William Higgins, Printer, of...'

Chase sat upright. "Enough, enough. That's legible for my purposes. So, this captain holds you from advancement? It's plain narrow-mindedness. Would you be willing to accept an offer elsewhere?"

"Who? Do what?"

"Me. I need an assistant for business in shipyards and lumber mills. I can't take time to run around. I assume you sail small vessels and can run paperwork up and down the Bay. It's much responsibility, but also much freedom. Does that appeal?

"Don't know, boss. Maybe."

"Come on, lad. With your advice, Kent and Chase will purchase a seaworthy sloop for you to sail. What do you say, is it a good deal?"

"What is job's name? No chief can be *servant*."

"You will be my officer, called a *steward*, like the Good Steward in the Bible."

"I tell captain to keep job. If I can't be 4th mate at sea, I'm *steward* on land."

Chapter Four

Town council commandeered Camden's commons with a latticed pavilion, festooned with red, white, and blue bunting. Flags with 24 stars hung on either side of the podium. A band played tunes from the Revolution and the War of 1812 as the crowd assembled on the green. Places of honor were accorded for ancient men, dressed in remains of uniforms and tri-cornered hats. *Sans* sight, *sans* teeth, *sans* hearing, the last vestiges of the Revolution hobbled to seats.

Girls in light dresses clustered among the benches. Harriet Norwood, her cousin Penelope, and friends sat at the back of the crowd, close enough to hear yet far enough to be inconspicuous. Each one sat under a splash of color in a parasol's shade.

Under the pavilion, George waited his turn while judging the crowd. Ladies chattered. Children skipped between relatives. Each orator would have to earn their respect. The mayor rose to introduce the main speaker.

"We have the honor today of hearing from one of Camden's newest lights. I would like to introduce to you today, Mister George Monroe Chase, Esquire."

George rose from the gallery of speakers and strode to the podium, a sheaf of papers in his hand. Penelope nudged Harriet.

"He's the one I told you about," she whispered.

Fellow Citizens, while you honor me with your attention, permit me to express my fears that your expectations of my services will not be realized. Should this be the case, I will successfully plead by apology before an indulgent audience.

He removed his beaver hat and placed it on the side table. He smoothed down his high sweep of black hair.

Need I ask the occasion of our meeting this day July Fourth, 1832? Why this assembly of people? Is it to celebrate the birthday of some prince? The coronation of some monarch? Or the death of some tyrant? Why this commixture of high and low? This fellowship of rich and poor? This union....

His voice rose... ***of bond and free?***

People clapped.

Harriet examined his costume. Jutting up to his chin and surrounding his neck was a winged shirt collar. A maroon cravat flared up to the knot.

A waistcoat covered the waist of George's trousers, which rose above his hips, held by lacing. The trousers, made of black calfskin, revealed the wearer's trim figure. Finally, the trouser legs tapered over his calves to end at the black shoes, polished and laced above the ankles.

The 23-year-old Harriet usually prided herself with tart judgment on most public speeches, but this one could be different.

Are the instruments of war awakened from this slumber of peace and safety in every part of our territory, to speak the terrors of alarm? No. We have met to commemorate the Sabbath of Liberty. The aged warrior on this approach of this day shakes off the drowsy habit of decrepitude and comes forward to receive the honors and gratitude of his nation.

George gestured to the Revolutionary veterans.

The middle aged quits the gathering of worldly acquisitions and goes forth to celebrate the birthday of his country and Independence with as much zeal, sincerity, and joy as the religionist gives to the duties of his altar. Even the youth, before the lullaby of the cradle, ceases to vibrate upon his ear, feels his bosom warm with patriotism and leap with joy. Such is the celebrity of the fourth day of July.

Harriet joined the crowd in spontaneous applause at the mention of the holiday.

Adhering to the principle recognized as well in English jurisprudence, that the right of taxation is vested in the people, we became obnoxious to British indignation; and the inalienable rights of man were about to be lost to a hardy, toil-worn people who had knelt before their Mother Country till their rustic dignity was ashamed, or that people, few in number, scarcity in resources and undisciplined in war, must rise and prepare to meet the invincible arms of Great Britain.

A breeze blew from the harbor into the Camden commons. George's hair was lifted and blown above his collar as he leaned toward the crowd.

We were proud to call her Mother and while we cherished this affection, it was with sorrow that pervades the youth's first lesson, when he lends a faltering hand to seal the parting with a mother that we dissolved the tie. He heard the Vulcan of British vengeance forging the chain of Slavery – a premonition of his certain fate, he saw his duty inscribed upon the monument of his country's independence.

Harriet remained transfixed while her cousin clapped at every phrase, shrieking, "Just listen to those words, so...so fantastic!"

Dragged to the Fourth of July celebration, still she had dressed well. A wide bonnet framed her face, ties hanging lose across her chest. Her green poplin dress, gathered in pleats at her shoulders, exposed her bosom with a low bodice. Below the bodice, the material drew to a high waist.

She caught Penelope eyes, smirking at her rapt attention. Little did the girl know Harriet's heart thumped, and her head swam. Her brow and armpits grew damp, and the poplin dress stuck to her skin.

It was on the banks of the Mississippi that the veterans of the great Wellington with the haughtiness of invincible warriors raised the standard of their many victories. It was there they found an enemy indefatigable in his exertions, masterly in his plans, and a Leonidas defending the pass to the liberty of America, Jackson, the hero of New Orleans.

Britain will long remember the fatal conflict. Her soldiers and statesmen, while they dazzle the world with the éclat of their victories, will spread the blanket over their wounded pride as the trump of fame shall sound the name of Jackson.

To the delight of the crowd, Chase shouted in full volume and pitch:

*To us, Fellow Citizens, this country is now committed to hand down its Liberties to our Children as our Fathers handed them to us, that if invasions should be made from without, the peace disturbed or our rights and institutions violated from within, there is a nerve sleeping in our very arm that will awake at the sound of danger **and Woe! To him that wakes it!***

The audience burst into applause and rose to its feet. All but Harriet. She crouched down. The muscles in her lower body tingled. She regained control and forced herself to stand.

"Come and I'll introduce you to Mister Chase, Harriet. Everyone is congratulating him," the girls laughed, bouncing in place. Avoiding Penelope's eyes, Harriet turned away and fought against the stream of faces. Upon reaching the edge of the commons, she walked home to change clothes.

Chapter Five

Winslow Norwood and George Chase walked through the great shed. Winslow showed George the naked frame so his lawyer would grasp the clipper project. Only a skeleton of braces, the hull seemed oddly narrow and long.

"Picture a ship capable of cutting through water faster than any ship in all history. The eight months it takes to reach Oregon will be cut in half with speeds of four hundred miles per day," claimed Winslow.

"But, won't paddle steamers overtake clippers?"

"Perhaps in time, but now clippers will dominate the trade between China and Oregon for many decades until those experiments stabilize," he explained.

Returning to the law office, George and Winslow drafted the contract, in familiar nautical terms. Although weak on shipbuilding, George realized that Winslow knew little about lumber, a key element of the industry. George would negotiate better prices and smoother materials delivery.

The clock struck six before they finished.

"Come home with me for supper. Mother is always prepared for a guest. We can finish business in the parlor." Winslow invited George to the Norwood home.

The two men entered the house to be greeted by Deborah.

"Oh, Mister Chase, having heard your performance on the Fourth, I am so pleased to make your acquaintance. Pardon my husband's absence. He captains his ship on a return voyage as we speak."

She called up stairs, "Harriet, we have a guest."

A head of curls bent over the balustrade, "Who's to supper tonight?"

"'Tis Mister Chase, hurry down. The meal is almost to table."

The head withdrew, and steps were heard. George turned and caught the sight of the young woman proceeding down the staircase, eyes focused on the treads. George failed to avert his eyes.

A cool evening, Harriet's ivory, muslin dress was full-sleeved to her wrists, flared at her upper arms, bodice close to her throat. The waist began just below the bosom. Such fashion, meant to enhance a small-figured woman, was unnecessary on the well-proportioned Miss Norwood.

Below the waist, the dress fell loosely to an embroidered hem. An apron of the same design and material complemented the front. Each step revealed an ankle. George drank in the sight, hoping her brother didn't notice the indiscretion.

Family and guest sat around a large teakwood table with matching chairs. Generous dinner plates, cups, and saucers were decorated with a glazed blue on white design. Exotic birds frolicked among mulberry trees. Heavy cloth napkins lay to the left of each plate under long-pronged, silver forks. To the right were pistol-handled knives and soup spoons.

Seated opposite, Mother Deborah carried conversation, irritated that her normally loquacious daughter sat silent, addressing the visitor only when necessary. Winslow and George discussed business until they withdrew to the parlor for brandy and pipes.

"Tell me about your father's China trade, Winslow."

"The family comes from seafaring people, George. It's in our blood, his father a blockade runner in the Revolution. Our father began to work the coast on a sloop at twelve, trading with the West Indies by sixteen. He made his first voyage around Cape Horn before Mother and he married in 1804."

"Does she not mind the long absences?"

"Mother's family also worked the sea from North Haven Island, so she knew what to expect. Trade can make captains wealthy. Twenty-five years ago, father traveled in nothing more than a sloop around Cape Horn through the

Pacific, up to Vancouver Island. There, they brought iron tools and British cloth to Indians, trading for sea otter pelts and lumber which they took to Whampoa by way of Hawaii."

"Whampoa? A strange sounding place."

"An island on the Pearl River in the Guangdong Province, near the city of Guangzhou, what we call Canton. All trade with foreigners is confined to Whampoa so the Emperor can control influence from "white" nations, it being their bias we are 'barbarians.'"

"Amusing. Chinese see us as 'barbarians' while we see them as 'heathen.' So, what are the sea otter skins to the Chinese, and what does he receive in exchange?"

"They make coat collars, gloves, and coats for the Mandarin nobles. Tonight, we dined on plates and sat at table and on chairs all made by Chinese craftsmen. Father, voyaging home now, is expected within the month."

*   *   *

The next Saturday, the Young Men's Society of Belfast sponsored a barn dance, which Ezekiel Kent encouraged George to attend.

"Take my buggy. Good to see a young man meet proper company."

George arrived late. The caller and fiddle were just finishing a robust selection. George entered and started for the refreshments when he recognized Harriet Norwood, standing among the crowd.

Her hair was arranged in ringlets, held by a yellow ribbon, her cheeks rouged, eyes penciled. Six young men hovered around her. George could hear them competing for clever remarks. Harriet laughed at their comments, but none asked her to dance.

Harriet separated herself from the men and walked to the refreshments. George made his approach, along the length of the table of food and drink.

"If we were to dance, would you dare speak with me tonight?" he asked.

Without raising acknowledgement, she slowly poured a half glass of cider. "Only if you speak on things other than old ships and arcane contracts, Mister Chase."

Chapter Six

George Chase began to call weekly on Harriet Norwood. Mother Deborah found room to include the young lawyer in family gatherings. Every time he arrived, Missus Norwood greeted him at the door, except for one night in January.

The wide door opened, and the portal filled with a heavy figure. The gentleman wore a dark, blue broadcloth suit, fixed by brass buttons. His broad shoulders were matched by a hearty girth, a full white beard, and a head of yellow curls.

"George Chase?" he asked, as his beefy hand pumped the young man's. "I am Captain Norwood."

"Glad to make your acquaintance, sir. Is Miss Harriet at home?"

"In the parlor with her mother, young man." The captain accompanied George into the room. He took his upholstered chair next to the stove while Chase sat beside Harriet.

"I hear you've joined Ezekiel Kent as a partner, Mister Chase. Has he much business with local shipbuilders?" the captain inquired, lighting his pipe.

"You know Cousin Ezekiel does, William. Why do you ask Mister Chase?" Deborah Norwood interrupted.

"Only curious as to the young man's familiarity with that side of the business," he returned.

"Indeed, the captain's correct in that I'm still learning the maritime business. My background is closer to the lumber industry." George explained.

Harriet concentrated on a cross-stitch project, pretending to ignore the men's conversation.

*   *   *

After George departed for his rooms, captain and wife found themselves in familiar chairs, stove embers aglow. Deborah sat in the loveseat next to her handwork. After the captain had stirred the fire, he sat back in the wingchair, pulling on his pipe.

"Young George seems to have made an impression on our Harriet," Captain Norwood began.

"He's been welcome in this house for several months. Good manners, proper speaking, well-dressed. The town, selectmen to pastors, considers him the future of Camden, maybe a senator or governor," she explained.

Whale oil lamps lowered, heat from the Franklin stove warmed the room. The captain propped the stove's door open. Light flickered around the walls.

"A good family? We ought to know his breeding before our daughter takes to a parvenu." Smoke blew puffs into the air.

"Cousin Ezekiel knows George's father from Dartmouth, class of 1793. That's how he's come to Camden. It's an old family, same as ours, but from Vermont and New Hampshire, inlanders. His father is a judge. Chases are even spread to Ohio where one cousin, Salmon, is a lawyer who champions fugitive slaves. Finally, his grandfather, Major Epaphras Bull, died fighting at Yorktown. Could the family have any better credentials, husband?" She put down her sewing and surveyed the captain's expression. "What the matter, William?"

"All right, all right, Debbie, that's enough. You've done a thorough job checking the young man's background. I ought to be happy that our Harriet's finally overcome her fussiness and found a man to her liking. I only hoped she'd chosen someone different," he whispered. The captain tapped the ashes from his pipe.

"Who different?"

"No one in particular, but a man more like our kind of people, close to the sea."

"A fisherman like your nephew Israel?" She laughed.

"Naw, someone worthy of her like a ship master, an owner, a captain." Norwood stood and stretched.

"Marry a man like her father? The girl has her own mind, William. Be happy she's found a lawyer." Deborah put away her sewing.

"Oh, well, you're right, I should be satisfied. By twenty-three, any girl's overdue for marriage."

*   *   *

The Belfast Gazette
January 6, 1834

Notice

Captain and Missus William Norwood announce the wedding of their daughter, Miss Harriet Green Norwood, to Mister George Monroe Chase, Esq. of the firm, Kent and Chase of Camden, Maine. Ceremony to be held at the bride's parent's home on July Seventh, one thousand eight-hundred and thirty-four, Reverend Emanuel Weathersby of Camden Congregational, officiating.

*   *   *

One night in February, George lingered to court Harriet in the parlor, while her father read his newspaper by lamplight. He rose to check his barometer. "'Tis true! My bones feel the change. We'll be getting some weather tonight, I predict," he said.

The evening wore on with conversation and Faro cards until the hall clock toned eleven times. George rose and apologized to the parents for allowing the hours to pass.

"The pleasure of your company makes time pass quickly, my boy," Harriet's mother soothed his concern. But, when the captain brought George to the door, they realized that a blizzard covered the ground with thick snow. Harriet peeked out past them.

"It's been snowing, Mother. It's too deep for George to walk. He'll be lost on the way to his rooms. He must spend the night."

"William, is that so?" Deborah called from the kitchen.

"I suppose. I'll fix a pallet on the parlor floor," the captain suggested.

"Heavens, that's hardly adequate. Fetch the bundling board from the cellar." She passed the others in the hallway and turned up the stairs.

"You mean...her bed?" The captain pulled the pipe from his mouth. "Is this...proper?"

"They're engaged, husband."

As the parents arranged their daughter's room, George and Harriet changed in separate locations and emerged in flannel nightgowns. Deborah bustled about with blankets. When the captain appeared carrying a pine board, she directed him to light a fire in the bedroom's hearth.

George and Harriet lay a foot apart, watching her parents arrange the room. Deborah drew up a single quilt to the couple's chins.

"There you are." She smiled. "Now, William, snap in the bundling board."

The captain leaned over George to fit a one-inch plank into grooves on the bed's head and foot. Their eyes met as the piece clicked into place.

The parents wished the young couple 'a good night' and left the room, closing the door. Harriet and George lay, alone, separated by an inch of unvarnished pine.

The fire warmed the air and bathed the walls in a golden glow. The two rested silently on their backs, adjusting to an abrupt intimacy. Harriet first broke the hush.

She laughed. "We've never been alone."

"Yes. I believe you're right. It feels rather odd, don't you think." He answered.

"Until the wedding, it may be our only time alone."

"Your parents respect our privacy in the parlor so we may talk."

"We've only just kissed and held hands. Don't you think it's a silly custom to keep couples so demure, especially when they plan to marry?"

George cleared his throat. Dim firelight sparkled on the walls. She persisted.

"Are we not betrothed? Surely, Providence has blessed our affection. I hunger for a foretaste of bliss, the reward of a happy marriage. How could a lady venture, except thorough her fiancé?"

She heard a rustle and felt George's hand on her face. She reached and kissed the palm as he stroked her cheek, ear, and hair. His hand played with the edges of her hair and probed her ear.

Harriet reached across the board and touched his face in the twilight. His eyes watched her from the pillow.

"Oh, I am so happy to have found you," she said.

"I love you, dearly, Harriet."

Stroking his cheeks and hair sleek against his head, she drew his hand down to her bosom, drawing back strings and offering herself. His hand came alive from her grasp and delved for the firm flesh.

Courage rose as her interest caught fire.

She pulled George's hand from breasts down into her smooth recesses. At last, the rapture surged through her body, and she sank back into the feather pillow.

But, soon Harriet propped herself on an elbow and looked into George's face.

She reached over the plank, but George thwarted her hand.

"I fear my seed will spill onto the bedclothes, stark evidence of our intimacy."

"Trust me. No one else shall see any 'evidence,' Counselor Chase."

She pulled off her pantalets and wrapped them about George's member.

"I shall wash them myself."

George could hardly believe his good fortune to find a wife with such pluck.

27

Chapter Seven

George walked from the law offices of Kent and Chase, through the green lawn of Camden's commons, past the Episcopal Church. Sun warmed the air, and birds played among the new green leaves in the park's trees. He strode across oyster-shelled Elm Street, through a brass-framed door into Camden Bank. The white marble counter reflected light from broad windows. The gray marble floor, lightly sanded, scraped under his leather soles.

Like a church, the bank gave off an air of solidarity, cool and rational even on the hottest summer's day. Like a church, banks caused people to speak in hushed tones, as if commerce had some divine weight. Bank managers reckoned a customer's financial worth as a pastor might measure a parishioner's moral value. That morning, the clerks, like acolytes, glanced up from ledgers at the young lawyer entering their sanctum.

George reminded one he had an appointment with the bank manager.

"Mister Kenworthy is occupied. Please have a seat," was the response.

George sat, pulling papers from his leather satchel to review the details of the whaler contract, a full 532-tons burden, on speculation for a Massachusetts' owner. The whaling industry in New Bedford, grown beyond its capacity, knocked on the doors of Maine shipyards.

As the agent for the contract, George would be due a clear five percent. Any bank should be eager to join and finance the capital. Tucking the papers back into the satchel, he examined his shoes.

"I need two new pairs before the July wedding," he thought. One would be for the office and the other for the ceremony. Marrying the daughter of William Norwood, wealthy captain and hero of 1812, bore some costs, but every pretty picture had its price. He had proudly written to his parents of the beautiful fiancée and his prospects at Camden.

"Mister Kenworthy will see you now," the clerk whispered.

George followed him into the paneled offices at the rear of the bank and entered where the portly Kenworthy occupied a high-backed chair. The bank manager offered no hand in greeting.

"Have a chair, Chase," said Kenworthy as the clerk slipped out. "I've been reviewing your papers regarding the whaling ship contract and I have some questions."

"Yes, sir," Chase sat forward.

"Your financial reputation is rather patchy, isn't that so, Chase?" Kenworthy peered over his glasses, with a reptilian gaze.

"I've a solid portfolio, sir, with mortgages on several properties in the town, and you know my regular habit of saving. I have a tidy sum in this bank."

"Ah, yep, and you're owed some back rent, but can't collect, I hear," his voice trailed off. "Have you collateral? Does your father own property, Chase?"

"A great deal. Houses, land, mills."

"And just where is this property?"

"In Vermont."

"Not Camden, not even Maine? Hard to assess from here. Is there a letter of credit from a Vermont bank?"

"My father has no bearing on my credit worthiness. There's good honest profit to be made on this project. What can be your objection?"

George's foot tapped on the floor.

"Control your eagerness, young man. We here in Camden have our ways. Perhaps one day you shall know them. For now, this bank cannot extend credit for your contract, a decision by the board of trustees." Kenworthy tossed the file back at Chase.

"How is that…possible?" George stammered.

"Unless you produce a local property owner and influential citizen to co-sign, this bank can not support this project, Mister Chase."

Chase fled the office, passing red-faced through the bevy of clerks. His stomach knotted, shamed like a schoolboy in rebuke.

*   *   *

"George Chase, in the middle of the day, my word, this is unusual," Deborah Norwood stood among her flowers. "Miss Harriet is up to her elbows in baking right now."

"Actually, Mother Norwood, I came to see the captain."

"He's down to the harbor this morning. You'll find him to the Davis yard."

George turned and walked to the harbor area where Captain Norwood talked to a brace of captains, wreathed in pipe smoke.

"May I speak with you alone, sir?" He touched the man's sleeve.

Stepping away, George described the bank manager's inexplicable behavior.

Norwood listened intently, tugging his grizzled beard, blue eyes blazing.

"My reason for coming to you, Father Norwood, was for advice. What would you do in my shoes?"

Norwood removed a pipe, tobacco gone cold.

"Have you considered their point of view? A young lawyer appears in town one fall and after ten months asks to borrow a small fortune with little equity and less reputation. I wish I could help you, Mister Chase. You shall miss this opportunity. Start with contracts for smaller vessels and work your way up."

George stood aghast. Pinpricks tingled down his legs, crawling on his skin. A surge of anger filled his chest. This wasn't the answer he expected. He thought, "All the old mossbacks think me an upstart."

George stepped back.

"Thank you, Captain Norwood. Give my regards to Harriet." He turned on his heal. Head down, as though walking through a snowstorm, George wound his way around the harbor and back to the office. Ezekiel Kent looked up as the door slammed.

"Damn, damn. 'Work your way up' 'Owed some, can't collect' 'A letter of credit' Damn them all to hell!"

"Watch you language, George Chase!"

"I'm only returning the favor, Ezekiel, since I feel cursed by some in this town. The bank wouldn't back the project. I even went to my future father-in-law."

"Norwood, himself? Perhaps you don't realize his position with the bank and his son, Winslow."

"Winslow? I'd expect his father's support."

"Norwood holds a large portion of the bank's stock and intends to use his power to finance Winslow's interests. Old Norwood wants to set up Winslow in Portland and off the sea, safe at home, wearing suit and dry shoes to work. It's the old man's mission."

"And his son-in-law, the husband of his daughter?"

"He might help, but you realize by this time Camden is a tight little society with plenty of sons to look out for."

"Her parents have been generous up to now."

"Not enough to offer you a part of the China trade, though, you ought to have noticed. As much as the Norwoods love Harriet, they and others have too many sons around this town, ready to inherit fathers' businesses. Too many old boys with young boys in the wings."

"So, my prospects here will be limited."

"Only by time. Give it some years. Once you've become a seasoned citizen of the town, it will be easier. Meanwhile, work with me to build up the practice."

George walked out of the office before speaking his mind.

Chapter Eight

The note read: *Mother expects you to dinner Sunday.*

Slipped under his door, Paul handed him the folded paper when he entered their apartment.

"Mother expects you …," he read out loud.

"'Expects'? What's that mean?" Paul asked.

"They assume too much." He saw Paul's puzzled expression. "It's…bossy."

"Americans let wife's parents be the boss?"

What had passed between the captain and his wife, perhaps George's being an upstart? Chase, too ambitious to rise above his station. Was the mother trying to smooth over the breech?

"I'm going out for a while, Paul."

Perhaps he would ride down the coast road to Rockland, away from Norwoods, away from the whole damned lot. Pushing his hat on, he stepped quietly down to the stable. The horse welcomed his attention, as he readied the tack.

"How about a little ride, Cindy?"

Over his shoulder, a voice spoke from the dark, "How about staying home?"

She had returned to find him. Harriet reached her arms around George and squeezed her body against his back.

"Haven't heard from you all day. Where are you going?"

He stood still, his back to her.

"What's the matter, darling, have I startled you? Am I too forward?" She laughed.

George turned to face his fiancée.

"I've had a disappointment, and I need time alone."

"What disappointments can't be shared with someone you love? I want to know everything about your world." Her hands caressed his chest.

"Huh, my disappointment must be the talk of the Norwood household by now." He stepped back.

"But, I know nothing. You have to tell me, now."

"I brought good business to Camden Bank, but was turned down. Old men are threatened by new men. I turned to the most influential man in the town, your father, and asked for advice. He offered one explanation: old men consider me an insolent upstart. "

"My father said that?"

"He implied as much. Since then, I've learned the real reason."

Harriet backed away.

"Mercy, Mister Chase, I've never seen you like this. What's come over you?"

"Your father himself deliberately blocked my access to credit to finance your brother at my expense. I can have only a shrunken future here in Camden as a minor lawyer."

"What has that to do with us? We are engaged. Surely, our love is worth more than business deals."

"If your family won't support my career, who else would?"

"Is that all there is between us, George Chase? Am I a vehicle to ride for your ambition? Horrible!" She backed away, her voice shrill. "I see through your motives, now, and want no promises kept between us." She spat the words. "Consider this engagement off. I won't tolerate being just another asset, a piece of property. Love has to come first, over family and wealth. If you were a true man, I would have followed you anywhere."

*   *   *

The office was quiet, too early for Kent to appear. George spread the Portland *Eastern Argus* over his desk to catch the morning light and marked stories of interest.

One: gold discovered in north Georgia...President Jackson removing Cherokees...settlers swarming to make claims, new town springing on the Chattahoochee River.

Circle.

Two: a new city on Lake Michigan...flat prairie...marketing grain and beef to New York and Europe through the Erie Canal.

Circle.

Three: new city at the confluence of three rivers...gateway to the west...coal and iron ore found together...air black with soot for iron mills...blast furnaces turn night into day.

Circle.

Four: Maine boomtown, lumber mills, foundries, fisheries, boatyards, land speculation, world shipping, international border...a frontier between two great empires.

Circle

The door opened and Paul burst into the office.

"Has the lumber order arrived from Belfast? What's the big hurry, Paul?"

"Oh, is it true? They say that you and Miss Harriet won't marry now?"

Chase sighed, "That hope has been dashed. Camden is not the city of opportunity for new men. It's time to move to greener pastures."

"What you mean, 'greener pastures?' You want to farm, now?"

"No, only another figure of speech. It means things have died for me here."

"If you leave, I ship back to Hawaii. My family will be happy to see Paul again. Warm there, no snow like Maine. Pastures always green. You come too; you see, Americans like Hawaii."

"I'll stay in America. I want somewhere fresh, to be a first citizen, a pioneer in a wilderness," he patted the newspaper. "I can't say I would like all these places. Too far inland. One has lumber, ships, fishing, land, all things I've learned already. Yet, it, too, is a wilderness, ripe with potential."

"Is this Maine?"

"Yes, the far east of Maine. My license lets me practice anywhere. It's an opportunity for you, too, Paul. Come along. We get rich together."

"As steward?" he twisted the paper around.

"Yes. With no old men to stop our rise, this Calais wilderness offers our best chance."

Chapter Nine

The sloop's mast held jib and mainsail. Its cabin was fitted with provisions and equipment for the short voyage – food, bunks, and extra clothing. In one cabinet, George tucked his precious law book collection, wrapped in oilcloth.

As dawn approached, Paul headed the boat out of Camden harbor across Penobscot Bay. They sailed through the 'thorofare' between Vinalhaven and North Haven Islands, through the rocky archipelago of Blue Hill Bay, past the Cranberry Islands into the Gulf of Maine. Strong breeze pushed from the west.

Paul's instinct sensed wind, current, and tide. He knew the vessel's draught, avoiding rocky shallows, never losing sight of land. Wind filled the sheets and sped the craft forward, racing 'down east' in the prevailing winds.

That evening, Paul furled the main sail and sought a deep cove far from current and wind. They anchored, hoping the keel would not bump bottom when the tide turned. Towering above the rocky shore, boughs of virgin pines created shelter; isolation in a quiet pool. On a moonless night, a window of stars opened above the trees.

Paul tugged on the anchor rope until it caught. He crawled down the hatch into the cabin. George hung a lamp over the chart, spread before them. They munched bread and cheese.

"Where you figure we are, boss?"

"Maybe Dyer Bay or Narraguagus Bay. Hard to tell with no towns along the Empty Quarter."

"We arrive tomorrow?"

"Maybe into the Passamaquoddy by nightfall. See here on the chart?"

"Camden watermen say watch for tides, say a big change."

"I hear that, too."

"What we going to find, Chase?" Paul lay back on his bunk.

"A wilderness."

"What's wilderness?"

"You've only seen port towns in America and local timberland up the Penobscot. Look, this chart only shows the coast. Inland, away from the sea, there's open country. No towns, no farms. Only Indians among the trees. That's wilderness."

"But, why go there?"

"For opportunity. To start a new community. If we start a life in a wilderness, we will be first in everything. First to buy the land, first to harvest the tallest pines, first to build mills, first to begin a law practice, first to bring refinement to a town. A Chase family would be at the top, like the Norwoods in Camden. Live in a fine house."

"What do Paul do in this wilderness?"

"You are my right hand, my steward. In this wilderness, I teach you to become a man of property."

"Property? Is it possible have property? I'm not even American."

The lantern swayed overhead, their shadows shuddering across the bulkheads.

"Does your family own property in Hawaii?"

"The king owns all the land with the nobles. Noblemen let farmers grow crops. The land is for everyone. We don't know property. Land is like sea. Who owns fish in sea? That is Hawaiian way, not American. If I am to be an American man, I must do American things, like own land. Now, I go sleep.

The teenager collapsed, curled up on a narrow bunk. George lay sleepless, listening to water lap against the hull and tug the anchor.

*　　　　　　*　　　　　　*

37

Chase woke to feel the boat jerk. Paul must be weighing the anchor, loosening its grip on the bottom. Light filtered into the cove from the dawn sky.

"Must get started, Chase, else we won't make port by night." Paul shouted down the hold.

George drank cold tea to wash down breakfast's salt pork and biscuit. Using a pole, Paul fended off rocks, inching the boat forward out of the cove into a narrow bay. In open water, he unfurled the sheets to the wind, and the boat leaped forward onto a dawn-laced ocean.

That afternoon, they entered the Grand Manan Channel, between Grand Manan Island and the entrance to Passamaquoddy Bay. Fortress-like walls rose on shore; ragged cliffs stood firm against the sea, the chart read, *Bold Coast.*

"Look for West Quoddy lighthouse." George peered over the swells, trying to pick out the tower; a striped red and white cylinder. Behind them rose the outline of Grand Manan Island.

"Look, there it is. Tack into the channel."

The sloop turned north toward the lighthouse. They could see the channel's mile-wide opening; Maine's West Quoddy Head on the left and Britain's Campobello Island on the right.

Paul turned, but made no progress. The sails were filled with wind, but the current flowed out of the channel so strongly, the boat pushed back.

"Current too strong, boss. What is this?"

They floundered, testing the current first on the American side, then the Canadian. Sunshine shrunk to a dim glimmer over the land. The coast's cliffs were unforgiving; no haven there. Darkness threatened to catch them at sea with the terror of waves dashing them against invisible rocks.

"Belay this. Head out. See if there's an inlet on that island." Chase gave up.

Paul set a course for Grand Manan, running before the wind, both sails full. Just as dark overtook them, a cove opened up and they slipped through the narrow breach. By starlight, Paul inched the sloop ahead until the channel opened to a tiny harbor, shielded from the sea by wooded peaks. Fires burned in the distance, light flickering.

"Is it safe?" Paul asked.

"We have no choice. Pray they're not sea bandits."

Paul let the boat approach the blazes. They heard shouts, saw shadows. Fire light cast on a hellish scene.

Open boats, sails collapsed onto the decks, lay on the beach. Bare shanties, leaning at angles, stood on pilings above the shore. White carcasses dried across rough laths. A dozen men and boys stood among worktables, slick with mire. The crew raised their heads, startled see a sloop enter their rugged sanctuary.

Paul stopped along a neglected pier, letting George step up to the group.

"Good evening, gentlemen, where would this place be?"

The clan stared in silence, blades poised above the slaughter of fish. The debris of their work – heads, fins, tails and guts – lay on the ground. The stink of fish mixed with the musk of dirty clothing. One man, holding a knife, walked around the worktable and peered into George's face.

"Ye'd be in Dark Harbour, mister. Where ye from and where ye headed in that there *boot*?" The man's swollen nose squatted amidst a coarse face. A stubbled beard surrounded his sunken mouth over toothless gums. The accent trembled with Scotch burr.

"From Penobscot Bay two days ago. On the morrow we would enter Lubec Channel, if possible."

"Possible? Why not possible?"

"Two hours ago, our sloop was pushed back by the current."

"Not familiar with the Fundy tides, are ye? See yer boat ridin' so high at the pier now? Wall, come low tide, she'd be down on the mud and rocks, all laid over. Best moor her out in the channel. The boy here will ride ye to shore on the skiff." He gestured to a boy to follow. "We don't have much, but we're happy to share with ye. We welcome all who drift upon the waters."

George and Paul walked back, followed by rugged fishermen shoeless over stony ground. Their clothing, damp with endless days of fishing, hung rotting from their bodies.

Untying the line, Paul let the boat drift into mid-channel, away from rocks. When they returned, the fishermen explained the Passamaquoddy Bay and inlets behind the channel expelled water like a hurricane; a 12-knot current. Local sailors timed entrances and exits with the tides.

"What have ye' fer tide on the Penobscot?"

"About ten feet at Camden."

"Look fer twenty feet here and higher up into the Passamaquoddy. If ye've come a distance, ye'd be longin' fer a hot meal," the leader invited the travelers to join supper.

Finished filleting the day's catch, the men shoveled debris into the harbor, blood washed off hands in the brine. A bucket of seawater thrown over a worktable swilled blood off onto the ground, and a steaming pot appeared on the wet surface.

"We have the best of home for our guests, don't we, Angus? Have ye the proper tools?"

"'Deed we do, Gregory," gap-toothed Angus produced two spoons from a dingy pocket. Presenting one to each, he invited George and Paul to stand with the others to attack a hearty potion of hot chowder. Large chunks of white flesh floated among onions and potatoes, skins still attached.

Ever-so-thankful for the fishermen's hospitality, ever-so-famished from their sparse supply, the two travelers ignored the bloody ground, ignored the filth, and ignored the raw dinner table as they carried spoonfuls of hot nourishment to their mouths, letting the broth and oil run down chins, laughing with the cod fishermen.

Chapter Ten

Next day, they received exact directions and returned to the channel off Passamaquoddy Bay. This time the sailors saw the signs of an incoming tide and threaded the sloop through the two points, as current sucked the boat between the headlands. The narrower the channel, the faster the current moved.

Ahead in the distance, they could make out a cluster of masts around a point of land. Eastport thrived with shipping and fish.

Paul weaved the sloop between the ocean vessels, finding a dock. Fishermen, back from their morning catch, stood around the harbor. An elderly gentleman, still decked out in his slicker, called out, "Best tie a long line from that boat, young feller, lessen you want the tide to strand ye'."

"We're just stopping for provisions. Can you direct us to the nearest store?"

George and Paul walked through the town's business district. Up narrow streets, they glimpsed sight of white clapboard homes and steeples. This easternmost town of the United States appeared well-established. On well-defined streets, elm trees shaded stately homes of sea captains. Offices, a haunt for lawyers, lined a row near the shipping warehouses. Sewn tight, Eastport welcomed no new men.

"Come on, Paul. We've nothing here for to tarry." They returned to their boat.

The elderly gentleman remained at his post, sucking on a full pipe, a cloud of tobacco smoke swirling over his head.

As George untied, he asked, "How far is Calais?" pronouncing the name the French way, *Cal-lay*.

"Never heard of it," the man said flatly. Taking out the chart, George pointed to the spot.

"Well, whyn't you SAY where you wanted to go?" he shot back, exasperated, "*Callus*," he said and aimed a finger north, "Up they-yuh 'bout twenty mile."

The men pulled away from the wharves and out into the channel, heading north, deeper into the Passamaquoddy Bay. The channel narrowed, and still, the tidal current bore them deeper. Soon, they came to a fork. "Keep to the left. That's the river, the American side."

"Boss, what's that mean, the American side?"

"We are between two countries, Paul. This is the United States, and that is Britain's colony, New Brunswick."

"Can you talk with them, do you understand their language?"

"They speak English. We were once the same country, but now separate."

"Did you fight and can't settle?"

"Yes, it's like that. We chose to go our separate ways."

"I understand, like a family. Like you and the Norwoods."

"They're no family of mine, neither now nor ever," George growled.

*   *   *

The channel narrowed with exposed rock on both sides, hemming in the boat. The hills, coming down to the river bed, had been cut clear of all trees. Farms were cut into the slope, house and barns on the rise, lanes led down to docks. Each property formed a narrow strip, each farm like a self-sufficient economy, supplying self-reliant families with all subsistence; the ideal of rural maritime New England independence.

Ahead in the distance, they saw a congregation of masts. Clusters of houses appeared along the shores; American on the left, British on the right. The closer they came, the fewer spaces were open to moor the sloop, so they pulled the boat into a creek on the American side. The water appeared to have reached the high tide, lapping against grass and shrubbery, but neither understood the contrast between flood tide and ebb tide. They tied the boat with ropes to trees, centering her in deep water.

"Have to find this boat a berth, Chase."

"Maybe I should turn her into cash."

They carried their few valuables – Chase's credentials, papers, money withdrawn from Camden Bank, and books. Paul Kamehameha carried the heavy trunk and two duffel bags.

Neither had seen an American town like Calais. Arriving from the Pacific by whaling ship, Paul only experienced old coastal settlements – New Bedford, Boston, Portland, Rockland, and Camden – where proud houses on flowered lots, set off by picket fences, surrounded a commons.

A stony road led into Calais. Houses of rough planks lined the street. Some construction used planks like clapboard, overlapping horizontally, while other construction used planks vertically, seams covered with lath. Yards were strewn with discarded lumber and trash. None were fenced. Animals roamed at will – milk cows, goats, and pigs.

The closer they walked to the business section, the muddier the street's surface became. Wagons and hooves had stirred up clay into a frothy muck. They skirted the center of the street, walking instead along the side, until they arrived at a plank sidewalk.

Toward the river, commercial buildings looked more like boathouses and barns, being warehouses and construction sites. Lumber was stacked on wharves. Opposite, buildings tried to present a proper commercial façade. All hastily cobbled of unplanned boards, the carpenters built the street side with an extra storey, a false front.

The double doors of a tippling shop opened onto the street. A drunk, ejected from the establishment, lay in the mud while others laughed. One rummy pointed out the coming pair; George Chase and Paul Kamehameha.

"Hey, look at that, an Injin usin' the white man's sidewalk. Hey, boy, get the hell off to the mud where you belong."

George stepped forward. "He's no Indian. He's from the South Seas."

"South Seas? You don't say!" they mocked the explanation. "Well, lookie here, a regular gentleman and a live cannibal, walkin' down the streets of Calais. Got any shrunken heads in yer pockets, big boy?"

Paul looked to George, putting down his burden in case a fight started.

"Tom Moore, Will Tanner, Ned Pike. You work to Murchie's mill over St. Stephen way?" A voice called out names. A gentleman in a business suit had stepped from an office. "Murchie won't take kindly to word his hands are cutting up in Calais, will he? If you men have to drink in town, it must be a quiet kind of intoxication. Now, back into the tippling shop with you."

The man turned to George.

"Sorry, stranger, Calais is a raw town with raw men. They work half the day in the cold and drink for recreation. What brings you to our town?" He drew them into the office, one with the only plate glass window of any establishment. Painted in Roman letters were the words, *Anson Chandler, Esq. Attorney At Law.*

"My name is George Chase. This is my steward, Paul. Thank you for saving us from a fight."

"You two draw attention." He smiled at the huge boy and short man. "Just arrived?"

"I'm considering re-locating for new opportunities," Chase muddled an answer.

"We're plain spoken up here in Calais, Mister Chase. Men live by the bare facts and unvarnished truth. A new man in town needs to be candid, if he's to be trusted. Everyone's from somewhere else, looking for those opportunities."

"Is it plainspoken enough to say I'm a lawyer?"

"That would have been my guess. Welcome to Calais," Chandler extended his hand. "Don't be wary, Mister

Chase. Rivalry between lawyers here is rare. The seven of us on the American side are swamped with business."

"Seven lawyers?"

"Seven lawyers spread over ten miles. Calais is only the narrow neck of the jug of the St. Croix Valley. Behind me is the full gallon of mills and foundries whose products pass through this narrow opening to the world. I suggest you take a tour up Milltown Road. Beyond Milltown, it becomes the Houlton Road which turns into wilderness. You'll find horses at the livery stable near international bridge. Good luck. Stop by to ask favors, don't be too proud."

*   *   *

The stable stood near the frame headquarters of the United States Customs Service, under the stars and stripes. One lone official in short billed cap, wearing a badge on a slovenly wool coat, stood in a wooden booth surveying a line of halted wagons. Traffic backed up while other officials moved aimlessly around the headquarters, ledgers in hands, keeping record of cross-border traffic. Informal, inefficient, and casual, the American officials seemed more a club than a corps. Neither soldiers, nor weapons, nor any attire resembled a uniform.

"Look, Paul, nothing but political appointees of the Jackson administration I bet the Whigs went kicking and screaming when those Democrats appeared in '29. It's the American way; to the victors belong the spoils."

Beyond the U.S. customs station was the international bridge; a wooden structure built on thick pilings, tree trunks driven into the silt river bottom. The river, full at flood tide, covered the supports like a lake, having no current. The bridge supports and roadway were unfinished logs, flattened roughly with an adze, leaving wide gaps. Blindfolded horses were led across, pulling wagons that thumped over each groove. Pedestrians jockeyed for space amid the horse traffic.

On the Canadian side, St. Stephen, New Brunswick, crown colony in the royal realm, the British customs service was housed in a stone arsenal. The Union Jack waved from a tall pole, facing the foreign shore. In crisp uniforms, Imperial British soldiers stood at attention bearing muskets, while their officers supervised the flow of traffic. A heavy pike swung down to halt each traveler in turn; a token bar to any invasion of the kingdom. Professional customs officials, trained by the Colonial Office in London, garbed in blue regalia, effected inspections of every saddlebag and wagon bed.

George and Paul walked to a promontory. From this vantage point, they could see the faces of the two towns beyond their separate customs posts. St. Stephen, frontier outpost of the British Empire, boasted masonry buildings along a cobblestone main street. Young elms planted in regular intervals edged the thoroughfare. Church steeples jutted into the sky among white clapboard homes on the hill above the town's businesses. Women and children strolled on a municipal common. St. Stephen bespoke common-wealth.

On the other side, Calais' commercial buildings were peculiar, hastily erected shacks set at various distances and angles from the muddy street, where men and horses passed brusquely doing business. Wharves, filled with industrial products, projected into the river. Workmen swarmed over dry-docked structures, hammering shapes of ships and schooners. Sooty vapor hung over foundries and smithies. On the rise above town, cabins crowded on a raw landscape, recently cleared of timber. No buildings of any institutional nature were visible, neither schools nor churches. Calais was busy producing wealth.

George couldn't have been more pleased.

Chapter Eleven

"You won't be racing them steeds," the stable hand eyed Paul sitting astride a tired plough horse.

"Not a chance," said George Chase from his gelding. "How far up river do the mills go?"

"Far as Baileyville, 'bout ten mile. Take you over two hours ta' get there. If ya ain't back by suppertime, it'll be another fifty cents."

"Plan on that, stableman. You will not see your horses again today," Chase turned his gelding and slapped his rump. They stopped for bread and roasted chicken.

The river road dipped down behind the town. Up stream from the international bridge, the quiet pool of the St. Croix turned into rocky rapids, useless for boats but perfect for turning machinery.

Ahead loomed the first mill. Built on the riverbank from plain planks the mill's roof and walls protected a whirl of machinery. A sluice carried water along a mill race. Water cascaded over a wheel where rectangular buckets caught the force. The pressure turned the wheel that powered gang saws. Workers pushed logs onto a trolley to bring the wood against the teeth of the blades.

The noise from the mill eclipsed all other sound. George and Paul had to shout to talk. The crankshaft thumped with every rotation. Metal squeaked against metal. Logs thumped, rolling onto their trolley, and when wood met blade, the saws screamed as they sliced through the white timber.

Up river from the mill, gangs of men pulled logs from the rushing river water, using great hooks. The log drive still filled the river with timber. Great jumbles of logs lay over acres; a stock of timber for the mill's work all summer.

Beyond the first mill, they counted eleven mills on the American side.

Some mills specialized in finished lumber, curing in the sun – shingles for roofs and siding, lath for plastering inside houses, rough boards for building shacks, planed boards for proper clapboard homes, and hemlock for tanning hides, pickets for fences, oak for floors and ship framing, hardwoods for furniture and paneling, and juniper knees for ship braces. In one yard a gang of workers hammered slats into boxes to be shipped to Cuba to hold sugar.

Up from the banks of the St. Croix, they saw communities of shanties; housing for the laborers, thrown together among a clear-cut landscape. The air was ripe with the stench of sewage. The ground, being so recently unprotected from rain, was scarred by eroded crevices where rivulets washed thin soil off bedrock.

*   *   *

The two riders found a trail leading to higher ground that took them miles into clear-cut, denuded land. Grasses sprung up between huge stumps, grave monuments of trees whose rings recorded hundreds of years of life.

Finally, ahead they saw a wall, a palisade; the border of the great forest, the frontier where the army of axe men halted their march and retreated. From a hill, they viewed the mighty barrier of evergreen treetops, an unbroken boundary of nature.

"Look, boss, so much more trees," Paul surveyed the endless forest.

"Never see the end of those woods. It stretches from Maine to a place called Minnesota, where the prairies start."

"Prairies?"

"A flat treeless place, halfway to California."

The two riders entered the forest floor. A hundred feet above them, green branches formed a roof, blocking sunlight. Flocks of birds called from the higher branches.

Flying squirrels floated on webbed flesh among the lower branches

Paul found a trail stamped out by heavy animals. They reached a clearing. Fresh grass grew in damp sunlight; grazing for the horses. A spring bubbled up from rocks, a brook's birth. Fresh water.

"Good camp, Chase," Paul's blessing.

Night fell and Paul scratched together a shelter of boughs. A deep carpet lay on the forest floor; pine needles mulched to cover and feed the tree roots. Paul gathered aromatic armloads to make natural mattresses. He found stones and built a hearth, clearing away the dry needles.

Paul brought out his tinderbox of striking stones and dry moss. He flicked sparks on the moss, transferring tiny tongues of flame to dry tinder. A tiny blaze began in a cove of stones and dirt.

They ate a cold supper, cross-legged, and tossed bones into the fire.

"Why we come here, boss, if we not work in mill?"

Chase lay back, head propped on a roll of clothes. Stars peeked through the canopy of evergreen branches.

"Just look up at those trees, Paul. See how they reach over a hundred feet. How many men would it take to join hands around that one, there?"

"Maybe five."

"If a man owned this land, owned a mill, and owned interest in a shipyard, he could transform these trees into great vessels to trade with Boston or the Indies."

"We going to do that?"

"Indeed! This is a young man's country, Paul. A wilderness. A virgin land. A place to start fresh, a place so new, so unconquered, that go-to men can build fortunes. Tomorrow, we take a house in Milltown. We'll furnish it enough to be comfortable, give me an office, and hang out my shingle – George M. Chase, Esquire, Attorney at Law. I'll tap on Anson Chandler's shoulder to find you a job in the ship yards."

The peace was broken by an eerie scream. Hairs on their necks rippled. The horses jumped.

"Mister Chase, a woman, a woman hurt. We go help her." Paul crouched, glaring into the woods.

"That's no woman, Paul. That's a panther. One of us will have to stand guard. That's right, pile on wood. It's going to be a long night."

"Is this Chase's *wilderness*?"

Chapter Twelve

"Gentlemen of the jury, every man of Washington County knows the dangers of the farm, the vessel, the forest and the mill. Which of you has personal association with the chance of accident?"

Their eyes followed George Chase, dressed in black suit, his full pompadour hair oiled to a sheen.

"Booms fall from rigging. Crewmen are lost at sea. Axes glance off timber and bite into a leg."

Twelve jurymen. Qualifications: Washington County voters. Ruddy faces, callused hands, church suits. Summoned to the county seat of Machias, to the brick courthouse on the hill, to fulfill their civic duty.

"Accidents happen to both the good and the wicked. For us, injuries and deaths due to accidents are happenstance – uncalculated, unwitting, unforeseen, and random."

The men sat forward in their chairs. A white railing separated the jury box from the court floor. Face illuminated by the room's high windows, Chase delivered his opening statement at the plaintiff's table.

"However, when injury is accountable, when blame is clear, then responsibility must be assessed and compensation paid to the injured party."

Chase gestured to the plaintiff behind the table. The man stood.

"When Patrick McShea arrived at work at Copeland, Duren and Company on the morning of February twenty-third of eighteen-hundred and thirty-five, he expected to put in a full-day's work for a full-day's pay, but he did not expect his employer to endanger his life and limb, intentionally."

Chase crooked his finger for the plaintiff to advance around the table. The man lifted two crutches from under the

51

table and hobbled out onto the court's floor. The jury saw the empty pant leg dangling.

"This husband, father, parishioner, citizen, can no longer support the family he loves. His children cry out for the sustenance he once brought by the sweat of his brow; each child's cry stabs his heart. He calls out, 'Oh, woe, from whence will come the salvation of my children?'"

Chase reached to support the elbow of his client.

"Gentlemen, we are gathered here to answer Mister McShea's question. I know you will deliver these children from a cruel fate.

"Let me turn from the matters of the heart to the matters of the head. During this trial, I will prove to you that Copeland, Duren and Company were culpable in causing Patrick McShea's loss of a leg. That their panting after profits led to dangerous conditions, which precipitated this so-called 'accident.' The only conclusion possible will be their liability for their employee's lost wages equal to his lifetime earnings."

*   *   *

It had been a March morning when Paul pulled on his boots and left for the ship yards. George Chase scribbled property transfers in rounded calligraphy. He brewed a pot of tea, carefully pouring away from the papers and allowed himself a half-spoon of precious white sugar, stirring the tea, when the knock came.

George opened his door to see a priest standing outside.

"May I have a few moments of your time, sir?" the clergyman asked in a lilting Irish accent.

"Certainly, Father. Step into my office. Would you like a cup of tea?" George offered the only other chair in the parlor room. The priest wore a black biretta divided into thirds, a tassel on top, a black cape covered his shoulders.

"Nothing, thank you. Allow me to introduce myself; I am Father Murray of Saint Anne de Beaupres in St. Stephen.

I realize you aren't one of our parishioners, but I have to appeal to someone and your office is located among my Milltown flock."

"Many of your people work in the mills and camps?"

"Yes, they do, and one has met with dreadful circumstances. Have you heard?"

"Was that a saw accident? How is he?"

"Doctor Porter had to amputate at the knee. It took four stout men to hold down the poor fellow, even after a quart of whiskey. The wound had to be cauterized, and none of us shall forget the stench of burning human flesh."

"You were present?"

"Sometimes the shock of amputation results in death, which case would call for the sacrament…"

"Extreme unction?"

"Correct. You are familiar with our faith?"

"As would any reasonably curious mind. But, what is the purpose of your visit this morning?"

"The corporation, Copeland, Duren and Company, is responsible for this injury, Mister Chase, and ought to pay restitution to the victim, Patrick McShea, who can no longer support his family."

"Just a minute, Father. It's a great leap from McShea's injury to Copeland's responsibility. Men are injured all the time in lumber camps, on the river drives, and in the mills. There wouldn't be an industry if every jack were pensioned off for every accident."

George Chase felt the eyes of the Father Andrew boring into his thoughts.

"Young man, one can understand the reluctance to question a corporation as powerful as Copeland, Duren and Company."

"You seem to know much about business for a priest."

"You separate the secular from the spiritual."

"Are they not two realms?" George enjoyed the parry and thrust.

"For me, earthly pursuits and the divine are a seamless fabric. For example, I once toiled as an accountant in a Dublin firm before I took religious orders. Now, I am about my 'Father's business.' I prefer to think it as advancement to a more prestigious firm. But, we digress from the 'business' at hand. Would you at least visit the home of McShea and listen to his story?"

"I would be interested in that account, but promise nothing. Understood, Father?"

"Yes, it's understood, Mister Chase."

*   *   *

The two men trudged through the heavy spring snow through Milltown; a community facing the St. Croix rapids above Calais. Workers' shacks scattered over the hillside overlooking the clutter of lumber and grist mills. Father Andrew Murray led the lawyer along the streets to upper cottages; small, one-storey houses, trimmed and painted.

Choosing one, the priest stood on its porch and knocked on the door. Either side of the door were white lace curtained windows. The door opened.

"Father Andrew, good morning," a beautiful woman greeted the men. Her strawberry blonde hair hung loose around her shoulders. She had not been expecting company, but stood aside as the men entered the cottage.

"Mary, I have brought Lawyer George Chase to speak with Patrick. Would that be convenient?" As the priest spoke, a girl in the first bloom of youth entered the room followed by three younger children, peeking around the older girl's skirts.

"Oh, Father," Mary spoke in hushed tones, "he's lowly, all withdrawn into hisself, he is. I'd have ta' see if'n he's receivin' coompany."

"Never mind that, Mary. Our visit will do no harm. I believe our lawyer needs a spot of tea, isn't that so, Mister Chase," a knowing glance.

"Ah, yes, good idea, Missus McShea. I would be so grateful for the refreshment on this chilly morning." Chase noticed the Franklin stove standing cool in the parlor corner. Only using wood for the kitchen stove, he thought.

"While you're busy, we'll make our way to see the patient, Mary," Father Andrew whisked through the doorways to the back bedroom. Chase followed.

He was shocked at the sight of the mill worker. Patrick McShea lay clothed under a quilt on a low bed in a dim room. No lamp lit the space, only decorated with a wall crucifix depicting Jesus in agony.

Father Murray acted as if the occasion were more party than pall. He called for Mary to bring a candle.

"Good to see the color returning to your cheeks, Pat. We missed you at mass so I brought the Host. We'll celebrate after your guest leaves. This is Mister George Chase, attorney-at-law, a new lawyer in town. I'd like him to hear your story."

"What fer, Father? There's nothin' to stand up against the likes of Copeland. I'm done, finished. What kind of man can I ever be with this?" He threw back the quilt to reveal a stump where his calf ought to have been. Even in the dim light, George could see the wound oozing fluid, like a grotesque leg of beef. McShea looked away, shamed by his disability.

"You cover that up, Patrick McShea," demanded the priest. "And stop feeling so damn sorry for yourself. You're whining like a limp-wristed woman. Count your blessings. Doctor Porter says it's draining well, no corruption. 'Choose life' as the Bible says. We're here to plan the next portion of yours."

McShea looked up at his fearsome priest.

"What do youse want from me, Father Andrew?"

"Prop him up and bring some chairs here before Mary arrives with the tea," he said to Chase. "You, Patrick, show your wife the respect she deserves. Act like a man."

They pulled McShea up against a bolster pillow. Mary McShea brought each man a cup and saucer. She set a plate of scones on the bed before she withdrew.

"Tell Mister Chase about the accident, Pat."

"It was late February, the twenty-third, during the thaw."

Chase asked, "But the sawing usually doesn't start until April or May, after the log run. Why was Copeland sawing?"

"He's always so eager ta outmaneuver the competition. Wanted ta deliver the first batch of deal lumber ta the docks and capture a contract with the Boston people. McKinley, foreman at the mill, tried ta talk him out of it."

"Just tell me what happened that day," said Chase.

"The river had opened with that thaw. Copeland opened the sluice gate. Inside the mill, the thaw ain't melted nothin'. Ice still over everythin'. Slippery as Hell, beg pardon, Father.

"But, it wasn't enough for old man Copeland. No, he was in a big hurry. Sayin' that the log wasn't bein' carried ta the saw fast enough. Me and Luke made a clean pass through the saw once and were drawin' back for a second pass when the blade jammed.

"Copeland acted like it was my fault, told me ta git up on that log and shake her loose. That's when I slipped and fell on the blade just when it started up. Ripped open my leg from ankle to knee.

"The worst part was when Copeland had me pulled to one side, bleedin' like some animal. Ordered the men back to work. That's my story, Mister Chase."

"Well, Mister Chase, does McShea have a case against Copeland's company?"

"It depends on whether witnesses are willing to talk and other factors, Father Andrew."

"Are you afraid of this Copeland?"

"Copeland, Hall, Gates, Lovejoy, all the mill owners here, Father. I'm a young lawyer, starting a practice. Dare I challenge the most powerful businessmen in the St. Croix Valley?"

"The situation isn't as simple as mill owners having a united front. Others resent Copeland," the priest replied.

McShea spoke from the bed. "I could show you that he pulls logs off the river with other mills' pollywog marks. He's been caught stealin' their timber."

"All right, gentlemen. I will investigate if we have a case to sue Copeland."

"Bless you, George Chase. I will return to your office in three days for an answer," the priest rose and shook his hand.

Chapter Thirteen

Sydney Saltonstall, from the Boston firm, Saltonstall, Saltonstall and Lodge, walked toward the jury box. His suit, shirt, cravat, and shiny shoes all spoke the image of a Harvard-educated barrister.

"Gentlemen, the very pillars of society are threatened, what's best is undermined by the worst. It will be up to this jury to protect what is most precious in this community from what is most cheap.

"The firm of Copeland, Duren and Company built a mill on the St. Croix River. That mill employs thirty-five men and produces four million feet of lumber, valued at thirty-six thousand dollars. Those men have families and value the twenty-eight dollars a month they bring home. The good derived from my client's company spreads throughout this county.

"But, gentlemen, this good is threatened. On the surface, the threat is cloaked by sympathy. You saw the display of cheap theatrics when the opposing party forced his wretched client to surrender your sound judgment to effeminate pity.

"We have a party injured by a chance accident. Or was it? How careless was the plaintiff? I will purport to prove two conclusions. One, that McShea's injury was a pure accident, not caused by my client; and two, that the company of Copeland and Duren is a solid business and ought to be defended for its contribution to this county."

Sydney Saltonstall resumed his chair.

Judge Thayer asked Chase to call his first witness. He brought to the stand the owners of mills on the St. Croix such as Lovejoy, Lamb, McAllister and Hall. All testified they dared not start machinery on February 23rd due to the harsh weather.

Chase brought forward another mill employee.

"I call to the stand, Peter McKinley." A man about thirty-five mounted the stand and took the oath.

"Would you please tell the jury your view of the events of February twenty-third last?" Chase stood arms folded.

McKinley described how Copeland insisted on operating the mill, although other mills remained shuttered. In his judgment, Copeland was directly at fault for McShea's injury.

"What words did he use to curse?"

"They was profane and blasphemous, sir."

"Nevertheless, the jury ought to hear them."

"Ya' want me to repeat them? There's ladies present, your honor." McKinley appealed to the judge.

Mary McShea sat behind her husband, employing her hands with cross-stitch. A bevy of elderly women sat in the back. Judge Thayer asked ladies to stand in the hallway during McKinley's testimony. They passed John Jackson of the *Calais Advertiser* scribbling notes.

"I ask you to repeat Copeland's words, and I remind you that your oath frees you from the statutes against blasphemy and profanity."

"The words were '*you god-damned shit-assed Mick.*'"

The men of the jury looked at Harold Copeland, sitting beside his pricey lawyer.

Chase turned to Judge Thayer, "I have no more questions for this witness."

"Mister Saltonstall? Do you care to cross-examine?"

"Yes, your honor."

Saltonstall stood at his table, shooting questions at Peter McKinley.

"Micks? Tell the court your definition of that term."

"'Tis the curse for Irish Catholic."

"Do I discern you are neither Irish nor Catholic?"

"Aye, Scotts Presbyterian," rolled out the answer.

"Like Mister Copeland, your employer. So, why do you take sides against your employer, Mister McKinley?

After all, he's recognized your merit with more pay and a high position."

"The word is that as soon as he wins this case, I'm to be tossed out, but that don't matter because James Hall's offered me an office job." He turned to smile at the jury and spoke in a loud whisper. "I don't need to wait for no pink slip."

The jurymen laughed and nudged each other.

"Order in the court."

"That's all I have for this witness, your honor."

Sydney Saltonstall called a series of expert witnesses. All testified affirming the company's contention that conditions on that February day were acceptable for operation of the mill. Chase let each one deliver his testimony without challenge, until the last.

Salmon Dyer was a Portland civil engineer, graduate of the military academy at West Point, junior associate of Peter Cooper's enterprises in New York and New Jersey. He had no objections to operating mills during a thaw.

Chase caught him on cross-examination.

"Have you ever operated a mill on the St. Croix, Mister Dyer?"

"No, but I am familiar with operations on the Kennebec River."

"At your mill on the Kennebec, do you start operations before April?"

"Actually, I have no mill on the Kennebec."

"Then, let me ask, did you view operations last April on the Kennebec?"

"No, I did not."

"If I were to read your office calendar for last year or the year before last, Mister Dyer," Chase's voice rose in mock exasperation, "just when *would* I find you visiting that river?"

"In July, I visited a site where I am designing a mill."

"Designing a mill without ever having operated a mill? How bold! I recommend you not try that on the St.

Croix." He swung toward the jury, fixing his eyes on the most robust man.

"Objection, attempt to intimidate the witness, your honor." Saltonstall was on his feet, hand poking the air.

The judge leaned over the bench.

"Make your point, Chase, and move on."

"Yes, your honor. Beg the court's pardon. Mister Dyer, you've come a long way to offer us expert testimony, true?"

"Yes, the steam packet brought me from Portland to Machias last night."

"How much is that round trip, Mister Dyer?"

"Six dollars."

"And, what do you charge for your time to attend this trial?"

Saltonstall jumped to his feet, "Objection, relevancy, you honor."

"Overruled. The witness will answer."

"Thirty dollars, plus expenses."

"More than a month's wages of a mill hand?" Chase spun around to face the jury. "Good pay for a day's work for a man with no experience operating a saw mill in any kind of weather, don't you think? I have no more questions."

The jurymen guffawed and nudged each other.

"The plaintiff rests, your honor." Chase closed his presentation.

After Judge Thayer instructed the jury, the men filed out to deliberate.

Saltonstall and Copeland fell into loud whispering at the defendant's table.

"Permission to withdraw to chambers, your honor?" Saltonstall was pulling Copeland's sleeve.

"If you wish, counselor." Judge Thayer drew the two into his chambers.

In a few minutes, the bailiff returned, motioning to Chase to join.

Saltonstall burst with an offer. "Listen to reason, Chase. Copeland is willing to offer a handsome award. But, everything must be confidential. Word can't leak out, otherwise the deal is off."

"That depends on the award, Saltonstall, and my client must approve. He must to raise his family. Do you have a figure?" answered Chase.

"One thousand dollars," the lawyer said slowly to enhance their value.

"I won't even convey that number to Mister McShea. You ought to be ashamed. That's only three year's wages." Chase scoffed.

"Looking for a big fee, are you, Chase? Gouging the poor Irishman?" taunted Saltonstall.

"Only what I'm entitled to and a lot less than poor Copeland's paying you, win or lose." Copeland's attention swung between the two advocates.

"Then, two thousand. That's final."

"Let's see what the jury says," George turned back.

"Chase, you'll regret that."

"Maybe, but my regret will be deliberate, not accidental," he said in the door's threshold.

The jury filed back to their chairs. Late afternoon slanted sunlight caught dust floating in the courtroom's air.

"Mister Foreman, have you reached a verdict."

"Yes we have your honor."

"May I have the slip?" He read the decision. "Now, tell the court, foreman."

"We decided in favor of Patrick McShea. Copeland, Duren and Company is liable for damages to Mister McShea." Patrick turned and reached for Mary.

"Have you named an amount for the award?"

"We have, your honor. We figure Pat has thirty years' work left in him. Not counting any wage increase, to be fair to the company, we fix the award at ten thousand dollars, plus Mister Chase's fee and court costs."

The plaintiff's table broke into joyful mirth. Mary ran around the barrier and hugged her husband, thanking George Chase. Chase shook the hands of the jurors. The defendant's table remained sitting, stunned by the verdict.

Chapter Fourteen

Summer 1835 arrived and George's fears about mill owners' antagonism were relieved when mill owner, James Hall discussed a retainer to advise the company on worker issues.

The Democratic Party needed strength for their field of state candidates. The chairman and state senator, Anson Chandler, called at the office.

"Chase, the men have their eye on you. Would you agree to stand for office?"

"It's time away from my practice, Mister Chandler."

"Believe me, George. The day I met you I saw that steel-sharp eye. I said, there's a *go-to* man. George, the common man is restless. He looks for leadership, young leadership. I guess your age at thirty."

"No, just twenty-six."

"Good Lord! All the better. Voting! The new immigrants think a vote makes them gentlemen, and without property qualifications, the native-born laborer feels it's a new privilege. They're all Jackson men, every one of them."

"But, the election is only next month."

"All the better," Chandler was indefatigable. "If you let us nominate you, we'll stage a rally in Milltown on Saturday night. Let me warm up the crowd. Then, at the climax, you'll speak. Let the common people see their champion of the working man."

*   *   *

The platform was constructed next to Milltown Road in clear sight of traffic. A band played marches and patriotic tunes. As darkness came, torches of pine sap were lit and arrayed along the platform's railings.

Local dignitaries warmed up the crowd with brief speeches. A Baptist pastor spoke sadly of the plight of the poor in the community. He touched on the rights of workers to associate and speak up about conditions on the job. In a brogue, a labor leader boasted of the spreading membership in workers' associations.

Finally, George rose to speak. The assembly cheered and waved their hats. George stood, startled by the acclaim.

"When ready, raise your hand for attention, George," Chandler softly suggested.

"Friends! Friends!" he leaned over the multitude.

"Chase, Chase, Chase," a chant began, "Chase, Chase, Chase."

One huge man in red flannel shirt, wide suspenders holding up broad trousers, turned to the crowd and shouted, "He'll chase out the masters from the State House. He'll chase off the bosses."

"Chase, Chase, Chase," they continued.

"Friends! It's time for a change in Maine, and it's time for a change in America."

The huge man in flannel turned, raised his hands, and demanded silence.

"The voice of the common man must be heard. He cries out for a fair share. His children need schools. His horses need roads. His family needs the protection of the law."

As he closed, he noticed one man seated at the back of the throng.

"Any good leader needs allies. We need to grow many leaders in our community and our nation. I want to welcome on stage a man rising to leadership in the Workman's Association. I believe he's been elected secretary. Mister Patrick McShea, please come on stage."

As McShea swung his crutches, the gathering parted, opening a path to the platform. Hopping the steps on one leg, he appeared above the crowd and waved. Then, he threw an arm around George Chase and shouted.

"Let's have a hand for our champion, men. Get out that vote on election day."

George Chase enjoyed a slim majority, elected to the twelfth legislative session of the State of Maine, session to be held from January 2nd through March 30th, 1836, in the new capitol building at Augusta.

Chapter Fifteen

"Why can't I stay home, Boss?" Paul frowned over his coffee cup.

"That would be irresponsible of me to leave an eighteen-year-old boy alone for three months. Besides, I need your mind attending to business while I'm at the legislature in Augusta. With Anson gone to be a senator, Missus Chandler looks to mother you a while. She's a better cook than either one of us."

A fist pounded on the outside door where a boy stood, holding an envelope.

"Invitation from Father Murray," he called out, running off with a handful of other envelopes.

Inside was an engraved invitation to a Christmas party at St. Anne de Beaupres's parish house in St. Stephen. Father Andrew Murray wrote a postscript that extended the invitation to George's steward, Paul.

"I can't do that, Mister Chase. I'm just a steward."

"It's only a parish party, my friend. The Father will have invited his flock, probably wants them to intermingle. It's good for us to make a brief appearance, shows we care to meet my constituency. I promise we will linger only a half-hour; after all, we're the only Protestants."

The parish house glowed with lights where the housekeeper had lit candles in every window and fires in every stove.

As they walked closer, they heard music.

"There's dancing."

"Oh, no. I can't. Not American dance." Paul balked.

The door opened and the two bachelors were greeted by Father Andrew in full canonical regalia – biretta cap, a red-edged cape, and, dangling by a chain, a simple crucifix. On his left hand, he wore a ruby ring.

"Aha, the new representative and his aide-de-camp, welcome to the party. Perhaps some wine, perhaps some punch. How does one say, 'Merry Christmas' in Sandwich Islanderish, Paul?"

"Mele Kalikimaka."

"Malay Kikimiki?"

"Very good, father," Paul allowed.

"The bowl to the right contains the magic potion. Friends," he announced to the party, "we have the pleasure to be in the company of the Honorable George Chase, soon to represent Calais, and his aide, Paul."

In the parlor, all furniture and carpets had been removed to reveal a light oak floor. Musicians played in the alcove, a violin and pianoforte, while couples whirled politely.

Chase found Patrick and Mary McShea seated among a group of other mill workers and their wives. Father Murray continued to greet guests at the door. Paul, the largest person in the room, shifted from one foot to the other, sweating with heat and anxiety. He watched guests arrive; so many people he didn't know. The door opened for a group that caught his attention.

Men in stovepipe hats, hair worn in braids. Women in head shawls wore long colorful dresses. All had copper-colored faces.

Father Murray brought the new guests to be greeted as the others. The older man was Chief Joseph Gabriel, accompanied by his brothers, their wives, and the chief's daughter, Mary. The father made a point of informing the company that the chief and his family were the pillars of the Catholic mission at Peter Dana Point, Indian Township. The message was clear: Catholic Indians were equal citizens in the eyes of the church.

Suddenly, the music took on a new character. The polite ladies in full dresses with close-fitting bodices and low décolletage withdrew with their male partners dressed in double-breasted tail-coats and tight-fitting trousers.

They were pushed off the floor by couples who threw themselves into a display of jumping and hopping. These ladies wore wide skirts and white blouses, the hems rising as they leaped, revealing calves and ankles crossing in time to the wild music. Each person out-did others in athletic prowess.

Paul laughed to see such show of unrestrained merriment. He pushed into the parlor; better to see the women's legs. He heard a voice behind him, someone tapping his back.

Paul turned to see Chief Joseph's daughter, Mary Gabriel, stuck behind others, trying to view the dancing. She jabbered words in another language. He shook his head, shrugged his shoulders.

"You know dance, maybe?"

"Oh, no, all new to me. At home, men and women dance separate."

"My people, too. Shame on Indian women to dance with men."

"We say its 'kapu.' That's like *shame*."

"Where you from? *Skincin kil?* (Are you an Indian?)"

"Havai'i. Far away."

"You come Indian Township?"

"Maybe. Is there someone for me to visit?"

"You come. I show you."

Father Murray greeted a couple, latecomers. A tall gentleman wearing an expensive beaver hat, his wife and daughter in winter bonnets. He waved a silver-crowned cane in the air. Someone important in the parish, no doubt, the way the priest fussed over the family. The accent, like Father Murray, sounded more British than Irish.

The mother wore a mantle, trimmed with fur at the wrist. Her upstanding collar and hem were made of wide fur, and around her shoulders she wore a fur shawl.

The daughter's dark red cloak gathered into a natural waistline then fell to her ankles. She wore white gloves and a soft red hat in a poke bonnet shape.

The priest's housekeeper offered to hang the guests' outer garments. As the young woman removed hat and cloak, she unveiled a black velour dress with a high neck and close-fitting bodice.

Her perfect pale complexion, small nose and mouth, combined with a small bosom all added to the perfect picture of purity. Upon her bodice, she wore a tiny gold cross.

The priest caught George's long look.

"Do come and meet the O'Neils, George. This young man is the new representative to Maine's state assembly. Mister O'Neil is a barrister who divides his time between St. Steven and the colony's capital city, St. John."

"Very pleased to meet you, Mister Chase. This is my wife, Missus O'Neil, and our daughter, Ellen."

"The pleasure is mine. Would the family permit me the honor to ask their daughter for a dance?" George asked.

The barrister glanced at his wife and nodded.

"The honor is ours, Mister Chase."

"May I have this dance, Miss O'Neil?" George extended his elbow.

Ellen O'Neil took his arm, walking into the parlor to join the spinning couples.

He made conversation, but her answers were mono-syllabic. Just as well for him to concentrate on her face. Her whiteness was extraordinary; only her high cheeks bore any color, and that was rouge. Her skin was a smooth as a child's, like his mother's Dresden dolls. Her hair, a high pile of raven held by a gold clasp, was as black as her skin was stark white,

She danced badly; a stiff jerkiness like a puppet on strings. Her palms sweat as she tried to push George around the room. Right foot back, left foot left, left foot forward, right foot right, repeat. She pushed off with a little bounce, mechanically like a spring toy. Her eyes focused at an invisible spot on George's shirt until George spoke up.

"What did you say?" she asked.

"I asked if you danced with your sisters."

"How would you know that?" she looked up for the first time, her brow wrinkled. Her little pink tongue darted to curl over her upper lip.

"Because you are trying to translate your steps. They made you dance the man's part, didn't they?"

She laughed.

"That couldn't be helped, Mister Chase. My parents wouldn't send us to the dancing academy."

"Why not?" he asked.

"Academy boys are Protestant. It's a rule not to mix with them," she said.

"How about school? Are Protestant boys there?"

"Not even Catholic ones. We went to the convent in Saint John. Only nuns and girls."

"Went?"

"I graduated last spring."

"That would make you about...."

"Eighteen, if that's what you're asking." He was charmed by her British accent. She smiled; the tongue remained in her mouth. Their dancing smoothed into natural motion.

"You live in Saint John? What brought you here?"

"It's our country home. Father has business here and knows Father Murray. Frankly, there's a dearth of acceptable society in either town."

"Meaning 'unattached Catholic men with prospects'?"

She smiled and nodded.

"I, too, feel frankness important in personal relations, Miss O'Neil," he hated to break the spell. It was unavoidable, "but you are violating your parents' rule."

"Whatever can that mean? What rule?" she pulled back.

"You are dancing with a 'heathen' right now."

"Heathen?"

"One of those forbidden Protestant boys, Miss O'Neil."

She hesitated in mid-step and looked at his face for the first time.

"Why are you here, then?"

"These are my friends. I value Father Murray's advice. Have you been swindled?" He laughed.

They resumed dancing, albeit slower.

"I'm only surprised."

"We Protestants are quite nice, you know, Miss O'Neil. No horns, no devil's tail. Look," he laughed, lifting his jacket and turning around.

"I've really never spoken to a Protestant before, and now I'm dancing with one."

"One step at a time."

She laughed. "That's funny. Are you all so interesting? Wait until my sisters hear about this!"

"Miss O'Neil, before we are interrupted, would you grant me one wish?"

"Is it reasonable?"

"Would you allow me to call at your home?"

"My father may have objections."

"I will respect that. I will come to your house tomorrow at three o'clock to learn the answer."

*   *   *

One hundred and fifty miles southwest of Calais, another Christmas party took place in the Norwood home in Camden. Harriet had assisted her mother, preparing food and welcoming overnight guests.

A shipmaster attended, who had amassed a fortune which afforded him everything except a patient wife.

Striding into the house, Jeremiah Follansbee's charm swept Harriet off her feet. By New Year's Day, they were engaged, planning a wedding upon his return from the next voyage, two years away.

Follansbee promised to send letters via returning ships; promised a full set of willow pattern dishes, direct from Whampoa Island in the Canton River; promised this to be his last voyage; promised a life of home and children; promised to be faithful when stopping for supplies in the Sandwich Islands. She saw his ship off, the hope of a twenty-four-year-old maiden departing on the ebb tide.

Chapter Sixteen

The sleigh sped through a bleak landscape, so cold that branches snapped like pistol shots. The three passengers, wrapped in bearskin blankets, sat huddled over a charcoal brazier. The horses plodded, slipping the runners over packed snow, dawn to dusk, broken by stops at way-stations. Senator Anson Chandler sat opposite George. When he spoke, the vapor of his words dissipated into the wind.

"I'll wager those downstaters are cursing; so comfortable when we met in Portland with its hotels and taverns. There, most arrived by packet and walked up the hill from the harbor. Now they're seeing the real Maine, our kind of Maine."

"What can we expect for rooms, Anson?"

"I've written the speaker of the House. He guarantees some rooms. We may have to rough it this session. Don't expect the capitol building to be finished either. It was difficult enough passing the appropriations for the construction back in '29. You know how tight-fisted these farmer legislators are. For them, it's the old adage: *Use it up, wear it out, make it do, or do without.*"

"What's wrong with that, I ask?" the third passenger emerged from bearskins. "I say, keep a firm hand on the purse strings before there's ruin. I read there's to be a library with books in the State House. My people on Vinalhaven want to know if representatives are there to browse through novels."

"And who is the representative from the fair island of Vinalhaven?" Anson looked over in greeting.

"Israel Snow, it is."

"Am I correct that this is your first session, Mister Snow?" said Anson, determined to facilitate an amicable conversation.

"Indeed, it is, and the people of the islands send me with a special mandate."

"A mandate for what, Israel?"

"To establish Maine's laws on chastity, morality, and decency."

"Do elaborate."

"In the years since statehood, the state house is yet to pass laws to protect public morality and cultivate decency. Instead, professional politicians dream up profligate schemes, such as the capitol building."

"Didn't Maine inherit the old Massachusetts' statues?" George asked Anson.

"Partly, but from Puritan times. Mister Snow is correct that Maine's morality laws need revision. To quote the 1780 Massachusetts Constitution, 'the good order and preservation of civil government depend upon piety, religion and morality.' I have a proposition. Since you both are freshmen members of the House, why not collaborate? Israel, this is George Chase. Though young, he is a lawyer with skills you need. If you gentlemen produce an acceptable document to the House, I would be honored to guide it through the Senate."

A gloved hand poked out from Israel Snow's cloaks. Slipping off his glove a long, narrow palm and fingers appeared, disfigured by scars, badges of a waterman's life. George gripped Israel's with his smooth palm.

"Pleased to make your acquaintance and cooperation on such a worthy project"

"For the glory of the Lord," answered Israel.

The sleigh slowed down a long slope. The frozen Kennebec River spread out before them. Across the valley, they saw the monumental splendor of the new State House.

The white granite set in a scene of white snow, neoclassical architecture in a raw landscape. The new State House stood on a hill above the Kennebec River, framed by an avenue between leafless elms. The party crossed the solid ice and trudged up the slope. They could see the grand columned portico above broad steps, ending with tall doors of brass. Above the first floor was a second portico. On each side of the columned porches were wings; the Senate to the left, the House to the right.

In contrast, the village of Augusta lay scattered. Shabby cabins and unpainted houses sprawled on the surrounding lots; board and lodging for the legislators.

George, Anson, and Israel entered the brass doors into a grand center hall. White columns, twenty feet tall, graced the interior, rising to the ceiling. Hallways to right and left led to offices. A grand staircase ahead rose halfway to a landing from which another stairway rose to the second floor.

"It's so high. They could 'a put another floor in between. I never seed so many stairs jest to git to the second storey." Israel craned his neck.

Leaving luggage, they mounted the marble stairs. Down a hallway, they found the Senate chamber. Evening sunlight from western windows illuminated the high-ceilinged room, with a dozen leather-cushioned chairs on ascending carpeted platforms before oak desks. Pens, paper, and inkwells were provided each member. Amid the wood paneled walls were patriotic paintings. All senatorial desks, each one representing a county, were arranged around a dais.

"Jest look at all that paper gone to waste. I sure hope you use it sparingly, Anson. Think of the school children with only slates and chalk to learn their letters."

As much as the Senate displayed luxury, the House displayed austerity. Although the same size as the Senate, the room crowded with pine desks and hard chairs on a bare oak floor.

Israel was ecstatic, "Surely the Lord's vineyard's where we shall labor. Plain as a church where we shall raise our state to be a shining city on a hill."

The man walked around the room, touching desks, making plans, posing as if he were making a speech. George drew Anson aside.

"How could you pair me up with this blatherskite, Anson? We have nothing in common."

"That's exactly why you are needed. There are many rustics in the House; good men but insular and narrow. For all we know, they may still be burning witches on those islands. Many are swept up by religious revival, a second Great Awakening, enthusiastic to hasten the Millennium through statute. You would serve this government well to involve him in the task of composing Maine's morals statutes. Temper down draconian language and, above all, keep their hands off public works projects. You'll be amply rewarded."

That evening, the legislators settled into lodging. Anson and George located a tavern in the village of Augusta where a hot rum concoction could be ordered with the meal. Israel found fellow Baptists to form a prayer group. All three met back in lodging; a large sleeping room filled with wide beds, sharing beds by threes and fours.

"George, are you awake?"

"Yes, Israel, I'm thinking about the opening session tomorrow."

"So am I. George, may I ask you a personal question?"

"Go ahead."

"Are you saved? Have you accepted the Lord in your heart?"

George hesitated, weighing his answer.

"I suppose so. I was baptized and confirmed."

"Do you know the moment you were converted? Have you felt gripped up by the Lord and completely changed by the Spirit, born again?"

"No, can't say that I have. I do try to lead a good life, though, and obey the Commandments. Can't say, though, that I've experienced religious ecstasy."

"I will pray for your soul, George. Perhaps the amazing grace of our Father in heaven will descend on you."

"Thank you, Israel. It's time for sleep. I suggest the Lord wants rest to descend on both of us."

Chapter Seventeen

George slept fitfully between Anson and Israel. After a full breakfast of meat, pancakes, and coffee, the legislators of Maine drifted into chambers.

The speaker of the house assigned each member to a committee to draft legislation. Appointed co-chairman with Israel, George addressed the Committee on Public Morality.

"Gentlemen, James Madison, father of the United States Constitution, said that 'to suppose that any form of government will secure liberty or happiness without any virtue in the people is a chimerical idea.' Therefore, it is incumbent upon us to apply the bulwark of law in the maintenance of public morals in order that we and our posterity will continue to enjoy the blessings of liberty and public order."

Israel Snow raised his hand.

"Yes, but any Justice of the Peace, any parson, any parent, any citizen should understand the meaning."

"Good point, Mister Snow. These offenses should reflect our community standards in plain language. For the sake of efficiency, we should divide into subcommittees. Every week, the committee of the whole will reconvene to review the work. Does everyone agree?"

William Larrabee of Saco spoke up.

"How do you propose to structure the subcommittees, Mister Chase? Perhaps each one named for a Commandment?"

"Hear, hear," called out several representatives.

"Mister Snow and I have anticipated your suggestion. Committees are based on the Commandments, but not limited by them," George answered. "Modern life presents us with issues unforeseen by the Bible. There needs be a committee on gaming, another on public worship, another on abortion, another on obscenity, and so on."

Reuel Williams from Bangor asked, "Shouldn't the topic of obscenity be covered by the committee for the Seventh?"

"There is too much work for Adultery. That committee would never finish writing law on incest, polygamy, bigamy, fornication, and crimes against nature, not to mention prostitution. Here are your committee assignments on printed lists with room assignments. Let us begin work. My committee is the Fourth Commandment - how Maine will honor the Sabbath. Israel, would you please close us in prayer?"

*　　　　　　　　*　　　　　　　　*

From the hallway, George overheard shouting outside the Adultery Committee. "Gentlemen, gentlemen, your voices are reaching the far corners of our fair state house. What is going on?"

The group hushed.

"It's about absent spouses. Some here know wives whose husbands abandoned them for the West, and they can't remarry. Others say having no proof of the husband's death is an excuse for polygamy."

"Write your polygamy statutes well, first, then compose the exceptions." Chase turned and left the room, leaving others to iron out the wrinkles.

*　　　　　　　　*　　　　　　　　*

"Mister Chase, would you to hear our statutes?" asked William Larrabee of the Prostitution Committee.

Larrabee expounded, "We assume no young woman would volunteer to prostitute herself. Instead, the crime uses young women through force or inducement. The weight of arrest and punishment should fall on the whoremonger, whether man or woman."

George chimed in. "I agree. Do we not postulate, as men, that Nature's God distributed lust unevenly between the sexes, granting males the greater proportion, therefore, the greater responsibility? Hence, there ought be no punishment for young women in prostitution."

"Well said," agreed the group.

"Please read the key sections aloud, Mister Larrabee,"

"There are two parts. The first reads *'Any person, who shall keep a house of ill fame, resorted to for the purpose of prostitution or lewdness, shall be punished by imprisonment in the county jail, not more than one year, or by fine, not exceeding five hundred dollars.'*

"Starting to write like lawyers," said young George.

They laughed.

"The second part deals with a person who induces a girl into prostitution. It reads *'Any person, who shall entice any female, before reputed virtuous, to a house of ill fame, or shall knowingly conceal any such female, so deluded or enticed, for the purpose of prostitution or lewdness, shall be punished by imprisonment in the state prison, no less than one year, or more than ten years.'*"

"Ten years? That's a greater term than the whoremonger receives."

"Exactly. The seducer destroys innocence, whereas the whoremonger only utilizes the results."

*   *   *

George entered his own committee room; the one designated to write law protecting the Sabbath. Israel Snow led the discussion.

"Yer right, Mister Brown. I never thought we'd have ta write law to protect one Christian from another. We can't let people disturb services in another house of public worship, even if they disagree, like the Congregational parson protesting at the Baptist Church against total immersion. Here's the wording at this point: *'If any person on the Lord's day, or at any other time, shall willfully interrupt or disturb any church, within the place of such* church or out of it, he shall be punished by imprisonment in the county jail, not more than thirty days, or by fine, not exceeding ten dollars.' Is that clear enough? Will that cover the offense?"

"Yes, yes, write that down, Israel," the others agreed.

"There is something else to consider for the committee." George added. "Besides protecting one Christian sect from another, we should also protect non-Christian worship as well."

"Non-Christian? Do you mean the Hebrews?"

"Hebrews or any other religion that doesn't use churches. Change the word 'church' to 'house of worship.'"

"Won't this encourage these people to inhabit our state?"

"Do we want Maine to be that 'shining city on a hill' or do we imitate old Europe before Napoleon opened the ghettos? I say, a generous attitude best exemplifies the spirit of our Lord. The people of the Book deserve a place in our communities; their health a hallmark of a civilized society."

"Shouldn't everyone be made to observe the Sabbath?"

George reached into his coat pocket. "I have written a special exemption. Here are copies so you may read along with me. I think you will appreciate the careful language of this Hebrew Exception.

He read slowly, *No person, who conscientiously believes that the seventh day* – Saturday – *of the week ought to be observed as the Sabbath, and actually refrains from secular business and labor on that day, shall be liable to the said penalties for performing secular business and labor on the Lord's day, or first day of the week; provided, he disturbs no other persons.*

"This permits the devout Hebrew, who observes his day of worship on Saturday, to conduct business on the Christian Sabbath. Our day will not be disturbed from that quarter. The law is spent circumscribing the behavior of gentiles, rather than Jews. Israel, what have you composed for the official Sabbath law?"

Israel read: *If any person shall, on the Lord's day, keep open his shop, workhouse, or warehouse, or travel or do any work labor or business on that day, works of necessity or charity excepted, or use any sport, game or recreation, or be present at any dancing, public diversion, show or entertainment, encouraging the same, he shall be punished by a fine, not exceeding ten dollars.*

"Thank you. Not only does it acknowledge the Commandments, but serves to protect the workingman from the unscrupulous employer, working employees to death, to release the farmer from his labors, to allow the school child relief from study, to encourage the busy father to know his children. Let every family practice their traditions on this special day."

George Chase stood looking pensively out the high windows at the western hills. "For me, the Vermont Sabbath tradition was walking through pastures with my father, noting tasks for the coming week. Sundays shall be safe in Maine for all time."

*   *   *

For his 58 days in the legislature to and from which he traveled 250 miles, George received compensation of $166. In recognition of his service to the party in chairing the Morals Committee, his name was attached to a public works project to build a second bridge from Calais to St. Stephen, the incorporation of the Bucksport and Calais Stage Company, the incorporation of the Calais Bank, the incorporation of the Calais Unitarian Society, and the act to incorporate the Calais Mutual Fire Insurance Company. George would return home to an office filled with requests for service.

*   *   *

At the close of the legislative session, Israel Snow returned to the coast of Penobscot Bay, first stopping by his cousin's home in Camden. The relatives were eager to learn about the new State House and their cousin's experience as a freshman politician. Israel regaled them at length.

"I admit to being encouraged. Aided by some very admirable young men, one in particular worked with me on the new Morals Law. That boy has a career ahead of him."

"Who was that, cousin?"

"A young lawyer from Calais, George Chase," said Israel.

Her face flaming crimson, Harriet Norwood spit into her napkin and fled the room.

"What's the matter? Did I say anything wrong?" Israel looked around the table.

Chapter Eighteen

It is Sunday morning, and Chase wakes to attend Mass with the O'Neil family. Important, so important to see her with her family. Leave the cottage, dash through the back streets of Milltown to Main.

Forward to the international bridge, but where is it? Bridge is gone, custom official gone. What to do? Got to hurry, Ellen waiting. Walk to the ferry. Boat is tied to the far shore. I ring the bell; I call over. They ignore me.

Urgent walk up to Milltown Bridge. Look ahead, Milltown Bridge gone, too. Back to Main, maybe bridge is really there. Have to cross the river. Low tide, maybe walk across through water.

It's deep, very deep, over my head. I lift off the hat, hold it above while my head is under. River wide, water dark. I can't see light. A long time crossing. So tired, feet drag in mud.

I emerge onto the opposite shore. Where am I? What is this town? What? How can this be ... Camden?

Jolt. Darkness. Crickets singing outside the window.

Great Caesar's Ghost, I'm abed in the dark. Got to get up, I'm late for Mass.

No. It's night, and there is no Mass. Paul's asleep. Snoring, too. Damn!

All a dream. Can I sleep again? Not to a terrible nightmare! Can't return there.

Must rise and dispel the fantasy. Leave the boy asleep, don't want company. Got to think. Restore the stove fire, careful not to bang iron on iron. Heat water, boil coffee, sit, and think.

Remember the dream. Why was I going to church? Haven't been for years, never been to a Mass. Why would I be on Main Street without clothes? Thank goodness Kalish was open on the Sabbath. Why did I dream the bridges disappeared and the ferrymen paid me no heed? And why Camden?

It's Ellen. I do wish I felt more comfortable with Ellen O'Neil. Such Catholic display. The home altar. The Mary statue. The pictures of saints. Innocence anchored in the church.

Preposterous that I, George Chase, would convert?

That perfect face, that child-like nose and mouth, that porcelain complexion, that delicate figure, that pure guilelessness. The very image of an angel, trained by home and school for a simple chasteness. She looks kindly upon me, this worldly creature, this fallen man, this outsider…but, also, I am a free thinker…this skeptic…proud of an open mind…an enlightened soul…an independent man.

Stop! Think of the advantages, man. Jerome O'Neil, "barrister." Quite a father-in-law! Wealth and influence. Entrée to British commerce and an international career.

Is all that not worth a weekly whiff of incense?

Bother!

*　　　　　　　*　　　　　　　*

"Margaret, Margaret, it's Mister Chase. He's come to call on Ellen. Poor thing. He doesn't know he's in trouble. Let's go down to entertain him until Mater and she return from the shops." Mary kneeled on the window bench in the girl's front bedroom. Bored with games, they took up time before supper.

The younger O'Neil sisters flew down the stairs to the presence of their sister's beau, all rustling of satin and bouncing hair ringlets. The maid let in the young man to the center hall, offering to closet his cane and hat.

George looked up and smiled at Ellen's sisters.

"What have we here? Two deer bounding through the house?"

"Dear? He called us 'dear,' Mary. Ooh, don't tell Ellen. Oh, Mister Chase, she isn't here just now, but don't leave. She's shopping with Mater."

"We have him all to ourselves, Margaret. Come, Mister Chase, come into the parlor. We have a new deck of cards. Mater lets us play. Do you know any games? We'll play for something. We'll wager on ha'pennies." The girls took Chase's hands and walked backwards, pulling the man into the parlor.

"Let's put him in Father's chair."

"No, if we put him on the sofa, we can both sit with him."

"Girls, girls. If we are to play cards, we must sit across a table. Why not the dining room?" Chase said to confuse the plan.

Mary looked at Margaret and shook her head.

"Cards were a bad idea, and isn't wagering a sin for Protestants, Mister Chase?" Margaret said, hand on hip, wagging a finger.

"No, Mister Chase, we ought to sit on the sofa and *converse*." Mary recalled her sister's term for proper entertainment of men.

The three sat on the sofa.

"Do you have family in Calais, Mister Chase?"

"Yes, my brother, Daniel, has arrived from Vermont to move in with Paul and me. He will be starting a business, dealing in land."

"And your parents? Are they well?" They asked, shaking heads affirmatively.

"Yes, the elder Chases continue to reside in Vermont, thank you for asking after them."

The door opened. Missus O'Neil and Ellen entered the house. George Chase stood to greet the ladies. Mary and Margaret scattered.

"Good afternoon, Mister Chase. I hope you haven't waited long. I'm sure Ellen's sisters found you entertaining meantime. Ellen, do help me with the packages. Please resume sitting while Ellen's occupied, Mister Chase." While Missus O'Neil had acknowledged George's presence, Ellen walked by without a glance. She headed straight back into the pantry.

George remained standing, examining the family altar off the living room, a chapel for family devotions. Would there be daily Mass here? Stained glass windows let in the afternoon sun, bright colors, bordering on gaudy. The statue of the Virgin Mary draped in rosary beads, a serene expression on a pure white visage. Prints of Renaissance paintings, naked Jesuses, writhing on crosses - scenes at once sensual and repugnant.

He realized Ellen had entered the room. She stood anticipating his recognition.

"Mister Chase, how disturbed you've made me."

"What can you mean, Miss O'Neil?"

"Here, take this filth away from my home," she threw a book at George's chest. Unprepared, the volume bounced onto the floor, landing face down, pages rumpled. He bent to pick up Cooper's *The Last of the Mohicans.*

"I feel desecrated, sullied, disgusted, my soul pierced. You encouraged me to start that novel and I finished the first few chapters until Pater informed me it is condemned by the Index of Prohibited Books as 'pernicious writing.' Do you know what I've had to do? Confession and penance. You had no right to contaminate my soul."

"But, Miss O'Neil, Cooper's books are universally admired as the new American literature. He has my greatest respect, and the message is certainly moral, the sadness of a noble race, now defeated. It's about natural people – settlers, the great struggle for this continent, and Indians – hardly obscene. What kind of literature is not on your Index?"

"Not Indians, that's certain. Natty Bumpo? Hawk-eye? Leatherstocking? What grotesque names! A greedy publisher pandered to man's basest nature and printed a novel about Red Indians. Worse still, isn't Bumpo a half-breed with a white mother?

"What virtuous maid would accede to marriage with a savage? The book masks as literature. True literature is uplifting, true literature is the life of manners and politeness. I prefer reading about ladies and gentlemen in polite conversation."

86

"Please, sit, my dear. Be calm. I'm so sorry to upset you," he encouraged Ellen to sit beside him on the sofa. She took a distant chair, instead.

"Please understand, Miss O'Neil, I meant no harm. I lent the book as one friend to another. Perhaps you would lend me some literature of your interest," he bent to take her hand. She tucked her hands among her skirts as she sat knees tight, body turned aside, lips pursed.

"Go, sit over there, Mister Chase. Be civilized. You have much to learn, if we are to continue."

The supper passed in stilted conversation. As he ate, he seethed over their quarrel. How vexing to find such small mindedness, such intolerance!

The Index of Prohibited Books? Surely, a vestige of the Middle Ages still lingering after a century after Voltaire's scorn.

The incident opened his eyes. The girl's beauty had blinded him to her irritating mannerisms, aspects once eclipsed, but now raised to stark relief.

He thought, let me count the ways she annoys.

She fasts.

This meal she sits, sipping water, while others eat. She takes pleasure in asceticism. Is that tiny figure merely the product of starvation?

She prepares no food. Family servants provide all domestic labor, including cooking, which she abhors. She takes pride in her ignorance of all baking, all ingredients, and all recipes.

She sews nothing, knits nothing, preferring only decorative pursuits, such as cross-stitch. All her clothes originate in a seamstress's shop, an expensive affectation.

She refuses to ride a horse, even finding a sidesaddle indecorous.

She eschews small boats, fearful of water. She prefers walking in manicured parks and gardens, never going near a woods.

Not only does she look like a Dresden doll; she acts like an ornamentation, adored but useless.

He speculated about intimate details. Do those Platonic characteristics extend to the marriage bed, as well?

George permitted himself a vulgar thought.

Are those legs under her parents' table ever to be spread in pleasure or only for grimacing propagation of little Catholics?

The absolute most infuriating quirk of all was this affectation to address her parents in a dead language, Latin, as *Mater* and *Pater*.

What a little prig! The meal ended, George and Ellen were permitted to retreat alone to the parlor.

"Having time to consider you actions, Mister Chase, can you express remorse for having desecrated my soul with your Cooper book? Are you prepared to apologize?"

"Much has been revealed this evening. Miss O'Neil. As mature people, we may have discovered an important difference between us. What desecrates your soul consummates mine. Madam, I can compete against any man, however, I have no chance against God."

*   *   *

Barbados rum or Monongahela whiskey? The whiskey rushed to his head faster, but the taste was bitter. Rum acted slower, but he preferred the sweetness.

He kept jugs under the cottage, away from Paul.

A drink at noon with the meal would do no harm. Maybe, one in the morning would inspire fluency of thought. No harm done.

"Paul, what have you been up to? Have you been under the cottage?"

"That rum is no good. I threw those jugs in the river. Mister Chase, you been drunk. You look like dead man."

"Damn you, boy. Dare you correct your betters and I kick your black ass!"

Chase attempted to reach Paul but fell against the hot stove.

"Jesus Christ! I burned my hand. Help me! I demand you help me."

"No, Mister Chase. Miz Chandler has a bed for me. I come back when you not sick with drink no more."

Chapter Nineteen

Clear weather on the Penobscot Bay, Harriet joins friends to climb Mount Battie above Camden. The path leads through copses and thickets, until the vegetation gives way to a rocky peak. Camden Harbor below floats miniature ships, moving like skimmers on a pond, independent of human will. Out in the bay, tiny white waves grace swells. Clumps of fishing dories work nets. Far in the distance, islets cluster around Vinalhaven and North Haven.

Everyone brings picnic food. Men spread blankets while women set out victuals. Everything tastes fresh and sharp. Among her girl friends, talk turns to her impending marriage. When will Captain Follansbee return? Will they have a home in town, near her parents, or will he ask her aboard, his helpmate for a voyage to the Orient?

One of the men brings a telescope, now shared by a crowd, calling out the sights. "I can see Rockland Harbor. Look, the village on Vinalhaven."

Harriet looks through the glass.

"Miss Norwood, look at that ship entering the harbor, rounding Spenser's Island. Is that familiar to you?"

It is Black Cloud, her fiancé's vessel. An early arrival, Jeremiah Follansbee safe at last. All her dreams came true.

She hands off the scope and starts down the slope. Her clothes catch on thorny bushes, leaving patches on the trail. Reckless, she pushes away branches, letting them snap behind her. She leaps from outcropping to outcropping, heedless of footing. Perspiration runs down her arms and legs, as her clothes became damp. The pleasant taste of excitement grips her throat. Her lips moisten. Her hair falls from the pins, loose around her shoulders.

Harriet reaches the level ground and runs toward the harbor. She sees Black Cloud tied up at the wharf, men lifting off casks. She searches for her lover, Captain Jeremiah Follansbee.

That man with his back turned. The broad shoulders, the bushy beard, the black hat, shouting gruff orders. My promise, my commander has come home!

Jeremiah! It's me.

The man turns.

William Norwood, bearded smile, opens his arms to hug his daughter.

      *   *   *

Oh, no. She opened her eyes. Laying face down in her sun-filled bedroom, her lace pillowcase was glued to her face with spittle and sweat.

Harriet jumped to her hands and knees, away from the wet sheets. She threw the pillow across the room! She tore the damp nightgown over her head and sat on the edge of the bed, waiting for the loathing to subside.

Didn't she want to be a captain's wife, raised for the role, a perfect knowledge of the expectations? Captains' wives, free of the pressure to provide a domestic haven for a husband's daily needs, were the freest women in America.

Yet, that freedom came at a price.

Were her parents ever companions, or were they mere associates, like distant partners in an enterprise? Neither she nor her siblings were born when Father was to home. She thought of the rumors among women whose husbands traveled the Pacific, each man having a dusky Dido to lure the lonely mariner to palm groves.

Harriet sat at her secretary and pulled out stationary.

Representative George Chase   June 1, 1836
Calais, Maine

Dear Mister Chase,

Please forgive my forwardness to inquire about your health and condition.

In March this year I learned of your rise to political position as representative for our grand state of Maine, my cousin being Representative Israel Snow, who related to my family his fondness of you. I do hope our Israel comported himself appropriately. At times he can display an excess of character.

Mother and Father are well, especially now that Father has retired from his voyages.

How is life up on your frontier region? I think life in a new country would be stimulating, especially for the ambitious. Are you standing for representative again?

I ask about Paul. In the past two years he would have changed from boy to man. I hope he makes you proud. You are so good to act the protective older brother. I pray no one misuses him.

If you have time, I would like to hear from you.

With sincerity,
Miss Harriet Norwood

*   *   *

Miss Harriet Norwood   June 10, 1836
Camden, Maine

Dear Miss Norwood,

Thank you for your kind letter of July 20.

Your letter found me well. Paul works, partly as shipwright, partly as my steward. He has become the independent man in Calais, often traveling to outlying areas in the wilderness. He has grown in stature and size as well, filling out his upper parts. Although some may confuse him with local Indians, he is respected among the tradesmen in the city.

I have stood again and hope to be re-elected representative for the district. My practice at times suffers for my political activities.

I remain grateful to your cousin, Mister Snow, with whom I worked on the morals legislation, both earning a name for sound law and honest brokering. I shall be in his debt. Will he stand once more? I suppose the good citizenry of his island would gladly return him to office. I anticipate his hearty voice booming through the marble halls in Augusta, announcing this year's mandate.

This region is most exciting in its transcendent beauty and its commercial potential. Ships cover the

Passamaquoddy Bay. Commerce thrives with lumber, ship building, and cross-border trade. Regional freight travels to Britain, the West Indies, as well as Boston and New York. Many fine shops have sprung up along Main Street in Calais and across the short bridge to St. Stephen, which, although a foreign country, is easily accessible. The ladies of Calais enjoy the comforts as they would in any American city.

      Your letter is highly appreciated. There are times in a man's life when he dwells on past decisions with regret. There are times when a man recalls having used words for which he later must beg forgiveness. There are times in a man's life when he doesn't know what he loved until that love was lost.

I am,
your obed't serv't,
George Chase

     *   *   *

Dear George,   June 16, 1836

      Forgiveness unnecessary.

In loving kindness,
Harriet

He read her brief letter as he sat amid a trash of bottles and discarded food. Maggots crawled around raw garbage in a bucket. The handsome face wore a growth of black beard. Hair, unkempt and tousled, formed greasy waves above the collar. A dirty shirt covered his frame down to exposed legs and feet.

"What a thorough mess of things I've made," he bent over and rested his forehead on the page. His shoulders shuttered, and he wept. The letter dampened with salty tears. George shuffled to the bed and fell upon grimy sheets, her letter in his hand. He collapsed forward and fell asleep in the afternoon light.

Hours later, awake, he rolled over in darkness.

"Must light a lamp," he searched the table for matches, knocking over bottles and sending papers to the floor. Scratch and light revealed the dismal room.

He carried the matches over to the stove, but realized neither kindling nor wood would be found in the cottage. Pulling on trousers, he stumbled to the shed, bringing back armloads of split oak, handfuls of twigs and chips. Soon, a fire roared in the stove.

Returning outside, George fetched buckets of water, several for the zinc tub and one on the stove to heat. In the firelight, he saw the desolation of empty bottles about the house; his soul's poison. Gathering all flasks, jugs, and bottles, he tossed them clattering into a grain sack. Pulling on a coat, he walked through the dark lanes of Milltown to the St. Croix. He stood on a boulder and flung the burden into the rapids. George enjoyed the shattering. Watching until the last thread of burlap sunk into the froth, he walked back to the bright light and warmth of the cottage.

George searched around a box until he found his straight razor. He lathered his face and scraped off the stubble, leaving beard from temple to ears. After drying his face, George opened a jar of pomade and slicked down the tousled hair with a comb, bent to the wall mirror.

By this time, the room had warmed to eighty degrees, and window panes dripped with steam. George removed the water from the stove and mixed it with the cold, heating it to a tolerable degree. Removing clothes, George slipped into the narrow tub, legs folded to this chin. With a body brush, he stood to lather his body with a bar of lye and ashes soap and dipped to rinse off the suds.

George dried himself and began dressing, first covering his body from neck to wrists to ankles with white underclothes. He pulled on his trousers, attaching buttons to suspenders stretched over the shoulders. His shirt, stiffened with starch, fit over the suspenders and buttoned with silver links from collar to waist. He tied a black silk cravat around the batwing collar that sat high on his neck. Searching wall pegs, he found the brocaded yellow waistcoat and buttoned it under his suit jacket. Plopping his beaver hat over the greased hair, he picked up the straight black cane before stepping out onto the road.

"Paul, Mister Chase wants to see you," William Porter, shipyard owner, had crossed the yard to deliver the message. Paul found George in the shipyard's office, dressed in black suit, shoes polished, face shaved, hair slicked. His eyes sparkled.

"I'm leaving for a few days. The cottage has been swept clean of all drink. Feel welcome to use it. Come outside. We should talk."

Paul followed him to the street, away from a crowded office.

"Boss, I can't believe. You look like new man, like my friend George Chase."

Chase looked into Paul's eyes. "Paul, I've been a cad and a drunk. Please forgive me. You have been my friend, trying to help. Over the past month I've gone from the street gutter to a re-birth, a higher order of person."

"A new lady? Be careful," Paul cautioned.

"It's been nearly two years since we left Camden, but…"

"Miss Harriet? You heard from her?" asked Paul.

"We've exchanged letters. She's written twice now in her lovely hand."

"Oh, Miss Harriet, she bold to say she loves you."

"Well, she wasn't that bold. She only hinted." Chase shuffled his feet.

"She still loves you, boss. Think the old captain will let you see her?"

"Nothing tried, nothing gained, lad. Come back home to care for the cottage."

"I keep house neat. You bring back Miss Harriet. I make best impression."

Chapter Twenty

The door rap brought Deborah Norwood's attention from the scene in her temperance novel - the child pleaded with her father to leave the tippling shop where he caroused among the town's scum. As she arrived at the door, her flush of anger at the father's selfishness was replaced by surprise at the identity of the caller.

"Why, Mister Chase, whatever brings you here?"

"The hope that I may speak with your daughter."

"No. That is not possible. If you must know, she is engaged to a man with high prospects, and she awaits his return from a prosperous voyage, when they shall be wed. When last I observed, she busied herself adding to her hope chest. You do your reputation harm, Mister Chase, by appearing at this door like a hound in heat."

"I do not deserve nor did I invite such a comparison, Missus Norwood. Had I no word from your daughter, I would have no business in Camden at all."

"Word? You've exchanged words?"

"There, madam, I've said too much already. Kindly communicate my regards to the lady. Good day," George turned and walked out the door. Stopping at the road, he stood for several minutes deciding his next destination, to the town to look up old friends or back to the steamer, returning that afternoon.

Harriet looked up from the close stitching on her bonnet. Her eyes stung with concentration. She stood and walked to the window. A man leaned, his back to the house, against the fence. Dressed in black from beaver hat to shiny boots, he looked quite formal for the noonday hour. He seemed preoccupied with thought, looking right and left. His movements looked familiar when he adjusted his gloves and spanked his left hand with the cane's gold head. She saw his profile when he turned to the harbor.

Mercy me, it's George Chase! What's going on?

Harriet gathered her skirts and rushed downstairs.

"Mother, did George Chase come to our door?"

Deborah looked up, flustered by the second interruption.

"What of it? From my point of view, the man has no business at this house and no cause to pursue. A young woman, promised to her betrothed, would be ill advised to threaten her future by communicating with a former lover."

Harriet burst into tears.

"My future? I hate my future, Mother. The stark future of a captain's wife."

"Stop that drivel. Have you read too many romances about trite husbands in homey nests of domestic bliss? Those romances exist only in the heads of silly girls. I know my daughter. One week of such so-called bliss, and you'd be raging against any husband. Those romances describe a hearth-side democracy that doesn't exist. It is the nature of males to rule their homes, my dear. They dole out the medicine of absolute monarchy, best taken by wives in small doses. No, do not trade your captain for this lawyer."

"Mother, your opinion of men is biased, entirely predicated on Father. That's unfair to George. He cares what I think and feel."

"He cares? You know his mind? How is that possible, since you haven't seen him for over a year? Have you carried on correspondence secretly behind our backs?"

Deborah stood and approached Harriet, who retreated, backing into the center hall.

"Am I not a grown woman, emancipated from my parents' control?"

"We shall see, Harriet. Go to your room and compose yourself. Fetch a basin and wash your face."

"No. I have more urgent business to conduct at the harbor."

"In my day, no lady pursued a man unless she were in the 'business' of cultivating a sullied reputation."

"I will always honor your opinion, Mother, and hope that you will come to respect my decisions. My mistake was to release George Chase. If I am to live my life as an honest woman, I must rectify that mistake. Now, I must hurry before I lose him forever." She slammed the door.

"Harriet, your hat, your gloves. Come back."

*   *   *

Chase reclaimed his stateroom, waiting for the afternoon departure. He flung his satchel down on the bunk and seethed at a gloomy return to Calais.

"Damn, damn, if I'd only known she was betrothed, I'd never have made such a fool of myself. Came all this way and turned back by her mother. Awful news, but what else could I expect. Harriet Norwood shall never pass into spinsterhood.

"Egad! In the arms of another man. I suppose old Norwood primed the pump with his bundling board again. What a thought! Could I expect otherwise?"

A tapping came from the stateroom's flimsy door. George rose, unlatched the catch, and opened the door to see a hatless Harriet standing on deck, the western sun illuminating her hair tossed about her shoulders. She reached and pulled him onto the passageway.

"Come out. I mustn't be seen entering your room. Is this visit about my letters?"

"Partly," he looked away, taking a breath. "You never mentioned any engagement. I am the fool to have come here."

"No! You mustn't say that. It's important that you took the risk. Yes, I am engaged, but it was a hasty decision. I never stopped loving you, George Chase. I ran down here this moment, a spectacle in my home town, to restore the possibility that you love me also." She pleaded.

George smiled at her earnestness.

"Heaven defend two fools, Harriet! It must be Providence that brought us to this point. If I cannot love and marry

100

you, my life will be a shambles. I could not choose otherwise. You invade my mind and soul."

"And you mine, also, dear heart, with a higher power than fate. It is truly the will of Providence that we should rediscover our love. What will you have me do? I am yours to dispose as you will. I would depart with you this day, sharing this cabin without shame."

"Whoa, keep your head about you. There is a certain captain who deserves a letter, and your parents deserve respect. 'Tis better to have their blessing." He held her hands.

"I will do all I can to leave my parents' house under favorable circumstances. Perhaps leaving with my trousseau and hope chest, perhaps not. But, leave I shall."

George and Harriet stood in full view of the busy wharves. Crewmen brushed past them on the narrow passageway, between the rail and the staterooms. Barrels, boxes, and packets were being loaded from the dock. A rumble came from the boat's interior, steam building up in the boilers, announcing imminent departure.

"I must return to Calais this afternoon. I shall write daily."

"I, as well," she started to pull away, disengaging her hands.

Chase pulled her back by the wrist, his hand reached for the small of her back. He pulled her willowy figure against him and kissed her mouth. Her arms reached to embrace his head. The kiss lingered, neither wanting to part.

Across the docks and decks, on barks, ships, schooners, and skiffs plying Camden's tight harbor, crew and stevedores halted to gawk. One seaman began to clap slowly, mocking sentiment. Other joined in, laughing.

Harriet stepped back, red-faced, and ran down the gangplank, a surefooted trot, skirts lifted, tresses streaming.

*   *   *

The widow opened her son's letter. A paper bank note fell from the folds. A seaman on the *Black Cloud*, Robert had written his mother from the outbound layover in the Sandwich Islands with much news. The bank note, official Maine scrip and easy to cash, was his month's wages.

Annabelle Tawdry read each passage slowly. Robert was a pious boy, wary of shipping out to heathen parts. Quotes from Scripture laced prose to assure his mother he remained a child of the Holy Spirit.

Robert remarked on the crew's scandalous behavior in the port of Lahaina. They caroused on the town's streets, danced, played cards, and visited the native women. Then, Robert wrote about the actions of Captain Follansbee. Annabelle forced her eyes off the text. Looking heavenwards, she recited Psalm Nineteen:

Let the words of my mouth,
And the meditation of my heart
Be acceptable in thy sight, Oh Lord
My strength and my redeemer

She knew her duty. Widow Tawdry, black hat and shawl in place, walked out of the modest frame house behind the harbor. She passed through the business section, past the church, and into the wealthier residential district on Elm. Walking directly up to the Norwood home, she banged on the door. Both Captain and Misses Norwood were present.

"Pardon me. Ye may not know who I am, but my son is seaman on the *Black Cloud*. I got this here letter from him. Something he writes should concern yer daughter."

In the parlor, the widow Tawdry handed the letter to the couple. She had marked the disgraceful passage with a pencil, but they read the entire letter, noting young Tawdry's forthright lack of guile.

He wrote: It warnt enough fer crew to run with the dusky doxies about this Sodom and

102

Gormorah, but the captain hisself took up with a Kanaka girl. He's bought himself her services for the two-weeks of our layover. Keeps her in his cabin to frolik. She cud not be mor than 12 yers old, Her bein only a child, I think he commits two sins - a crime genst natur as well as fornicatin.

"Pardon me for askin'," the widow said, "but warn't yer daughter betrothed to this Captain Follansbee?"

Chapter Twenty-One

Captain Norwood stood in the hallway, head swathed in billowing tobacco smoke, displaying the patience of a wise man waiting on womanly preparations. Norwood wore the blue wool suit, garb for commanding the helm of a three-masted ship. Today, he would receive, not give, orders.

Before his feet lay boxes arrayed by wife and daughter. Luggage and trunks, some family heirlooms like the hope chest. This luggage contained the accumulation of more than twenty years of female costume, crafts, collections – a daughter's paraphernalia, emptied from her room, soon to become a guestroom, perhaps serving visits from future grandchildren, should the captain live to see the day.

"Father, have you the tickets for this steam boat?" Deborah Norwood demanded to know.

"Yes, Mother, since days ago. The horse cart stands ready on the road. If I may only begin loading...?"

"Patience, Father. I need to survey everything at once. If anything is loaded, I couldn't.... Now, where is that hatbox?"

"Right here, at my feet."

"No, that's the other one. Harriet! Harriet! Come to the banister. I have a question."

Harriet Norwood leaned over the railing from the second floor, looking at her parents in the center hallway. Her hair fell in ringlets about her face as she leaned on the banister.

"Yes?"

"Bring the other hatbox and every thing from your room. Father is waiting."

Harriet appeared at the top step, holding a box in one hand and a parasol in the other. Captain Norwood watched her negotiate the crinoline skirt down the stairs. Her summer dress had a close-fitting bodice with tight, elbow-length sleeves. Her 'bertha' collar accentuated the sloping shoulders. Her full skirt was gathered at the waist and fell to the instep. On her head she wore a circular bonnet, drawn with an internal decoration of live flowers. The bride was outfitted to meet the groom.

Once the horse cart was loaded, Harriet and her parents walked to the steamer dock beside the mare, Father holding the trace while mother and daughter chatted.

On the docks, crew scrambled to load the belongings of Captain Norwood's family into the two staterooms. Her father deposited his grip into his cabin and started to explore the boat. Deborah settled Harriet's belongings into her paneled compartment.

"One of our wedding gifts, my dear, is a leather-bound copy of Missus Child's *The American Frugal Housewife*. Do not expect a young husband rising in his career to afford extravagance in the household. A young wife should not be ashamed of economy.

"Also is a year's supply of wick string. Do not buy sperm candles this winter; they're too dear. Missus Child calls for ten ounces of mutton tallow, a quarter of an ounce of camphor, four ounces of beeswax and two ounces of alum. Those ingredients always assure candles burning with clear light. Wait for the first cool day in September to make your winter candles.

"A young bride should take care of her health. Bathe often, rubbing your skin with a hard brush. Do not read or sew at twilight. Air your bed-chamber, never heat it. On the other hand, never let the night's miasma blow in from an open window."

They heard a rumbling from the bowels of the vessel, the boiler fueled, ready to engage the great paddle wheel. Deborah calmed herself by removing Harriet's bonnet, unpinning her hair to brush. The ivory handle flashed in the blond tresses.

"Your fair hair will always be your crown, my daughter. Remember, too frequent use of an ivory comb injures it, and only wash your hair in rum.

"If you are scratched by a nail, a rind of pork bound upon the wound prevents the lock-jaw. Dysentery is cured with a porridge made of boiled flour and milk as well as a tablespoonful of West Indian rum, molasses, and sweet oil.

"Mister Chase has a pale complexion. He may suffer chilblains in winter. Bind his feet and hands in suet or rub with Castile soap and honey."

Harriet pulled away from her mother, to brush herself.

"Mother, I'm sure this is all worthy guidance. I promise to read Missus Child."

"I know. I'm prattling on. Please forgive you mother's old-fashioned advice. You've always been my independent child. I should have no concerns, except for your happiness as a new bride. After all your experiences, I respect your foresight in choosing George Chase. You are marrying for love, not expediency, the free choice and honest preference of a mature woman."

Deborah halted, as if she required a pause to accent the importance of the next topic. Looking away from Harriet, she addressed, finally, the most sensitive issue.

"You and I have always shared confidences on delicate subjects. Have I ever put off your questions with lies or mysteries?" Harriet shook her head, and Deborah continued.

"As your natural curiosity peaked, we had frank discussions, to prevent your recourse to domestics or immodest school-companions with minds filled with anecdotes of vice and vulgarity. You deserved a rational explanation about intimacy from your mother.

"When a young woman embarks on marriage, it's her mother's duty to prepare her for private affection. A couple is to enjoy mutual bliss, but do not exaggerate expectations to suit romance novels. Complete marital joy develops over time in nature's own course. Assume husbands know nothing about a wife's body. Her duty is to guide his clumsy ventures. Is there anything I've left unsaid, my dear?"

"Nothing," Harriet blurted.

"Has Mister Chase made all the arrangements with the parson?"

"We are to be married by the town clerk."

"No parson? Then, no church? What kind of wedding is this?"

"A civil ceremony, mother. Mister Chase is a skeptic. He attends no church."

"Mercy, my first child to enter a marriage without a church home. Your nieces and nephews, at least, are being raised in a faith."

"Yes, Methodists, and, as I recall, you complained bitterly that my sister-in-law was not Congregational."

"Help your dear mother, Harriet. What am I to expect? Will there be vows? A ring? What time of day is the ceremony?"

"A ceremony and reception in a home. We chose Anglican vows, and George has the ring."

They heard a rap on the louvered door.

"Mother? Harriet? The steamer is about to depart. Come out and watch."

The women stepped onto the promenade.

Smoke belched from high black cylindrical stacks. The boat's firemen flung split chunks of wood into the flaming furnace from the deck's pile. A gear kicked the paddle wheel into rotation, propelling the boat away from the dock.

The Norwoods watched the town of Camden recede from view as the *Belfast* sped across Penobscot Bay, headed for Castine; the first fueling station. Father eagerly studied all functions of the boat.

"Do you mind my gadding about the vessel?" he asked.

Harriet answered. "That's fine by me, Father. You know my weak stomach for open water. I shall lie down and ignore the yawing. Knock when it's time for supper."

"Do as you wish, Father." said Deborah. "Look for me in our stateroom. Harriet, look to your wedding dress.

See that it's folded right. We may not be able to iron out any creases."

The *Belfast* offered comfortable accommodations for over-night travelers.

Harriet let herself into her stateroom with a little brass key, opening a light louvered door that protected modesty but permitted fresh air. She closed the window shutters, adjusting the movable louvers. Her room's walls were paneled in carved white birch. One wall held a narrow bunk with drawers beneath. A table swung on hinges, attached to the wall, which, when released, stood on one leg, its surface inlaid with gold leaf. A chair allowed the traveler to sit, reading or writing at the table.

She lay on the coverlet, head on pillow, looking at the ceiling's design. The rafters, supporting the boat's upper storey were exposed. An oil lamp swung from one rafter, moving to the boat's lurching. The side wheel churned in liquid rhythm. The stomping of the crew grew fainter. Voices receded. She allowed her mind to range free among errant thoughts, fantasizing she were an English princess in a Middle Ages fantasy being transported across the channel by King William to marry the French prince, the Dauphin, in royal splendor.

Except for breakfast and supper, Harriet's father spent the voyage poking around the steamer while it churned from Camden to Castine to Machiasport to Eastport. There, they transferred to a smaller open steamer, the *Tom Thumb*, for a quick ride up the St. Croix to Calais. At the steamer dock in Calais was a delegation of gentlemen, dressed in suits and beaver hats.

Paul Kamehameha, in elegant black, advanced to greet Captain Norwood.

"Would this be the Norwood wedding party?"

*   *   *

Calais society had prepared for the wedding of the summer. The family of George Downes, senior lawyer and president of Calais Bank, welcomed the Norwoods into their home. Lydia Downes insisted that the bride and her family rest that Tuesday evening, postponing any calling by ladies of the town. Wednesday would provide plenty of time for introductions, the wedding to be on Thursday morning at the Chandler's

All day Wednesday, wives and daughters from all levels of Calais society called at the Downes' home. Elizabeth Ann Chandler arrived early, conferring with Deborah on seating and serving. Harriet and her mother asked Missus Chandler to assume the role of Matron of Honor. After several other wives of prominent men stopped to offer their congratulations, Mary McShea, wife of the injured Patrick, George's first client, sat primly on the edge of her chair, introduced to the bride and family, as her youngest daughter, Theresa, listened to instructions. She would be the flower girl.

Father Andrew Murray, attired in black, stunned Deborah Norwood when he appeared in the Downes' parlor. She resisted his cordial manner, having preconceptions regarding Catholic people. Father Murray bore the message that he permitted his parishioners participation in a ceremony, smacking of Protestant ritual.

Later that afternoon, upstairs, Harriet and Deborah prepared the bridal trousseau. From one trunk, she gathered her undergarments; light materials sewn during the past decade. From another, she pulled the wedding dress, a design she duplicated after studying the newly popular magazines for women's clothing, Louis Godey's *Lady's Book* and Sarah Hale's *Lady's Magazine*.

Harriet laid the gown over the bed sheet, admiring the details. Using generous yards of pink silk, she and her mother had created a high-waisted full gown, gathered in pleats, with a matching puffed yoke. Imitation lacing appeared on the bodice, rising from the waist. Over each shoulder of the yoke were six buttons, defining the scalloped edge. Sleeves came to the elbow, ending in a lace cuff.

Inside the bodice was linen backing, secured at the nape with string. String also secured the gown's back. The simple garment's sole ornamentation was a silk cord, attached to the high waist, dangling two feet from the sides. The silk cord ended in matching bells, tied at the back.

Meanwhile, Captain Norwood transacted business. He and the groom's father, Moses Chase sat with George Downes in the offices of Calais Bank. Using notes from a Portland bank, he funded an account of five thousand dollars, a dowry, under the groom's name, George M. Chase.

*   *   *

Morning of Thursday, July 7, 1836 brought a day of warmth and sunshine. After a light breakfast, George, accompanied by Paul, his brother, and father, and various male friends, assembled at the Chandler household. The groom's party wore tight-fitting, swallow tail, double-breasted jackets, uniformly black. Each wore a high collar, attached to a dickey, a false front, with white satin cravats.

At ten o'clock, a carriage pulled up, bearing the bride's wedding party. Captain Norwood assisted all ladies as they alighted from the vehicle. Finally, Harriet Norwood emerged, bearing a bouquet of sweetheart roses and baby's breath. George's friends boisterously blocked his view of the entrance to prevent even a peek.

The bridal party lined for the processional, while George stood with his brother, Daniel, and the town clerk, Thomas Rice, before the Chandler's mantle. The parlor had been arranged with two groups of chairs and a center aisle. Guests crowded the small room, spilling out into hallway and dining area. Other guests, less formally attired, Chase's rougher constituents, lounged around the yard, watching the pig roast. The aroma of Chinese and Double-musk Roses vied for domination of the parlor, blocking the odor of food.

The bride's process started into the entrance hall. Gentlemen of the Calais bar escorted Deborah Norwood, followed by bridesmaids and matrons. Elizabeth Ann

Chandler led Theresa McShea, the flower girl, whose tiny hands strewed rose petals over the carpets. Finally, Harriet, right arm entwined with her father's left, stepped pace by pace up the aisle. The pair halted at the mantle, facing Clerk Rice.

Speaking to the assembly, Rice asked, "Who is to give away this woman?"

"I am," said the captain, and he placed Harriet's right hand into George's. Bowing at the shoulders to his daughter, he stepped back and took the chair beside Deborah.

Rice carried out his brief offices.

"Dearly beloved, we are gathered here today to celebrate with George and Harriet as they unite in marriage. May they honor and cherish each other through long lives."

Turning to George, Rice asked, "Have you the ring? Are you ready to say your vow?"

George turned to Harriet, looking into her eyes. Slipping the gold ring over her left hand, he recited the ancient words, "With this ring I thee wed and this gold thee I give and with my body I thee worship, and with all my worldly chattels I thee honor."

Turning, Rice addressed Harriet, "Are you ready to say your vow?"

Holding George's hands, Harriet looked up at his face.

She recited her antique pronouncement.

"I take thee to my wedded husband, to have and to hold, for fairer for fouler, for better for worse, for richer for poorer, in sickness and in health, to be bonny and buxom in bed and at board till death us depart."

Stepping back, Thomas Rice said, "I pronounce you man and wife. You may kiss the bride, Mister Chase."

Family and guests burst into applause, and all rose to congratulate the couple. The party would last far into the night, even at the bridal window.

*   *   *

Their privacy was soon broken by midnight revelers, come for the traditional *Shivaree*. Dozens of young people crept close to the cottage, pulling a wagonload of trashed crockery and cheap tin pots. At a signal, they tipped the wagon bed, smashing the old plates and cups against the house, nearest the bedroom window, while banging the pots together. The sound of dishes smashed mingled with bawdy verses, the noise wafting clearly through the neighborhood's open windows on this warm July night. Finally, George took a bottle out to the crowd, to make them relent and depart.

As the revelers drifted away, the mantle clock struck one. George found a match and lit a candle on the dressing table, checking the curtains. He offered Harriet a last sip from the goblet. Wedding gifts lay on tables in the room.

While she lay, ringlets arrayed over the pillow, her head propped, George sat on the bed's edge, one leg tucked under, one over the edge, all the better to see her face. He stroked her cheek as they recollected the day, the mirth, the generosity, the friends, flirting between men and maids in the entourage.

George stood and reached for the candle to pinch the flame.

"Oh, don't, George. It's a serene bath of light. Let me drink in the sight of my new husband."

With such a welcome, George slipped inside the sheets to consummate the experiment begun in Camden two years before, no longer confined by any bundling board. By May 15, 1837 Harriet and George greeted their first child, George Monroe Chase Junior.

Chapter Twenty-Two

From his father's arms, wide-eyed with awe, Georgie watched the children in costume; small ones in white angel robes with garland hair; large ones in dark shepherd garb, golden robes and crowns, one face blackened with burnt cork. Two comely youths played the holy couple, the girl mature enough to handle the baby Jesus, her own sibling. All actors stood in silent tableau upon the song's conclusion.

The three-year-old squirmed in George Chase's arms, but father held on, knowing his bold son would bolt toward the crèche scene. Harriet whispered, "Next year, Georgie."

In unison, all raised candles at the last lines of each stanza, casting a glow around the plain, prim interior, reflecting from the flat white plaster, gleaming from the glossy white trim.

...sleep in heavenly peace, sleep in heavenly peace.

Starting a new verse, candles were lowered, shadows rising on walls. The boy turned to watch, over father's shoulder, the congregation's faces distorted by the shimmering glimmer into grotesque masks.

...Christ the Savior is born, Christ the Savior is born.

The carol ended, candles extinguished, room lights raised. The nativity tableau returned into ordinary village children. Released from father's grasp, under his parent's watchful eyes, the boy slipped out of the pew into the aisle and walked up to examine the transformation from drama to everyday.

From the pianoforte, the recessional tune began, and the congregation burst into song:

...Joy to the world! The Lord is come!

Afterward in the aisle, George turned to Harriet, "Well, was it all you dreamed of? Was the magic still there?"

Harriet looked up at her husband's face, confirming her impression.

"Your sarcasm takes nothing away from this moment, George. It's really a shame that you can't enjoy the simple pleasure of a Christmas pageant. The music, the costumes, the lights, the message of hope and joy. You can see how our son is enthralled. Enjoy the time for his sake, if not for yours."

"Horsefeathers, Harriet. It's all a great humbug."

"Enough. Come and greet the minister. We must return home. I am exhausted, and we want nothing to happen here."

Reverend Edward Stone, recent Harvard Divinity graduate, greeted the worshipers on their departure into the snows of Christmas Eve. Although young, he already had the knack of all good pastors, calling out everyone's name and touching the faces of every small child. When the Chase family reached the door, George tried to brush past.

"I believe this would be the Chase family. Merry Christmas to you and welcome to our services at Calais Unitarian." Stone's eyes shone with intensity, arresting George's attention.

"I don't recall our being introduced," George sniffed.

"Ah, but your reputation precedes you, Representative Chase. Perhaps you would grace me with an introduction to your family."

"This is my wife, Harriet Chase, and our son, George Junior."

"Have a very merry Christmas Day tomorrow. We do hope to see you for our regular worship services," intoned the pastor.

Without responding, George stepped away, but she remained standing, attentive to the clergyman.

"Yes, Reverend Stone, you shall see our family at church."

*   *   *

Riding the sleigh back to Milltown, George seethed until he broke the silence.

"Why did you have to commit us to that confounded church?"

"George! That is just the kind of comment I can't tolerate. Our child deserves a wholesome life, besides hearing proper language. Your attitude toward religion fits more the college sophomore than the mind of the head of household, the father of a rambunctious boy and a soon-to-be-born baby, a state legislator, a man of property. Your deism, your atheism, whatever term you apply is a disruption to our family."

"But, Harriet, my principles! I would be breaking my personal code to participate in religion."

"How important are those principles; enough to deny your children an ethical foundation? Husband, we are only two people, soon rearing two children. We have not power enough to provide this bumptious boy with a moral foundation, a sense of right and wrong.

"Did not Father and Mother Chase raise you in church?" she asked.

"Yes, and a harsh Calvinism, cold as the snows of January. With their religion, it's damned if you do and damned if you don't," Harriet held the boy's ears. "From a sadistic and arbitrary God who saves only those he chose before time, no matter what good works they perform during their lives on earth. What incentive is that for the Christian life?"

"Can't you discern the difference between Reverend Stone's branch of faith and the old Puritanism? Stone is thoughtful, joyful, offering a salvation for all who accept Christ, more Ralph Waldo Emerson than Jonathan Edwards. You believe in "open-mindedness," in the "brotherhood of man." I am asking you to apply those principles."

"This is not a fair argument, using my words against me. I ask for a new hearing."

"Home is not Court, sweetheart. Please confine your lawyering to the bench."

A healthy baby girl was born January 4, 1839. That spring she was baptized Harriet Norwood Chase at Calais Unitarian Church.

Chapter Twenty-Three

George reined in the horse and stopped the black chaise for Harriet to see. The awning shaded from the summer sun.

"That's the property. A corner lot, fifty feet wide, more than two hundred feet deep. Almost a half-acre. The fir trees to the north provide a windbreak. But, it's a busy part of the town, maybe you'd prefer a lot on Calais Avenue, something more fashionable."

Harriet turned around on the upholstered leather bench, to view the street scene. The lot's location would be central to town traffic and business, just yards away from the Unitarian Church, a block from Main Street, on Milltown Road, across from the intersection with Washington Avenue. The Jewish community planned to build a synagogue opposite on a lot owned by Kalish, the clothier.

"Look, George, the ship masts show above the downtown buildings. We could look out and see them from our front rooms."

"Would that remind you of Camden?"

"Yes, it would. Always the captain's daughter, though I've lost him, Lord rest his soul. May I never be so far from the sea that a ship mast isn't framed by a window. Those ladies on Calais Avenue see only their neighbor's houses, competing as to whose columns are more Ionic. Or is it Doric? I forget the distinction." She laughed.

George watched her, light hair poking from the bonnet's edge. He loved those times when they came to decisions, delighting in the process.

"Which way is south?" she asked.

"The front faces southeast."

"If the house is built in line with the street, it allows a quarter acre for garden facing south. Oh, George, I can picture it all. How much is the lot?"

"A thousand, and the bank will take paper notes. That leaves our specie intact."

"Have you a builder in mind? I hear Mister Sawyer's done the fine houses on Calais Avenue. "

"And along Main, too, in the Greek style."

"Not too elaborate, though. This is still New England, George, long winters, heavy snow. No two-storey columns, no pediment, looking like a slave plantation or a pagan temple. It should reflect our character. What will the house cost?"

"I've budgeted four thousand."

"That's too much. Make the design less elaborate."

"Still, though, today, in 1846, a new house ought to have more details than a plain saltbox from Camden's Elm Street, all due respect to your parents."

Harriet pouted, "Elegant simplicity, dear. Understated taste, not like these upstart shipping barons displaying intemperate extravagance, magnifying resentment by the poor. The Chase family has an obligation to be the exemplar."

"It's only a house, Harriet."

"No, it's our home, a legacy to our children. Speaking of which, ought we to be returning to them?"

"So," George tapped the horse's flank and shook the reins. The chaise's high wheels began to turn. "Shall I close the sale tomorrow?"

"Yes, and set an appointment with that builder; Sawyer."

Dear Mother,   June 3, 1846

How have you been faring at Elm Street? We think of you often, it being a year since Father passed on.

The children are well, although young George presents his teacher with little effort. I fear he is no scholar, although to his friends he is the boon companion. Little Harriet puzzles me and her father, quick with lessons, yet set upon by catty girls.

The new house is rising from its foundation. As I write the high pitched roof receives her tin cover, necessary before the finish carpenters and plasterers address the interior. Already we see the classical fashion emerging from the raw materials, like a sculptor brings a figure from a block of marble.

Mister Sawyer, the builder, brought books to our house before the first shovel dug the root cellar. He favors the architect, Minard Lafever, for his projects. Lefever published two books, The Modern Builder's Guide and Beauties of Modern Architecture. Mister Chase and I chose some modest designs, fitting our taste.

I attempt to draw a word-picture.

Looking from the road, the front has four second storey windows, each four-over-four double-hung sashes, nicely framed in the clapboard siding. A large entrance porch, supported by Tuscan columns, leads to a paneled door with sidelights to illuminate the center hall. Tall six-over-six double-hung sash windows on either side of the porch provide balance. Finally, Tuscan pilasters at the ends of the house appear to hold up a plain entablature and cornice, framing the entire front. All wood, each pilaster has plain pedestals and capitals. As Greek as is the style, above the cornice is a practical Maine roof, steep enough to support heavy snow, and topped by two chimneys.

As you may well imagine, I plan to establish a garden on the property, between the house and the corner, possibly a quarter acre in size. I asked Mister Sawyer, how is it possible to enjoy the garden while inside the house?

He suggested a bay with three sides, attached to the library, having three tall windows, one facing directly south, bringing light summer and winter. Every window will admit the sight of my flowers. The library shall be my favorite space, my private sanctuary.

New furniture shall arrive by late August, when we take possession. All should be settled by mid-September with children in new schools. Please, do come for the fall months, starting October first until New Year. A bedroom is yours. George will escort you back to Camden on his way to the legislature.

There is so much to do. Outside, laying out the garden until frost hardens the ground, inside, sewing curtains and all the other meticulous detail. No woman needed her mother's wisdom as much as I.

Affectionately,

Your Daughter
Harriet Chase

*   *   *

"Sensitive? Is she injured?"

"No, Mother. I mean she has sensitive feelings. The other girls shun her."

Deborah Norwood enjoyed visiting her daughter's family in their new home on the Milltown Road. Sometimes, though she disagreed with Harriet's childrearing.

"Yeah, they pick on her 'cause she won't fight back." Young George added from his seat at the breakfast table.

"'Course I can't fix it none, else I'd be in trouble with Miss McKinley. If Sis only smacked one of those..." He thought of a choice term, slung around by swaggering sons of mill hands. "...hussies."

"George! If your father overheard you use foul language, there'd be a caning in the shed. Your sister, grandmother, and I don't appreciate such words."

Meanwhile, the object of their discussion sat downcast, picking at her toast. Seven-year-old Harriet, legs dangling from the outsized chair, turned away to hide welling tears. She dawdled to ward off the inevitable departure for school.

Grandmother Norwood reached over, pulling the girl to stand straight beside her chair. She held the child by her bony arms.

"Listen, child, pay those girls no heed. Take your own amusements for recess time. Doesn't teacher praise you enough?"

The child nodded, her body frail inside the pinafore dress.

"Miss McKinley calls her the best reader in the primaries," her brother prompted. "Come on, Sis, we got to go."

"'HAVE to go' or 'MUST go', never 'got to go'" Harriet scolded.

"Yea, Okay, Mother."

"There's that awful word, again. *OKAY* What does that mean, Georgie?"

"I dunno. Maybe 'alright' or just 'good.' All the fellas use it. Everything's 'okay' with us. Bye, now"

Young George pushed his sister out of the front door and up the hill, holding her hand through the road traffic.

"That's a new childhood malady, Harriet."

"What do you mean, young George's language?"

"Heavens no! That's just boy-talk, testing your resolve. It's easier to turn a savage into a gentleman than to give pluck to the meek. I don't like your word, *sensitive*, Daughter, sounds like a virtue. That girl's plain *timid* and that will vex you more than ten rascally boys."

"Missus Chase, *paadon,* but a man's at the kitchen door, says he's here for the *gaaden,*" Colleen Sullivan curtsied to the seated ladies.

"Oh, thank you, Colleen. Please tell him we'll be right along." The maid returned to the back section.

"Don't you mind having a foreigner as a servant?" Deborah whispered. "Isn't Paul enough as an extra hand in the house?"

"Paul's too important to George for housework. And such a prim young lady. She and her sister, Mary, arrived this winter, penniless from Ireland, but displaying the best manners and domestic talents. Now, Mary works for Minerva, Daniel Chase's wife, and Colleen's with us. It won't be long before young men from Ste. Anne de Beaupres Church come calling and these girls have homes of their own. Meanwhile, Colleen's help permits me time to support important causes in our community. Let's greet this workman George found."

Tossing knitted shawls over shoulders against the October morning chill, the women walked outside through the back kitchen. A man stood on the side lot, facing the corner property, holding a spade. The ladies approached.

"Good morning, sir. Did my husband send you?"

The man startled, jumping forward, his hat falling.

"Gol-darn, you ladies spooked me, creepin' up like that." He hopped around, scooping up his hat.

"This is my mother, Missus Norwood, and I am Missus Chase."

"Pleased to meet ya, both," he grinned, revealing various gaps among his teeth.

"And you?"

"Me?"

"Yes, your name?"

"Oh, yes, my name. Otis Gault, at your service," he poked his hat brim with two fingers. Gault wore canvas trousers, tied with a length of ship cable, a collared shirt and waistcoat. His face hadn't felt the scrape of a razor for a fortnight.

"What did my husband say about the work, about what we want done here?"

"He warnt too pacific 'bout it. Says somethin' 'bout a garden. Otis Gault's good for that, I am. I worked all them gardens in St. Stephen an' on Calais Avenue properties." Gault learned on his spade.

"All right, Mister Gault. Shall we survey the property? Let's stand at the corner."

Harriet and Deborah strode several steps toward the road before they realized Mister Gault had fallen behind. Looking back, they saw the man walked with a limp, using the tool as a crutch. Deborah shook her head at Harriet, scowling.

Harriet slowed to a stroll until reaching the corner. She looked over the proposed plot until the gardener caught up.

"Sorry to be takin' my time, ladies. I been palsied since a child, lucky to have lived a-tal these thirty-nine years."

"Is it possible this project would be too rigorous, Mister Gault?"

"No more than the other twenty gardens I tend. I come recommended, Missus Chase, by the likes of the better people on the St. Croix, the older families."

Harriet detected a trace of snobbery in Gault's voice; a hint the Chases were only "new money" latecomers, upstarts. Gault presented the *coup de grace.*

"My granddaddy served gardener for the Loyalist families down to St. Andrews, Church of England people."

Then, Gault softened, "My work will please ya, Missus Chase. People ridin' by here know a Gault garden when they see one."

"But, will a "Gault garden" permit my plans, too? I have some firm ideas."

"Can you commit your plans to writin', drawin' up a pitcher?"

"It will be ready by morning," promised Harriet.

Chapter Twenty-Four

"Gee, gee."

Harriet heard the cry outside the kitchen.

"Git, git." Otis Gault's mule team at work, churning up the soil.

"Ha, Ha."

Looking out, she saw the gardener standing on the harrow frame. He'd already cleared off brush and scrub trees, stumps of the original forest having rotted into mulch. By mid-morning, the quarter acre was smoothed to a rumpled surface, even furrows like heavy corduroy.

After his work in dirt, Gault limped toward the house. He stripped to the waist, undershirt wrapped around hips, skin as white as linen, and plunged his torso into a barrel of rainwater. Clothes removed, the twisted trunk obvious, his left arm shook with tremors. Harriet and Colleen fled inside, out of sight, until the gardener restored decency. Still smelling of sweat, Gault sat, shirt saturated, in the kitchen's heat opposite his employer's wife, looking over a well-marked sheet of tablet paper.

"Rose hedge all along the road? How's the public to look inside yer garden, all hidden from view."

"That is the main point. I wish privacy; an opportunity to muck about in the dirt as I please, Mister Gault, to dress in old clothes and wear odd hats. What business has the public looking into my garden?"

"Okay, Missus Chase, whatever your say. What is that?" he said, pointing to an octagon.

"A gazebo, hidden among the hosta, asters, phlox, and alyssum."

"A ga-what-bo?"

"Gazebo," she enunciated. "Ga-zee-bow. A little roofed hut with a raised floor."

"For tools and such?"

"No, the tool shed is hidden among the fir trees. My gazebo is a private escape where a lady may read while enjoying her flowers and shrubs."

"What's this s'posed ta' be?" he pointed at penciled tuffs.

"A hummock, a little hill built up with extra soil, from the pond you will dig. See that oval figure?"

"You mean everythin's not flat and in line? Are these paths? They're jest as crooked as the rest of the plan."

"Mister Gault, just who's the patron and who the employee? Are you taking liberties over a woman?" she demanded to know.

"Jest don't want a lady to have regrets 'cause she don't understand," he answered.

Deborah Norwood entered the room, seeking refreshment. After a morning of sewing curtains, a cup of tea would relieve a nagging headache. She pinched the bridge of her nose.

"What are you arguing about, dear?" She examined the paper.

"It's my garden plan, but I believe Mister Gault objects. It doesn't meet with his approval. He would prefer more old-fashioned gardens with white picket fences, gravel paths, straight raised beds, white trellises, marble benches and statues."

"As would I, Harriet. Order. That's the ideal garden design. Create an ordered space in this disordered world. Conquer and correct nature. Mister Gault has the right idea."

Harriet leaned forward, grasping the man's attention. "Mister Gault, my drawing shows a new kind of garden design. I shall provide nature a space where she may grow free and where my family may experience that freedom. Mixing flowers with herbs. Mixing the wet with the dry, rocks and soil, flat and round. The natural cycle of life should prevail – generation, growth, life, death, and decay. Lots of decay, and all surrounded with walls of rose hedge. Will you follow my design?"

"Yes, Mam." Gault acceded.

"First, there's to be mint around the kitchen steps, where it's moist and the aroma will rise as feet pass." Harriet reviewed the directions. "Colleen knows to add mint to teas."

"Next, build frames against the south, under the bay windows, so I may sprout my flower seeds in sets for transplanting in May. Use these old windows, set at angles."

"These are the Wrinkled-leaved Rose bushes, the Rugosa Rose. Plant them at three foot intervals on the property line. They will grow eight feet tall, very hearty, standing hard freezes. Their roses will bloom from spring through fall. These bushes are marked by color; some white, some yellow, some pink, others red – all fragrant. Mix the colors to look random."

"You sure about that?"

"Mister Gault, do not quibble with me!" she turned on the man. "Here on the plan you can see the space dedicated to roses. My special treasures are the Pale China Roses, so recent to the United States. They will need protection to survive winter. Please surround them with the Double Musks, the Red-leaved, and the Austrian Brier."

"What's to go around the pond?" Gault wondered.

"Water cress at one end. We'll see how it fares over winter. We'll plant the Siebold Weeping Forsythia beyond the pond for the burst of yellow in spring. Do build a trellis over this path, nothing painted, only using cedar wood. We'll let Japanese Honeysuckle root there."

"Are you having no herbs?" he questioned

"Yes, indeed, the herb garden will be within sight of the bay. Some other herbs will be portable, brought into the library over the winter. I have seeds from the Shaker colony for Sweet Yarrow, Pimpernel, Marjoram, Summer and Winter Savory, and Thyme."

"Where are the bulbs to go? Snowdrops, crocuses, hyacinths, and narcissi?" he asked.

"In the beds along the front against the foundation."

"Other than mint and herbs, are there another other edibles?"

"Just some beans. I shall also try to raise tomatoes, so rare are they sold this far north, but only as a hobby."

"What about this *decay*? Where do you want *decay*?"

"A compost heap will turn kitchen refuse and cuttings into useful fertility," she insisted

"That'll stink," he observed.

"So, it's best far from house and neighbors."

"Wall, let me git started on the shrubbery. Make me a copy of that drawin'. I promise to follow every idear."

Chapter Twenty-Five

George Chase wrote bank checks on his portable writing desk, placed atop one of the card tables. *To: Joseph Meeks and Sons, New York,* the steel tip scratched flourished script.

"There, the last payment to Meeks." George wiped off the remaining ink from the pen tip and returned the pen to the tambour, a compartmented niche above the writing surface. As he slid the paper drawer back inside the box, a flexible screen of thin dowels rolled down to hide the tambour. A key locked the drawer, securing the legal papers needed at court the next morning. George carried the small device from office to court to home.

Harriet sat in the armchair, next to her worktable, repairing a tear in her son's trousers. Heat from the stove radiated across the parlor. Firelight, peeking from slits in the cast iron, danced over the oriental. Aside from the oil lamp next to George's portable desk, lighted candles before a mirror provided the only other illumination.

"Do you think that Colleen's drawn the bath, yet, dear?" George looked around the pages of the *Calais Advertiser.*

"She began filling the tub after supper with cold. The hot was just steaming for the dishes. I'll check." Harriet folded her sewing back into the worktable's fabric bag hanging under the box. She returned promptly.

"It's ready. Let's get our night clothes."

The couple walked up the main stairs and, while George alerted the children to prepare for weekly baths, Harriet withdrew into their bedroom. She untied the wide collar's neck ribbon, unbuttoned her bodice, unhooked her belt, and removed her gingham dress. Opening the armoire, she hung her outer clothing on hooks.

Turning her back to the mirror, Harriet pulled her chemise over her head, unbuttoned the camisole shirt, removed three petticoats, and, finally, removed her corset with the whalebone stays. She redressed herself with a nightgown and dressing gown, a quilted housecoat. Having covered her body, she was comfortable to step out of her drawers, white knee length flannel.

A tap on the door, "Are you presentable, dear?"

"Quite. I'll see to the children while you dress, George." She pulled the gown over her hips.

George opened the bedroom door, stepping aside as Harriet swept into the hallway. George removed his jacket, untied the cravat from his throat, unbuttoned the collar from his shirt, and removed his waistcoat and shirt.

George unbuttoned his fly and, sitting, removed each leg from the pants. Standing, back to the mirror, he unbuttoned the full-length flannel suit of underwear, replacing it with his nightshirt and dressing gown.

"Are you children ready?"

"Is Mother washing hair tonight?" Young George asked.

"I don't believe so, but I'll ask."

George returned to the first floor, but encountered a closed door, baring the kitchen. He rapped three times.

"Colleen, is Missus Chase in her bath already?"

"Indeed, I am," Harriet called out through a cascade of water. "Colleen, do ask what Mister Chase wants."

"Sir, madam asks what ye want." Colleen shouted through the door.

"Only if she's washing the children's hair tonight."

"Tell him, yes, and I don't care what Master George has to say about it."

"Sir, she says..."

"Never mind, Colleen, I can hear perfectly well."

George delivered the awful news to his son. Then, returned to wait in the parlor for his turn at bath. Soon, the kitchen door opened and the entourage of Harriet and

Colleen emerged, the maid rubbing her mistress's hair with a towel. They fled upstairs.

Taking his turn alone in the kitchen, George poured more hot water into the long zinc tub, adding to his wife's bath, and lowered himself in. Scrubbing with soap and brush, he washed away a week's worth of dirt. Keeping water away from his dark, oiled hair, he sunk to his shoulders, relaxing in the heat, skin tingling from the brushing sensations.

Ah, yes, Saturday evening, the start of the Sabbath, no bustle of business, no pressure from clients. Supper, bath, a nice brandy, a little Sir Walter Scott romance novel, and then sleep. Tomorrow a service, hoping the young pastor sticks to something spiritual and inspirational, followed by the family dinner.

"Father, we're waiting." Loud knocking on the kitchen door.

Dried and dressed, George opened the door to find a delegation in the hallway. Both Harriet and Colleen shepherding the children, all in nightshirts.

"Father, please tell Mother I don't have to take my bath in front of Colleen and the girls," the boy complained.

His mother answered, "Oh, bother, Georgie, you're still a child. Colleen and the girls aren't paying any attention to you. Now, march into that kitchen, young man." The assembly left the head of the house standing outside the closed door.

George entered the library and lit the whale oil lamp. A chill draft crept from the bay's windows, making him stir the stove's coals. He looked along the shelves at the collection, all green leather and gold lettering, published in Edinburgh. Shall it be stories of the Scottish clans or Middle Ages knights and ladies, *Rob Roy* or *Ivanhoe*? The tissue paper covered the prints, two detailed illustrations before and after the title page. He studied the sketches, opening the fronts of every volume.

Castle Dangerous, a short one, sharing a volume with another brief novel, would be an easy read for the evening.

George studied the pretty maid etched on the title page, her costume slightly out of fashion.

George reached for the shelf holding the Norwood Bible. Fumbling behind the Scriptures, he found a tiny key which he inserted into a low cabinet door. He took out a squat bottle of brown liquid, followed by a small glass and poured the first dram.

George settled into the book. It wasn't long before interest waned.

"George, George. The clock struck midnight. Come to bed."

*   *   *

Reverend Edward Stone delivered a beautiful sermon on the inherent goodness of the human spirit. Eloquent and erudite, the young minister swept a verbal wave of serenity and contentment across his church. Young George sat between his father and Paul who nudged the boy when he fidgeted.

Service over, the family strolled over to Daniel's house, knowing the uncle, aunt, and grandfather may not have returned from the Congregational Church, a sanctuary of long sermons. The children, running ahead, reported no one home at the Church Street house. It didn't matter. Harriet knew to begin the meal, not waiting for the Sullivan sisters to return from Mass. Colleen and Mary Sullivan arrived to finish preparations, releasing Harriet to manage children, now becoming noisy in the family parlor.

Soon, other family members returned from services. The Sullivan sisters served the meal, after grandfather, Moses Chase, delivered a long blessing. The Sullivans were anxious to leave, having learned other Irish were gathering in St. Stephen at the lyceum.

George and Harriet sat facing across the table. George took the opportunity to watch his wife. Harriet's golden hair, wrapped in a swirl above her neck, had worked loose from pins and hung about her shoulders, frizzed curls washed out, and tresses natural. Her Sunday clothes, designed to convey piety, rendered the opposite effect on her husband.

While passing butter or pork gravy their eyes met. George held her gaze, his head cocked to one side. Harriet blinked, her fingers seeking a loose hair around an ear.

The meal over, Minerva took the children upstairs to a playroom with a dollhouse, dolls, and wheeled toy vehicles. Finally released from reading Bible passages, they reveled in imaginative play.

The Sullivan sisters cleared the table and disappeared out the kitchen door, leaving dish washing for night. George stepped from the entry, walking to the street, waiting in the afternoon's fading light. Harriet soon followed, wordlessly, to walk beside her husband on a circuitous route. They entered the rear of their property.

George opened the kitchen door, "Missus Chase?"

A tip of the hat. She brushed by.

She whisked through the kitchen, up the stairs, and into the bedroom. George followed, making fast the door.

Familiar touch
Smooth skin
Close faces
Exploring eyes
Caress-hold-arouse-release
Shameless passion
Rapture
Bliss

Chapter Twenty-Six

Peter McKinley called dinner hour early, gathering the yard workers – wrights, blacksmiths, coppers, caulkers, and apprentices. They met between two hulls, one skeletal, one complete.

"Listen up, now. I'm proud of ya and yar work. Progress on the *Arabian* has been swift since winter in the mould loft with the drawn patterns through laying the keel. Look aloft, boys, take pride in the shrouds rigging all three masts. Take pleasure from sturdy rudder to narrow bow. Soon we launch the *Arabian* down the slipway. The crew tarries; the course of the maiden voyage is set; the owners fret in their New York counting house."

"All right, McKinley, come around to yer point," a grizzled caulker groused.

"Well, the point, which I was coming to, is that, while finishing the *Arabian*, we've been a wee bit lavish with the materials. It's time to economize, especially lumber. Here's an example. Just look at this oak plank I pulled off the trash pile."

McKinley looked over the crowd and called to the tallest shipwright.

"Paul, come forward." He handed Paul a length of plank. "Do ya see some use for this?"

The brown hand of Paul held the rugged eighteen-inch board as if it were a slat, revolving an examination of its possibilities.

"Yes, Mister McKinley, she would fit the taffrail on the new schooner, I believe. But, do you want us using up time combing through the trash?"

McKinley was distracted by the cry of an apprentice.

"Look at what she's got."

All eyes swung around to see a dark figure bent over tugging on a board amid discarded debris of wood, caulk, and bits of ironwork. An elderly woman strained, yanking a red oak board. Her tattered dress lifted to reveal torn stockings. A black shawl hid face and hair. Suddenly, the board loosened, and she fell back onto the muddy yard.

McKinley called out, "Get away from our wood. That's just the kind of waste we can't afford." McKinley charged at the old woman.

She stood her ground, unflinching as he approached. He stopped when he saw her face, eyes glaring above gaunt cheeks, a thin mouth set over a whiskered chin. Her mouth opened to speak, words distorted by toothless gums.

"Doan' ye have wood to spare? Thompson and Sons always let widows pick over trash afore now."

"It's a new day here at Thompson's. That's valuable lumber you have, and none in excess. Move along with ya, old woman."

Keeping her gaze on McKinley's face, her arthritic fingers opened to release the lumber to fall back on mud. She walked toward the yard's exit, taking a path past each vessel sitting in its launching way, bowsprits protruding over the yard. As she passed each unfinished ship, brig, or schooner, she touched a portion of the bow like a priest might bless supplicants at the communion rail.

McKinley marched back to the workers, slapping his palms to wipe away some irritant. The crowd of workers remained apart, grumbling. Paul spoke for the men.

"You don't know what you done, Mister McKinley. That's not just any old woman. That's Hagar Clooney, the witch of Calais, they say. "

"Phooey." McKinley walked away.

*   *   *

The children returned home from school at four o'clock. Washed up from her afternoon in the garden, Harriet directed Colleen to set the table for supper, a light fare but still requiring plates, bowls, and utensils.

At six o'clock, both George and Paul entered the house, eager for supper. After George said a grace, platters were passed of potatoes, bread, and fish. Everyone drank milk.

"Trouble today in the yard," Paul opened the conversation.

"What sort of trouble, work stoppage?" George stirred pork gravy and spooned it on boiled potatoes.

"Seems like McKinley crossed an old woman picking wood scraps. Chased her off the property. You know the one? Hagar Clooney. Lives back by the tracks, next to the lath mills."

"The old witch?" young Georgie piped up.

"Young man, no one addressed you," George reprimanded.

"That's what the men say, too, Chase," Paul pointed out.

"Why does the poor thing collect wood like that?" Harriet asked.

Paul lifted an extra portion of broiled fish from the platter. He shrugged. "She's a widow. Scratches a living, but, they say, you better not cross her or bad luck comes your way."

"People who would hurt an old woman deserve the luck they earn. Witchcraft, nonsense." George intoned. "Georgie, no matter what the children say, there is no such thing as a witch. A long time ago, people believed in witches and the devil. Hysterical girls accused innocent people at Salem, Massachusetts, and grown men believed them and hung about twenty innocent people. Many more were arrested and imprisoned – not just elderly women, but men, too. Rich and poor, young and old, the weak and the powerful, even children like you. It's a dark stain on the Christian religion."

"You need not start that, Mister Chase," Harriet broke in.

"Sorry, dear. The boy must understand it's irresponsible to toss around such accusations. Perhaps the Ladies

Guild should consider this Hagar Clooney worthy of charity." Harriet smiled at the suggestion.

*   *   *

Reverend Edward Stone looked out over his flock as they sang the processional hymn:

> *The generous feeling, pure and warm,*
> *Which owns the rights of all divine,*
> *The pitying heart, the helping arm,*
> *The prompt self-sacrifice, are thine.*
> *Beneath thy broad, impartial eye,*
> *How fade the lines of cast and birth!*
> *How equal in their sufferings lie,*
> *The groaning multitudes of earth!*

This morning Reverend Stone counted the lawyers among the congregants. There's Dwyer. There's Samuels. There's Chase. He noted Jackson and Owens; competing newspaper editors. Pews filled with bankers and clerks, mill owners, and bookkeepers. Men in high collars and tasteful cravats, their wives in demure bonnets. Even one colored parishioner, the South Sea Islander, was indistinguishable in dress. The minister thought, any clergyman would be proud to have attracted the cream of Calais society.

Sometimes he loathed this smug herd.

Not only did they accord him the paltry salary of five hundred dollars per annum, these paragons worshiped for entertainment. His sermons provided stimulation for clever conversations in drawing rooms. His liberal opinions confirmed their self-righteous largesse.

Hymn ended, scripture read, and Reverend Stone mounted the pulpit. He wore a white surplice over a cassock; a loose flowing vestment of linen. His broad sleeves flowed over the pulpit's railing. Prematurely bald, wisps of hair floated above his forehead, which wrinkled as he warmed to his subject.

135

"My text this morning comes from the fourth chapter of Colossians, first verse: *Masters, give unto your slaves that which is just and equal; knowing that ye also have a Master in heaven.*

"This morning I see before me the proper citizens of Calais, Milltown, and St. Stephen; an array of good-doing, well-educated men and women worshiping a God who blessed them with the fruits of the earth. For the few moments of a Sabbath, their business is quiet contemplation. Empty are the shops on Main Street. Silent are the shipyards. A ghostly calm pervades the lumber mills. The iron locomotive sits cold on its tracks. No pen scratches contracts. It is a day of rest for these good people. But, do they deserve such a day?

"Is the Sabbath a luxury that all enjoy? Hardly.

"For millions in America, there is no Sabbath, for they work seven days of the week. Of course, these are the Negro slaves, suffering in our Southern states."

The minister reddened from his cheeks to his bald pate.

"The passage I read exhorts the master to provide justice and equality for his slaves. Absurd! What did Paul mean? There can be neither justice nor equality between master and slave. When masters use such passages to excuse their 'peculiar institution,' no wonder skeptics question the authority of the Bible.

"I see the look of shock on some faces and I hear your thoughts...No! Not again! What does this have to do with us? Plantations are far away from the St. Croix. Aren't we exempt from such concerns, here next to the British border? Does not the virtue of our British cousins, whose monarch, Queen Victoria, abolished Slavery in their empire in 1833, somehow shine upon us, in proximity?

"We New Englanders, We solid Maine folk who long to emulate high civilization. But, wait. Have not 'lesser' nations also removed this stain?

"Argentina in 1813. Columbia in 1821. Mexico! Yes, that backward nation, outlawed Slavery in 1829. But, stop. I run ahead of myself with mere facts.

"Let us begin with the original premise, the Right. There is but one unfailing good, and that is fidelity to the Everlasting Law written on the heart and republished in God's Word.

"A simple examination leads us to certain conclusions. One, Man cannot be justly used as property. Two, man has sacred rights, the rights of God, and inseparable from human nature, to which Slavery is a crime. Three, if the rights for the free to liberty is founded, not on their attributes as human beings, but on certain accidental circumstances – the hue of our skins or the place of our birth – then every human being by a change of circumstances may justly be held and treated as property."

The minister learned forward, gesturing toward youths from the Academy sitting under the pulpit.

"Indeed, every one of you could be rightfully seized, and made an article of property; subjected to whipping at another's will."

Turning to a group of ladies, he continued.

"And, every one of you could be made a passive instrument of another's will for his pleasure." The ladies shuddered.

"If I were to read the sharp minds of my lawyer friends, I might hear the plea, what business is this of ours? There are no slaves in Washington County, Maine. The Almighty has no quarrel with us.

"I answer that the Almighty does ask us to examine our souls for any contribution, however indirect, we may make to such evil. Look to the next lumber contract. Where are those boards destined, perhaps to build slave quarters in Maryland?

"Look to sponsors in the *Advertiser*. Any notices for runaways?

"Look to the purpose of that new ship. Is she to be refitted as a slaver?

"Let me close with the thought that Christianity is terrible in its simplicity. It is absolute, pure Morality, the love of man, the love of God, acting without hindrance."

Harriet Chase's head snapped up at these words, her face peering around the bonnet's brim to see the minister.

"Christianity only demands a divine life, doing the best thing from the highest motives, all summed up in the Great Commandment, *Thou shalt love the Lord thy God with all they heart, and with all they soul, and with all thy mind, and thou shalt love thy neighbor as thyself.*"

*   *   *

George and Harriet waited their turn to speak with the minister. Reverend Edward Stone smiled at the Chases. George spoke in a low, rational voice, almost a confidence to the younger man, advice from a mature point of view.

"Reverend Stone, surely there are other topics more pertinent to this community than Slavery. Look about you. The advantage of employers over labor. The plight of the Indians. The low standards of education for our poorer classes. Unscrupulous purveyors of quack medicines. Why always Slavery?"

"Negro bondage is America's Original Sin. If slavery were abolished, other reforms would sweep our nation clean. Slavery is key to solving all others you mention. We ignore Slavery at our peril."

"I wish I were so convinced," George said with a shiver.

Harriet reached out to grasp the young pastor's hands, greeting and gaining his attention.

"Reverend Stone, your conclusion greatly affected me. I wish to call a meeting of the Ladies Guild about a pressing problem. Would you please lend us your presence? We meet tomorrow morning at our home."

*   *   *

The *Arabian* squatted on her cradle, the timber frame holding the ship upright on the launching ways. A full-rigged, three masted vessel, a huge exposed hull, like a land-locked Ark awaiting the arrival of a forty-day deluge. The ways, rails leading down the riverbank, were greased for sliding cradle and ship into the St. Croix.

On this Monday morning, Clara Thompson stood on the little platform facing the bow, listening for the signal, a wine bottle poised in her hand. Paul Kamehameha and another stout carpenter stood on each side of the ways, sledgehammers at the ready.

William Thompson called out, "Strike the blocks!" Clara, holding with both hands, waited for the ship to edge away.

Paul and his companion slammed their sledges, knocking away the keel blocks. Then they turned and knocked down the dog shores, two timbers on the sides, holding back the hull. Clara tensed. Daughter of a shipbuilding family, she knew the routine of such launches.

Ship and cradle remained steady. Clara stepped aside to let the yard crew put their shoulders against the bow. "Ready men? Shove!"

Again, nothing moved. All men, gentlemen in frock coats and silk hats, engineers, shipwrights, and apprentices reached for parts of the hull to add their strength.

Still, nothing moved.

"Mister McKinley," Paul spoke for the crew, "the men say they know what's wrong."

"Well, let's have it. We have a contract to fulfill."

"It's not going to be that simple."

"Eh?"

"It's that thing with Hagar Clooney, the old woman."

"What?"

"Remember she touched the ship after you drove her off? They say it's been cursed. They say, you've to make amends to her. Take her stove wood, apologize."

"That's crazy."

139

"Well, the men, they say, aren't too partial toward pushing this *Arabian* into the water, she being cursed and all. You better do your duty, else all our work's in vain."

"Damn, if I'll apologize to no witch." Peter McKinley's strong words belied his wavering tone.

Chapter Twenty-Seven

The Ladies Guild began at nine o'clock. They arrived to find young Reverend Stone seated on an upholstered armchair, spoon in hand, stirring a cup balanced on his knees. Three of the ladies sat on the curly maple and satinwood veneer sofa, where they could place their cups on the mahogany sofa table. Others sat among the side chairs. The minister intoned a brief prayer.

Harriet Chase brought their concerns to the minister's attention.

"Reverend Stone, others may choose to debate the fine points of Sunday's sermon, but it struck home with the Guild. We thank you for such bold thoughts."

"Oh, let us be grateful for like minds. If this be so, Guild members demonstrate true Christian nature in their resolve to free the African slave from his Southern masters."

"Indeed, Reverend, a good cause. However, being mere women and so far removed from direct contact with slavery, we thought our duty may be found a bit closer to Calais, to relieve suffering among those within our sight."

"Suffering here in Calais?"

"On the lonely lanes, far from public view, are dismal shacks where live the poor of Calais. Among them are many single women, aged and infirm, unsupported by husbands and adult children. Do you know the widow Hagar Clooney?"

"No."

"Her condition is a scandal, harassed by the ignorant as a witch, followed by gangs of urchins. The shack sits among the river mills where she ekes out a living."

"Do the town authorities know her situation?"

"Perhaps, but the welfare of elderly women is not their concern. It is ours. Didn't the Lord say *Insomuch as you have done it unto one of the least of these, you have done it unto me.* Hagar Clooney qualifies as 'least' in Calais."

"I applaud your charity, Missus Chase. I encourage you to look into the situation."

"Won't you accompany us, Reverend, were we to visit the widow? Were we to complain at a public meeting, it would only be a gaggle of silly women making noise. If a clergyman witnessed the condition, he would receive the respect of a hearing. Can I count on your accompanying us this afternoon?"

"I suppose I can delay my studies."

"Good. We'll stop by your office at three."

      *   *   *

Master of Thompson and Sons shipyard, Peter McKinley, slouched, hat drawn over his brow, walking the back streets near the lumber mills. He had slipped away unnoticed from the shipyard. No use alerting the others.

The thirty-three mills along the American side were in full cry on this Monday afternoon. Lath machines screamed. Gang saws buzzed. Iron clanged against iron in foundries. One of the two steam locomotives, this one the *Calais,* chugged through the industrial landscape, spewing burning embers from her balloon stack and steam from her boiler.

He hoped to take care of this nasty business with the widow and slip away, unnoticed. Such foolishness to think she prevented the *Arabian* from slipping down the launchways. Like Irish and leprechauns. Like ghost stories. Better that McKinley be seen as generous, inviting the woman to pick discards from the heap. Then, the men would put their shoulders to the job.

"Bah, witches," he said to himself.

McKinley halted. Ahead among the mills and tracks, walking through the mud, he saw crinoline and lace, swallow tail jacket and cravat, bonnets and a silk top hat. Workmen

142

from the mills stopped to gape at the delegation, a bevy of ladies led by a gentleman, rapping at a dismal shack.

A tiny woman stood at the door. Hagar Clooney, herself.

"Excuse me, ladies and sir, excuse me. Missus Clooney and I have some urgent busy-ness."

"Eh, 'tis the hard-hearted one," the widow looked up at the yard master's face.

McKinley worked up a smile.

"I've come to announce that Thompson and Soon has reconsidered the company policy regarding discarded lumber. We welcome yer removing any scraps ya find on the heap, we do."

"Well, now, ain't this a turn of events. I wonder what caused this change of heart." Hagar's thin mouth wrinkled into a wary smile. "Could it have been some hindrance with the *Arabian*?" Her eyebrows, bushy with white, rose like two frosty caterpillars.

Fear gripped McKinley's body. He backed away.

"Don't worry, Mister McKinley. Go back to yer yard. Things will return to their proper places. I'll be along for me scraps, meanwhile these lovely people and I have busy-ness, too."

       *   *   *

Paul Kamehameha started out for home on a dark December evening. He bundled his cloak collar around his neck and crossed Main Street, hoping the shelter of the buildings would break the wintry blast. A lone figure walked up the river road from the Ledge.

"Paul, Paul, it that you?"

Paul halted mid-street.

"Wait up for me. I'm desperate." The man drew closer. It was Toby Dunn in light sailor's pants and tunic, his slippers under caked snow. Paul reached out and grabbed his cold arms.

"Come inside Calais House. Get warmed up."

Light from the tavern shone through frosted windows, guiding Paul up the steps onto the plank sidewalk and though wide doors. The crowd at bar and tables looked up at the pair, the town's tea-totaling 'colored' man and a skeletal figure in summer clothing. The faro card game, Buck the Tiger, halted.

"Get him some hot soup and bread. Get him a whiskey. Get him a blanket." The crowd mobilized.

"Didn't you ship out with the *Arabian* last summer? Remember the launching trouble? He left on her maiden voyage. Where is the ship, Toby? Is she come back with ya?"

Toby gripped the hot bowl, exposing palms to the heat, slurping nourishment and ignoring the questions. He drank all liquor offered. Finally, he slumped back.

Senator George Chase entered the saloon for a pint of beer before walking home. He drew up a chair next to the youthful sailor. His fatherly voice reached into the realm of Toby's consciousness.

"Tell us what happened, Toby."

The boy rolled out of his chair and into Chase's arms. He hid his face and sobbed. The crowd backed off, afraid.

"There, there, son," Chase patted his back. "'Tis better to get it all out with friends. You're home now, son."

"The *Arabian.* It's gone. All hands, 'cept me."

"What?" The men gathered closer.

"Horrible. Such sin I never knew existed."

"Sin? What are you talking about? Make sense, man." Angry voices.

Chase commanded the men to back off and not badger the boy.

"Things went real well on the voyage to New York. She showed her best qualities, every man jack proud to be aboard. Every head turned in New York Harbor when we tied up at the Brooklyn yards. My only mistake was to continue on for the first merchant voyage. I thought she'd be a China or California trader. But, the owners had other plans.

144

They outfitted her to be…" The boy looked around the room and hung his head, whispering, "…a slaver."

"A slaver? You mean goin' to Africa?"

"At Brooklyn they removed all partitions, from steerage down to the orlop floor of the cargo hold. Bolted down chains with leg and wrist irons. Seein' those irons, I tried to break my contract but the bucko' mate and his bully boys locked me up until we was at sea, sailing for the Guinea Coast."

A hush fell over the group, none here having sailed beyond the Maritimes and New England.

"There ain't no real harbor there, just a beach. I thought, oh boy, we've got to land and hunt down the black Africans, but, no, out they came to the ship in long canoes, five paddlers to a side, fetching us through the surf to the beach, to this great fortress built by the Portugee. In its dungeons were hundreds of men and women, all captives, one tribe captured by another, brought to the castle and sold."

"They sell each other?"

"God's truth. Trussed up like so many pigs, ready for market, kept in low dark dungeons, taken out a tiny door into the tide, thrown into a surf canoe, blinded by sunlight, hoisted onto the deck, thrown into the hold and clamped in irons."

"The men didn't fight?" they asked.

"The slavers know how to confuse the captives. The menfolk are separated from their women, kept chained hands and feet in the deepest hold. Tribes are mixed, a babble of languages, and they're all naked. Even heathen know shame.

"The passage is worse than the loading. Guns always ready for a revolt, they dare not ever release men, except singly. For a month, the men eat, sleep, and lie prone in their own dirt."

"Did it stink?"

"Like a sewer. After a week they began to die. Sharks followed the ship, awaiting the next body."

"What about the women?"

Toby looked down. "Can't rightly talk about that."

Chase put his hand on the boy's shoulder.

"You've seen the worst in human character, haven't you, son?"

"Tried to stop it. They think it's their right, extra wages. Some girls flung themselves overboard."

"Where did the ship make land?"

"Havana on the island of Cuba. Slaves harvest sugarcane. The crew washed down the holds, pumped out the filth from the bilge, then holystoned the floors. After taking on fresh water and supplies, we headed back to New York, glad to be free from fear and abomination.

"The first night out of Cuba, fire broke out in the galley. We threw a few buckets of brine, thought it out, and went to sleep, having a healthy ration of grog. It must'a been still alight 'cause around two bells, there's alarm. The fire raged, tar on ropes, shrouds, and canvas aflame, men crushed by masts falling. By daylight, the *Arabian*'s burned to the water, and we in the Gulf Stream, clinging to flotsam."

"Were you picked up by other ships?"

"Not right away. Fate hadn't punished us enough." He sat back, looking at his hands. The men waited.

"Must'a been about mid-morning when one felt something brush past him and made a funny comment, next thing he's screaming about his leg and the water's turned red. Sharks. I started kickin' and movin' away from the others. Found a spar and stabbed 'em when they come close. All day long there was screaming and crying as seamen was attacked. By the time night came, all was quiet. I clung to my spar and flotsam. At first light, I felt myself being pulled over a gunwale onto a deck. I looked up and saw all black faces. Thought I died and gone to Hell with black devils to torture a slaver. Punishment to fit the crime, but they was kind fishermen off the Bahamas, instead, and delivered me. It's taken a month of hopping ships to make home."

Paul spoke up, "if it's okay with the Senator, you'll be needing a place to stay until you find work and all. I have room to spare."

"That's right, son, come along home with us. Missus Chase will fix supper."

Toby followed Chase and Paul into the night. Men broke into groups, rehashing the story. A tiny figure behind the curtain finished her dram and slipped out the rear door.

Chapter Twenty-Eight

Deep winter arrived at the inland towns of downeast Maine. Snow filled the silent forests upstream, silencing lumber camps; workers scattered to town or holed up, snowbound, in snug cabins. The great work of spring; floating the pine and hemlock, waited. Saw mills would be silent until the thaw, when rivers ran logs downstream. Even Calais harbor lay iced over. Real work ceased in commerce, leaving only pen and paper to grind slow and fine.

Harriet Chase sent out the invitations, decorated the house, and supervised the food for her Christmas party on Saturday at three o'clock.

The late December lull permitted Paul Kamehameha the freedom to help with the celebration, George happy to have Harriet supported in her Christmas projects and released Paul from responsibilities. After sixteen years in Maine, Paul had adapted to the cold and wet climate, accepting the weight of gloves, thick coats, heavy boots, and woolen caps, all specially ordered for his large frame.

Being the largest man in Calais at six feet four inches, heads turned when the Polynesian walked beside his boss. The Chase family provided a room off the kitchen which always stayed heated, the fire in the wood stove lit from September to April; a respite from the frigid Maine temperatures, a sanctuary for a Hawaiian to bask.

On Wednesday before the party, Paul hitched up Nell to the sleigh, bringing handsaws and hatchets, and drove Harriet into the nearby forest to find the right pine boughs for the garlands over the front door, the inner doorways, and down banisters. Both had only coffee for breakfast. Harriet wore a heavy woolen dress, gray with many petticoats beneath, and a soft bonnet tied with a wide band at her chin to protect her ears, but the freezing air still stung her face.

Horse hooves moved in silence, only the tinkle of bells and jiggle of traces warning pedestrians. Paul and Harriet sat on and under bearskin blankets for the miles into the forests on the logging roads Paul knew so well, away from the St. Croix Valley and its maritime climate. He felt the air grow sharper the deeper they traveled.

"There's a new woods off the Princeton road, Miss Harriet. It burned off some years ago. It got many young trees. You like those branches. I weave them into garlands to look like they're growing down the banisters." He enjoyed the Christmas custom of bringing greens into the houses, like Hawaiians' celebration of life.

"This year we will try a new custom I read about, Paul. It's an idea from Germany, cut the prettiest little tree in the woods and stand it up in the parlor, then decorate it with bows and candles. In Germany, the parents light the candles on Christmas eve, alerting the "Kriskind", to bring presents. When they bring the children into the room, their eyes are dazzled."

"Miss Harriet always knows the best ideas. Young George can help me build a stand for the tree. Who is coming?"

"All of George's business associates, of course. The Murchies, the Thompsons, the Campbells, the Pikes, the Greens. The foremen and their families from the mills. The pastors and church friends. Judges and county commissioners. It's easy to know who to invite in Calais."

The sleigh reached the new forest of pine, spruce, and fir, planted by squirrels and birds, grown above a man's height. Paul slid down off the sleigh into snow reaching his knees and pulled out the tools. He walked around to reach for Harriet's arm, helping her down, skirts catching on edges of the vehicle. She walked ahead of him in long strides over heavy powder, eyes scanning the crowded host of young trees. Meanwhile, Paul covered Nell with a horse blanket against the chill in the woods.

Paul followed, saw and hatchet in hand, cutting those boughs she designated, piling them on the path back to the sleigh. She moved back through the low woods, choosy and enthusiastic.

"Miss Harriet, wait for me." Paul carried a pile back to the sleigh, filling the box. She ranged farther, her voice calling out. They had left town two hours, now. Paul noticed the clouds lower, the air chillier.

He found her waiting beside a Douglas fir. "This is perfect for the Christmas tree. Look how all branches are even and full. Please cut it carefully, close to the ground."

On his knees, Paul swept the base as clean as possible, getting a clear path near the ground. He sawed as Harriet held the branches, tipping the tree away from him. They dragged the fir back, each holding a side. Paul noticed she walked slower, stopping after a few steps. When they reached the sleigh, Paul lifted the tree onto the boughs, tying down all the evergreens. He turned to see Harriet hold onto the frame, a stationary figure, eyes fixed on her feet.

"Miss Harriet, look at me."

She continued to stare at the ground.

Again, "Look at me."

She lifted her head.

"Miss Harriet, your cheek, your nose. They're white."

"I'm just a little tired."

"Miss Harriet has frostbite." Paul threw his gloves on the snow and reached for her face, feeling the cold, exposed skin. She drew her head back at the touch.

"Whatever are you doing?"

"Get up into the sleigh. We go now."

"Oh, Paul, I can hardly lift my feet." Then, she collapsed, falling into the snow.

He swept her up, his burly arms about her back and knees, onto the sleigh bench, laying her across the length. He wrapped her in the bearskins, covering her face. Jumping down, he grabbed the reins and gave a shake. "Go, Nell, go fast."

Running beside the sleigh, Paul directed the horse farther up the logging road, and, turning into the forest, followed a dim path for several yards, down a slope, halting at a clearing. No brush grew under this canopy of Douglas fir. Shielded by the dense, snow-filled boughs, trees spaced widely apart, a log cabin sat at the center of the clearing, drifted snow banked over the roof.

Paul lifted Harriet, a limp form, from the sleigh and carried her to the door which he shoved open with a hip. Carrying her to a pallet of evergreen, he laid the woman down and, after covering her with bearskin, turned to light a fire in a waddle-and-daub hearth. Soon, heat warmed the cabin's frigid air. Taking a tinned pot, Paul fetched snow to heat water over the fire. Once water boiled, he threw in coffee grounds.

The noise brought Harriet to hazy consciousness. From the pallet she looked around. Log walls, caulked with clay and moss. Split shakes exposed above rafters. A rough abode, like a Grimm's folktale or Natty Bumpo's cabin in a book by Cooper. Table, two benches, split pine, puncheon furniture. Rough but orderly. She propped herself on an elbow.

"Is this yours, Paul?"

He spun around.

"Miss Harriet, you lie down and drink hot coffee with sugar. Rub your face with hands to make warm."

"Very well, then, but where are we?"

"Indian camp. Please lie down."

Harriet lay back and allowed herself to relax.

The aroma of coffee, slightly burnt, filled the room. Paul spilled cold water into the potion and stood up. Knocking debris out of an enamel cup, Paul poured the coffee, and then stirred in a spoon of brown sugar. Kneeling on one knee, he lifted Harriet to a sitting position and brought the cup to her lips. She watched his face as she sipped, but he would not meet her eyes.

"Is this where you go when you disappear for days?"

He said nothing. When she finished, she lay back, but her curiosity came back as the coffee renewed her strength.

"Paul, would you be about thirty now? When Mister Chase and I married, you were maybe eighteen, still a youth when you came to Calais with us."

"In Sandwich Islands we have no birthdays. I was born the year before grandfather, King Kamehameha, died; maybe 1819, when all taboos were broken. The pagan alters were smashed and missionaries came to save us."

"Calais must be hard on you. Who are your friends? The mill hands? The watermen?"

"Mister Chase, you, little George, the girls."

"Are the Passamaquoddy Indians friendly?"

"Indians think I'm some kind of Indian. They helped me build this cabin, showed me the woods, hunt, fish with them. It is good. I like the wilderness."

"Do you have a sweetheart among the Indian girls?"

Paul rose to his feet, face rigid. "Not to marry. Indians are a defeated people. If I marry in America, I marry into a strong family, a woman with power, schooling, and property."

"I am so sorry, Paul, I pried into your life. I have no right to ask such questions." She stood, revived enough by the warmth and drink.

He looked at her eyes. His body relaxed. Both smiled.

She lifted her chin and said firmly, "Let us start back for town before dark overtakes us. I think Mister Chase shan't hear about your cabin, Paul. Your secret is safe with me."

Chapter Twenty-Nine

Saturday arrived, and everyone in the Chase household had prepared for the Christmas party. All males – the senator, Paul, and little George – were dressed formally, but with some bright red or green article of clothing. All the girls and women were festively attired. On the first floor, candles, bows, candies, and garlands spread through every room. Candles were lighted against the evening's gathering gloom.

The guests began arriving promptly at three o'clock. The pastors and their wives were the first to enter. Pastor Edwards, the Congregationalist, glared at the Chase's house decorations, sniffed at the rum punch, and departed disturbed at the deviations from strict restrictions on Christmas gaiety. Reverend Stone from Calais Unitarian attempted to interest a ship captain in the finer points of Transcendentalism. Father Murray conversed with one of the Catholic parishioners, while Father Lamb, rector of All Saints Episcopal and a collector of fine china, examined the bottoms of cups and plates. Pastor Evans, the Methodist, sipped punch as his wife played the pianoforte, leading the party singing the most popular carol, Deck the Halls with Boughs of Holly.

Harriet and Colleen had worked for days preparing foods. Pies, cookies, fruit cakes. Rare green oranges shipped from Florida. White bread, sliced and open, lay on the sideboard with slabs of beef and a mayonnaise, ready for guests to make open-faced sandwiches. A goose, stuffed with oysters and surrounded by devilled eggs, sat in a huge platter on the dining room table. A suckling pig lay spread-eagle on a wooden cutting board, neck bent back, jaws propped open by a green apple.

At four o'clock, Harriet and George greeted the Thompsons - James and Patience. The Thompsons brought their daughter, Sarah, who had just been "introduced to society." The nineteen-year-old had returned from the young ladies academy at Portland the previous summer, having studied education for a year at Teachers College. In her first year at a Calais elementary school, teaching grade one, Sarah caused a stir among the old maid teachers, proposing to maintain order without flogging six-year-olds.

"Thank you so much, Missus Chase, for including my name on the invitation. Many parents of my students may also attend the party, and I find it helpful to know them socially," said the Thompson's daughter, stepping forward.

"I could hardly snub you. We've known you since girlhood, Sarah, you are welcome. Take your place among the adults."

The young woman sauntered into the house, her coat among the other wraps, but keeping her scarf. Over the scarf, her blonde hair fell in ringlets to her neck ribbon, a jeweled fob hanging in a little crevice at her throat. Her holiday dress was forest green velvet with white lace at wrists and collar and red piping at the seams. Sarah's figure was slight, her frame tall and movements lithe. She walked with agility and poise.

Paul stood by the sideboard helping guests when Sarah approached. Handing her a plate, Paul asked her which food she wished. She pointed, vaguely at each item, and upon receiving a full portion, she remained standing nearby, not joining her parents among the other guests. She faced the party, but spoke to him.

"And you would be Paul?" she asked.

"Yes. I live here with the Chase family."

"I know who you are. I've watched you since I was a girl. You are Senator Chase's assistant. You manage his businesses, don't you?"

"Yes, but who are you, may I ask?"

"Sarah Thompson. My parents and I live on Washington Avenue. You have passed me on the street."

"I beg your pardon, if I don't recall."

"It's understandable. You were talking about really important business."

Patience Thompson, realizing her daughter had not joined the others, motioned with her hand from across the room. Sarah pretended to not see the gesture.

"Is it true you came from some Pacific island with palm trees and warm weather?" she asked Paul.

"Yes, I am from the Hawaiian Islands, one called Maui."

"But, you speak English, and you are educated. Otherwise, the senator wouldn't have given you such responsibilities."

"Six years at the Lahainaluna School, reading our language, then English," he said.

"They call you Paul 'K', but what is your family name?"

"No *haole* here can say it. Don't bother."

"*Haole.* What's that?" she huffed.

"White person."

"Let me try. I studied French, learned to pronounce foreign words."

"Very well. Kamehameha."

"Kamehameha," she repeated fluently.

Patience came up to Sarah, reached for her elbow, and said, "Time you joined other guests, dear," without acknowledging the presence of the young man. Sarah allowed herself to be drawn away, but glanced over her shoulder at Paul and smiled, their first eye contact.

Chapter Thirty

Missus Patience Thompson drew back the curtains, better to see the street. She stared. The tea brewed in the pot and cookies sat out on the plate. All was ready.

"Bridget, did my daughter come in the kitchen door?"

"No, mum," came the reply, "Else I a-would 'a' heard her step, mum."

Missus Thompson decided to control her impatience and drew a novel from the shelf. Her mind refused the distraction.

Patience walked again to the front door and stared out. A pair walked up Washington Avenue, a man and a woman; small steps, too far away to see faces, but walking without purpose, stopping to talk in the cold February air. The male, wearing gloves, tall, black stovepipe hat obscuring his face, towered over the female. What was she carrying? A satchel, a familiar light satchel.

"That's Sarah! What's she doing talking to a man in public, for all the neighbors to see? By now, everyone is talking."

She clasped the knob, intending to step outside and hail her daughter, but stopped.

"No, that would embarrass her. She'd be angry, and I must respect her independence. Why is my daughter so strong willed?"

Sarah and the man walked up to the house, continuing to talk, the man's back turned to the house.

Sarah looked up to see her mother staring from the door and ended the conversation. As she walked up the flagstones, Missus Thompson could see the man's face. It was Paul "K".

Patience backed away from the door as her daughter entered. "Hello, Mother."

"Had I known you would be late, I would have delayed our tea, my dear," she said, her voice icy.

"Sorry, I will try to inform you when to excuse me from our tea time, Mother. Is there some brewed now? I don't mind it lukewarm."

"Well, I do mind. One should always think of others' feelings. Please try to control your impulses and act like a lady."

"Shall we sit down, Mother? I have stood all day with the children."

The women entered the parlor, pouring and spooning sugar in silence. Sarah sat, staring at her cup. Her mother fussed at the tea service.

"It's been a trying day, so many of the boys were out of sorts, fisticuffs and all."

"Girls break rules in their own way, my dear daughter."

"Mother, is there something you want to say to me?"

"Indeed. No young lady from a good family ought to entertain young men beneath them. It's simply a waste of time, lowers a young woman's prestige, makes her less sought by the better sort."

"Would you be speaking of Paul Kamehameha?" Her voice rose.

"It's a principle, not a person, of which I am speaking," said Patience to avoid her daughter's superior skills of argument.

"If it's a high principle, perhaps we agree."

"Oh, yes, I'm sure we can agree," Patience fell into the trap.

"Paul Kamehameha qualifies on all counts as an eligible bachelor, according to all the principles by which you and Father live."

"How is that possible?"

"Let me count the ways. Religion: he and we are Congregationalists. Fortune: managing Senator Chase's properties and businesses, investing himself, he has accumulated wealth and owns property. Education: as much schooling as father. Breeding: he is the grandson of King Kamehameha the First and an aristocrat from the finest family of the Sandwich Islands."

"But," Patience sputtered, "That's it. He isn't white. He's a kind of colored man."

"Mother, everyone knows some of the finest families of New England descend from Indian tribes." Placing her cup and saucer onto the silver tray, she started out of the room.

"Before things advance further, young lady, you ought to know the laws of the state of Maine forbid marriage between whites and colored."

*   *   *

The mounted woman walked her horse past the edge of town, cottages set on large lots, freshly blooming with May lettuce, fenced against deer. The forest began at the last dwelling, a wall of secondary growth, brushy and dense. The horse guided herself, happy for the exercise, trotting beyond sight of town.

She sat sidesaddle, both legs draped left, left foot in a high stirrup which she had used to mount. Her right knee was hooked over an indentation at the center of the saddle, her right foot and ankle hung, covered by a duck riding skirt. She dug her heel into the horse's ribs and shook the traces. "Get up, go." The horse leaped into a gallop. The rider leaned forward, her slender body synchronized with the animal's motion. She savored speeding ever closer to her destination.

Soon, horse and rider were miles down the Princeton road before they turned off onto the logging lane, and slowed to a trot. Trees grew across the track. Branches brushed the girl's clothes and hat, threatening to knock it off. She pushed it back to hang by the ribbon. The motion of the horse loosened her hair, tresses falling to her shoulders.

She noted landmarks – a lake with a lone island, a burnt-off area with new growth, a deepening gloom, virgin forest untouched by men. She had never ventured so far into the wilderness. The horse continued down the path as she looked up at trees' height and breadth, each standing distant and apart like columns in a cathedral, roofed in green and paved with a carpet of brown needles. Finally, she turned right down a slope to a clearing near a stream. The cabin stood on a rise. Another horse, free of halter and saddle, grazed on ferns sprouting near the water.

The cabin door opened and Paul emerged, ducking at the low threshold. He came to the mounted woman and reached up, inviting her to throw herself off the mount. She flung her body into the huge hands.

They embraced, her back leaning against the horse, motionless, savoring the moment, until the horse stomped impatiently. Paul removed the horse's tack, tossing it on the cabin porch with his equipment. Slapping the mare's rump, he sent her off to graze.

Sarah wrapped her arms around his bulk, pressing her breasts against his back. She ran her hands up and down, chest to waist. She laid her cheek between his shoulder blades, against the rough texture of the woolen shirt. Her chest heaved, pulling in the scent, filling her lungs with the man-odor. When he reached back to pull her hips against his buttocks, her cheek felt the muscles flex in his back.

"You come inside." Paul turned, circling her with one huge arm to guide Sarah into the cabin.

"I only have a few hours," she said. "I have dreamed of this so long I don't know what is real. This isn't the same as walking and talking, is it?"

"Sit down, Sarah. I made a meal, but cabin food. Are you thirsty? I have water from the spring." Pots hung over the fire in the hearth, steaming. Strips of meat were draped over a grate, sizzling.

"Might you have some spirits, Paul?"

"Have you ever drunk rum? I think you only drink a little wine, like other town ladies. Maybe rum is not good for a lady."

"Maybe you can add a little rum to spring water. The effects would be milder."

They used spoons for utensils, with tin plates and cups. Paul's hunting knife cut the meat and corn bread. They picked at a bowl of blueberries, tiny but plump, each one's eyes taking in the other. They sat on the same side of the puncheon table, he astride, and she with both legs inside. Sated with food, warmed by confidence, Sarah reached out to stroke Paul's knee.

"Sarah, your parents are strict. I think maybe you were never with a man."

"That's true, but I have never wanted to be alone with a man unless I were to love him. You are that man, Paul."

"I love you, too, Sarah. I think you are the right lady for me."

She clasped her hands in her lap, "But, I am a little worried. We must be careful."

"Yes. I am careful."

"I know you are a careful man in business, careful in work. I mean in society."

"Society? What does that mean?"

"Mother and Father would not approve of us, courting and all; not yet. Not until I change their minds. Meanwhile, we also have to be careful in another way, wouldn't want to start a baby."

"Children come after a wedding."

Paul moved down the bench, putting one arm under her knees and the other behind her back, lifting Sarah into the air, he stood for a moment looking at her. Then he knelt and lay her down on the pallet, cushioned with evergreens. Kneeling beside the bed, he held her and kissed her mouth, her cheeks, her eyes, her ears while his hands stroked her back. The hearth fire crackled and hissed as small pockets of sap exploded in the heat. The weight of their bodies crushed the pine needles, releasing the scent of wet mornings.

Sarah's hands explored Paul's shoulders as she relaxed in his arms. She felt the full muscles, the curve of the blades, and the architecture of his back. Her hands reached his neck, darting under his shirt, stroking the smooth dark skin, tanned to a deep red. A sigh came from her throat. Parting her lips, her mouth accepted his tongue, a wet intrusion, welcomed and reciprocated.

Holding her with one arm, a hand moved to her front. Slowly, it plied over her willowy figure. Breathless, she unbuttoned her front with nimble fingers. He reached in, lifting her chemise and found the naked breasts, each one cupped in a palm. Paul pulled her dress from her shoulders, down her arms, and off her wrists. The chemise lifted, he surveyed her bosom.

"Kiss them, please. I dream of your lips on my nipples."

His tan face fixed to her creamy skin. Shuttering, she arched her back.

Sarah's hands explored the front of Paul's trousers, a buttoned flap, a laced fly, too complicated, her fingers fumbled.

Paul's deft hand loosened fasteners and returned to its task. Reaching under her bottom, Paul tossed off Sarah's skirts into disarray. Returning his mouth to her breasts, his hand invaded her golden mound, probing deep, while she delved at his throbbing hardness.

"I want your body inside me," her voice hoarse and throaty.

"That would be dangerous. Better my hands, then no babies."

Thoughts errant, Sarah allowed full access, curling back her long legs. His fingers stroked exquisite surprise. A force rose in the whole realm of legs, bottom, shoulders, sweeping up the back into her head. She voiced the elegant current, a supplication, a cry.

"Oh, God, yes, please." The force exploded. She clutched, released, and her body fell back, spent. He smiled, teeth grinning. "Now, you learn about mine."

Chapter Thirty-One

Patience Thompson appeared at Harriet Chase's door that afternoon, her face swollen. "I must speak with you about my Sarah."

"Come in, Patience. How can I help you?"

"James and I are quite upset. I don't know where to begin. Please keep my confidence. We are so ashamed."

"Oh, my, you *are* very upset. Whatever this problem is, Mister Chase and I would keep our silence. No word will spread in the community."

"We believe our Sarah is having a liaison with your Paul. She is seen riding from town weekly when he is nowhere about. She excuses herself with lame fibs." The woman began to cry, squeezing a soaked handkerchief, her shoulders heaving with each sob.

"Please calm yourself, Patience. Where could they be meeting?"

"Rumors say Paul has a cabin near Indian Township. Such a beautiful girl, such prospects, all ruined now. Always unconventional and outspoken, but we assumed that would change with adulthood. The school board will dismiss her for moral turpitude, and what young man would touch her now?"

"If this were true – and I emphasize IF – I would be disappointed in our Paul. He has always been forthright and trustworthy. A shocking rumor, but do be calm, Patience, it's only a rumor. On the other hand, if true, young people's impulses ought not to condemn them. This may prove an opportunity for reconciliation between you and Sarah, she having been such a little rebel."

"Rebel, she? What about your Paul? A lewd savage leading my virgin daughter into voluptuous depravity."

"Lord, preserve my forbearance." Harriet, moving her lips, looked toward heaven. "Are we not women, dear neighbor? Have we forgotten our flirtatious youth? To be frank, if these young people pleasured each other, their carnal knowledge was consensual and mutual. You and I must cease casting aspersions and begin planning."

"What do you propose?"

"This will be brought to Mister Chase's attention this evening. He, not I, shall address Paul. I shall entreat Mister Chase to protect Sarah's interests with the school committee. You must enlighten Sarah about her reputation, if this nasty rumor spreads. Now, go home and bend to the task. We will meet again tomorrow."

*   *   *

The hour was late. Questions would be asked unless she started for town.

"Sarah, I will ride with you, and I speak with your father."

She stopped tying the ribbon under her bonnet. "No, Paul, not now. Not ever, maybe. Why can't this all go on?"

"I want to marry you, have many children, a house in town. I want this now. I do not like hiding our love from town. I am always honest with George Chase; he trusts in me. My word is true. I have respect."

"Your words, your honesty, your respect matter little, my darling."

"All that does so matter."

"To whom?"

"George Chase, for one."

She laughed at him. "That's stupid. Chase's ambitions won't let him champion you beyond his own craven interests. Whatever he says to your face, you are still his "boy" – loyal, like a retriever fetching ducks. Chase's loyalty is to Chase and maybe to his imperious Harriet. He's not one to stick his neck out and challenge prudence."

"You are wrong," said Paul, and he walked out the cabin door and into the woods to let her fix her own saddle.

*   *   *

Paul – stop by the office. The terse note lay on his bed. Paul walked to the business district, testing pedestrian faces.

He stepped into George Chase's office. The lawyer looked up from papers.

"You've come already," he said, shuffling pages, pens, ink, books. The windows facing the St. Croix emitted a cool light. "Have a seat, Paul."

"Is this about business, Chase?"

"Ah, well, no, it is not. It is a personal matter, unfortunately."

"What is it?" Paul asked sharply.

"Have you been courting Sara Thompson, Paul?"

"Many months."

"Many months? Why have you kept this a secret?"

"Her wish. Lady teachers must be unattached."

"That's the least of it. This is all very complicated, Paul. Yes, lady teachers cannot court, but more so, her parents do not approve, and there are lewd rumors. Is she indeed your paramour?"

"Does that mean, do I love her? Yes, I love her," Paul's voice deepened. "Does this make a problem for you?"

"Man to man, Paul, inside this room, with the doors closed, I say 'enjoy the carnal delights of the flesh.' Outside, in society, your situation makes a muddle. How will we clear this up?"

Paul sat forward, smiling, "I have asked her to marry me."

Chase's face remained tight. "That's not possible."

Paul sunk back, "Why not?"

"Have you ever heard of the miscegenation laws? Those forbid legal marriage between whites and all other races. The State of Maine will not issue a marriage license for you and Sara Thompson. It's that simple, and the Calais School Committee will dismiss her from teaching, unless I use my powers to prevent some puritan witch hunt."

164

"Sara's no witch."

"No, not a real witch hunt, I have to shut up the old maids, some in trousers, from casting her out," insisted George. Paul noticed flecks of gray on Chase's temples and lines beside his eyes. White people aged so early, he thought.

"But, those marriage laws were meant for Africans and Indians, not Hawaiians. I am her equal, maybe higher, since the Thompson's have no royal blood. All you New English were peasants when you came here."

"Yes, but now after two hundred years we've devised our own forms of pretension, haven't we?"

Paul stood up and pointed. "You, George Chase, state senator, rich businessman. You can fix this law. You have the power. "

"What? I can't change the words in the law for one case."

"What case? No 'case' at all. You say to State of Maine, Hawaiians are white people, just darker. You made the lumberjacks and mill workers obey me. George Chase has power to fix this law."

George looked up at the robust man, his student of business for sixteen years like a younger brother. Chase weighed the profit and loss in the calculus of his social and business interests. "What woman wouldn't want you? Handsome, mature, rich with trade. The law can not envision a couple like you and Sara. We will not solve this. Calais is not ready for your marriage to a white girl." He waved his hand.

Paul studied his mentor's expression. "Then, Calais is no longer for me. I cannot any longer live among *haoles.* I will sell out and return to the Sandwich Islands, my Hawaii."

Chase shuffled papers. "I regret your decision. Harriet and I will be very disturbed to lose you. Young George thinks of you as an uncle, as does little Hattie. Let us move cautiously and sell off your property with an eye to the market. I want to see you off with all your assets. A rich man in Hawaii will have many options."

At the holiday season of 1850, Miss Sara Thompson accepted invitations to parties. Former friends found excuses to avoid her company, afraid to be tarnished by her 'reputation.' Proper young men looked through her. Finally, at a church function, she was introduced to a newly ordained minister from Bangor, Unitarian pastor to the Union Street Brick Church, who suggested she attend his services and who was thrilled to discover her in the front pew the next week.

Theirs was a whirling friendship, culminating in an engagement announcement and subsequent resignation letter to the Calais School Committee. The June wedding, Boston honeymoon, and housekeeping in the Bangor manse was followed by a first baby in February of '52. During the fifty years of marriage, the pastor wondered how his wife managed to transform him from a starched prude to a lusty sybarite, as she sat primly beneath the pulpit Sunday mornings, to be followed by matrimonial bliss Sunday afternoons.

*　　　　　　　　*　　　　　　　　*

In New Bedford, Paul found his old whaler, *Saratoga,* prepared to sign on seamen. He offered himself as 4th mate to hunt sperm whale in the Pacific and departed from wintry Acushnet River for Hawaii.

Chapter Thirty-Two

Harriet threw herself at the flower garden, turning over the beds, pruning before new growth began. In an unbelted frock, she kneeled on the path and stabbed loose earth with a trowel. The broad brim of a bonnet shielded her face, her body warmed by a weak April sun. A foot scrape meant George had entered the brick path from the house, home early from court.

His steps halted. Did he wait for a hint of recognition? At last, he broke the silence between them. "My dear, you seem to have made progress. This shall be a splendid summer garden."

"Thank you, George."

"What a pleasure to come home to such a well-kept house. I have some thoughts I would like to share, dear."

"What are those?"

"Do you recall Daniel and Minerva's excursion to Boston last fall? They had six wonderful days – visiting theatres, hearing lectures, and shopping. I propose that we take a journey there in May, when the weather calms."

"Wouldn't such a journey be expensive?" Harriet rose to her feet and craned her neck to see past the bonnet's brim.

"My dear, we have never visited Boston, yet you read articles from magazines on the city's culture. When fashions reach Calais, they're already passé in Boston. A few days in Boston would grant us months of memories. Besides that, it might provide a diversion… "

"Diversion? You patronize me, George Chase," she spat. Her bonnet fell back on her neck. "You've tiptoed around since Paul left, afraid to mention his name. You know how much I was offended by your cowardice."

"I regret his decision to leave, but it couldn't be helped."

"Helped? Any defense of Paul collapsed before your overweening ambition for high office. State senator isn't enough for George Chase. You hope to ride someone's coattails into a national office, and you didn't want any rumors to reach southern Democrats that you'd 'lubricated' a mixed-race marriage." A finger, soiled by earth, wagged in the man's face."

"Harriet! What language you've harbored these months! Think how much I encouraged Paul over the years. The young man simply assumed too much. I had no choice, and you attack my integrity."

"Indeed, I expected better from the man I married," she turned back to her garden, walking away from her husband. "But, now that I've had my say, I shall agree to the Boston trip."

*   *   *

Minerva Chase, with her niece and nephew, saw the couple off at the Bridge Street wharf on a sunny May morning, the side-wheeler packet belching smoke into the clear breeze. The boat backed away from the wharf out into mid-channel, turned, and churned downstream. With luggage secured, George and Harriet took seats on the rough wooden benches inside the protective main cabin. That night, the Chases stayed with Harriet's brother, Winslow and his family in Portland. The next morning, leaving early, they continued on the Boston packet, arriving on the second evening.

Seated in a cab, the couple arrived at the portico of the Tremont House. The cabbie hopped down and reached for the lady's hand. The Tremont was surrounded by a bricked sidewalk with curbing of cut stone, so that Harriet could alight from the horse-drawn cab without a step into the muddy street. George followed, allowing the driver to pull out luggage. The weather was balmy as they stood on the street after the cabbie pulled away. They looked around at Boston's buildings, all native granite and two stories tall. In comparison, the Tremont House was an enormous four stories, dominating the entire neighborhood, a half-block with two wings.

The front of the hotel presented a grand visage of Greek Revival. On each storey, eleven windows faced the street, deep set into the stone front. Windows on the first floor were at street level and plainly cased, while second storey windows were each topped by stone pediment that overhung the frame. Above fourth storey windows was an elaborate, fluted, stone cornice running the length of the building, the façade a rich palatial appearance.

The hotel's portico sheltered the sidewalk halfway to the curb. Inside the columned portico was the two-storey entrance, framed by fluted semi-columns. Inside this elaborate entrance was a double-door made of brass and glass panes.

"May I help sir and madam with their luggage?" A doorman touched his cap.

While George dealt with the clerks, Harriet turned to view the lobby. She stood on a polished marble floor with oriental carpets. Pink marble framed door and windows. A crystal chandelier hung from the two-storey ceiling, giving the lobby an airy height like a church interior.

"Welcome to the Tremont House, Senator and Madam Chase. Allow me to ring the boy." Then, he struck a small bell with a hammer. A youth appeared, dressed in a red jacket with matching cap and black trousers. The boy carried their luggage up the stairs to the third floor rooms.

"Sir and Madam, I am Bobby, your bell boy. I will introduce you to the Tremont House this evening."

Bobby pointed out that each door at the Tremont had its own lock. George and Harriet looked in amazement. Not even houses were locked in Calais. Inside the room, he pointed out the water pitcher and wash bowl on the marble topped sink, soap and towels provided. Harriet noticed the high, wide canopied bed and upholstered chairs. George noticed the small fireplace, logs and kindling ready for lighting, but he did not recognize the device under the window, heavy iron tubes in a row.

"Young man, what purpose has this?"

"Indeed, sir, that device heats the room in cold weather. That's called a *radiator*."

"How does it generate heat?"

"The Tremont has a coal stove in the basement which heats steam to circulate around the rooms."

"Take me to see this apparatus."

They followed the young man under street level to a basement floor. They saw eight bathing rooms with metal tubs. Beyond the bathing rooms were a men's and a lady's privies, four toilets to each. Lamps hung from walls.

"What fuel feeds these lamps? I see no reservoir for the oil."

"Coal gas is piped in from a plant outside Boston. The gas comes by pipes inside the walls. You have such a lamp in your room."

Drawing the bellboy into the men's privy away from his wife's hearing, George asked, "But, how does the House clean the privies? I detect no waste here. Everything smells clean."

"Several rainwater cisterns on the roof hold 2,000 gallons. When a gentleman is finished using the facility, he pulls this chain..." Water gushed through the porcelain bowl. "...and water rushes down from the roof to wash waste into pipes, carrying everything to street gutters and hence, into the Bay."

"Astounding! How efficient and sanitary!"

"Sir, with three hundred guests, the House had no choice but to utilize the latest device. If you wish to bathe, please inform the desk and the same clean rainwater will be heated for your bath."

Bobby escorted the Chases onto the first floor. He showed them a reception hall, the bar, the ladies' drawing room, the gentleman's parlor, the ladies' dining room, a gentlemen's smoking room, a reading room and a dining room. On the second floor was a large ballroom which could seat 200 for dining.

After tipping Bobby, the Chases returned to their room. The hour was late and both were fatigued by the journey and excitement. They decided to call for sandwiches in their room instead of dressing for dining. Harriet was fascinated by the bathing rooms in the basement, so George made arrangements.

An hour later, a light knock was heard on the door. A slight girl in a maid's outfit stood in the hall holding thick towels and an oil lamp

In a brogue, she introduced herself and curtsied, "Go' evenin', mam. My name is Kathleen. Is madam ready for her bath?"

Kathleen helped to carry Harriet's clothes and, opening the reserved room, showed her the drawn bath and stepped out to the hallway to await the lady's pleasure. Harriet felt the water; hot but not scalding. She undressed and hung her clothes on the wall pegs. The gas lamp on the wall lit the room with a steady flame, enough to find soap in water.

The tub surface was off-white enamel, set into a wooden frame. She sat on the side, arranging her soap and washcloth within easy reach. She tested the water with a foot, finding the temperature acceptable. The heat was tolerable. Easing into the water, she gradually lowered her hips and torso until she lay up to her neck. She scrubbed away the dirt of the journey. Then she scrubbed away her fatigue, her worries and cares, and when the scrubbing was over, she was content to lay, neck deep, until the water turned tepid, fingertips wrinkled like raisins.

Rising, she patted dry, bound her hair in a towel, draped herself in a nightgown, and tied a robe around her body. She followed Kathleen and mounted the stairs to their room. She entered the room to find George asleep. She laughed, no hurry. Several delicious such nights lay ahead like promises.

The assembly hall was lit by gas lamps along the walls, seating limited to straight-backed benches. The lecture hall had the austere interior of a Puritan church. Columns, panels, and ceiling were painted grays and white, the floor, varnished pine. George and Harriet took seats in the center, back three rows, to be close without being conspicuous. Nearby, a couple introduced themselves as Captain Fordyce Haskell and his wife, Sylvia Haskell, of New Bedford.

At the appointed time, the speaker walked slowly and deliberately onto the platform elevated by three steps. He wore an elegant blue suit with matching waistcoat, a high collar held a bowed cravat. Standing erect, his hand rested on the podium.

Harriet leaned over to whisper into George's ear, "He looks like an angel. I can see the power of his soul." The speaker stood waiting, without gesture, for the audience to appreciate his presence. A hush fell on those seated on the floor, while the balcony of apprentices, young clerks, and youthful merchants with damsels provided the last titters and scrapes.

Ralph Waldo Emerson finally spoke.

"Tonight I wish to extemporize on my themes of Character and Self-reliance. Young America is rising, and she should trust her instincts, thrusting off the restrictions of old Europe as the slave throws off the chains of bondage. A man should learn to detect and watch that gleam of light which flashes across his own mind from within, more than the luster of the firmament of bards and sages."

The audience sat still. Having read his essays, Harriet heard familiar ideas. Missus Haskell and she exchanged nods.

"Trust thyself: every heart vibrates to that iron string. Accept the place divine providence has found for you, let the eternal stir at your heart. But, society is everywhere in conspiracy against the manhood of its members. Whoso would be a man, must be a nonconformist."

Emerson counseled against reliance on learned culture, against rank and class and institutions. "Whence this worship of the past? The centuries are conspirators against the sanity and majesty of the soul."

Without notes, the podium only a prop for his elbow, Emerson's features were strong, eyebrows thick, nose beaked, the face of a Boston aristocrat. As he spoke, Emerson provided examples and illustrations from history, politics, literature, mathematics, and science. The man's erudition was inexhaustible, as was the listeners' hunger for further display.

"Character is nature in the highest form. Divine persons are 'character born', to borrow a phrase from Napoleon, they are victory organized. Nature never rhymes his children, nor makes two men alike. Character wants room; must not be crowded on by persons."

"Tonight I wish to introduce a young man of character, who, though low born, has risen above his peers. Though once in chains, now he releases the minds of free born as well as those in bondage. I have asked him to share this podium. I give you the hero of the African people of America, Frederick Douglass."

The audience gasped.

A light-complexioned black man stepped from the shadows and walked to stand beside Emerson. The man's physique was athletic, broad shoulders and deep chest, standing a head taller than his companion. The brown, homespun suit, contrasting with Emerson's elegance, revealed his masculine build. His features were striking, a mix of European and African, a bold nose, high cheeks, deep-set flashing eyes, tight mouth. His hair was a massive bush; his complexion the color of freshly minted pennies.

"Good evening, ladies and gentlemen. Thank you, Mister Emerson, for this opportunity." He shook hands with the eminent orator.

Douglass turned to the audience. "Ladies and Gentlemen, a great movement is sweeping the nation. You may be expecting me to refer to the institution of slavery, but I am expanding that cause to include other areas of our national life. Tonight I see before me an assembly which would identify itself as free people, but I would disagree. Many here are women. Theirs is a life in bondage, no control over property or children, none in political office, no more enfranchisement than African slaves."

The rich baritone voice resonated across the audience which had to strain to hear the delicate voice of Emerson. A practiced orator, his accent revealed his Southern roots, his enunciation sounded as crisp as an actor's.

"This great movement will not be satisfied until we have shed those laws and practices which keep us from fulfilling our destiny as a nation with full civil liberties for all. This movement will not only free the oppressed but also free those who must struggle to keep the oppressed in their places."

George struggled to understand who Douglass was referring to. Looking to Harriet, he found her eyes fixed on the man.

"Three years ago my friends in Great Britain collected one-hundred and fifty pounds to purchase my freedom. From 1838, age twenty, until 1847 I lived in fear of slave catchers returning me to bondage."

Frederick Douglass recounted his experiences, born on a plantation on the Eastern Shore of Maryland, child of a slave mother and her owner. He witnessed the sexual exploitation and brutality of black women who, like his own mother, were separated early from their babies to be raised with insufficient clothing and food in clay-floored shanties.

"I never saw my mother, to know her as such, more than four or five times in my life."

He described beatings and killings as casual deeds of impunity. Being mulatto, Douglass lived with the extra suspicion and hostility of masters, evidence of their carnal relations with slave women. To remove this evidence, his master sent the boy to relatives in Baltimore.

"My kind Baltimore mistress found me a bright boy and took it upon herself to instruct me in reading, until halted by her husband, it being a crime to teach a slave to read, but I continued self-instruction through the aid of neighborhood white school boys."

Douglass's voice rose as he closed. "Politicians tell me to be patient. Apologists say slaves are happy in bondage, that there's a sunny side to plantation life. They speak of property rights. They speak of the difficulties inherent in abolishing slavery. They tell us chaos will ensue if millions of blacks are freed." Douglass's hand waved in dismissal. "But, I tell you..." He paused for effect. "...no person has a right to own another person."

The crowd broke into wild cheering.

When the speech ended, the audience members collected funds to support Douglass' work. Young men and ladies poured forth onto the main floor, shaking his hand. Harriet and Sylvia Haskell wiped tears from their eyes.

Harriet was outraged. "How could we allow slavery in the United States? Douglass is as much a human being as any white man and more intelligent than most."

"Madam, that's not the issue," Fordyce Haskell corrected. "Douglass is an exception. The vast numbers of Africans are incapable of citizenship, like draft animals, and must be directed by others. I speak from experience, my friends, having commanded whaling crews from the four corners of the earth."

"The captain has a point," agreed George. "Abolition is too idealistic a proposition. Douglass would sweep away the law and rights of property in one stroke."

"You men...how can you not be affected by his testimony? Take me back to the Tremont, George, before I speak my mind." She tugged her husband's sleeve and excused herself from the Haskells.

*   *   *

"It must have been too much walking," he said.

"Or sitting on benches at the Emerson and Douglass lecture," she offered.

George had awakened with painful knee joints. Harriet fed him breakfast in bed. After he forced himself to stand, the pain subsided until he could hobble around the room.

"Today should be a time to take the omnibus tour, my dear," he suggested.

The remaining days the Chases slowed their pace and returned to Calais according to schedule. Harriet insisted George take his ailment to Doctor Porter, but the problem passed from his mind.

Chapter Thirty-Three

The problem re-appeared December of 1851.

Mornings were the worst.

Harriet carried up cups of coffee as he lay in bed, flexing legs against the stiffness. He blamed the frigid bedroom so Harriet tucked heated soapstones under the quilt, brought from the kitchen where young George stoked the oven. Later, able to rise, the man shuffled into a business suit.

"Not since Boston has this happened."

"Well, darling husband, you were forty-five last year. Be thankful to have lived so long without misery. What did Charles Porter tell you at the examination?"

"I'm ashamed to report nothing."

"Nothing? Your doctor found nothing wrong?" she asked.

"My shame must be that I never brought the condition to Charles, and when Madam mentions my birthday she risks a challenge, insinuating her husband has lapsed into old age. Perhaps he should demonstrate some feat of prowess." George rose on his toes.

"Not until he's warmed his bones in the kitchen where a pot of oatmeal awaits. Come down." Harriet vanished.

Over the next week, the morning stiffness became acute and migrated up to hips, shoulders, and arms. Walking around the office became a chore. Finally, George visited Doctor Porter. His friend asked him to pace the floor, and he manipulated George's arms.

"It would appear to be a case of rheumatism. Hopefully, this will pass, but cold can contribute to worsening. Try salt baths; bring the water to near scalding, as much as you can stand. Return next week. I want to know how you're progressing."

The stiffness and pain only increased that winter. By January, George experienced pain in the small connections of hands and feet where every joint swelled so that he could barely perform his duties. How much further could the illness progress?

One morning before an April dawn, Harriet realized George was gone from bed. She flung a housecoat over her gown and ran down stairs to find him in the kitchen, heating coffee.

"What are you doing? How did you get here?"

"The pain and stiffness are gone, dear. My malady disappeared. I can move without pain and look at my joints, no swelling. My hands feel so flexible."

"All well and good, but I insist you see Charles again."

Doctor Charles Porter admitted Chase to the examining room and listened to his report. He tapped a pencil against a globe, each continent arrayed in colors.

"Yes, George, rheumatism arrives and leaves without cause, but you will despair should another episode appear. Many suffer this debility in cold climates. It shall worsen."

Chase grimaced at the thought.

"Didn't some Maine Congressman suffer from rheumatism?" George asked.

"Luther Severance, Congressman Whig from Augusta. President Taylor appointed Severance Commissioner to the Sandwich Islands in '50. Oh, yes, the man suffered all those years in Augusta's cold. I do hope the salubrity of the Hawaiian climate salved his joints," Porter explained.

"Severance isn't the only Maine man in the islands. There's Elisha Allen from Bangor who was also a Whig Congressman and a widower with several children. He took them all to be consul in Honolulu." Chase recalled. "A most pleasant assignment."

"Does that interest you, George?" Porter smiled. "I shouldn't mind such duty myself. Do you plan to support that man from New Hampshire, Pierce, in the election? If

Pierce wins, he'd be obliged to grant requests from someone who delivered Maine's electors."

"To replace Allen at Honolulu? I see you've researched this through, Charles. Might there be a medical position involved?"

"Head of a seamen's hospital, either one in Honolulu or one at the royal capital, Lahaina. The doctor is appointed by the local American consul, a plum job."

"What about the children, the house, the law practice?"

"Your health supersedes all else, my friend. A couple of years in the tropics may resolve your rheumatism, and the appointment would be of short duration. As to your career, posts overseas provide opportunities for ample rewards. Do you recall Shakespeare's *Julius Caesar*? Brutus says to Cassius that line about flood tide when you get only one great chance in life."

"Yes. 'A tide in the affairs of men, which, taken at the flood, leads on to fortune; Omitted, all the voyage of their life is bound in shallows and in miseries, on such a full sea are we now afloat.'"

*   *   *

Honorable George Monroe Chase
November 17, 1852
Calais, Maine

Dear Senator Chase,

As President-elect, I am writing to thank you for your support of my candidacy for President of the United States within the State of Maine.

That support was recognized by the citizens of your great state with an overwhelming plurality of votes, contributing to my election for president earlier this year.

My success was due to the many efforts of loyal Democrats, especially you in Maine. I write to inform you of my gratitude and to offer you a post commensurate with your ability. My associates will be contacting you in the near future to discuss such an appointment.

With sincerest thanks,
Yours truly,

President-elect Franklin Pierce

*   *   *

Honorable George M. Chase   March 5, 1853
Calais, Maine

Dear Senator Chase,

By the authority of the United States, as Secretary of State, under the auspices of President Franklin Pierce, I am writing to announce your appointment to the post of consul, in the Sandwich Islands on the Island of Maui at the royal town of Lahaina. The Lahaina consul serves the interests of the American whaling fleet.

As you well may be aware, although the lugubrious climate and manifest opportunities abound at this location, your appointment indicates the strategic importance of these Islands to the Pierce administration. Due to the malfeasance of your predecessor, both in the capacity of fiscal as well as diplomatic responsibility, it is incumbent upon you to come to the city of Washington, District of Columbia, for instructions, cachet, and letters of introduction.

Your appointment at my office is arranged for the thirtieth of June 1853 at eleven in the morning. It is the honor of every Consul at Lahaina to appoint his own doctor to the Seaman's Hospital. Please inform us when you have identified your choice to this position.

Enclosed is a draught for your expenses, negotiable at the Bank of Boston. I suggest you travel railroads from Boston to Washington.

This office has made arrangements with the Calvert Shipping Company of Baltimore, Maryland for your voyage to the Sandwich Islands. You will sail on the Queen Anne. Please arrange to send your luggage directly to Calvert. Details will follow during your visit on June 30th.

Y'r ob'nt servant,

Honorable William L. Marcy
Secretary of State

Chapter Thirty-Four

The rail car's motion and the stink of coal smoke made Chase sick. The train couldn't arrive in New Bedford fast enough. Only the view compensated for the ride, as the Taunton and New Bedford coaches crossed the countryside of southern Massachusetts along the Acushnet River. Farm patches spread along the river, each house near the water prospering from both land and sea. Dairy barns were separated from the white farmhouses by an open yard, he noted, unlike Maine farmsteads with house and barn attached.

As the balloon-stacked locomotive steamed south, the Acushnet widened. Farms gave way to factories with high windows to light the lathes for mechanics or looms for girls. Simple docks with skiffs gave way to elaborate piers with schooners as the estuary widened.

How lush Massachusetts farms were compared to Maine's! Harriet would enjoy seeing so much fertile pasture, and fertility led him of to recall their last conversation.

*   *   *

George watched Harriet leaning against a station pillar. The carriage's open doors awaited passengers.

"Darling, look at your condition. I'm ashamed to leave you."

"Silly man, you know I'm quite capable of managing, and mother arrives to share housekeeping. You forget your wife's the daughter of a ship captain whose mother thrived alone for months. With infant in arms, I will soon appear beside you in Hawaii."

"Travel can be worse than bearing this child, I fear, and then, too, I worry about young George and Hattie once you've gone. Off to school under the care of strangers."

"Too late to worry now. They'll manage until the family re-unites in Hawaii. Hurry, the conductor's calling all aboard."

*   *   *

George fished out the locket from his breast pocket. He sprung open the catch and looked at the miniature portrait of his wife. A fine likeness, he thought, though the checks displayed more rouge than necessary.

The train slowed to the speed of a stagecoach, as the city appeared. Clusters of factories skirted railroad yards on entering New Bedford. A new odor permeated the air like rancid butter, the smell of whale oil.

The porter lifted his articles onto a cart and pushed it down the platform toward waiting carriages. A black carriage driver stepped forward to meet Chase. "Carry you somewhere, Sir?"

"Yes, I would like to go to Captain Haskell's house on Union Street."

"Yes, sir, I know it well. The corner of Union and Cottage. No one could miss Captain Haskell's home, sir. It's one-of-a-kind." The driver lifted trunk and valise onto the boot of the carriage while Chase climbed into the rear seat.

"Let me ask, what would a tour cost?"

"A tour? What would you be wantin' to see?"

"The wealth of New Bedford. What makes this town rich?"

"Well, sir, this carriage's time is valuable."

"Go on, man, name your price."

"A dollar an hour for the carriage and another fifty cents explainin'."

"Very well, carry on," ordered Chase

The driver steered his horse toward piers jutting into the Acushnet River. Whaling ships crowded along every available spot like a forest – masts as trees, spars as branches, rigging as foliage, from shore to shore.

183

Chase asked to stop beside a busy wharf filled with huge casks and a strange display like hairy trees.

"They be raw baleen, sir, from whales."

Then Chase understood baleen to be the long fringed plates hanging in overlapping rows from the upper jaws of most whales. The baleen, pliable and flexible, made frames for umbrellas, corset stays, skirt hoops, buggy whips, carriage springs, and fishing rods.

Teams of men plied among the casks, bearing clear glass bottles, opening the top plugs, and dipping out samples of whale oil to test. Some wore the Quaker broad hat and butternut homespun, others wore expensive black suits and silk hats. Ordinary workers looked dark skinned.

"Driver, excuse me but where do those workmen come from?"

"Some be Indians, some be Portuguese from Cape Verde. We got all kinds here in New Bedford. We even got cannibals."

"You mean Sandwich Islanders, come from the whaling fleet?"

"Yes, indeed. Then, there's us colored."

"All runaways from slave states, I suppose?"

"Not exactly, sir," the driver corrected, "many of us are free colored, like me. Others may not have their papers yet, fugitives from slavery. You heard of Frederick Douglass, sir?"

"Indeed! My wife and I saw him lecture."

"Mister Douglass started right here on these wharfs, sir, rolling them casks. He had the skill to be a ship's caulker, apprenticed in Baltimore harbor, but the white ship carpenters would'a struck if a colored was hired. So, Douglass worked day-labor until he brought his wife up north."

The carriage drove into the city, along cobblestone streets and up a slope from the river, rising above the smells of oil refineries and spermaceti candle factories, to the shipping businesses. They passed the Seamen's Bethel

Chapel where sailors prayed before a voyage and a seamen's home and hospital.

"Where is the Friends Meeting House?" Chase asked.

"That's over on Maple Street." He turned left.

Chase noticed how stately the homes were in this section; large houses and gracious gardens, and remarked about it to the driver.

"Oh, yeah, these are Friends in the whaling business. They tend to build on the south side of Union, the rest live to the north. The AME is on North County Street."

"The what?"

"African Methodist Episcopal, the colored church."

Finally, they arrived at the home of Captain Fordyce Haskell.

The driver pointed up at the Haskell house, said, "Didn't I tell you this was different? Ain't nothin' square about it, kind'a spooks me."

Chase turned to examine the house. While all other houses were squared, clapboard two storey homes, the Haskell house had no right-angled corners because, instead of four sides, it had eight – an octagonal house. The front door faced the corner. Flower gardens filled the large lot beyond the house. Each of the eight sides, presented a different façade to the street, some with balconies, some with overhanging gables, and others, plain clapboard.

Chase rang the bell. A young woman came to the door. She smiled and called to her mother in the kitchen that Senator Chase had arrived. Missus Haskell led George through the parlor and into the conservatory.

The conservatory was entirely glassed in. Exotic plants grew in great pots set on the marble floor, small trees with broad leaves and delicate flowers, voluptuous in their design. Chase wondered how hot the room became in a summer's afternoon.

Soon, Captain Haskell entered.

"George Chase, welcome to New Bedford. Glad to learn of your consulship in Lahaina since our chance meeting at the Emerson lecture in Boston. How can I help you succeed on this new venture?"

"Please tell me about Lahaina from the perspective of a ship's master."

Captain Haskell settled back, lit his pipe, and took two long draws. "Very familiar with that port, spent several pleasant months anchored off Lahaina, provisioning the *Mercury*. You have an important post that can be rewarding if you manage."

"Manage? How challenging could it be?"

"From October to December and from March to May you will be busy. Four to five hundred ships arrive at Lahaina, each with a crew of twenty to thirty. Whaling is a dangerous business. Men get injured, and you oversee the seaman's hospital. There also, captains dismiss seamen for incompetence and insubordination. If those men find no other crews to join, they may become beachcombers and malcontents among the Sandwich Islanders, rioting and – he darted a glance about– whoring.

"Also, you will require from the captains three months' wages for dismissed seamen for their support, $36, which is deposited into a seamen's relief fund that you administer. You are the sole representative of the United States to these men. In the event of a shipwreck, you are expected to clothe them, care for them, and find them berths on passing ships. Captains will need paperwork, at $2 each – certificates of entry, certificates for warehousing oil and whalebone until it is trans-shipped on clipper ships back to the States. "

Chase interjected, "And the opportunities?" He sat on the seat's edge.

"Ah, yes, Senator Chase. The islands are prospering and opportunities for investment abound. California buys Maui potatoes, sugar, beef, and pork. Men are starting plantations on the rich volcanic soil. Buy property. Then, there's money in trade. Find a trusted agent, set him up in business, and let your purchases be from him alone.

"The whaling business has brought prosperity to my family. I spent from 1836 to 1848 on four voyages, harvesting sperm whales off Japan. Those four voyages allowed me to retire as a young man, investing my savings in the voyages of still younger men.

"Sperm oil was my 'gold.' One sperm whale might boil down to two thousand gallons of oil. A barrel fetches some days $41.42 at the dock. Today, I invest $30,000 per voyage. Compare that with the cost of a farm at $2,500 or a manufacturing firm at $5,000. A huge investment. Why bother, you may ask? Because it earns a 15% an average return. I ask you, what does a good bond earn?"

"About six percent," answered Chase.

"You see our pretty town. Twenty-six agents, living among these proud houses and flowery gardens, earn as much as the President of the United States and six times the salary of a U. S. federal judge. The Pacific beckons to those who would take calculated risks."

Chase interjected, "You make it sound easy."

"Only strong men survive the whaling business. You see me now a gentleman of culture, but I was the devil on the quarterdeck. Younger men now dominate their ships in the Pacific, for example, Thomas Dallman, master of the *Mary Ann.* When first mate, he single-handed put down a mutiny, beating the ringleader within a hair's breadth of life."

Sylvia Haskell called the men to dinner. The captain proposed a toast for the evening. "To the Honorable Senator Chase and Missus Chase and all their posterity on this great venture to the Sandwich Islands."

Chapter Thirty-Five

George Chase emerged from the polluted confines of Union Station to the hill overlooking the classical architecture of the Capitol of the United States of America. White Roman columns of Congress floated above the squalor of low office buildings.

He arrived this day before his appointment at the State Department, wearing a black traveling suit and a beaver hat to match. He slung his canvas coat over one arm while the other carried a valise. Chase checked his pocket watch and sighed, perhaps there would be time tomorrow to tour the national capital before his appointment with Secretary of State William Marcy.

Chase hailed an omnibus and asked for the Willard Hotel. The bus, drawn by two workhorses, stopped at intersections when passengers called out. The city was less than majestic beyond the Roman imitation government buildings. Telegraph poles marched up dirt streets, each pole festooned by slack wires. The driver shrugged when reminded about the hotel and, finally, stopped the bus, and mumbled "Willard." Chase got off.

Before him stood the hotel with columned entrance and marquee. A plank sidewalk surrounded the building so that pedestrians could walk around and peer into the shop windows lining the first floor. Doormen in livery greeted guests as they alighted from carriages while black servants met horsemen, offering to stable their steeds. Outside, the Willard Hotel hummed with activity.

Chase accepted the doorman's greeting and entered. The portal held not one set of doors, but two in sequence, that insulated the street's dirt and noise from infecting the carpeted interior. The lobby of the Willard was hushed and formal. A uniformed attendant directed him to the front desk.

"Thank you for visiting our hotel, Mister Chase. A servant will carry your luggage. Boy!" A line of black men stood to attention. One stepped forward, touching his hat brim, and took his bags. Chase waited for the man's lead.

The desk clerk intervened, "Mister Chase, our servants aren't allowed to touch the keys. The boy will follow you." The clerk slipped Chase the key.

"Very well, please follow me." Chase led forward up the stairs to the room, through dimly lit hallways. The servant followed without comment as the hotel guest checked door numbers.

Finally, Chase located the room, opened the door, and directed the man to place the luggage on the settee. He offered change for a tip.

"No, Sir, nothing, Sir," the servant backed out of the room, eyes lowered, bowing down, and closing the door after himself.

"That's no servant," Chase said aloud. The District of Columbia, capital of the 'land of the free', was a slave-owning city.

*   *   *

A soft knock on the door came at dawn. It wasn't necessary; Chase had lain in disturbed sleep. Thick hotel walls softened the cries of other guests, but a window open to the building's interior court let in teeming human nature from drunken spats and sexual encounters.

His appointment with Marcy was at eleven, but Chase rose early and washed in a basin brought by his "servant" who replaced the chamber pot. Today, he dressed in his senatorial claw hammer jacket, black suit, white shirt, dark cravat, high button shoes and spats, topping off the ensemble with his silk hat and gold-headed cane.

Chase stepped into the hotel's restaurant for breakfast. Long tables groaned with food. Eggs, yolks red, swam in grease. Chicken, potatoes, corn fritters, and mush were all fried in batter. Diners piled up food and ate with spoons and knives. Nauseated by the liquids and solids intermingled, revolted by the lack of cutlery, George craved privacy.

Chase stepped out of the hotel onto the plank sidewalk and checked his watch. Six o'clock. Lighting a cigar and surveying the early morning traffic, he inhaled. His appointment was five hours away. Time to tour the city, with the White House only a short distance. He strolled past shops and offices for two blocks when he heard a strange sound.

A rhythmic clinking noise, each separated by an interval of ticks. Was it approaching? Was that another noise, pulling something across a wooden surface?

Then, he heard a tone; deep, underneath the clinking at wider internals. Instrumental or human? It came from some wide hollow cavity. Was this music, a chant?

Now, he knew the direction came from 14th Street, but nothing was visible.

The noise grew closer, more distinct. The clinking became louder, more metallic, and the deep tone became several voices, one bass and several baritone. The bass voice called and the baritones answered in muffled words. Chase slowed.

Suddenly, a sight exploded around the corner of 14th Street coming fast upon him. Six African men shuffled toward Chase on the plank sidewalk in close formation, stripped to the waist, shoeless, attached by heavy chain, linked to iron ankle braces. An armed white man in a broad brimmed hat guarded the squad. The line maintained a pace, timed so that the loose portions of the chain lifted together. All right feet came off the wood surface simultaneously and all returned down with a hard "chink" as links hit links.

One man lifted his voice in a call as the right feet hit the planks. The other five answered, eyes focused on the flooring. Only the overseer cocked an eye toward their course.

The gang approached Chase square in the path, cigar fumes curling around his hand.

"Stop. You, damn"

The overseer grabbed the first man's arm.

"You 'most ran into a gentleman, damn your black ass."

The first African came to a halt, but the other five crashed into him.

"Pardon me, sir, but we 'spected you to step aside. Otherwise, I would have pulled these here niggers into the street, but seein' how's the streets nothin' but mud and their master wants 'em clean fur the slave market..."

The explanation was lost on Chase. He stared at the six bondsmen. He had never been this close to so many bare-skinned black men. Could he distinguish their features? Skin, noses, lips, hair – so alike and so unlike whites'. One was a tall youth, the age of Chase's son.

"Now, sir, if you'd be excusin' me," the guard turned away from Chase. "Y'all get up and move out," the gang started once again down 14th Street.

Chase watched the rhythmic walk start up.

Market? A slave market?

All thoughts of touring the White House fled his mind.

Do I dare look at such an auction? Half our nation depends on slavery. All the better to understand fellow Democrats in the South.

He hurried to follow the bondsmen to an industrial area of Washington, near the Potomac River. Long, low buildings warehoused products for sale. Stacked lumber, baled cotton, crated chickens, all competed for space. Corralled cattle waited for city slaughterhouses.

At the horse auction, Chase stopped to sit on bleachers in an arc-shaped arena. Others watched animals led through the gate and bid from their seats with small gestures. Black grooms walked each horse, guiding with the bridle.

The auctioneer shouted and appealed to the crowd on the stands. "Fine piece of horseflesh" as the handler held the bridle of a thoroughbred stallion. "This boy will sire a whole new stable of colts for your herd. Just look how attentive those ears are, how straight those legs. This stallion is a prime breeder, gentlemen."

The heavy Virginia dialect was difficult to follow, but George understood the terms. The handler walked the animal around the corral, showing off its perfect form. Men leaned over the barrier for closer inspection. Bids rose until exhausted, and a Virginian claimed the horse, sending his personal groom to collect the prize while he settled payment.

Following the sale of the stallion, other horses – Clydesdales, Belgians, Percherons, and Morgans – were sold. "Years of service left in this animal. Just look at this healthy mane." Quarter horses for cattle herding. "This one is agile and quick." Palominos and Shetland ponies. "Your little daughters will be delighted to ride this around your estate." Then, an old mule was led into the circle. The auctioneer lowered his voice. "Gentlemen, have you a tenant? Does that man need a plow mule? A small investment in this mule will parley into a greater return from your tenant."

Chase watched as the auctioneer worked to shed the best possible light on every beast for sale. He wondered where the slave gang had gone. He left the auction and passed beyond vendors hawking vegetables.

He saw a set of bleachers which provided seating for a male audience of buyers who faced a platform. George stood to the side and refrained from taking a seat.

On a raised pulpit, an auctioneer took bids, extolling the qualities on a dark young man, a little older than George Junior. A tunic to his knees, the bondsman faced his audience, manacled at the wrists. "Fine Guineaman just arrived from the Bight of Benin's Ebo tribe. Well-beaten and prepared to perform for your overseer. By the looks of his teeth, this boy could be about twenty. At this time, he's months from female company, gentlemen, and ready to runt your wenches." Using his cane, the auctioneer lifted the tunic, exposing the young man's penis. "Putting that tool in your workshop will add much to your property." The crowd guffawed.

The slave looked straight ahead. George gawked. Breakfast churned in this stomach.

From his pulpit, the auctioneer suggested, "Do I hear $2,000 for his fine specimen?" Buyers raised the bid, the process moved quickly to its conclusion. The highest bidder, upon concluding the transaction, sent a slave to collect the young man from the stable.

Chase checked his watch. Eight o'clock. He turned to leave when the attendants brought forth a pretty girl. She stood, a black book pressed to her chest by crossed arms.

"Gentlemen, there are times when the misfortunes of others become your good fortunes. This wench belonged to a prominent family fallen on hard times. The Thigpen estate of Perquimans Quarter on North Carolina's Albemarle must sell property at distress prices. This here saucy miss was raised in their genteel home among the master's children, learning all their high-class manners. She sews, lays out table service, and knows to fix a lady's hair. Your wives and daughters would be well-attended."

The young woman stood awkwardly at the back of the stage. Unlike other slaves, she wore a full dress, puffed sleeves and hemline to the ankles. Her pink complexion and gray eyes bespoke generations of secret liaisons between upstairs maids and planters' sons. Light hair fell in tight curls about her shoulders.

Chase thought, had she walked down a Calais street, none would have noted her African heritage; but standing on the dais, identified, and marked for sale, the girl was *black*. Indeed, could this young woman be considered "black" at all?

The auctioneer's voice cut through his ruminations.

"Git up here, you little minx."

The girl missed the command and searched the crowd for sympathetic eyes. Tears ran down her cheeks.

"Earl, move that tart to where the gentlemen can get an eyeful." Pug-faced Earl pushed her to the front of the stage. The audience moved forward. Chase squirmed. He felt weak.

"If a lucky party were to take this girl today, the wife would think herself fortunate with well-trained maid, but that's not what's on your mind, is it? This gal has many fine attributes that are hidden, such as... cross-stitch?"

The men laughed.

"Gentlemen, I believe in displaying my merchandise as honest business."

"Yes, yes," they said.

"Earl, display the goods."

From behind the girl, in one fluid motion, Earl ripped open her buttoned dress, forcing the top down to her waist, exposing her breasts. Embracing her to trap her arms, pelvis against her buttocks, Earl leered at the crowd. The girl turned away and closed her eyes. Her book fell to the floor.

But, the expected effect was lost on the crowd of southern gentlemen; all eyes drawn to the man puking in spasms next to the stage.

"Sir, will you not move your illness away from my sale?" shouted the auctioneer.

George gripped the edge of the stage.

Wiping a kerchief across his flushed face, George tried to answer, "Sorry, gentlemen. A bit shocking, the use of the girl."

"And who might you be?"

"Senator George M. Chase, Washington County, Maine"

"Well, looky what we have here, boys. A jinuine Yankee abolitionist. A male Harriet Beecher Stowe, writtin' another *Uncle Tom's Cabin*, interferin' in a lawful procedure," he sneered. "Maybe he's fixin' to buy her and use her hisself!"

Chase ignored the taunt and turned to the tidewater gentlemen.

"Hardly an abolitionist. I'm only curious about your peculiar institution. I do caution, however, against purchasing this young woman. She'll contaminate your other slaves. My friends, this girl reads."

Chase left for his appointment at State.

Chapter Thirty-Six

William L. Marcy, Secretary of State for the United States of America, worked in a small office in a dismal two-storey structure. The State Department's staff comprised seven political drones and fifteen male clerks to maintain the records of all twenty-seven United States ambassadors, 197 consuls, and agents in scores of wooden drawers.

The staff worked with natural light, streaming in through high windows, whose upper sashes were lowered to admit fresh air. Clerks, using steel-tipped pens, wrote correspondence to overseas American officials, for which the Secretary would, using cursive script, handwrite cover letters.

Marcy earned his position after a long career. Author of the motto, "To the victors belong the spoils," Marcy served both as Senator from and Governor of New York. As Secretary of War during the triumphal Mexican War, he had tasted power and commanded men. For him, the Department of State under the Pierce Administration was early retirement to a swamp.

On this June 30, 1853, Secretary Marcy was in a foul mood. The unpaved streets of Washington and spring rains conspired to soak the clay into a morass. The carriage from his apartment had bogged down in the muddy street, leaving him no option but to walk through the sucking muck. Trousers soiled to the hips, the Secretary of State stood shoeless behind his desk when a clerk ushered in George Chase.

"Chase? What do you want, Chase?" the Secretary barked.

"Sir, I am under the impression we have an appointment to discuss my assignment to the Sandwich Islands." Chase held his hat in both hands.

"Yes, yes, that's right," Marcy's eyes scanned his desk, eyeing the appointment book, "McCalla!" he shouted for the clerk, "Fetch me that damned folder on Lahaina from the Sandwich Island drawer."

McCalla brought the file immediately. The Secretary shoved on a pair of glasses and leafed through the papers, scanning correspondence to remind himself of the post's recent history.

"Sit, sit. Why are you standing?" He shouted.

"But, sir, I wait for you." Chase protested.

"Oh, all right, if I must." The Secretary eased his wet buttocks onto the desk chair, grimacing. "Chase, are you prepared to handle a difficult situation?" Without waiting for a reply, he continued, "the United States has interests in Hawaii – the Sandwich Islands – national interests, commercial interests, and spiritual interests. Are you aware of this?"

Marcy squinted over his glasses.

"Yes, Sir. I am aware of the work of the Missionary Board, and my wife's family, too, has interests in the China trade."

"Good. We like your background, Chase, law, politics, and business, and being a Yankee – all what we need on the island of Maui. King Kamehameha the Third or whatever and his nobles respect New Englanders."

"An honored consulship." Chase interjected.

"Honor? Hardly the word to describe your predecessor." Marcy slapped his palm on the file. "We hope you can restore our country's good name."

"Please inform me…." Chase crossed his legs.

"Listen well, Chase. New England seafarers were the first Americans to visit the islands for ship provisions; so it's natural that most consuls and commissioners were chosen from that quarter. Hawaiian consulate positions are choice, and a man may add to his fortune in a comfortable climate with many appurtenances of civilization."

William Marcy spoke with vigor, delivering the orientation without notes. His mane of white hair shook when he made points.

"The duties of all consuls include providing relief for sick or stranded sailors, shipping them back to the U.S. if necessary.

"You will support American planters as they organize a sugar industry. Of course, you will encounter the usual problems with Americans. Womanizing whalers, drunk and rowdy sailors, captains who dump white crewmen and hire natives."

Chase blurted, "Is there slavery on the islands, Mister Secretary?"

"Good heavens, what brought on that question?" The Secretary stopped.

"I ran into a slave market this morning. First time ever saw such a thing." Chase fingered his hat brim.

Marcy cleared his throat.

"Yes. That can be a nasty shock for a northerner, but many a shock awaits you in Hawaii, too. For example, you may have heard scandals about whalers and Hawaiian women, *waheenies,* as Melville calls them. I am told they have no sense of sin."

"But, Mister Secretary, shouldn't we allow for differences between our nations? Even within the United States, customs differ between North and South. For instance, liberties enjoyed by slave owners over females in bondage would never be tolerated..."

"Young man, your liberal notions may serve you well in the salons of Boston, but not in the harsh light of reality. It may please you that slavery in Hawaii has been abolished. However, the races mix in shocking social equality. The United States could never digest those islands." Marcy thumped the desk. "But, I digress. To return to the official account of American consuls in the Sandwich Islands. In '38, Brinsmade was the first Maine man, who was followed by a Vermonter who was in turn followed in 1850 by Elisha Hunt Allen from Bangor. Know him?

Chase nodded, "Elisha served in Maine's House of Representatives and then one term in Congress. In '43, his wife died, leaving him with four children."

The Secretary ignored the comment, "Now we come to your predecessor, Charles Bunker. Since Allen had already been appointed to Honolulu, Lahaina, the royal capital, was awarded to Bunker." The Secretary examined the file.

"However, Bunker proved to be improvident, padding expenses at the seamen's hospital. The Treasury brought this to our attention and suggested an investigation. Bunker caught wind and skipped out."

Chase broke in, "I heard Allen resigned from the Honolulu post."

Marcy leered. "Your friend went native and married a dusky damsel from the royal family and accepted the position of Minister of Finance for the royal government, a very nice arrangement. Climate, wealth, power, affection."

A large black fly buzzed around the ceiling of the office, bouncing against surfaces. The insect missed the open window. Shifting in his chair, George began to crave food, but Marcy droned on.

"As consul, you will also report quarterly on all American shipping at Lahaina, Ship names, dates of arrival, captains, home ports, barrels of whale oil, barrels of spermaceti oil, pounds of whale bone, tonnage burden, number of American crewmen and foreign crewmen, and recent origin of the ships. You commit all this to memory?"

"Yes, Mister Secretary."

"Ah, gone are the days when I could have said the same. Time befuddles the mind, boy. Well, your ship awaits you in Baltimore harbor."

McCalla entered, "Beg pardon, Mister Secretary, you're called to dine at the White House at noon."

"Damn, Franklin needs a whip to lash that naughty cabinet. Always calling an old war horse to pull his chestnuts out of the fire, to mix metaphors," Marcy chuckled. "Never accept any post where you command a rabble, Chase."

The Secretary of State stood and reached for George's hand.

"Congratulations, Consul Chase, no longer Senator Chase. How does the new title sound? A bit like a Roman prefect, assigned to a barbarian outpost, eh?"

Chapter Thirty-Seven

As Chase entered the Willard, a hotel clerk hailed him by name. "You have a telegraph message."

The clerk drew a piece of paper from a pigeonhole and handed him a handwritten note. *Will call on you this afternoon, meet in lobby. Cousin.* Chase recalled no cousin in Washington. A paperboy passed through the lobby, hawking penny copies. Chase bought one to read while he lunched in the Willard's dining room.

Dissent in the administration!

Word that Attorney General Caleb Cushing of Massachusetts, and Secretary of War Jefferson Davis of Mississippi came to blows over the Fugitive Slave Act.

Papists threaten America!

Monsignor Gaetano Bedini, papal nuncio visits America and meets with Postmaster General James Campbell, first Catholic in the cabinet. Campbell kneels and kisses the Monsignor's ring! Nativists, arise while America is yet a Protestant nation!

Immigration Crisis!

The arrival of foreigners on our shores during this decade has already exceeded their arrival during the whole of the 1840's. Beware! Most foreigners are arriving from principalities of the Holy Roman Empire. Will your grandchildren speak German?

Over the rustle of the newspaper, George Chase became aware of a presence. A low voice said, "Return to your room. Someone wants to meet with you."

He spun around to see a young man put a finger to pursed lips and melt into the lobby's crowd. Chase gulped lunch, walked to the grand staircase, and climbed to his floor. When he slid the key into the lock, the door opened itself.

"Come in, George Chase."

Afternoon sun reflected from the central courtyard to reveal two men, one seated, and the other holding the knob. The seated one, older, balding, elegantly dressed, stood and extended a hand toward Chase. He towered over the short Chase.

"Welcome to Washington, cousin."

"I'm sorry but I don't recognize..."

"Not since grammar school at Cornwall, New Hampshire."

"Salmon Chase? I recall your father died, and your mother sent you away"

"Yes, mother could not manage all of us on the farm. My uncle raised me in Ohio with advantages beyond my poor mother's means."

"My God, man, I've followed your career from 'attorney-general of fugitive slaves' to junior member of the United States Senate from Ohio. Are you really such a zealot as the papers portray, all for the cause of ... abolition, Salmon?"

"More than all the preachers of New England. It shouldn't shock you, George. Many join our ranks."

George flopped into a chair and glanced at the young man still standing by the door, a bulky build and flash of metal under the jacket.

"It's still extremely radical. I'm grateful this meeting's secret," said George.

"Secrecy is mutually advantageous. What brought you to Washington, George?" asked Salmon.

"I'm appointed consul to Hawaii and sail soon from Baltimore," he answered.

"Oh, and what prompted Pierce to offer you that plum job? Did you deliver Maine to the Electoral College?" Salmon raised one eyebrow.

"My qualifications speak for themselves, and further my health requires a less rigorous climate," George sniffed. "At least my reputation is intact."

"I apologize for nothing," said Salmon. "In fact I boast to be one of only three senators to vote against the Fugitive Slave Law. As you may well imagine, I have many enemies," he paused to nod toward his bodyguard. "Sources tell me you had a singular experience this morning."

"If only you'd been there...oh, but how would you know about the young woman?" George glanced up at the sentry who crossed his arms.

Salmon, too, turned toward the young man, "Will?"

The bodyguard sprang to attention, "Yes, Senator, they were selling a pretty mulatto, named Matilda Thigpen. Your cousin's comments ruined the sale. Seems he suggested that she reads books and might influence other slaves. The girl remains locked in the stables."

Salmon faced his cousin, "George, will you at least admit the slave market offended you?"

"Only regarding this Matilda. She ought to be free, as light complexioned as she is. Hardly one-eighth or one-sixteenth African. What an absurdity!"

"Yes. Doesn't seem right." Salmon grinned. "Should someone step forward and break her manacles?"

"Certainly." George agreed.

"I think you're on to something, there, George." Salmon tapped his cousin's knee.

"If you are suggesting... No, not I. Violate the Fugitive Slave Law?"

"Aren't you leaving on a ship for the Hawaiian Islands? Once that ship's twelve miles off the shores of the United States, she's a free woman."

George rose from the chair and looked out the window. In the courtyard below, black maids hung out sheets from clotheslines.

"Six months' imprisonment and a thousand dollar fine; the penalty for aiding an escaped slave. A fine way to end a career!" Gesturing out the window, he asked, "Why can't the girl be whisked up to Canada?"

"Exactly what slave catchers would expect," answered Salmon. "There'd be a high price on her head."

George fumbled in his jacket for a cigar. His fingers found the locket with Harriet's portrait.

"It'd ruin my reputation as a family man, alone with a young woman all those months. It's impossible," said George, striking a match and lighting the cigar.

Salmon's voice soothed, "So normal, a government official on an important mission with a servant. She would pose as an emancipated woman to cook and clean for a gentleman. Once in Hawaii, she'd melt into that mixed society. This girl's got only this one chance. Tomorrow, they send her south."

"It's dangerous. Why should I accept such a risk?"

"Are you familiar with the James Russell Lowell poem?

Once to every man and nation,
Comes the moment to decide?"

George finished off the verse:
In the strife of truth with falsehood,
*For the good or evil side...*But, Salmon, this moment's just not practical, as much as I'd like her to be free."

Senator Salmon P. Chase clasped his cousin's shoulders.

"Don't give me your final answer now. In two nights, my agents will deliver Miss Thigpen to your ship. Time enough to examine your conscience. Delay your decision until then."

*   *   *

Twilight strode across the District on a warm night. Two forms moved from the market's shadows, one large, one small.

Large wore trousers; small, a long skirt.

Small darted between overhangs; large lumbered from shadow to shadow.

Small's hair was wrapped in a rag; large wore a brimmed hat.

Large blackened his pink skin with charcoal, while small's complexion required no darkening.

Together, they watched a sentry slumped in a chair, leaning against the stable door. The larger shadow moved forward and clamped a hand over the guard's mouth and nose. His eyes opened wide.

"Make a noise, and you die, son-of-a-bitch," said Will, Salmon Chase's bodyguard.

Will dragged the man into the stable and laid him on the straw. With a length of rope, he hogtied ankles to throat and jumped up to admire his work. The body, chest down, twitched, testing tautness on windpipe.

Turning, Will gestured. "Get her, Tubman."

The small shadow passed across the floor to a lone figure cringed in a stall. Matilda looked up.

"Ready to run, girl?" The voice barked the question, then gasped. "Oh, you is a real yellow gal. These men fool with you, honey?"

"No, ma'am."

Suddenly a door banged open at the end of the stable.

"Who's in here, besides niggers?" yelled Earl, the auctioneer's assistant.

Earl approached the two cowering women. The small black woman's hand cocked a pistol's hammer, but before the gun fired, a pick handle whistled through the air to connect with Earl's cranium. His body slumped, and the three figures vanished.

Chapter Thirty-Eight

The Baltimore taproom hung heavy with the odors of cigars and sawdust. Beneath the bar spittoons squatted among misaimed rancid expectorant; above the bartenders, over the display of bottled spirits, hung a huge painting, a nude woman, floating over serene waves, smiling, hair of seaweed. Her full breasts, tipped by swollen nipples, beckoned viewers.

The restaurant appealed to the better half of the maritime population. No common crewmen present, customers included ship's mates and officers, carpenters, coopers, blacksmiths, and other trades.

Chase sat with Captain James Scattergood, master of the *Queen Anne*, and First Mate MacClintock. A buxom waitress carried three steins of light beer, shoving each across the polished table.

"So, vat vill you haf?" the waitress took orders.

"Crab feast," MacClintock said. "We're breakin' in a Maine man, introducin' him ta the wonders of Chesapeake's finest. Don't hold back on the seasonin'."

"Comingk raght oop," she turned toward the kitchen.

His back to the nude, Captain Scattergood pushed his beer to MacClintock, "Thou hast a great venture ahead, Consul Chase, between Hawaiians and whalers. I don't envy thy task." A stout Quaker, Scattergood wore the plain broadbrimmed hat of his sect.

"Yes, there's work ahead. Any suggestions, Captain?" Chase sat bareheaded, his cravat loosened.

"Appreciate when an opportunity presents itself for redemption, my friend," the Quaker looked into Chase's eyes.

Chase watched his beer's foam subside before responding.

"The question is who is the redeemed and who the redeemer," he finally answered.

"Sometimes 'tis the same person. If I were thee, I'd meditate upon the essential goodness in every man...or woman, when you can save one person." He gave Chase a knowing look.

"Hoot, mon," MacClintock burst in, "ya' think too liberally of human nature bein' capable of reason or – beggin' yer pardon, Captain – of goodness. Human nature's depraved and requires restraint, especially on board a ship." MacClintock pushed back his peaked cap to the hairline. The Scot's long legs stretched far under the table.

"I feel, Captain Scattergood, a positive decision would be well-protected in confidence on the *Queen Anne*." Chase searched the Quaker's gaze.

"Thou are protected by a great cloud of witnesses, George Chase."

MacClintock looked at both men's faces. "Eh? What's that you're sayin'?"

"Private business, Alex. Needn't pester your mind," assured Scattergood.

Soon, a meal spread across the table – a heap of steamed crabs and corn fritters. The men plunged into the food. Chilled pilsner appeared every time Chase emptied his stein. He ate quickly as words of a letter formed in his mind, his conscience pricked anew. The *Queen Anne*, docked on Fels Point, would cast off tomorrow. No way to tell when the next opportunity for mail would present itself.

Back in quarters, Chase snapped open the locket and propped up Harriet's likeness. He pulled open the drawer of his traveling desk, the tambour's screen scrapped back, revealing ink and pens. Lighting the oil lamp, he drew out paper and envelope. With ink bottle and a fresh copper nib for the pen, he composed the letter:

31st June, 1853

Dearest Beloved Companion and Wife,

It is a pleasant evening in Baltimore Harbor as I await the departure of my ship, the Queen Anne. She sails on the morning tide, for the Isthmus of Panama.

The captain seems a congenial chap, James Scattergood, who indicates belonging to the Society of Friends, the Quakers, full of "thee" and "thou." He wears plain dark garb, no cravat, no color, no collar and an unadorned hat.

How is your condition? What does Doctor Benjamin say about the due date, still August or September? So glad that your mother can attend to your needs, please give her my best regards. I do hope the baby is strong enough for the voyage in October.

The past few days have been disruptive to my constitution, my mind a whirl of thoughts. Life in Washington County seems a distant Elysium of reason and order when compared to the speed, commerce, teeming masses, corruption, and cruelty of life from Boston to Washington. By chance I encountered my cousin, Salmon Chase, Senator from Ohio, while in the national capital.

Looking forward to the journey ahead, I know the fog of the past days will lift, once underway, and my mind will again focus on the great opportunity that this appointment affords. After you follow in October, you will miss your garden, friends, and cozy home in Calais, but the world that lies ahead, over the horizon, promises us a wealth of prosperity and new beginnings.

Your loving husband,
George

George paused. He tapped his teeth with the pen top, and then wrote a post-script.

Since you will need a housekeeper at Lahaina used to American standards, I consider bringing a colored girl, recommended by Salmon.

The June night closed over the docks of Fels Point. The clipper ship sat, sails furled among the rigging, tied to pilings, a lone lantern hung on a post. Crewmen lounged on deck, seeking a breeze, sleeping in odd postures. Due to an easterly wind, air flowed free of mosquitoes.

Two wagons, pulled by stout Clydesdales, rumbled through Baltimore's darkened streets. Traveling slowly, hooves and wheels padded, the wagons' route skirted the city's center. A block before the quay, the wagons slowed and two figures emerged from the back of one, slipping through a warehouse door.

The ship crew did not hear the wagons approach until the driver called a halt to the horses. Lights emerged from the ship, as the captain roused his men to unload bolts of dark blue sailcloth. Each bolt was covered by brown wrapping paper, firmly bound with twine, and labeled *Levi Strauss, San Francisco.* The crew lined the dock from quay to ship hold, passing the bolts down into the bowels of the clipper. One of the drivers approached the captain.

"Captain Scattergood, the special cargo is ready."

"Take me to Miss Tubman, Will"

The pair passed to a warehouse opposite the quay and entered a small door. Inside were a pretty girl and a stocky black woman.

The captain addressed the older one, "Tonight, thou come on a peculiar mission, Sister Harriet. Usually, I carry thy cargo north." He nodded at the girl.

"Brother James, let me talk to this white man, Chase. There's somethin' just ain't right 'bout this. White men all alike to me – 'ceptin' you, 'course, Brother James – They lookin' to fool with a young black girl. Let me see this so-called gentleman."

"Will, fetch thou Mister Chase in his cabin."

Will found the consul at his desk, addressing an envelope. Recognizing the bodyguard, he rose and followed him off the ship. The two entered the warehouse, approaching a tableau of three others lit by lantern light. Chase nodded at Matilda, and the girl lowered her eyes.

"Ah, yes. I see the young woman from the auction has arrived."

"Mister Chase," Scattergood gestured at Tubman. "Allow me to introduce another lady. Harriet Tubman brought this girl out of bondage. Regardless of a price on her famous head, she toils to free her people. As the Lord has chosen her for his huge mission, He recommends you for a small one."

Tubman stepped up to examine Chase. His space invaded, the lawyer stepped back until his back bumped into a column. The squat woman peered up into his eyes. Chase returned the gaze, curious the short oddity took such liberties.

"You the gentleman in the slave market?" asked Tubman.

"Yes, it was I." His eyes strained to see an expression on the dark complexion.

"What's so particular 'bout this gal?" Matilda shrunk back.

"Why she's nearly white!" Chase insisted.

"If light-skinned wrong to be made a slave, why be it right for dark-skinned to be a slave?"

Chase looked away from Tubman. "Those are issues of legality and public policy. Presently, United States laws..."

"Laws?" she cackled. "Ain't no law for colored, 'cept what whitey make it. What's different about this gal's skin to make her free and me a slave?"

"Sister Harriet, you badger the man," Scattergood intervened. "He's offering her escape to Hawaii."

"So he say," she retorted. "Know what bother me? I worry on some warm night you be takin' 'vantage a her."

"What? How dare you insinuate I have any such intention! Her innocence shall be inviolate."

Tubman's voice altered from baritone to falsetto. She stepped closer and her huge breasts bumped Chase's waist.

"Watch out," she mocked, "when massa' take him a nip of da bottle an' come on down to da cabins, horny as a dog wit' a little pink hard-on."

"Harriet, that's enough," Scattergood protested.

Tubman resumed her normal voice: "The good Lord be watchin' you, Chase. This Matilda," she wrapped her arm around the girl's shoulder, "leave Baltimore a lady, but will she arrive in Hawaii your slut?"

With that, she turned and walked out to the wagons.

The Captain and Chase escorted Matilda onto the ship and into officers' quarters. A closet between the Captain and Chase had been prepared as her berth, away from crew and passengers. The girl collapsed onto the pallet and found comfort in dreamless sleep.

Chapter Thirty-Nine

Dawn appeared over the Chesapeake Bay, light reflecting off the flat metallic surface on this windless morning. Flocks of sand pipers coasted upon sandy stands on the Western Shore of the Bay, looking for the bubbling holes of concealed mussels. Wheeling, turning, startling, a flock settled onto one beach and began flicking shellfish out of the sand.

Chase emerged from his quarters onto the *Queen Anne's* deck. As the clipper ship pulled out of the confines of the Patapsco's mouth, she sped in an arc to the main channel of the Bay. To the east, great forests of oak, bordered fields between water and farm fields, left by wise landowners, protecting land vulnerable to storm waves. Their imposing homes, encompassed by garden and hedge, appeared alike with brick with white trim and great columns supporting porches. At the plantation docks, gangs of black men worked, loading and unloading.

The course down the Bay took the day and most of the night until the ship entered the ocean on the second morning. In the shelter of the Bay, Matilda had remained below, out of sight. Above, Captain Scattergood drove the crew to prepare the ship for open ocean travel, securing cargo against shifting.

"See that point of land, Chase? It's the last glimpse of Virginia, Cape Henry. Thou may release the girl on deck once we've passed into the Atlantic. Best display her before the crew and belay suspicion."

Escorted by captain and consul, Matilda mounted the companionway and stepped out. The crew worked on deck, intent on their tasks until Matilda's slipper appeared, followed by her slim ankle. Behind her feet appeared a lace-fringed dress, encompassing narrow waist and full figure, in turn, supplanted by a narrow chin, aquiline nose, gray eyes, and pale skin, all framed by light curls.

Work halted.

Captain Scattergood spoke, "Stations, men, stations." Activity resumed amid low chatter and side-glances. Matilda walked to the railing and looked out on the ocean. Chase strolled behind the cringing figure.

"I don't see no land. Where's land?"

"Well, Matilda, we're going to be out of sight of land on a long voyage."

Matilda looked around at the parts of the ship while grasping a rail, unsteady on the rolling deck. A redheaded crewman, on his knees holystoning the oaken planks, gaped at the girl from his position, amid a lake of soapy water. Shipmates' whispered warnings had no effect until the captain's shadow fell upon his hands.

"In prayer, Mister O'Malley, I presume?" asked Scattergood, morning sun framing a blinding aura around his Quaker hat. O'Malley gave the captain a black scowl amidst crewmen's derisive laughter.

The sailor stood – pockmarked face, gnarled nose, ruddy with rage – and sneered, "no one said we was havin' women on board, captain."

Scattergood moved not a muscle, "Crewmen ought not be concerned about passengers or passenger's maids on the *Queen Anne*. Concentration on work is the best cure for impure thought, Mister O'Malley."

"Quaker, don't preach at me!" he threw back.

"Mister O'Malley, thou art new to the *Queen Anne*. Crew will inform thee that I am a fair master, but, in return, I expect discipline. On this vessel, we treat each as our Lord would ask – by the Golden Rule. As to my faith, yes, thou know I cannot strike thee. But, First Mate MacClintock, has no such compunctions. He's Presbyterian."

O'Malley blanched, returning to his knees to resume work. Scattergood strode on.

*   *   *

Holding her stomach, Matilda returned below decks and sat in Chase's cabin. He assured her that first-time ship passengers recovered from seasickness after a few days.

"Those men up there, they be starin' at me."

"The captain and I will protect you from any seadogs. But, you must agree not to wander away from our sight. Alone, you are too tempting a target." George remained standing. "Do you understand what's happening to you?"

She burst into tears. "I just wanna go home. I miss my momma and all of them."

"Matilda, stop. That's not possible." He searched his pockets and found a fresh handkerchief. "That part of your life is over. You have to make new friends."

Her sniffles quieted, and she looked up.

"Who are you, sir? My new master?" Wet eyes rose to his as a tear trail traced her full mouth.

"I am George Chase, and I am taking you away from bondage to the island kingdom of Hawaii. My wife remains at home expecting childbirth in three months, but she's to follow. In Hawaii, you can pose as her lady's maid. I am no slave master."

She gushed, sentences lifted girlish-like questions, hands fluttering in air.

"Back home, Mister James was my master, his real name James Thigpen, and in front of other white folks and in front of field hands we call him 'Master', but if he spoke, direct like, we call him 'Mister James' or 'sir,' like the boys who have to call their daddy 'sir' anyway. Do I call you 'Mister George'?" All in one breath, the sum of words tumbled out like marbles.

"No, I am 'Mister Chase' to you." He sat down opposite the girl. She twisted the linen, wet with tears. "So, a master and a mistress on a plantation?"

"Yes, sir."

"Was it harsh and cruel? Were you beaten?"

"Once. I was eight; broke a plate foolin' around when I was supposed to be settin' table and Miz Betty spank me hard."

"And the master had children?"

"We was reared together. Back in the day, Miss Sara and me was playmates, slept in the same bed. But, when our monthlies start, we stop sleepin' together and then, I be addressin' her 'Miss' and the boys 'sir' or 'Mister' Jimmy and 'Mister' Tommy." She laughed "That's how I can read, like you said when you shamed the slave market, Mister George." She giggled.

"Just how did that come about? And what kinds of things do you read?"

"My Bible and all Miss Sara's novels. Thigpens got a tutor, a good-lookin' boy outta William and Mary. Law don't allow colored to learn to read, but Thigpens don't see harm in colored girls sittin' aside Miss Sara. Perquimans County, who's goin' to arrest Mister James? He *was* the law."

Her face changed. Her smile evaporated, and she buried her face in the linen handkerchief, shoulders shaking with sobs. "Maybe they sell me because I read."

"No, Matilda, the Thigpens went bankrupt, out of money. I'm sure they regretted having to sell you. Please stop that crying." Chase patted her shoulder. "I am not your master, but let me propose you to be our maid in Hawaii."

She daubed her face and tried to smile.

He rose and looked through his belongings in a trunk.

"Here's a new popular book, perhaps unfairly dense...but you might show me how you read," he opened to the first chapter. She reached out and took the book. She read, sounding out strange words, syllable by syllable.

"What this bout, Mister George?" she asked.

"It's a novel about an adulteress."

"What's that?"

"A story's about a married woman who fell in love with another man, and she had a baby by him. The town arrested her, because she wouldn't disclose the father's identify on threat of punishment."

"They beat her?"

"No, worse. They made her wear a red letter 'A' on the front of her dress to call attention to her sin. In the end, she shames the whole town."

"Oo, a man tellin' a woman's story? Y'all got to let me read this, Mister George." The matter of Matilda's name for Chase seemed to have been settled.

Chapter Forty

Cabins under the quarterdeck provided space for privacy and shelter for four persons to sleep and dine. The captain and Chase's rooms had generous space for sleeping and storage. An officers' mess had a table and benches. Matilda's room allowed her to stretch out on a pallet, keeping her few belongings on a shelf. First Mate MacClintock's room held a high desk to maintain the ship's log.

Twice a day, cook and cabin boy brought meals to the mess. Meals under the quarterdeck were eaten with the captain's own dishes and silver service. Eating with three men, Matilda remained silent for two days. During the third noon meal, she waited for Chase and Scattergood to finish, then, slid out from the bench. Matilda cleared the table, stacking everything in precise order while they watched in rapt silence. When Tommy, the cabin boy arrived, she asked if she could follow him back to the galley to fetch coffee.

"Provided you speak to no one and stay in the galley," Chase cautioned.

Moments later, she reappeared bearing a pot and the captain's cups. Setting everything down, she poured each man a portion, turned, and left the stateroom.

"What do you suppose she's up to, Captain?"

"The poor thing finds us dull company, Consul. If thou were eighteen, would thou prefer to sit with two old men?" he laughed.

*   *   *

Joseph was the master of his galley. When James Scattergood advanced to ship's master, the Quaker had found Joseph destitute, a free 'colored' without employment, hanging around a Maryland courthouse. Scattergood

216

discovered Joseph's kitchen experience and took him on the *Queen Anne.*

When the girl tried to enter the galley, Joseph stopped her at the door.

"What you want?" he demanded.

"Captain wants his coffee," she said, looking past him at the tight room.

"White girls don't belong here, missy. Better get your little self back in that captain's cabin."

"They call you Mister Joseph?" She persisted.

"What if they do?"

"Mister Joseph, they always said I was a big help in the kitchen at home."

"What of it? This ain't home."

Lowering her eyes, she pleaded, "Mister Joseph, I'd do whatever needed doin' like clean those dirty dishes."

"Hell, girl, them dishes has got to be done jest right, otherwise my boys gets sick. I don't let no helpers do them, no way."

"Sir," she begged. "Would you let me try, just this once?"

"Okay, girl, maybe once. Take the captain his coffee and then git right back here."

Matilda returned to the galley and set metal buckets of water on the stove to heat. At first, Joseph nitpicked details, but, as the dishes were stacked onto drying storage racks, he saw she matched to his fastidious standards. Hands raw from the soap and hot water, Matilda asked if she might return the following night.

Joseph nodded in agreement.

*   *   *

Her quarters, a windowless space off the gangway between two gentlemen's staterooms, Matilda asked permission to read in the open light of Chase's cabin. He left her there to join Scattergood at the helm. As the ship plied through the Caribbean, the room's windows were open to warm breezes.

After sun reached overhead, George left the quarter-deck, to seek shade, possibly read or begin an afternoon's nap. Opening the cabin door, he saw the sleeping form of Matilda, sprawled across his bed, *The Scarlet Letter* propped open on her stomach.

He backed out into the passageway.

He tarried, hand on the knob. Absurd. He would find his book and read elsewhere.

Chase re-entered the cabin to find his book on the chair. Changing his mind, he sat and opened his novel, so that light fell across the page. Matilda moaned in her sleep.

Chase glanced at the girl. A breeze blew the curtains, and he thought to find her a cover. She lay on her back, face turned toward the bunk's wall, neck exposed. Her shabby cotton dress lay limp on her shape. Her knees spread apart in sleep, dress wrapped close to calves and thighs. Below the laced hem, her feet and ankles carelessly protruded. Her feet, like her hands, tan on top and light bottomed, small and delicate, juxtaposed like a dancer; one vertical, and the other horizontal.

Her white soles had smooth callused surfaces on heels and balls. A high arch made a perfect cavity from heel to ball. He imagined her silent footfall on a mansion's hardwood floors, running down dusty paths, and across damp lawns, skirts hiked up, laughing and skipping.

Matilda's toes splayed out, rounded and long, the nails even and pink. The toes of an innocent rarely confined as prisoners of shoes. Her ankles, improbably thin, stretched up to calves with smooth muscles. All visible parts of her were covered in smooth complexion. The sleeping Matilda's skin, an unblemished copper where sun-tanned, was the cloak of childlike purity.

What pleasant innocence! Chase recalled youthful days on corners at Lyndon after a rainstorm, watching girls lift skirts to cross puddles as youth strained to catch a glimpse of nubile ankles.

Then, he noticed her open eyes watching him.

"Are y'all readin', too, Mister George?"

"Ah, yes, yes, I have been reading. Were you asleep?"

Heat rose in his face and chest, flushing his pallid complexion.

"I suppose so. I had the strangest dream. We was alone together, and..."

George interrupted.

"Young lady, your English is deplorable. It's 'we *were* alone together. "

"Oh, y'all had the same dream?"

$*$ $*$ $*$

Beyond kitchen duty, the officers and Chase realized Matilda started keeping house in their quarters. Beds made, clothes washed, every surface gleamed, but she brought Chase a problem.

"Mister George, my clothes are dirty, but I have nothin to wear while I do laundry. Besides that, I need a bath to wash off that slave market."

"Perhaps the captain can prevail on a small seaman to loan you something while your clothes dry."

MacClintock surveyed the crew quarters for spare clothes. "Would any man have spare 'troosers' and 'bloose' for the young lady? Seems she brought little on the voyage and needs to do her wash. I'm only askin' the youth," said MacClintock. "The girl's a small figure."

"Here, sir," a boy came forward with canvas pants and linen shirt.

$*$ $*$ $*$

Inside the officers' quarters, the crew filled a laundry tub with heated water. Matilda stripped off her clothes and washed the garments, hanging them along the captain's transom windows. Then, she crouched over the tepid water and washed herself. Drying her body, she stepped into a sailor's white duck trousers, bell bottomed and laced at the fly. Once she figured out how to close the trousers, they fit too snugly around her hips. Twisting to look, she clucked disapproval.

She slipped the sailor's blouse over her head and shook her arms into the sleeves. Her breasts stretched against the thin cotton. She laced up the stringed bodice to cloak cleavage and tugged on the shirt's tail to cover her derriere.

Tommy had been posted outside the door, sworn to guard Matilda's privacy. A thin waif, refugee from Baltimore. The boy squatted, hollow eyes staring ahead. Never mothered, the boy wedded his loyalty to the ship family. He noted the redhead working his way aft.

O'Malley pretended to check cleated lines, as others worked the canvas rigging. He slipped up beside Tommy.

"Yer wanted below in the galley, me boy. The cook was askin' about ye."

"Yer a friggin' liar. Joseph knows what I'm doin'."

"Git on wid' ye, ya' little shit."

"MISTER MACCLINTOCK!" The high-pitched scream brought up heads.

"What's up, Tommy boy," the first mate's rapid steps approached.

"O'Malley's tryin' to get by me."

"No, I ain't, you little...."

The mate grabbed O'Malley by the collar and twisted him around. The seaman tried to swing a fist.

"Attemptin' to strike a ship's officer, O'Malley? Stand up, like a man," the mate's face inches away from him. "What do I smell on yer breath, mon? Moost 'a' been sneakin' extra grog. Well, it's distorted yer judgment. Confined to quarters, ya' are."

A boot in the butt sent the man sprawling. From the floor, he departed, hurling curses at all authority.

MacClintock reported the incident to Captain Scattergood. "Be careful, Alex, he's like mad dog. Dost thou think he has comrades on board?"

"Don't worry, Captain, he's a loner."

Old Joseph gaped when the galley door opened and Matilda stepped through, dressed like no sailor he'd ever seen. She announced she would make her Aunt Macy's bread pudding. Joseph brought out the requested supplies and food, leaving space for her preparation.

A passing supply ship had provided creamery milk and eggs. Bread, baked a week before, had hardened beyond use. Matilda called for sugar, vanilla extract, cinnamon, nutmeg, raisins, coconut, and pecans. She shredded the coconut and chopped the pecans. Combining the half-cream milk, sugar, grease, eggs, vanilla, and spices, she mixed them well and stirred in bits of bread, raisins, coconut and pecans.

Having Tommy heat the oven, she poured the mixture into several pans, baking the pudding an hour before the meal. Now she was ready to fix the sauce. Pushing aside a curl, she rested her hands on her hips and approached the old cook.

"Mister Joseph, I need to use the rum tonight."

"Captain be strict 'bout that rum."

"It part of Aunt Macy's recipe – bread puddin with rum sauce, heat steam off the liquor anyway."

"I'll have to ask, first."

"No, do like we say at home: 'easier to seek pardon than to ask permission'."

The old man unbuttoned the top of his shirt, reaching into the folds, and brought out a silver chain, which he pulled over his head. A key dangled on the end. "The key to the kingdom. Now lez see what you do with rum, gal."

While the pudding baked, Matilda made up the sauce with confectioner's sugar, butter, egg yoke, and the rum, heating sugar and butter in a saucepan. Stirring a small amount of the hot mixture into the egg yolk, then reversing and stirring the yolk into the mixture. Next, she added the rum. The sauce thickened as it cooled.

Supper over, a dessert was announced. The entire ship's company was present in the mess for the occasion;

men, officers, captain, prospector passengers, and George Chase. The galley doors swung open for Joseph followed by Matilda, each bearing pans. All eyes fell on the girl.

Matilda raised a hand. The room fell silent.

"If y'all want dessert, y'all sit down and wait turns."

Fifty men took seats like schoolboys waiting for mother's pie. She and Joseph passed among the tables, spooning out the dessert. Leaning over, pot under arm, curls around her face, watched by surreptitious glances, Matilda exchanged comments with every man.

Chapter Forty-One

Matilda and Chase had finished the noon meal, the captain and first-mate gone to duty on deck. The voyage neared its end, and the tropics pressed a humid hand on the ship. She got up to clear the table.

"Sit a while, Matilda. We have work to do."

"I'm tryin' to do my work, Mister George." She kneeled on a chair, hand on hip.

"It's more important than dishes. We have to prepare for Hawaii."

She flopped into a chair. "What do you mean, ain't ships takin' us along this journey? What's there to do except enjoy the ride?" She wobbled her head.

"That attitude's going to get us into trouble, young lady," Chase answered.

"Why, what's to happen in Hawaii?"

"We have to conceal your identity so no one guesses you escaped slavery. If they do, there would be dire consequences for both of us. For me, ruination. For you, a return to the auction block."

"But, ain't I white enough, already? What more can I do?"

"Your accent, your speech pattern has to change to pass as a white girl."

"Well, Mister George, that's just how we talk. Can't do nothin' about that." She flounced her arms helplessly.

"Not so. Two years ago in Boston, Missus Chase and I heard a lecture by the colored Abolitionist, Frederick Douglass. He, too, learned to read as a child, taught in secret by his mistress. He sneaked on a train to New York City and dashed to freedom. Since then, he's become an important writer and public speaker. White people flock to listen to him. He owns a magazine and wrote a famous book."

"A colored man wrote a book?" She sat up and her eyes grew large. "He looks white, too?"

"No, he couldn't pass as white, but that didn't stop him from speaking standard English." Chase taped on the table.

Matilda looked at her hands, head lowered.

"Tell me more about this Hawaii, what it like."

"Like a storybook for you. Just imagine this, Hawaiians are colored – dark-skinned, black-haired, even the king and queen!" he said, leaning forward.

"But, if Hawaiians be colored, why do I have to talk like you?"

"Because they speak another language, and since you're American, my dear, you have to blend into the American community. Don't worry. You're not alone. We both have much to learn, child."

"It's all so confusin'. I should write a book, too, so to remember all that's happenin' to me."

"Ah, splendid, keep a journal about your experiences like a proper lady."

* * *

After dinner, Matilda had returned to the galley to work alongside Joseph. The old man's hips ached for rest. Watching the cook strain, returning all gear to proper places, the girl tried to send him away.

"Mister Joseph, there ain't much left to do in this galley. You go on and rub that liniment on what ails you."

"You such a blessin', 'Tilda. What you goin' to do when this trip over?"

"I be told I'm Missus Chase's maid in Hawaii, but maybe the Lord has bigger plans for me, Mister Joseph. Can you keep a secret?"

"Yes, missy."

"I'm not really Mister Chase's hired maid. He's helping me escape bondage. I'm *colored* like you."

Joseph froze. "I guessed you wasn't no white girl, but I didn't figure you for a fugitive. Your secret's safe with me. I'm so glad you headed to a new life."

*   *   *

Chase and Scattergood lingered over dinner. Smoke from the Quaker's pipe and Chase's cigar sought escape through transom windows out the ship's stern. Phosphorescent plankton churned in the vessel's wake and she plowed through the western Caribbean. The remains of cups and saucers cast movable shadows from the swinging lamp. Matilda fussed at their lateness.

"You men just have to empty those coffee cups. Mister Joseph…is wantin' to close the galley for the night." She collected crumbs into a wet rag, banging against the crockery.

"Consul, you finished? Yes? Very well. Let's not offend the boss of the kitchen," chuckled Scattergood.

Matilda gathered up the last dishes and stomped up the companionway.

"Astounding Chase, what's going on? 'Mister Joseph *is wanting…*' What's happened to Matilda?" the captain whispered.

"I suppose she's making a point to me," Chase answered in a low voice. "It's that she can speak Standard English if she chooses."

*   *   *

Quiet fell on the vessel; crew asleep in hammocks, only helmsman and watchman, faces silhouetted by lamp, stood on the quarterdeck. The moonless night cast no shadows, stars guiding the ship's course.

A form crept through the bowels of the ship, secreting through passageways and steps, unobserved by any waked soul, seeking shadow, fearing light. Like a specter, he slipped by sleeping sailors, leaving no silhouette to see, no

225

rustle to hear, and no touch to feel, only a reeking odor from glistening sweat. Shoeless, stripped to knickers, Bowie knife in teeth, his agile hands and feet braced against bulkheads to counter the sway and yaw of the vessel. Like a rabid dog on a heinous mission, O'Malley's eyes glimpsed his quarry through a louvered crack.

Closer to the door, careful to plant each foot, he waited for Matilda to assume a vulnerable position. Finally, he beheld her kneeling, head buried in a cabinet, and he pounced.

"Call out and your throat is slit, bitch." He pulled her down, hand over mouth, and flashed the blade before her eyes.

"Get your ass on that floor." He pushed her on her back.

Stabbing the knife into the deck, O'Malley knelt between her legs, hot for his work. Matilda regained her wits and fought back.

"No, you can't, you won't, stay away, get off a' me, damn you, white trash." Her sturdy body twisted away to kick and arch.

O'Malley loved the fight and fury; terror on her face aroused him. He slapped her until blood ran from her mouth, while he chanted words of hate: bitch, whore, cunt, slut, sow. Pressing her chest with one hand, he tugged the strings on his trouser fly, fixing to cut her quiver.

Matilda tore at the soft flesh of O'Malley's face. Her nails ripped nostrils and gouged eyes to make O'Malley pay dear for his pleasure. Her feet flew furious kicks, one landing against a bucket that held a shovel butt that sent the iron blade into stacked plates which rained down to shatter on the deck. The sleeping Tommy next to the galley woke with a start; hearing voices he recognized the sound of sexual violence. In seconds, he flew to the officers' mess and burst into the room.

"Mister MacClintock, it's O'Malley again."

Chase flew up the companionway, across the deck, and burst into the galley.

Seeing O'Malley mounted on the girl, Chase flung himself against the body to send both men rolling across the floor, a tumult of curses and blows. The irate O'Malley snatched his knife as they rolled and stabbed Chase in the arm. He drew back for the kill.

Only one hand to fend off the blow, Chase grunted against the seaman's attack. The blade closed, Chase's hand weak, when the figure of MacClintock appeared. A butcher knife snatched from the galley's rack, the first mate fell full onto the sailor, piercing through skin, muscle, bone, heart, lung, bone, muscle, skin, and into the wood deck. Chase watched as his enemy's arm weakened and scowl turned to peaceful countenance. The three lay still, among the gore, taking accounts, until MacClintock looked over at Chase, smiling, "a wee bit of a close one, eh, Consul?" Then, gesturing to the open-eyed remains, "He won't be agitatin' no more. Let's have look at ye, mon, back in captain's quarters."

"Never mind me. What harm came to the girl?"

Captain Scattergood ministered to Matilda, covering her nakedness with his jacket. Drawn away from the butchery, she allowed herself to be brought into the staterooms, where the captain applied wet cloths to her swollen face. She sobbed, her face pressed into the Quaker's bosom. Soon, she fell asleep in the arms of the gentle Scattergood who carried her into his own berth.

Meanwhile, word passed down the gangways, men nodding assent for the rough justice administered by the adroit Scot. A piece of canvas wound O'Malley's body, tying the corpse inside for later disposal. Joseph led a crew to wash out the galley. Lucky for Chase, the wound was superficial, requiring only astringent and stitching. Tomorrow would bring the inquest.

*　　　　　　　*　　　　　　　*

The long table was unscrewed from the officers' mess and carried onto the main deck, before the crew. Being the only man aboard with legal training, George Chase sat beside Scattergood as counsel for the court of inquiry. Never having any serious crime on board a ship and being a Friend, James Scattergood was ill at ease with the proceedings. Both men wore formal dress, George his best black stovepipe hat. Matilda's presence was excused.

"Hear ye, hear ye, the captain's mast is called to order. Captain James Scattergood, presidin'," called out MacClintock.

"Gentlemen, we are called by God and the maritime laws of the United States to hold an inquest into the death of Seaman Patrick O'Malley, who died yesterday, July 27, 1853 of wounds inflicted by First Mate Alexander MacClintock. It is alleged that O'Malley was engaged in forcible and aggravated attempted rape and, when interrupted, attempted to murder the Honorable George Chase, whereupon First Mate MacClintock, in effort to save Consul Chase, used appropriate measures to subdue O'Malley. An officer of the courts, Consul Chase will direct the inquest."

Recording testimony from all witnesses such as Joseph, Tommy, Alex MacClintock and himself, George Chase interviewed Matilda "in chambers," shielding her from salacious curiosity. Only too happy to report that the attacker never completed his intentions, the young woman was relieved her words would enter the record. Chase ended the inquiry by declaring the death as justifiable homicide.

A brief service followed for Seaman O'Malley, committing the body to the sea with a reading of the Gospel, whereupon the sailcloth cylinder was tipped, allowing the corpse to splash into its saline grave.

Chapter Forty-Two

Chase and Matilda arrived at the port of Chagres during a tropical deluge. Chase found rooms for himself and Matilda in the best hotel Chagres could provide, a colonial structure, stucco rotten from mildew on the outside and inhabited by huge insects inside. Bed sheets, clammy and damp in the humidity, gave scant comfort.

The Isthmus of Panama, narrowest waist between two oceans, provided a bridge for world commerce. When Conquistadores looted gold from the Inca Empire, a paved causeway, El Camino Real, was engineered for pack animals and slaves to carry the hoard from Panama City on the Pacific to Porto Bello on the Caribbean. From there, Spanish galleons carried the plunder to the Spanish treasury, ruining both conquered and conqueror, one by destitution, the other by debauchery.

That first morning, Chase contacted the agents of the transportation company Hurtado y Hermanos, to be told there were several routes. Chase chose a twelve-hour journey, taking rail service from Manzanillo and then riding mules over the peaks of the Sierra for $30 per person. As the mule trail reached the summit, Chase caught a glimpse of vast water through the trees. His heart jumped, the Pacific.

Once in Panama City, settled into a hotel, Chase contacted the American consul, William Nelson, to arrange for transportation to San Francisco. After giving Matilda strict instructions to remain in her room, he paid his respects to the consulate, bringing credentials. Nelson greeted him at his desk, flustered with the demands of the Gold Rush prospectors.

"Welcome to Panama City, Senator Chase, I imagine you find the hordes of prospectors as disgusting as I. Their demands are impossible, and they expect me to rule over the locals. They can't accept this is a sovereign country, Nueva Granada."

"Yes, Mister Nelson, not much stands in their way. Tell me about ships to San Francisco."

"When this Gold Rush began, our country commissioned a transportation system, the Pacific Mail Steamship Company, to accommodate the expected numbers of travelers to California. The city overfilled quickly. Finally, a tent city sprang up on the outskirts, since all prospectors packed tents. That month, the Pacific Steamship Company began service with only one side-wheeled steamboat, woefully inadequate."

The American consul looked out from French doors beyond a veranda to the harbor.

"The ship was the *California,* captained by Cleveland Forbes on its maiden voyage from New York, a record for speed around Cape Horn, leaving New York on October 6th and arriving in Panama on January 17th. Here in Panama were waiting 700 gold-seekers armed with guns. They rioted to find the *California*'s capacity was only 400. Finally, the ship steamed out of Panama on the last day of January with 565 passengers, 165 over capacity, and all the coal she could carry. She ran out of coal on the voyage and had to burn the beds and mattresses, then the chairs, then the paneling, then the spars and bulkheads."

Chase laughed at the image of a ship consuming itself.

"With all that, they got only as far as Monterey where they took on 30 cords of wood. The final blow happened when the crew abandoned ship, joining the prospectors to the Gold Rush. That was our first experience with passenger service to San Francisco."

"Amazing! Did the *California* recruit a new crew?" asked Chase.

"Ah, yes, and more ships have joined the fleet, and service is now regularly scheduled and predictable, but Captain Forbes had to raise wages to $150 a month. Upon her return to Panama, she brought almost $350,000 in gold specie. You're on time for the *California* to leave in two days. May I make arrangements for you in the official suite? I would be honored to book you. Is Missus Chase tolerating the journey well?" Nelson fussed at papers on his desk.

"Missus Chase remains home in Maine. She is with child, due to be confined in September, following which she and the children will join me in Hawaii."

"Will she travel with a male escort?" asked Nelson.

"I am ashamed to say, not. Only a babe in arms." Chase looked out on the harbor.

"May I take the liberty to greet her and the children at Chagres, escorting them to their Pacific vessel? It would be an honor to serve a fellow consul. May I now book you into the suite on the *California*?"

"Yes, but include another passenger, my wife's maid. She's accompanied me and should be berthed in the women's section. I am deeply grateful to you."

Nelson raised his eyebrows.

"Oh? Everything proper, Consul Chase. Glad to be of service here on the remote reaches of American diplomacy. Who knows, but perhaps it will be my turn someday to pass through the islands and need your kind attention."

Returning to the hotel, Chase released Matilda from the confines of her room, suggesting a walk through the city. It was early afternoon, and shadows appeared in the narrow streets, beside the high walls surrounding family compounds, creating pastel canyons along cobble-stoned streets. Chase bought Matilda a parasol, to shield her complexion. He noticed pretty dresses, reasonably priced. He felt chagrinned not taking notice of Matilda's plight. A lady's maid for a consul should have adequate clothing.

Returning to the hotel, Chase asked for the assistance of an English-speaking woman to accompany them shopping. A gnarled crone in widow's black, Señora Lopez, appeared and led them to a tiny shop set off Cathedral Square. After asking for spending limits, she pulled Matilda in the shop, directing Chase to stay outside. From inside, he heard high voices, a whole imbroglio, and then silence.

Finally, the door opened and a smiling beauty emerged, Matilda, disguised in Spanish costume with a lace mantilla over her head and clogs on her feet.

"Señor has been very wise," said the gaunt lady "for his money bought her two dresses. His wife will be proud of her lady's maid." George gave her a generous gratuity, only too happy to reward the shrewd Señora Lopez. The trio returned to the hotel to secure the new wardrobe.

"Shall we walk? The evening's cooler," he asked Matilda.

Dressed in formal garb, George walked beside Matilda, in colorful frills, through exotic Spanish streets. The crowds took no recognizance of the dignified gringo gentleman and his young female companion. Indeed, they soon realized why they were ignored. The port of Panama received human cargo from all humanity – Asians from Manila, Peruvian Indians, Negroes from the Caribbean, and gradations of Europeans from blond Britons to swarthy Iberians.

A couple approached, the man mature and attired in a light suit, the senorita in bright dress, puffy sleeves, hemline displaying legs. As the two couples passed, the señor doffed his hat to George, "*Mis complementas a su hija. Ella es encantadora y me imagino que sus padres lo son tambien.*" (My compliments to your daughter. She is enchanting and I imagine she is such to her parents also.)

George managed a mumbled "Gracias," and, turning to Matilda, asked, "what do you suppose he said?"

They passed the ruins of the old city. A granite wall surrounded the newer city, built by the Spanish crown, and now a promenade, Las Bovedas. They passed the city's cathedral and palaces, theaters, and schools. Matilda's only experiences in a city were the worst of Washington and Baltimore. The majesty of Cuidad Panama dazzled her.

The odors of food wafted from a brightly-lit restaurant. Seeing the gringo couple, dumb in Spanish, the staff brought out a mildly spicy meal. George found it intolerable, stunning his taste buds. Matilda, used to southern spices, giggled to see him gulp red wine, trying to remove the sting.

At the hotel, George escorted her to her door, returning to his quarters to prepare for the next leg of the journey. First, he composed a letter to Harriet to be posted back to Maine in the morning.

August 1, 1853

Dearest Beloved Harriet,

Just a brief note today, hoping this reaches you. We have successfully crossed the Isthmus of Panama, and now wait in Panama City for our ship to California.

I have great news today. The United States consul, William Nelson, will meet you in Chagres upon your arrival. I have confided to him about your condition. Nelson will receive word when you land, coming to escort you across the isthmus. Once on the Pacific Coast, the consul will arrange for the next leg of the journey.

Please wish the children well for me. I miss you and them so very much.

Your loving husband,
G.M. Chase

Chapter Forty-Three

The next morning, George alone explored shops, seeking articles, rare or expensive, in California and Hawaii. Since Panama was a center of world commerce with cargoes flowing across the Isthmus, agents made prices cheap. Hats, clothing, shoes, dry goods, food staples, and trinkets were hawked from vendors. Entering a stationer, he found a variety of drawing and writing paper in folios. Delighted to purchase a paper supply, he carefully stored it in calfskin binders.

After supper, the two checked out of the hotel and walked through the dusk to the docks of Panama City. There stood the *California,* its gleaming black hull of copper sheathing visible above the water line. Above loomed white upper works, red paddle wheels and polished brass. Despite her elegance, the ship was utilitarian, built of oak and cedar. The hull was reinforced with diagonal iron straps to withstand the pounding of the paddle wheels. Just in case power failed, the ship was also rigged with three masts and full sails, ready, if necessary, for auxiliary wind power. Captain Fulton offered Consul Chase a tour of the ship after securing Matilda in the women's quarters. The following morning at dawn, the *California* steamed her way into the Pacific, headed for Acapulco; the only scheduled stop.

Matilda joined Chase in his state room the next morning. She had chosen another new dress, white with colorful trim. Her curly hair hung loose about her shoulders. Chase wore a satin dressing coat. He placed her on a chair before a desk.

"Now we shall make a more conscious effort to address your language so you blend into the American community. I hear two mistakes that have to be corrected," he began.

"Mister George, Don't this boat look different from the *Queen Anne*?"

"Ah, ha! A third mistake. Listen to your own words. What should you have said?"

"Oh, dear, Mister George, sorry. It's *doesn't*, isn't it?"

"Yes. What are the other two cautions?"

"*Am, is, was,* and *be,* are the ones I mix up. The other is finishing my *i-n-g* words. But, how am I ever to speak like you? Back on the Albemarle, even Mister James talked more like me, dropping his g's and saying *ain't*. You Yankees talk flat like you're reading out loud."

"Yes, young lady, you are correct. I may have to modify my ideas. There's naturalness in your speech. While I've taken the girl out of the South, I can't get the South out of the girl," he laughed. "There's much that's attractive in your character..." he leaned close, "...that should not tolerate uprooting. Your charm, your voice, your coquettish nature...why set limits on..."

He kissed her curls, his hand embracing her shoulder. His robe bulged with tumescence. Matilda placed a flat palm on Chase's chest.

"Do sit down, Mister George." He took the divan. "Mightily flattered by your compliments, all of which remind me of your wife. Just where would that locket be?"

"Oh, yes. There beside the bed." He tightened his robe's belt.

"After your baby's born and she follows, what's she expect when she sees me?"

"A lady's maid. When I wrote, the letter had to conceal your story of escaping slavery, in case it fell into the wrong hands," he said.

"So, when she comes you're going to tell her the truth?"

"Certainly, we keep no secrets between us," he explained, an open palm.

"And with the other Americans?" she asked.

"A secret forever. Your pose as our maid should convince them." He sat back, avoiding her eyes.

"Once a maid, always a maid," she crossed her arms. "I don't like that."

Chase sat back.

"What do you mean?"

"Why do I have to be a maid? Why can't I pass as your niece, some relative?" she explained, hands on hips.

"Well, because I have no nieces from the South," he said firmly.

She ignored the rebuff.

"Yes, just suppose you had a girl cousin who visited the South during cotillion season. She met and married a dashing bachelor, a Mister Thigpen, and had a daughter, but the girl's parents died in an influenza epidemic, leaving her an orphan. The poor girl's all alone with no dowry, except to fall upon the charity of relatives." Her voice droned in a sing-song.

"You've read too many novels, Matilda," chided Chase. "What if someone from North Carolina knows the Thigpens? You'll have to change that name.

"Never. 'Thigpen' gots respectability."

George slumped, head in hands, while she continued the fantasy.

"Tell them I'm from another part of the country. Where's Alabama? Is that in the South? What's that state's capital city?

"Montgomery," Chase groaned.

"Oo, what a nice name! Yes, the Montgomery Thigpens," she cooed. Her fingers wound around a blond curl.

"Very well, then. If it must be, you will pose as my niece and..."

"You will take me places as my uncle? You will call me your niece in front of other Americans?"

"Look here, young lady. Don't push me beyond...Never mind. Any niece of mine would speak and write like a lady. That being said, you have hard work preparing to pass as a southern belle. I remember you wanted to keep a journal."

"Oh, yes."

"Look here," he opened the calfskin folio, displaying two notebooks, "One for your private diary and another for writing exercises."

"Mister George, thank you, thank you," She reached out to hug his neck, planting a wet kiss on his cheek.

"That's not necessary. That's enough. Please, stop, sit down."

She returned to the desk chair.

In late afternoon, they stepped out from the stateroom, Matilda wearing her mantilla against the ocean chill. They watched the giant side-wheel turning, spilling water over her great paddles, churning the sea into a strange wake. Other first-class passengers watched, fascinated by the mechanism, including two girls in their late teens. Matilda, dressed in Panamanian style, they guessed her to be Latin American.

"Speak a little English?" one asked, eager to talk.

"Of course, I'm American, too," she answered.

George stepped away, hoping her grammar would stand the test.

Matilda chattered with the girls for fifteen minutes, but at last, she glanced at George and frowned. He stepped forward, suggesting she come inside away from the evening chill.

"Those girls like you, Matilda."

"I know, but it makes me so tired, Mister George, to talk right, to think about what I say before I say it. Those girls asked if I were French. Are French white?"

"Usually, but some are darker than other Americans."

"Maybe you could say my mother was French."

"That's a good explanation. Very well, I shall introduce you as my ward, a niece who's lost her parents. You've joined our family to travel. If necessary, I'll invent a whole damn background to throw off the overcurious.

"Our first test will be on our arrival in Honolulu. An acquaintance from home, Elisha Allen, has an important post with the Hawaiian royal government. He'd been a United States consul before. We have to pay a courtesy call. Is that reason enough to practice?"

The week went by as the lessons continued. Every evening concluded with a promenade among upper deck passengers, some nights conversing with other young people and some nights being an object of admiration of bejeweled matrons, too polite to inquire about Matilda's relationship to Chase. Her conversations eased, speaking at an even pace, her vivacious nature became natural in standard English.

*   *   *

Passengers gathered along the starboard railing to watch the headlands of the Golden Gate approach, the Presidio guarding the hilltop. The *California* turned into the Bay, drawing up to San Francisco's Embarcadero. On slopes, a ragged city of frame buildings covered the hills, a ramshackle clutter. Piers jutted out into the brackish water. Plank sidewalks covered where solid ground and marsh melted.

Hills surrounded the Bay, filled with the remains of hundreds of wooden ships, rigging cut away, rotting as anchored, abandoned by their crews like a ghost fleet never to sail again. A forest of wasted New England white pine languished, useless.

Chase ventured into the city, taking hotel rooms, one for himself and one for his "ward." He left Matilda while making arrangements for Honolulu. She was to remain in the room, practicing her writing. A hotel employee would inquire for meal service.

After purchasing two tickets to Honolulu on the bark, *Francis Palmer* for eight dollars each, he walked along the dock area near Market Street.

Walking back to the hotel, Chase passed a saloon, *The Stockton House*. He stepped inside the dim entrance. A long bar stood at one side of the room. Behind the barkeep was an elaborate mirror, the length of the wall. He sat down at a table on the opposite wall to watch activity in the room.

Wood shavings covered the floor in a thick carpet to absorb the tobacco juice and spit. The far wall had a stairwell and door to a kitchen. Men stood at the bar, each propping a foot on a brass rail inches off the floor. Several men's hips held holsters with a variety of pistols.

A waitress approached Chase. The brunette appeared only half attired, wearing petticoats and a wasp-waisted corset. Beneath the petticoats, reaching to her knees, net stockings covered her legs, her feet arched into thin slippers, heels high and tapered to a point. George judged her age to be near George Junior's, 16.

"What you wan'?" she asked.

"Is there a menu?"

Lips and cheeks rouged, dark eyes outlined with pencil, she answered in a Spanish accent.

"We got lots. Bean soup? Roast beef? Grizzly roast?"

"Good God! How much is the grizzly roast?"

"One dolla', bean soup is one dolla', but the roast beef is a dolla' fifty. A square meal is tree dolla'." Tiny papers and a cloth bag appeared from beneath her clothes. She tapped tobacco onto a paper, twisted it into a cigarette, and stuck it into her mouth.

"You got light?" she bent forward for Chase to strike a match. He looked down her generous bodice.

"Just bring me a beer."

The waitress came back with a pint of yellow liquid, "fifty cent'." Chase pushed coins across the table.

"You no big spender, meester. I like big spender. You spend big, and we go upstairs," she gestured to the back of the Stockton House.

"Some other time. Right now, I'll just drink beer."

George settled back against the wall. A man sitting at the next table leaned over, "The girls are a little forward, ain't they."

Chase laughed.

"New to Frisco?"

"About one day. Leaving this week for Honolulu"

"The city ain't all that rough, mister. It's even getting kind of refined. Although we got over five hundred saloons, we also have eighteen churches, and we got lotsa law and order. Vigilante committees. Did you hear of Joaquin Murieta and his gang?"

"No, can't say papers back East mentioned him."

"Joaquin Murieta was a *bandito*. Robbed miners of their gold. Governor Bigler posted a thousand dollar reward for Joaquin and his banditos. Just last month, the rangers ran across a group of Mexicans near Panoche Pass, trapped 'em and killed two of 'em; Joaquin and Three-Fingered Jack, they claimed. Since they couldn't bring their whole bodies back, they cut off parts, so as to collect the reward. Want to see 'em?"

"You mean here?" Chase sat up.

"Joe, show this dude the jars." The stranger brought George up close to the bar.

Reaching under the shelf, the keep lifted out two large beakers, full of clear alcohol and placed them before Chase. A human head floated in the first jar, hair tousled, eyes staring, mouth agape over a hacking decapitation, dangling blood vessels. The other jar contained a hand, indeed, having only three fingers.

Chapter Forty-Four

Clunk. George cracked his head on the companion-way threshold.

"Damn, damn." He rubbed his scalp, cradling a mug of coffee. He gripped the handle and found his footing.

Twenty days out of Frisco on the bark, *Frances Palmer,* George stepped onto the deck to take in a bright morning's clear air. A folding canvas chair on the quarterdeck let him face forward to watch the full sails and plunging bow. He eased his frame into the chair. Ah, so easy. His joints moved without pain, like oiled machinery.

"Today, we'll reach the islands, sir, at this speed," called out the helmsman. "It's been ten knots all night."

"Can you tell that we're approaching the islands soon?" asked George.

"Look up, sir, the birds."

He hadn't noticed sea birds surrounding the ship, hovering over the galley, hoping for tossed garbage. Overhead, the sky was a deep blue, and to the east, the sun crept over the horizon in a bronze glow. To the west, darkness still filled the sky, and a vapor of haze lay over the surface of the Pacific, shortening visibility. Yesterday, the color of the ocean had been a gray impenetrable mass, but today, a sparkling azure, lucid to keel depth where schools of fish darted.

To the west, George spied a single sun-lit cloud. It hung steady, unmoving. The bowsprit swayed side to side, but the ship's course aimed for the cloud.

"Sailor, tell me, do you see that distant cloud to the west?"

"Yes, sir."

"Why is it fixed in the sky?"

"Sir, you might say it's hooked, like a doughnut."

"A doughnut?"

"Yep, it surrounds a mountain."

"But it's so high. What kind of mountain is that?"

"That's Maui's Haleakala volcano, ten thousand feet. Congratulations! You're the first to spot the Sandwich Islands."

The "cloud" took on a new dimension; not a normal cloud at all, the crown on a mountain, the base wrapped in mist. He scanned the horizon below the summit, straining to comprehend the dimension. His eyes made out a monstrous mass, based squat on the ocean's skin, and rising into a ringed cumulus.

The *Francis Palmer* skirted Maui's northern shore, close to the dormant volcano. The mass dominated the ship's portside.

"Great Caesar's Ghost, sailor, look at the size of that mountain!" George stood involuntarily. Haze dissolved revealing the vast hulk of Haleakala. Until the *Frances Palmer* passed beyond Maui, Chase stayed planted on deck.

"Truly, the largest mountain I've ever seen. Ten thousand feet, you say, rising out of the sea, higher than any peak in the Appalachian range, even New Hampshire's Mount Washington."

He sniffed a strange new scent from morning breezes floating off the island, perfumed fertility, bloomed soil drawn deep into lungs. He turned to the helmsman.

"Do you catch that odor?"

"Well, sir, that's the smell of life from Hawaii. Strange flowers, red earth, trees, animals, and burning cane. A whole new scent, a surprise to the nostrils after two thousand miles of ocean."

The *Frances Palmer* entered the narrow passage of Pearl Harbor at dusk, all passengers crowded against the portside rail. The ship docked for the night, next to the town. Most passengers remained on board for the night, some gentlemen, coaxed by tars, disembarked and explored town attractions. Chase remained on board with Matilda to plan the days ahead.

In the morning, George arranged a warehouse near the docks for luggage and supplies, a base to collect additional materials for Maui. He sent a message to Elisha Allen at the Royal Palace, asking for an appointment. The messenger soon returned with an envelope. Its note read:

George: So glad to know another Maine man has joined us in the Islands. Do finish your business at the harbor quickly, and I shall expect you at 10 this a.m. Anticipate remaining for the evening.

Eli

*   *   *

Unable to leave Matilda, George directed her to bring her parasol. She and George dressed in formal summer garb; she in full-sleeved linen, he in off-white suit including waistcoat. He hailed a carriage and directed the driver to the Royal Palace.

The carriage climbed streets above the harbor overlooking the city of Honolulu. The business district, on flat lands near the harbor, had plank sidewalks under arcaded shops like San Francisco. Downtown businesses served the maritime industries with ship equipment, food, and clothing. Asian and Polynesian women, hair loose, garments tight, leaned against railings, sucking cigarettes and gawking at the dressy couple.

Above the fray, a residential area began with lush gardens on streets with large homes, each residence surrounded by porches, balconies, and verandas. The horse strained up the incline, properties growing larger as the elevation rose.

Finally, the carriage turned into an iron gate. A circular drive ended at a set of steps below a white stone building. Flowering trees bordered the property. Muscular Hawaiians in livery danced down the steps to open the carriage door, offering a hand to Matilda as she alighted on the white shell driveway.

"Consul Chase, I presume?" asked an official, "The Minister is expecting you."

George and Matilda were led through cool hallways. From every office, French doors opened onto courtyards where fountains and flowers graced the landscape. The official opened a door where gold letters marked the title, Minister of Finance, and informed the Hawaiian secretary that the visitors were present.

A tall, slender man strode, smiling, "George, George Chase, wonderful to see you. Welcome to the Hawaiian Islands and Honolulu."

Elisha Allen, dressed in white duck trousers and white shirt, wore no cravat. He brought George and Matilda into his inner office where he turned to look at Matilda.

"Please introduce me to this delightful young lady."

"My niece, Matilda Thigpen, is our ward and attends me on the voyage. I could hardly leave her among the seamen on the docks." George announced.

"Certainly not, but young lady, how would you entertain yourself while old men talk business?" Glancing at the novel clasped next to her bosom, he continued, "Much too pleasant a day for a pretty miss to be reading."

Matilda curtsied to Allen's compliment, a deep low bow, tips of her fingers tugging shirts wide, and the right foot placed toe down behind the left. She floated in air, perfectly balanced. "Whatever the gentleman has in mind, sir," she replied in a soft Tidewater accent.

"Would you prefer to join my wife and children, Miss Matilda? Our home is a short distance, and the secretary can walk you there. The consul and I will join the family for lunch."

"That would be so kind and thoughtful, sir." Turning to Chase, she asked, "May I, with your permission, Mister George?"

"Certainly, a young woman listening to two lawyers would be absurd."

Matilda left to enjoy the rest of the morning.

"Wherever did this creature appear from, George Chase?" Allen, eyes wide, began. "A niece? Is that true? She's too sensual to be from New England, George!"

Chase stiffened, "My distant cousin married an Alabama man with a hint of French ancestry. The girl was orphaned just as she approached womanhood. Missus Chase and I decided she would have better prospects here."

"Do I detect a rather familiar form of address?" Allen teased.

"Southern young ladies address their male benefactors by first names," Chase sniffed.

"A curious custom. Watch her, though, my friend. Single white women are rare in the islands, and many Americans are unattached. She'll be courted hard, once they catch her scent," Allen cautioned.

The Minister of Finance gestured to a comfortable chair and took a settee opposite Chase, a low table between them. The furniture in Allen's spacious office – large desk, chair, side tables, and bookcases – all matched in design and color. Allen explained the set had been made in a shop in Canton, a Chippendale imitation costing a fraction of British manufacture.

Allen's office overlooked the palace property. To the south, facing the harbor, French doors opened onto a wide veranda, shaded from direct sunlight. To the north, the wall was a curtain punctured by doorways opening onto a center courtyard of fountain and flowers. No stove was visible because, Allen explained, the temperature was temperate year round, but, if chilly, braziers would be brought to warm the room.

"George, it is a pleasure to have another Maine man. You shall enjoy your duties."

"Eli, are there more of us?"

"The United States Commissioner is Luther Severance. Do you recall he was editor of the Kennebec Journal, served a couple of terms at Augusta?"

"The State Department must think there's a Maine conspiracy cooking."

"Indeed! State is suspicious already. Back in '51, when France was threatening to annex the Islands, the monarchy drew up a deed of cession. The Hawaiians wanted United States protection by annexation. Luther asked me to carry it to Washington, but State was appalled. Pure bigotry. 'How can there be a part of America with races equal in status? You Americans in Hawaii have gone native!' They already knew about my marriage into the royal family," explained Allen

"I thought you were still a widower, Eli. You married royalty? You mean a Hawaiian woman?" Chase sat back, failing to conceal his surprise.

Allen laughed.

"Indeed, old boy. Astounded by the news as well? No such concept as 'miscegenation' out here. If dismissal from the Department of State's consulship was punishment for some supposed indiscretion, justice prevailed when Kamehameha the Third named me Minister of Finance." Allen's arm swept, gesturing at his office.

"Tell me first hand about the consulship, Eli."

"Although the post salary is modest, you're entitled to certain fees for paperwork to certify cargoes, to ship and discharge seamen, and to defray expenses. I earned over four thousand dollars in '52. As a side venture, you earn a five percent commission on expenses for the care of seamen in the Lahaina hospital. That's where your predecessor, Bunker, ran into trouble.

"Bunker may have been overcharging the U. S. Treasury. Lahaina is dominated by the whaling business, and, perhaps, Bunker was in collusion with whaling captains from Nantucket. Whatever the case, Bunker abandoned the post in February, skulked back through Honolulu, never informing Luther or me, and returned to Nantucket. The Department is counting on you to straighten out the accounts. Meanwhile, you are free to develop your own trade, George, as long as it does not compromise your position."

The minister and the consul were served tea as they talked, the secretary fixing the cups as the gentlemen wished. The morning passed quickly, no sense of urgency, no other business, a few papers left unattended on Allen's desk. A Minister of the Treasury for an entire kingdom?

Chapter Forty-Five

"Daddy, come home." A tan boy stood at the office door.

"Come here, son," Eli called him to join them. "This is my son, Charles. Charles, meet Consul Chase." The boy stepped forward and offered Chase his right hand.

"Good morning, sir. How do you do?" the words formal and halting, as the hand pumped three times and released. George studied the little figure – gray eyes, brown, wavy hair, skin tanned – a darker version of his father.

Eli stood, "My wife is expecting us for dinner. Come, she's impatient if I'm late."

They walked beyond the palace lawns, through a garden, and across a narrow lane to Allen's home. The two men and the boy filed up a path through a bushy area that opened onto an open lawn where children played with a flock of ducks and a tethered goat. Matilda led the children in a game of *blindman's wand*. A young boy, blindfolded, held out a stick, grasped by an older girl to whom he was asking questions.

Beyond the lawn was the two-storey house of white stucco with French doors surrounding the upper floor, opening onto decks, above which the red tiled roof pitched steeply into copper gutters. All windows and entrances to the first floor were shaded by overhangs and porches. The lavish home lay open to surroundings.

A tall, dark woman of thirty approached the men, her statuesque figure wearing a brightly printed, loose-fitting dress. Raven hair fell down her back, a clip at her temple held one side above her right ear, while a flower graced the temple over her left ear.

"Aloha, welcome to our home, Consul Chase."

"George, I am pleased to introduce my wife, Mary Koahumanu Allen."

"I am pleased to meet you, Missus Allen. I hope we aren't imposing, not giving prior notice of our arrival, and I hope my niece has not been difficult"

"Since her arrival this morning, she has taken over the entertainment of the children. She bursts with energy stored up over the voyage. Thank you for allowing me to be the hostess to introduce you and your niece to a Hawaiian home."

Chase looked to Allen who smiled broadly.

      *   *   *

The dining room had been prepared for dinner. The meal included a small pig, served whole, garnished with onions and potatoes. Baked fish was served on a slab of wood, head and fins still attached. Among the meat and fish were vegetables that Chase could not identify. Sliced fruits were brought out as desert.

As the dinner was announced, children and adults arrived from several parts of the house; young children, youths, girls, older youths, other adults, a mix of whites and Hawaiians. Matilda arrived in the company of another young woman, white and dressed as elegantly. All chatter ceased when Eli asked all to bow their heads.

"Heavenly Father, bless this meal to our use and us to thy service. We give our special thanks for the save arrival of Consul Chase and Matilda Thigpen and ask your protection on Missus Chase and the children on their journey. Pardon our sins and grant us salvation through your son, Jesus. Amen."

Plates were passed to Eli who served the meat and fish. George surveyed the gathered collection of mixed peoples at the table. Mary sat opposite Eli, and near her were two young children, lighter than she, but obviously, the product of their marriage. Also, there were white young people, introduced as "our" sons and daughters, but apparently born to Eli and his first wife. Also, there were other Hawaiian adults, introduced as Mary's brother and sister. Matilda chattered with everyone.

Following the meal, Mary and the two men retired to the porch, sitting on high-backed wicker chairs and sipping rum punch. The children were dispersed, younger returning to school, youngest to their nanny, and oldest to conversations. Matilda joined the nanny, taking the children onto the lawn to lead games. She kicked off her shoes.

"How long can you stay with us, Mister Chase?" asked Mary Allen.

"I should depart in three days. Although I'm anxious to see Lahaina, I need to introduce myself to several people in Honolulu."

"Wonderful, leave your evenings free for me to fill. There are many others to meet the new consul and his niece."

*   *   *

My Jurnal

I can write whatever I want in this here jurnal cause this is privat.

We on a ship, see no land, but expect to make San Francisco soon.

The womens quarters are some mess with clothes hangin down and fights startin up. They call themselves <u>working girls</u> - but I can't figure what work they do. Can't sew, can't read nor write. No good children's nannys. They be talkin like sluts.

Daytimes, Mister George makes me work on my lessons, writing and speaking. After lessons we walk decks. He calls it prominaid. Scared of folks talkin to me - might say somethin wrong. I am glad when he takes me back to salon.

Dear Momma,

I miss you very much.

I can not send you no letters - but I can write what I think. I do send you my prayers.

Mister George bought me two copybooks - and teach me to write better. One copybook for my lessons - this one for my jurnal. Mister George says ladies keep private jurnals.

I really do miss you and back home - but not that plantation and being told by Mister James and Miss Betty.

Since that low day when Mister James sent me off so much good has happened to me.

I have a new life now. My own bed. Two sets of nice clothes. Shoes. My own books.

The ship took us to a hot rainy country - had to cross to the other ocean.

I was glad when we came out the other ocean to a beautiful city. Like a story book. Mister George took pity on my old clothes - bought me new. Fixes for me to have my own room in hotels and ships. Wants me to learn to talk like a lady so as I can fit in. Calls me his _neese._

This is the hard part - Momma. You always said because I was so fair I could pass for some kind of white woman, but passin is not easy - makes me lonely. There are no colored people here - leastwise no colored people like home. Most are dark - darker than me. Americans think I am mixed white and French - they call it creole. The Hawaiians think I am white. Only Mister George knows the truth.

Dear Momma,

Last night I went to a party and danced.

Miss Mary is the Hawaiian wife of Mister Eli. Yes, colored and white marry!

I had so much fun. It was just like the parties Miss Elizabeth gave at home. Music. Food. That funny dancin white folks do. All except they didn't serve no drinks - no whiskey - no wine - no nuthin.

Every one dressed up. Miss Mary gave me a hoop dress to wear - showed me how to sit sos it don't flip up. Her maid did my hair. Mister George took me aside. He borrowed Miss Mary's silver service and made me show him which fork and spoon to use. He was surprised I already knew. Remember I always served at dinners back home? I could always tell which guests have class.

Mister George wanted me to sit near him - but Miss Mary said <u>the boys should have a chance to meet the new girl</u> so I sat with other young people - but Mister George kept watching.

I met lots of people - whites and colored all sitting together. Hawaiian names so hard to say. When they talk their language -it's like bird calls - all up and down -repeating the same sounds. Some take English first names, but their real names are different. Like Princess Victoria Ka-ma-ma-lu - she daughter of Governor Ke-kua-na-oa - I hope I spelt right.

They can't speak regular English, neither. Guess my speech lessons are over.

We ate supper real slow. The servants brought just a little at a time - a soup. Greens. Shrimp. You have to use a fork or spoon to get it to your mouth or just leave it on the plate. The main course was a roast beef. That was hard for the Hawaiians - I laughed to see them eat with their hands.

Before the last food came out music started, surprised when Miss

Mary's brother came to my chair and asked me to dance.

At first I shook my head - but he insisted. Remember watching them white folks dance at home? Movin round like clocks.

I never told you about the time Master Thomas offered me dance lessons. I should have knowed better when he took me to the barn. Just wanted to diddle - but - stopped when I said I would tell his momma. Miss Elizabeth didn't want her boys forcing no colored girls. Would believe us if we told on them. None of those white boys ever messed with me. In all this time I never laid with no man - I swear - Momma.

Miss Mary's brother is Edward Kamehameha - the biggest man I ever did see. Tall. Only come up to his chest - twice as wide as me - arms like the legs of a natural man. But, when he asked Missy want dance? I supposed maybe I knew more about dancin too.

He took my hand and led me to the dance floor where we could see the orchestra. I was so surprised to see a colored American, Mister George Hyatt, leadin the players - That Hyatt played a clarinet, real good.

What a terrible dancer Edward is! Too big and heavy to move on his feet. Wanted to hug me - no lady and gentleman dancin. Like Jonah in the Bible - little me all swallowed up by a whale. I thanked him - curtsied - and tried to sit down again. Except that other boys were waiting their turns. I danced with them all until Mister George said the evenin was over.

I slept til noon today.

Tomorrow Mister George and I leave Honolulu for Lahaina on the island of Maui.

Tonight we visited the theater where we saw a play. It was real hard to understand - tho the actors spoke a kind of English. Mister George tried to explain the story.

All about kings. Princes. Courts. War. A shifty foxy man swindles everybody out of their rightful inhairtrance so he can become king. You felt sorry at first because he's crippled - but then you hate him when he drownded two little boys in a barrel.

As bad as he was they still made him king - but in the end the good men surround him. He's trying to escape - crying for a fresh horse. He yells at the audience, "My kingdom for a horse" like they was going to bring a horse into the theater - then they stab him like a dog.

May God forgive me for sayin I was glad cause he deserved it. I never hated nobody so much.

Mister George said it was a real good play an we were lucky such a famous actor came to Honolulu. His name on the program - something - I think - like John Wilkes Booth.

Chapter Forty-Six

Lahaina Roads was a protected anchorage formed among four islands: Maui, Moloka'i, Lana'i, and Kaho'olawe. Gentle waves lapped facing shores, tides rose and fell a mild three feet, and the West Maui Mountains blocked heavy rains. Between the islands, the sea floor rose from trenches, miles deep, to a shallow three hundred feet between islands, a feeding ground for whales and dolphins.

When a man walked along the placid beach, minnows darted in transparent surf around his feet. Coral sand beneath the man's sole colored a foot tan at foot depth, yellow at hip depth, and green farther out. Farther still, the sea became darker shades of blue until black against an opposing island's cliffs.

Although the Roads were only twenty degrees north of the equator, the cold Pacific modified the day's heat, and night brought cool breezes. Occasional rain fell on the forested mountain height of Pu'u Kukui's rugged ridge, watering lowland plantations with streams cascading down slopes to the sea. The ancient volcano provided rich red soil, reliable water, and a wide seaboard.

Vegetation grew with little effort. Sugar cane, taro, mango, and bananas provided food. The breadfruit tree, the cocoanut tree, the koa and the hau provided shade, food, and wood for calabashes. For the pleasure of eyes and nostrils grew the white hibiscus, the red mountain apple, the yellow lehua mamo, and the red coastal kou – all flowers for house garlands and neck leis or delicate color in raven tresses.

Here, a thousand years before, the Polynesian roy-alty, the Ali'i, established their recreational capital, Lahaina, central to the six major islands. Here, for a thousand years, this aristocracy refined their divine pantheon, led by *kahuna* priests. Here, they worshiped their benevolent ocean, perfecting worship by riding surf. Here, they perfected expressive arts, dancing hulas and chanting genealogies. Here, they enjoyed sexual liberties.

But, here, also warriors, costumed in bright feathered capes, planned bloody war, and *kahuna* priests imposed death penalties on women and peasants for breaking *taboo* codes.

Until James Cook's expedition of 1778 revealed the islands to the western world, Hawaii stood outside the path of history. Soon, events accelerated. Unscrupulous traders bartered trinkets for Hawaiian resources and Hawaiian women, throwing traditions into chaos. The gods were overthrown the same year that Yankee missionaries from the Calvinist twig of the Protestant branch of the Christian religion would arrive to bring Jesus. Yankee missionaries faced Yankee sailors from the whaling fleet; one group to capture souls, the other to capture wealth. These New England cousins, one bringing faith and learning, the other bringing business and technology, would change Lahaina forever.

In 1853, Chase would confront them both.

*   *   *

The peaks of Oahu Island passed beyond sight as the packet boat floated on Pacific swells. They entered the Kalohi Channel between two islands with collections of huts fringing the shores.

Dolphins played at the bow, keeping up with the chugging steam engine and side wheel. Birds darted overhead. Native dugout canoes, some paddled, some with peculiar triangular lateen sails, passed across the steamers bow.

"Mister George, just look at those mountains ahead." Matilda pointed in the distance.

"That's your new home, Matilda. That's Maui. We'll be there before dark. My assistant, Snively Willington, should be waiting for us. We'll be in our new home tonight."

"It's all so beautiful. Sure enough, there's plenty of fish in this bay, Mister George. You've said it's summertime all year round with fruits and vegetables. You have been kind on this voyage, Mister George, but it will be good to stop traveling, to stand on land again, to walk among trees and flowers." She looked at the passing islands, while Chase looked at her.

"You must remember this day, September 20th. When this boat touches at Lahaina, a new Matilda will disembark."

"Mister George, what do you see in Lahaina?"

Chase leaned his forearms on the railing, pushing his hat back to his crown. He smiled at the approaching island.

"Missus Chase and I have been dreaming of this for a long time, only we didn't know its name, its location, or if it were an island at all. Only that it would be remote, a frontier, a new society, the potential for a family fortune, our 'main chance' to build an estate. This is not our first such experience; no, when we married, I carried my bride to the frontier of Maine, to an "island" of a town in the forests, remote from civilization. There, we built our fortunes, schools, businesses. But, Calais had limits, and so I have brought part of that fortune to plant at Lahaina, to start again. My position as Consul will permit us an entrance into Maui's society. By the time President Pierce leaves office, we shall be well invested in business here. I will end my days among the ship owners and planters while my children marry among the children of shipmasters and missionaries. That is my dream."

The sun bent low over the western horizon, setting between Moloka'i and Kana'i, lighting a bank of clouds. Sunlight lit the slopes of the mountains and the palm-fringed shoreline. Lahaina was only visible as a small collection of white-washed buildings in the distance, framed by mile-high peaks. From the water, the mountains loomed over shoreline. Only grassy slopes gave perspective, setting the peaks miles inland.

The boat engines cut off half a mile from shore to avoid the reef. Longboats appeared from a cove. Chase, dressed in stovepipe hat, and Matilda, protected by parasol, stepped onto a longboat with luggage and were rowed to shore, passing into a canal. Each longboat pulled beside a wharf built beside the canal and hands pulled passengers and belongings up to the plank surface. Chase looked up into the faces of Hawaiian, Chinese, and white workers.

A small white man holding a palm leaf hat approached George Chase.

"Would you happen to be George M. Chase, sir?"

"Yes." Chase squinted at the figure.

"I am Snively Willington, your assistant consul. Welcome to Lahaina. Please allow me to take you to your new home. Is this lady, Missus Chase or perhaps Miss Chase?"

"Neither. Allow me to introduce my ward, Miss Matilda Thigpen. She will be staying with our family. We expect the rest in a few months."

Matilda stepped forward and curtsied to Willington.

"Pleasure to meet you, Miss. I'm sure the *haole* ladies will be pleased to have another partner for their socials."

Matilda let out an imperceptible sigh. George restrained a smile at the remark.

Workers carried the luggage to a waiting carriage, while the crowd continued to bustle about. Manufactured products loaded off the steamer as agricultural products were carried out. A market covered the banks of the canal, extending to the main street of Lahaina. A rough superstructure covered the length from the beach to the street, a hundred yards, on which tradesmen and farmers hawked wares.

The carriage pulled onto the shore road, Front Street, and passed several stores, all with balconies and porches, creating an arcade on the land side of the street. On the ocean side, low buildings clung to the road. Red dust floated into the air stirred up by hooves and carriage wheels. Soon, clothes and luggage looked reddish-brown from the cloud.

Willington pointed out landmarks.

"But, the seamen's hospital and Charles Porter?" Chase inquired.

261

"That's at the north end of Lahaina. Doctor Porter arrived in July."

"Thank God." Chase sighed.

"However, the crisis at the seaman's hospital should receive your attention immediately. The doctor complains constantly to me."

"Just as soon as we can leave our baggage at the consul's residence. How close...Wait, driver, who's that?"

A large Hawaiian man, dressed in American clothes, approached atop a tall horse. Face shaded by a planter's straw hat, his eyes looked straight ahead.

Chase stood up and shouted, "Stop the carriage."

At the sound of Chase's voice, the rider swung around in the saddle and yanked on the reins. "Chase? You did come to Maui. It was no rumor." He dismounted and led the horse back.

George leaped onto the ground, meeting the rider halfway.

"Paul Kamehameha, you're here in Lahaina? How prosperous you look! But, then I had no doubt when you left Calais..."

Paul ignored the offered hand. He towered over Chase.

"You forget so easily. The voyage back home gave me a long time to think. Leaving Maine wasn't voluntary. I was pushed, Chase." The face glowered darkly under the hat brim.

"Had the issue been up to me, Paul, you'd be a married man in Maine."

"Another *haole* lie." Paul re-mounted his horse. "As consul, keep your missionaries out of our affairs and your whalers off our women. The Kanaka Maoli resent your presence." The horse wheeled around and trotted down the road.

"Who's that, Mister George?" Matilda asked when Chase climbed into the carriage.

"One of the hostiles from the palace," answered Willington. "Another insolent darkie."

262

"Troubling, troubling." mumbled Chase. "I knew him a long time in Maine. Damn, never expected this kind of reception,"

"More than white men should tolerate. The sooner we put them in their place the better," remarked the assistant.

"I can't abide that attitude, Willington. We must be diplomatic," the consul chastised.

Willington's answer was to beckon the driver continue.

"Willington?" Chase nudged. "Your assent?" He wouldn't let the matter alone.

"Give yourself a month in Lahaina. You'll come around to my point of view," he shrugged. "Let's go to your residence, Mister Chase."

The carriage rolled south on Lahaina's Shaw Street, passing ever more humble grass huts and adobe houses. Finally, they entered a large property. Chase stood on the carriage floor.

A plantation house was surrounded by high grass untended for months. Large trees bordered the property. Walls of coral rock covered in stucco, a half cellar poked out of the earth. Above, the stucco needed a coat of whitewash.

The first floor stood, surrounded by a wide veranda, like a shady skirt. Protected from rain and sun by a thatched roof that hung over the first floor, the veranda needed repair. A wide set of steps led up to the porch floor with a Dutch door for an entrance. Every side of the first floor sash windows opened to catch ocean breezes, and two dormers facing the mountain and two facing the sea served second floor bedrooms.

George sprang to the ground and mounted the stairs. One tread collapsed under his foot. He pushed open the Dutch door. Interior walls were plastered white above wainscoting, and around the ceiling, well-mitered crown molding met walls. Four large rooms, separated by wide thresholds, comprised the first floor.

The second floor bedroom floors were littered with dry thatch, fallen from the ceilings. Birds and insects, burrowed through the roof, infested the house, leaving webs, trails, dirt, and scattered dead on floors and in nooks. Lizards scurried across walls, floors, and ceiling. Some sticks of furniture had been left – beds in the second floor, chairs and tables on the first. A cookhouse, a partly thatched shelter, stood apart twenty feet from the house.

"Mister George, I'm feared to look into that cellar. Never can tell what's slithered into the damp." Matilda had followed him upstairs. "But, first have this roof fixed."

Snively Willington waited on the first floor. Chase listed some immediate repairs for him to arrange. Matilda added to the assignment.

"Would your men also cut down that grass around the house? That just invites snakes, rats, and other critters to come too close for comfort. I want no snakes in my cookhouse," she said to Willington. "While Mister Chase is busy at the office, have the workers call on me for directions. Mister Chase need not trouble himself with no household details. Also, we will need a girl for chores, and finally, so that Mister Chase can attend to business tomorrow, please take us to a green grocer so I may serve him supper and breakfast."

The assistant looked at the young woman, hands on hips, feet planted on the dirty plank floor.

"Would there be anything else?" he sneered.

"Miss Thigpen's request seems to be in order, Willington. Is there a problem?"

"Just curious to know if I'm to take direction from the woman as well as from you, sir," he asked, unsmiling.

Matilda lowered her eyes, and Chase stiffened.

"Any gentleman would recognize a lady looking to the welfare of her family. Now, escort her to a green grocer. I shall expect to find a swept home with a full larder by darkness. Get started. We all have work to do."

Chapter Forty-Seven

Matilda rose at dawn, waking Chase with the rich aroma of coffee. He walked to the Consulate. As he left the property, a cart filled with fresh thatch, pulled by oxen, came up the lane, accompanied by five men. Women walked behind the cart, holding brooms and carrying buckets.

Leaving his property on the first morning on Maui, Chase realized his joints felt new. Knees and hips moved without clicking pain. He rotated his shoulders. No resistance. Wrists and hands grasped the cane tightly. On reaching the road, he began to forget the rheumatism and concentrated on colors and smells.

He passed gardens filled with an assortment of flowers, the scent palpable. Birds filled the air like an aviary. The United States Consulate was located on Front Street, across from the busy Hawaiian Customs House, near the canal market, a low brick building made grand with Doric columns supporting a porch.

The United States had stationed an independent consul here for ten years, on the insistence of the Hawaiian government, after violence broke out between American whalers and Hawaiian police.

*   *   *

Chase found Snively Willington already at work at a ledger, seated on a high stool, catching light from a high window. The Consulate contained two rooms, an outer office with a street level door and an inner office with a back door. Willington's was the outer office where he greeted clients, while George's inner office's door allowed private conversations. A map of the Hawaiian Islands decorated one wall, and a bookcase against another wall held the statutes for consuls.

"Good morning, Willington. Already at work?"

"Oh, yes. How is the consul today?" the assistant chirped.

"Rested and ready to address the work. What is our business this morning?"

"Registering the two vessels that arrived two days ago, the bark *Oscar* and the ship *Saratoga*."

"How are the records laid out?"

"On this sheet, I record the date of arrival, class of vessel, name, ton burden, the ship master's name, the crew – Americans and foreigners, and where it has been hunting whales. Over on this sheet, I record its homeport and cargo. Those two vessels arrived from the North Seas. The bark has a crew of 19, the ship a crew of 29."

"There are so few vessels here now. When do we receive the body of the fleet?"

"In a week or two, several vessels will arrive every day, bringing us a heavy workload. Then, there will be much to do. On your desk you will find things as Mister Bunker left them."

"Good. Until then, I have much work introducing myself to the Lahaina community, preparing for my wife's arrival, and buying a horse. Do you have any suggestions?"

"The Chinese merchants are good for such commerce. I also suggest that the Consul be reserved toward any Sandwich Islanders. The American community frowns on fraternization with natives."

Chase stared at the clerk.

"You've made that clear yesterday. Before I leave, I better attend to correspondence." George began his first official act; a letter to William Marcy, Secretary of State:

Dear Sir

By virtue of an appointment of the President of the United States, I have this day entered upon the discharge of the duties of consul at this place.

I arrived at this place via San Francisco and Honolulu yesterday and have today taken possession of the consular archives and property by virtue of the order sent me by you, directed to Chas. Bunker, Esq. late consul, a schedule of which is herewith sent. Also this day upon the discharge of the duties of said office of consul by virtue of my appointment by the President and the exequatur granted by the Hawaiian Sovereign, as published in the newspaper called the Polynesian at Honolulu.

List of Government property in the U. S. Consulate, Lahaina. Sept. 21st 1853

Viz.

One Government Press and Seal

Two sets of arms

The Statues at Large

The Archives.

Very Respect.
Your Obt. Svt.
Geo. M. Chase
U. S. Consul

By noon, George Chase had secured a large reddish sorrel horse, Mexican saddle, heavy stirrups, and bridle. The merchant, Wong, promised to find another horses appropriate for his niece, Miss Thigpen.

George rode past the wharf area to a large house with wide porches and verandas set behind a spacious lawn. As he approached, the front a native woman, rotund and smiling, came forward to greet him.

"Would the Reverend Baldwin be at home?" Chase asked.

"He is seeing patients in his office now. May I ask who's calling?"

"George Chase, the new United States Consul."

Chase scanned the townscape and the shoreline. A creek ran past the springhouse down to the shore where a dismal house stood, surrounded by an open lot. From the front of Baldwin home, the whole wharf area was in clear view where merchants' stores lined Front Street. Reverend Baldwin chose a strategic location. George thought, this must be an active type of minister, not removing himself from the business of the world.

What did that native woman say? Reverend Baldwin is seeing "patients."

A man's voice interrupted George's thoughts. "Mister Chase, you have at last arrived at our station?"

George turned to see a tall man dressed in ministerial black, with white collared shirt and cravat. Reverend Dwight Baldwin invited the new consul into his medical dispensary.

"Reverend, you minister to the body as well as the soul." Chase took a chair.

"I took some medical training with my divinity studies at Harvard. All in order to bring more service to my Sandwich Island mission to deliver modern medicine to these people. The key is prevention, of course, and I'm concerned this morning to read the Honolulu Friend. It seems there's a smallpox outbreak on Oahu, and it's spreading rapidly." He waved a newspaper.

"We haven't seen smallpox in New England for years."

"Americans are inoculated while native people are not. Would you accompany me to the Palace today? The King may be available by early afternoon."

"Why not now?" asked Chase.

"King Kauiheaouli, you will learn, reigns but does not rule and suffers from extreme melancholy. He may be seen only after he wakes at noon. Let us plan to ride over to the Palace grounds after dinner. Meanwhile, have you visited your Seamen's Hospital?"

"My next destination."

"Please alert your people there, the seamen's chaplain, Reverend Sereno Bishop, and your doctor, Charles Porter. I'll inform young Doctor Dow at the drug store. Pardon my manners, Mister Chase, for not having introduced my wife. Please step into our home."

The Reverend Doctor Baldwin led Chase onto the veranda to the house front and into the front door. An American woman was directing several native girls, ironing bed sheets. The interconnected rooms of the first floor were bustling with many men. Rooms with beds could be seen off the center hall, a colorful garden lay beyond the open back. Several children, young adults to primary ages, worked and played among the chaos.

"Charlotte, dear, allow me to introduce a new resident of Lahaina."

Charlotte Baldwin was irritated at the intrusion, she said, "Will he be a boarder as well?"

"Hardly, my beloved. This is Consul Chase. He has the consul's residence out toward the Palace grounds." Charlotte looked up and smiled at George Chase, wiping her brow with a white handkerchief.

"I apologize for my unchristian greeting, Consul Chase. I'm in the midst of laundry day."

"But, Reverend and Missus Baldwin, where are your quarters?" asked Chase.

"We have the upstairs and the former Masters' Reading Room next door for our family. That leaves the first floor for our mission and medical dispensary," Charlotte answered

"Where is the church?" George looked outside the high windows.

"It's Waiola Congregational Church, near to your consul's home. I do hope you will attend. Are you a Christian?" Her face brightened and her voice rose on the term, "Christian," as if she were asking his preference for refreshment rather than his theological persuasion.

George measured his answer, careful to be both honest and tactful.

"My wife and I have many Congregational friends, but we are of the Unitarian persuasion. Missus Chase has remained at home for her confinement expected this month. If all is well, she plans to leave for Maui in October. Please do expect my appearance at the Waiola Church this Sunday in the company of my ward, Miss Matilda Thigpen."

"A young American lady as well as the Consul's wife? It will please the ladies of Lahaina to welcome your ward and your wife to our little circle, Mister Chase."

*   *   *

Doctor Charles Porter had arrived at Lahaina in July and began service at the United States Marine Seamen's Hospital. Having practiced small town medicine in Calais for eighteen years, a graduate of Bowdoin's medical school, Porter brought, along with his instruments, high standards for medicine. He had found a two-storey frame building, hardly recognizable as hospital and infested with twin corruptions: neglect and fraud.

Chase tied his horse to the hitching-post and walked in the front door.

Looking up from his desk, Charles Porter called out, "Oh, thank God," as he saw George Chase enter. He rose to shake George's hand and began to blurt out his frustrations.

"George, it's either incompetence or malfeasance, but this hospital is a damned cesspool. I have no authority, undermined at every turn, unable to bring any discipline. Worse, I cannot control the finances. More has been charged per patient than at any U. S. hospital overseas. Yet, we are short on medical supplies, short on food, too little for maintenance." The doctor tapped his index finger on a ledger book.

"Come into the wards." Porter tugged on Chase's sleeve.

The two men stepped into a large room. The odor rocked George on his heel. Dozens of young men lay on pallets, laid on wooden flooring. Their clothes hung limp and filthy. Some moaned, some played cards, some begged for water.

"These men are suffering, and death itself doesn't end the chicanery. I can show you the names of sailors still listed on the manifest who lie up in Sailor's Graveyard next to Maria Lanakila Church. Somebody's been collecting a tidy sum and I think I know who is the scoundrel, too. But, you're not going to like my deduction."

George looked up from papers rumpled by Charles' finger. He responded in one dry word.

"Willington."

"My God, George. How did you guess him? You've only just met."

"The man managed to annoy me within the first fifteen minutes. We'll get to the bottom of this in time, Charles. Right now, we have bigger fish to fry. There's been an outbreak of smallpox on Oahu. Natives could die in swarms. Baldwin is bringing a delegation to the king this afternoon at the Palace. You, Baldwin, and young Doctor Dow should propose mass inoculations."

"You won't find the king there."

"Where is he?"

"Here in the hospital gardens, escaping his supervisors."

"What?"

Doctor Porter smiled, "Have you ever met royalty, George? Queen Victoria, the Russian Czar, and the Prussian Kaiser perhaps?"

"Of course, not."

"Prepare yourself to meet his royal highness, King Kauikeaouli, Kamehameha the Third. You need not dress up for this audience," he laughed.

Leading George out of the office, Doctor Porter walked behind the hospital and into a shaded garden area. They approached a group sitting under a koa tree, cross-legged. They were laughing, a bottle passing among them like familiar friends. They ignored the two newcomers.

Most of the group were young white men, but two were Hawaiian, one older dressed in American clothes, the other in a loincloth.

"Your majesty, King Kauikeaouli, your majesty, please your attention this way," Porter shouted above the conversation. "This is our new consul, Mister Chase."

The older of the Hawaiian men looked toward Chase and Porter. The eyes were blood-veined, the irises dilated. Chase could tell that the king has reached a state where he, the garden, and the entire company had begun to spin. He tipped over.

"Charles, the king must return to the palace if we're going to address this problem. Get that driver and the king into the carriage. You drive and I'll ride my horse. Take us to the palace by way of the Baldwin's home. There, we'll pick up the minister and young Doctor Dow."

The crowds on Front Street parted, allowing the company of horsemen and carriage through the business section. King Kamehameha the Third did not rise to greet his subjects; instead, he slept on the carriage seat, lulled by the ride's rhythm.

Chapter Forty-Eight

Horsemen and carriage raced south on Front Street to the royal palace. From his mission, Dwight Baldwin joined the entourage, riding beside Chase on his dappled gray mare.

"Consul Chase, prepare to enter the royal compound, once a forbidden zone and as ancient as this island's origins. It's the inner sanctum of heathen practice and nobility. Careful not to mock any outlandish customs or design. Christian that I am, I always show respect for the customs of the royal house."

The cantering pastor loped on his horse's broad back.

"The Ali'i is an aristocracy, tall and handsome, lording over a feudal system. Somewhere in their wanderings millenniums ago, there had been a mythic island guarded by a dragon. Upon reaching these islands, they fulfilled that legend with a sacred royal park."

Chase noted, "Maui is an island already."

"Yes. The sanctuary is a complex surrounded by a fresh water pond called Loko o Mokuhinia, legend says, the home of a lizard goddess, Kihawahine, who guards the island, Moku'ula. The king lives on the island in a grass house, the Hale Pili, although a recent coral block palace, the Hale Piula, serves on the beach side of the road."

"Sounds like hocus-pocus to me," Chase scoffed. Baldwin glanced over, unsmiling.

"Try to think of our British cousins Chase. Doesn't their modern Queen live behind a moat at Windsor Castle when she isn't at Buckingham Palace, tapping shoulders with a sword to award knighthoods?"

"Well, that's all about history," Chase defended.

"How enlightened is that for England, the most progressive nation on earth? No wonder the Hawaiian royal family prefers the British."

"If you don't mind my asking, Reverend, isn't it a contradiction against Christ to ally your missionary efforts with this Hawaiian aristocracy? 'Blessed are the poor' and all that?"

Baldwin shrugged. "That certainly was an issue with the 1820 missionaries, but they soon discovered the peasants wouldn't accept Christ unless the Ali'i led the way."

The horsemen approached a masonry building along the beach. Baldwin led the group across a causeway to the building and dismounted. The king, removed by a swarm of native attendants, was ushered inside. Baldwin spoke to them, gesturing for the Americans to remain outside.

"Gentlemen, let us give the attendants time to call their council together."

The Hale Piula palace, built of coral rock, paralleled the sea for about one hundred twenty feet. The palace stood on several acres, surrounded by a wide piazza, within sound of the washing tides. Across the road, past rows of trees, was the expanse of the Loko O Mokuhinia pond, covering several acres, surrounding the mysterious island. Lake water extended to both sides of the road, a sluice under the roadway permitting an escape to the sea. On the island, Chase could see several structures under groves of palm trees.

"The council is ready for us, Consul," said Baldwin.

The three doctors and Consul Chase were admitted to a large room on the ocean side of the Hale Piula Palace. The king sat on a dais, raised against the far wall, windows and French doors open on either side, emitting cool wind and the sounds of surf. Chairs were offered to the Americans while the king's attendants stood. George saw Paul, standing among the council. Paul ignored Chase's nod.

A royal spokesman addressed Reverend Baldwin, who responded. Chase and Doctor Porter exchanged looks. The men were speaking Hawaiian. Chase watched amazed at Dwight Baldwin's fluency.

King Kauikeaouli began the audience, directing a question to the minister to which Baldwin responded in length. The king turned to Paul and the other counselors who in turn spoke to the minister. No one smiled. Only when the counselors spoke among themselves did Dwight Baldwin turn to Chase and the doctors.

"They realize the seriousness of the situation. I am asking for quarantine of Oahu, letting no one off the island, until everyone has been inoculated and the disease subsided. Meanwhile, we must start mass inoculations on Maui and the other islands before the contagion reaches those populations. If we can't prevent ships from leaving Oahu and Honolulu, perhaps we can bar landings here."

Again, the counselors conferred with Baldwin in Hawaiian. Then, a debate broke out among the counselors.

"What are they saying?" asked George.

"Some represent the commercial interests on Maui. They say they will lose business to shipping if we bar landings. Some say the whalers will avoid Lahaina. Some complain their relatives are visiting Honolulu and must return home. We need a month to inoculate."

Baldwin stepped forward and bowed his head in silence, clasping his hands reverentially. The native counselors immediately halted the argument and turned to him in unison. Slowly, the minister lifted his head to heaven and began to intone a prayer. Most of the assembly slowly sunk to their knees, heads bowed, and hands together. Only the ocean could be heard above the minister's prayer.

Finally, all joined in unison. Chase thought, The Lord's Prayer, perhaps?

The prayer ended, Baldwin sat and the counselors rose. One counselor stepped forward and spoke.

Baldwin whispered to Chase, "The governor of Maui, a reasonable man. He proposes a compromise. The king will declare Maui, Lana'i, and Moloka'i *kapu*, off limits for two weeks, and all royal authorities are to be at the service of the doctors for mass inoculations."

"Will that be enough?" asked Chase

"It should suffice. At least the king supports us," answered Baldwin.

The royal audience ended and the doctors gathered to plan their campaign.

Baldwin drew Chase aside. "Consul Chase, your cooperation is essential. Only you can forbid American ships from landing crews, and bar landings of packet boat passengers."

"Count on my cooperation." He started to leave the room, but the missionary held his arm.

"Please wait, the king wants to speak with you."

Baldwin escorted the consul out of the throne room.

King Kauikeaouli had withdrawn to a small, elegantly decorated anteroom. Seated on a cushioned couch, he gestured for Chase to sit beside him. Dwight Baldwin hovered between the two men, Paul Kamehameha, the only other attendant present.

"I say you many thanks, Consul. You act like man in charge. Good for the Kanaka Maoli. Save them from another *haole* sickness."

"For my part, your majesty, I must apologize for my abrupt and discourteous manner, bringing you from the Seamen's Hospital. That treatment was not worthy of a monarch. I hope you can accept my sincere apology."

The king turned his weary eyes toward Paul and lifted his brow, questioning. Paul spoke rapidly.

Paul turned to George. "His majesty says he understands the circumstances called for extreme measures. He apologizes for his condition, his lack of dignity, a loss of *mana*, being intoxicated."

The king followed Paul's translation. "Very sorry, not to have learned English. My young cousin here is my voice. Would you please follow us to my island home across the road?"

"I am at your service," said Chase.

"Would you please excuse me, your majesty?" Baldwin interrupted. "We doctors must begin our work. Consul Chase, on the other hand, will learn much from a visit to Moku'ula."

The retinue crossed the causeway from the Palace onto the island. King Kauikeaouli and Consul Chase, shadowed by Paul, were leading a line of attendants; males in the native *malo*, a one-piece loincloth, and women in loose dresses. The king led Chase to his dwelling; a large grass house with open sides, surrounded by gardens filled with flowers. The king explained his preference for the open traditional house, all one room containing an extended family.

"Good air. No closed rooms like American house."

Then, he led Chase and the retinue to the other end of the island. They entered another building.

"This house of the dead," he explained, "many famous kings, and some very special princess."

The interior was designed as a mausoleum, a tomb, the center of which was the large burial chamber. The walls were covered in mirrors and velvet draperies. The floors held chairs, couches, tables, and stands holding feathered staffs. Every few feet were ornate coffins.

"All *Ali'i* here from before *haole* come."

The king came up to one coffin; he stood, laying his hand on the lid and gazed at the decoration. Slowly, his body began to shake, sobs becoming audible. Gradually, his body lowered onto the coffin's lid. The king of the Sandwich Islands lay prostrate across the tomb, waving away the visitors and attendants. Paul took George's arm and brought him out into the light.

"Whatever happened, Paul? Just who is buried in that coffin?"

"Princess Nahienaena."

"Was she the king's wife?"

"Perhaps, Mister Chase, if that were true, our king would act more like a monarch. They loved one another. A baby was born to them, but died. She died young, torn between two worlds. It is a hard story."

"Why did they not marry?"

"Princess Nahienaena was caught between two worlds, our society taught her to love the king since childhood but Christian teachings forbid their love."

"Why so, Paul?"

"The princess was the king's full sister."

*   *   *

George Chase nudged the reddish-brown sorrel toward home, the sun setting over the channel. The twelve-hour day ended with the American consul enforcing a strict royal *kapu*, shutting down the port of Lahaina with a company of native police. Shadows crossed the dusty lane, altering the path so that he struggled to recognize the turn into the Consul's residence. Twenty feet onto the property, he stopped, surveying the house and lot.

Was this the same property he left this morning? The day before, Chase had seen the residence from this vantage all neglected and overgrown. Now, he saw the inherent beauty of the house and grounds. So much changed and new: fresh thatch on the roof, grasses trimmed up to property boundaries, windows clear and sparkling, white paint on railings, and new treads on steps. George tethered the horse among the grass.

Matilda rushed down the veranda steps. She held two cups.

"Mister George, I was so worried. Where have you been all day? You must have been doing some important things. Come inside and rest. Your supper is ready. It's special, but first you must have refreshment to stir the blood."

She handed him one cup, smelling sweet and fruity, garnished with a green sprig. He sipped a nectar. He sipped again. The sugars rushed into his body, pleasant sensation tingling his extremities; something more than fruit juice.

"Matilda, I do believe there are strong spirits in this libation," he grinned.

"Rum from the grog shop. A whole gallon for the household for medicinal purposes," she giggled. "The shop keeper asked me 'bout being something called 'temperance.' Says most white ladies don't drink here 'cause they "temperance." What's that?"

"The pledge. They pledged not to touch strong drink."

"Why is that? Can't hold liquor?" Matilda started up the broad steps to the porch.

"Missionary whites and their native followers are Congregationalist. People in those churches swear off drink. Pure Puritan self-denial." He held up his cup.

"Back home, no body goin' to take no pledge. Folks, black or white, enjoy drinkin', Mister George."

Chase laughed, "Matilda, you fell in with the right family when you joined the Chases. Now, what's for supper?"

"Mister Snively said for me to buy *alalauuea*, said it's sweet-tastin' fish. You also have potatoes and for your desert I sliced some kind of fruit, mango, from your tree. This here town's got the best food in the world."

Matilda waved George into the house. Where there had been an empty room, a table stood with four chairs. Plates and utensils surrounded heaping platters of food.

Chase rushed over to the table. Two plates, two forks, two knives laid on cloths, flowers stood in a discarded rum bottle. The room smelled of lime from cleaning and fresh whitewash, all droppings from insect, bird, worm, or reptile vanished. New rattan covered the plank floor. Evening breezes flowed through windows.

George reined in his hunger until Matilda served herself, sat down, and said grace. He had never tasted such fish – only cod, shad, and salmon. He ate with relish. Matilda enjoyed refilling his plate. He also asked for a second drink, although he could barely keep his eyes open.

"My dear Matilda, I am so happy you are here. A toast to Matilda and her masterpiece supper! The best cook and the best housekeeper in all Lahaina!"

"Now, Mister George, you need your rest. Take your-self upstairs. Your bed is ready," she said and avoided eye contact, busy clearing the table.

"A wise suggestion," and Chase lumbered over to the stairs. The last conscious sensation was numbness on his face as he fell into bed.

Chapter Forty-Nine

The mother stirred about the cooking fire as the family slept. She had slept fitfully among the children on the mat, the visiting cousin kicking and turning in the night. What was the matter with that girl? Maybe we have a look this morning. The baby on her back felt like a calabash of hot poi, listless face pressed against her skin. Why aren't these children awake yet? Usually, she was hushing them and the dogs at dawn.

"Auntie, auntie, look at my belly."

The girl stood at the hut opening, staring at her abdomen, pulling down her skirt to reveal red pimples over her brown skin. Were they flea bites? Each one seemed to be bleeding. She looked up at her aunt. The woman screamed. The girl's face was covered in lesions; pus-filled eruptions over her cheeks, ears, and neck. She bent down for a closer look. More pustules had crept into her hair. The aunt hugged the child to comfort her. The skin was burning with fever, worse than the baby. What to do?

She woke her husband.

"We take her to the missionary doctor."

*   *   *

"Oh, no, Mister George, not the pox. I seen folks wit' pox. Their skin is all marked up."

Matilda's morning coffee and cornbread ended with a description of the crisis.

"Come with me. Reverend Doctor Baldwin will administer your inoculation, a scratch. It gives you a small pox on your arm, like I have. See?" George rolled up his sleeve to reveal a deep pockmark on his shoulder. "That was five years ago and keeps me safe. He will scratch your arm, giving you a little infection, so your body can defend itself."

"Don't it hurt?" She pouted.

"Yes, silly girl, you have no choice. Grit your teeth and think of that pretty face."

At the dispensary, Dwight Baldwin was already giving inoculations to the Maui constables and all royal administrators, those most exposed to the public. Doctors Porter and Dow scoured back streets for any cases of people who had recently landed from Oahu carrying the disease. Baldwin wore this "plague clothes," a worn black suit and stovepipe hat, clothing kept for a contagion, otherwise hung in a shed.

"Good morning, Chase. I see you've brought young Miss Thigpen for her variolation. You seem upset, young lady."

"Yes, sir, I'm afraid of your cure."

"This isn't a cure. There is no cure. There's only a good chance for prevention. Please sit here." Matilda squatted on a low stool, her left shoulder toward the doctor. Baldwin asked her to lift her sleeve above her elbow.

"Is that the cowpox serum for a vaccination, Baldwin?" Chase asked.

"No, unfortunately, there isn't time to search the herds of cattle for any outbreaks of cowpox. The Doctor Jenner method will be the best solution for the future, once we convince the government to vaccinate the entire population, but today, Hawaii has an emergency. We have to use the old direct method, *variolation*, transferring the pus from the scab of a victim or the fluid from a newly inoculated person's papule or vesicle. Gives them a mild case. It's dangerous, but it's our only chance."

Having prepared a bloody serum of scab, pus, and fluid – the varioloid – in the bottom of a teacup and turning back to his work, Baldwin scratched a one-inch opening across Matilda's shoulder with the point of a scalpel, already used on the entire Maui police force. Using the same scalpel, he scraped a tiny portion of the smallpox variolation onto the blade and smeared the mix into the scratch.

"There, young lady. Now you will have a brief fever. Go home and lie down. Chase, take care of her. Is the port blocked? Have landings from Oahu stopped?"

"The royal constables have been chasing off the packet boats. No one is very happy. After returning Miss Thigpen home, I am due back at the Consulate."

*   *   *

For two weeks, Chase and the Hawaiian constables fended off all shipping. Produce rotted in the market's heat. Every day, a ship master slipped through the screen, screaming for services.

"Where's that damned consul?" a gruff voice boomed from the outer office. George could hear Willington calming the visitor, perhaps to take a seat.

Looking up from his ledger, George waited for the clerk to appear at his door. The man came around the threshold, flustered, glasses fallen down his nose, pen shaking between ink-stained fingers.

"There's a Captain Dallman from the *Mary Ann* demanding to see you, Judge Chase. He rowed himself to the beach. Sorry, but he wouldn't take an appointment for office hours."

Chase looked up from his work.

"Send in this Dallman, Willington," he said closing an inkwell and cleaning off the pen's metal tip.

In strode a tall, broad-shouldered man dressed in a dark suit of heavy duck, topped by a varnished black hat. Wearing his hair in a queue, his face set, lips tight in a frown framed with a flaming red beard, Captain Thomas Dallman was all business this morning.

"Good morning, Consul. I'm Thomas Dallman of Fairhaven, Massachusetts, master of the *Mary Ann*, recently returned from the Japan coast and loaded with sparm oil."

"Good morning, Captain Dallman. I am George Monroe Chase, recently arrived Consul of the United States. Please state your business."

283

Dallman slammed his fist onto the consul's desk.

"Chase, yer costin' me time. I can't land my casks for transshipment. The steward says provisions are running out. What's left of the fresh water ain't fit for beasts. Some men got scurvy, and the rest are horny as hell and thirsty for grog. If I can't land the crew, I can't scrub down my ship and leave for the South Seas for the winter. What can you do for me?"

"You know we're quarantined, don't you, Captain? It's the king's orders and it's for your crew's safety. What good would it do you to sail with the pox on board? Let the doctors do their work, man, and give us another week."

"My steward says our provisions are nil, consul. How about getting up a tender with some victuals and fresh water, rowing out to the *Mary Ann*, and heaving on board? We'll keep the men apart. My crew will stay out until the danger is passed. If you're inoculated, like me, you can come aboard and witness our conditions yourself."

"Captain Dallman, I will inquire among the royal constables to round up a rowing crew. Leave money and a list of provisions with the clerk. Keep in mind the capacity of one boat is limited. I will come with the tender in the morning. Meanwhile, I must insist upon your return to the vessel and your promise to hold that crew offshore until danger is past."

Dallman looked at the consul for a moment, sizing up the consul's determination.

"Expect you at dawn, consul." He turned on his heel.

Chapter Fifty

Dear Momma,   October 5, 1853

Church today, first time since home.

Mister George and I got dressed up, light dress for me, but he wore a dark suit.

Most Hawaiians don't dress at all, six days a week, especially in fields or town, but things is different Sundays.

We walked to Doctor Baldwin's Waiola Church. Mister George and I stepped into the lane, me holdin my parasol against the hot sun burnin my skin. My, the lane was crowded wit Hawaiian people - all dressed like Americans in dark suits, stiff collars, cravats, closed shoes; womens all dressed in gingham to the feet, puff sleeves to rists, hooded bonnets covering the faces- like a city in America - cept they steppin out of grass houses, walkin on dirt.

The church is regular size cept there's no walls. Breeze blows through. Wondered how they going to fit all these people, more than a thousand in that church, but then I see most people happy to sit outside on the grass. Hawaiian people smiled, greeted, and brought us into the sanctuary to a pew, with the other white people - Doctor Dow, Doctor and Missus Porter, Missus Baldwin and her children. The royals was there, all proud up front.

When service started, I didn't understand what Doctor Baldwin was sayin cause he Hawaiian jabbertalk. Sometimes he speaks both first English then Hawaiian like the Lord's Prayer. One line in English, next Hawaiian. Then, he opened the Bible for the Readin.

Jest not right to hear Philippians 4:13 in jabbertalk!

"I can do all things through Christ who strengtheneth me." Seems that Hawaiians take this wrong, think that Jesus will stop accidents, prevent all disease as long as they believe in him and do right. Bad things happen only to bad people, they think.

Hawaiians listen up, cause they losing too many kids in accidents.

Then, Pastor Baldwin turned to whites. Said they have little faith, think they're saved by Good Works. Then, he explained to the Hawaiians he had scolded the whites to be fair about it. Royal Paul liked that.

This kind of church, isn't like All Saints in Perquimans. Too much sermon, tired of listenin.

Last night, I attended the ladies Bible class. Sometimes white ladies mix with Hawaiian ladies, so as to teach the Hawaiians, but missionary wives speak only a little Hawaiian, not like the men who learned it good so's to write the Bible in Hawaiian.

Last night only the white ladies met. We read some Bible verses. Free choice. When it was my turn, I chose the third epistle of John, fourth verse:

"I have no greater joy than to hear that my children walk in truth."

Miz Charlotte ask me why I pick that verse. Cause I love all the children, the brown ones and white ones, want to see them grow up right, say I. Miz Charlotte smiled, said I was a <u>blessin</u> sent to Lahaina, said I might have a special mission.

Dearest Momma,   October 8

A girl came to work today. Leilei. Royal Paul Kamehameha brought her to the house, says she's a good girl from a church family.

Leilei may be about twelve or thirteen, she doesn't know. Likely thirteen cause she womanly, and I make her cover up her titties. Can't have no hussy. Girl needs to learn, but Lord knows she's tryin. Sewin, cookin for Mister George, cleanin house, settin table. Hard to make her understand English.

E ko makou Makua I loko o ka lani
That's how the Lord's Prayer starts.

Mister George bot me a pony from Wong. Coat like buttermilk, gold to match my hair. Says they call it palomino. So's I call her Pal. Now I can go riding, too, but white ladies not sposed to spread theys legs over a saddle, you know, so I has to sit sidesaddle an that's hard.

Dearest Mamma,

Paul took me riding on the mountain over the town tonight.

Chapter Fifty-One

Dawn and the shadow of the mountain lay over Lahaina's mooring, momentarily a protection from the heat. The American flag flapped on the consul's pole above a yellow banner warning of plague.

George Chase walked briskly to the canal where Hawaiians were loading the tender with firewood, fruits, vegetables, melons, pigs, and a barrel of water. A burlap bag filled with the sailor's favorite, Lahaina sweet potatoes, sat in the bow. Holding his stovepipe hat, Chase took a seat at the stern, next to the tiller. The Hawaiian crew heaved oars, speeding them out of the canal's mouth and into the low surf. The *Mary Ann's* black hull lay in the clear morning light, a mile from shore.

As the tender drew closer to the *Mary Ann*, Chase saw the ship's figurehead under the bowsprit, a barebreasted maiden with golden tresses and ruby lips. The ship's crewmen lined the portside railing, all in shiny black porkpie hats. Ships master, Captain Thomas Dallman stood among his crew, distinguished at a distance by his taller hat and broad shoulders.

"Hallo, Consul Chase, yer as good as yer word. The light is yet to hit her crows nest." He pointed to the top of the mainmast's ringed perch.

Chase's Hawaiians received the hauling ropes thrown down from the railing. Heavy rope was lowered from a pulley system to lift the water cask. Once the ropes were secured around the cask, the crew turned the windlass, winching the heavy weight from the tender's deck, swinging away from the ship's side, and onto the *Mary Ann's* mid-ship deck.

"No man gets a drink until all's aboard," roared Dallman. "Consul Chase, heave aboard yerself."

Quickly, all else was lifted from the tender. Pigs by ropes under shoulders, squealing in fright and pain. Fruits and vegetables in baskets. Finally, Chase himself crawled up a rope ladder, pulled over the rail by crewmen.

"Welcome aboard. Always a pleasure in the company of a representative of Old Glory among the heathen. Give our consul a cheer, boys." Dallman called out to his crew.

"Thank you, Captain, but I can stay only a moment. The men on the tender will be back with a second water barrel presently."

"Hurrah for our consul," shouted the seamen. Chase's eyes scanned the crew. Their faces surprised Chase. They included the usual range of New English, but also swarthy Latins, tan South Sea Islanders, copper Indians with earrings, and Africans so dark their blackness hovered on the edge of blue.

Dallman invited Chase to his cabin for a toast. They walked to the stern on the sloped deck. At the rear were the cookhouse on the starboard side, the wheel at the center covered by housing, and a covered companionway on the port side. The stairs in the companionway led to the officer's quarters.

An oil lamp swung overhead beneath a glass skylight. Dallman invited Chase into his personal cabin, built along the ship's stern, complete with a window. Now that the sun reached the water, bright light danced on the surface channel, giving an illusion of space to the tiny compartment. The men sat on a red upholstered horsehair divan, built into the rear bulkhead. Dallman poured two glasses of rum.

Chase lifted his glass, "To the *Mary Ann*. May she prosper and return with full casks."

"Aye, that, and also to the United States and her far-flung interests." He continued, "so, yer the new consul here. How have you been received, so far?"

"Pleasantly surprised by the civility of Hawaiian people and our relations. The whaling industry rises. From past consuls' records, barrels of oil and the pounds of whalebone increase every year."

"Those relations weren't so cordial years ago. Back then, there were four parties in contention – the whalers, the missionaries, the nobles, and the commoners. Just when the Hawaiian nobility stripped away the heathen religion, discarding the old gods, who appeared but the missionaries and the whalers, one offering western religion and the other western commerce."

"Yes, whalers shot cannon at the missionary's home. Something about a *kapu* against the Hawaiian girls and the sailors."

"Indeed. Thirty years ago, Lahaina was wild. The missionaries had just converted the Hawaiians while the whalers wanted ta exploit their child-like simplicity. The girls would give themselves for an iron nail. For our boys, such easy virtue was too attractive. The missionaries' crusade ran smack into the whaler's motto – 'we hang our consciences on Cape Horn'"

Chase smiled. "Or 'there's no God west of Cape Horn,' or so I was warned." He swallowed the last drop of liquor. Dallman refilled the glass and continued.

"The Hawaiian nobility grasped the value of Christianity quickly as the only way ta' prepare their people for the onslaught of the western world. On the other hand, the common people remain attracted to American trinkets. Meanwhile, the demand for whale oil is met by more production. The *Mary Ann* sits at anchor with nearly a full hold and time yet for more hunting. That's when yer embargo stopped us, consul."

"And after your unload?"

"Store them in Lahaina with an agent. Let a clipper ship take our barrels to New Bedford. 'Tis a small expense, and the owners would appreciate realizing an early return."

Suddenly a face appeared at the cabin door.

"Sorry to disturb you, Captain."

"What is it, Swain?"

"There's a native boat alongside, very excited. Peter William says something about a whale."

"Let's go up ta see what's the ruckus, eh, Chase?"

On deck, the crew finished enjoying fresh water. One of the pigs had been slaughtered on deck, blood washed into the scuppers. The top corner of a native sail peeked over the portside railing. Peter William exchanged flowery vowels with the Hawaiians.

"What's this about, William?" Dallman demanded.

"They talk 'bout whale, capt'n. Lots whale, a shoal. T'other side Lana'i. Deep water."

Dallman spun around, surveying the deck. He signaled First Mate Abraham Swain. "Prepare to sail. We've got space in the hold for one more good haul."

"Wait, Captain," Chase objected, "I can't accompany you and the tender is still at Lahaina. I'm stranded aboard ship. I demand you row me to shore."

"No time. They'll know where yer at. Consider this a free education, Consul. After this tutorial, ye'll be the expert."

Chase watched as the deck exploded into action.

Chapter Fifty-Two

"All hands on deck," Swain called out down the forward companionway.

Word passed among the crew, last chase before shore leave.

Eight men, handspikes in windlass holes, weighed the anchor, winching up chain until snug to the bulwark. The three masts and cross spars swarmed with men loosening ties and releasing sails to catch wind.

Lines of men pulled on ropes to raise spars, singing in unison and jerking the rope when the mate joined on the last word:

The last time I saw her she was down on the strand
As my boat passed by her she waved her hand
Saying when you get home to the girl you love,
Remember the maid in the coconut grove.
Now I am safe landed on my own native shore
My friends and relations gather round me once more
Not one comes round me not one do I see
That can be compared with the lass of Mowee*

The three mates directed their watches, First Mate Swain, Second Mate Thorn, and Third Mate McLane. Swain's men climbed the main mast, unfurling the topgallant, the topsail, and the mainsail. Thorn's men hoisted the three most forward sails. McLane's men loosed the stern's mizzen sail. The youngest greenhand, Alvin Gunnison, was sent up to the crows nest to sight the shoal of whales.

The *Mary Ann* sailed south, rounding the high cliffs of Lanai Island, and then headed west toward deep water. Sailors readied whaleboats dangling from davits over water.

---

*Gale Huntington, Songs the Whalemen Sang (New York:Dover, 1970) Permission: Martha's Vineyard Historical Society

Chase noted the boats hardly looked up to the challenge of killing anything. Flimsy, with only a thin skin of half-inch planks shaped into a double-prowed canoe.

The ship gained speed, and George braced against the foremast. Crewmen bumped the consul as they scurried about the deck, causing Chase to seek any nook where he could watch.

Captain Dallman called out encouragements. "Gunnison," he shouted up at the lookout, "look about, they could breach anywhere."

He gathered the boat crews.

"Men, we have just one last whale to harvest before shore leave. Ye've worked hard and endured hardship. Ye deserve a good time on the strand, so I advance every man a portion of his lay ta cover entertainments."

Cheers from the crew.

"Today we have a special guest, our consul from Lahaina. Unlike us, he's here against his will, accidental-like." He laughed. The men turned and eyed the pale Chase in office clothes.

"We want ta give him a good show so's he knows about the life of a whalin' man. Maybe even when a tar slips up and gets rowdy ashore, our consul may come ta the man's defense." He winked.

"Victorino, what's Jose saying?" Jose had asked a question in Portuguese.

"He axe, 'Consul come, kill whale?'"

Dallman looked at Chase.

"Well, these clothes, my shoes," Chase floundered for excuses, shaking his head.

"We could use another oarsman, Mister Chase. Put that hat, shoes, and jacket in my cabin. You'll never get closer to a livin' leviathan."

Chase pushed off his hat and shed shoes and jacket. The crew cheered, and a call broke from the crow's nest.

"Thar she blows!" All hands ran to starboard. Faintly, fountains of spray leaped in the distance as a shoal of whales rested on the surface.

"Boats away, boys," Dallman ordered. "Time be wastin'."

Each boat lowered off the overhung davits. Each commanded by a mate, each steered by a harpooner. Victorino stood with Swain, Antonio with Thorn, Whampanoag Charley with McLane. Chase joined McLane's crew and climbed down the hull on a knotted rope until pulled into the bobbing boat feet first.

At the stern, the Whampanoag crouched at the tiller, black eyes burning. At the bow, Mate McLane sat on the harpoonist's brace shouting orders. Between the prows were four thwarts where men sat amid oars, paddles, and harpoons.

Chase, barefoot, took an oar, coordinating strokes with the others. They pulled away from the ship. McLane called the rhythm. "Pull, pull" until amid the other whaleboats, a hundred yards from the *Mary Ann*. Chase panted to match the younger men, bracing his feet against the next thwart. To his left, the harpoon bracket bristled with weapons.

McLane called orders to the backs of the oarsmen who blindly pulled toward the shoal of whales. Then, he called to ship the oars, his voice a harsh whisper.

"Take up the paddles, boys. Quiet now." The rowers rotated to face the shoal, paddling the craft like an Ontario war party. Chase saw only the green swells of the Pacific Ocean and the other whaleboats. On the nearest boat, the swart shape of Victorino stood at his tiller.

The boats closed in on their quarry. Spray sprung into the air, and a shiny black mass emerged from the green water to rise alongside, huge as the hull of the *Mary Ann*. Chase's stomach spasmed, and he tasted bile in his mouth.

"Faster, now."

A signal to change places, McLane and Charley crawled, passing amidships, beside rowers, feet and hands only touching thwarts. The Whampanoag lifted the harpoon from its cradle, threading a portion through the bow pins with yards slack for the thrust. The rope snaked past each rower, a creeping serpent to tangle the unwary boatman.

Whampanoag Charley knelt at the bow, naked to the waist, copper skin taut. McLane guided the craft to the animal's left side. Chase smelled the scent of the beast, an odor of rotten fish. The monster lolled about, unaware of the tiny men in the frail boat.

Chase could have touched the creature's shiny black mass. A great eye rose from the water; incomprehension. The huge hulk blocked their view from the others. Chase froze.

"Paddle, damn you," McLane demanded and Chase stabbed into the brine.

Charley rose on the bow brace, aloft against the boat's pitching. He lifted the harpoon above his head, right hand on the butt, left on the stock, inches from the whale's black mass. At a moment only he knew, he thrust the weapon deep into the black hide and jumped down onto the boat's deck.

"Paddle back." The crew reversed, and the whale's mass gave a sudden quiver. Its tail rose, flukes towering, to slam on the surface, and water cascaded over the boat's sides, soaking Chase and the crew. The rope sung through the bow's pins, spinning from the tub, as the whale tore away.

"Steady men. Stay low."

The rope played out, reaching her end. The boat jerked forward, following the whale, throwing men back. Chase clung to his thwart. Speed increased. The delicate hull slapped against each wave. Faster, and the boat became airborne over a swell. Chase feared the boat's strength. A slam landing, spray pelted the men; then a stretch of smooth water, breaking a frothy wake.

"It's a Nantucket sleigh ride, boys. Careful, Charley. Cut, if he sounds."

The Indian crouched, knife in hand, ready to cut the rope if the whale dove for the deep. But, instead, the beast dragged men and boat for miles, beyond sight of the *Mary Ann*.

Gradually, its speed slowed. Charley and McLane, hand over hand, brought the rope back into the boat, pulling themselves closer to the harpooned whale, until they floated beside the hulk. This time, the Wampanoag took up the lance and mounted the bow's brace to deliver the deathblow.

Hands above his head, Charley thrust the tool deep into the whale's side. The animal shuddered in pain as the lancer's arm worked the tool back and forth inside the body, probing for the lung. Suddenly, the blowhole spray burst forth red seawater and blood rained down. The whale quivered in its "flurry" and rolled over.

Chapter Fifty-Three

"Ye've had yer fun, now the hard work starts." Dallman shouted over the swells.

Together, the four boats rowed the leviathan back toward the *Mary Ann*. Smoke swirled over the ship where the cook had fired up the tryworks and a cauldron sat ready to boil the blubber.

The whale's carcass was brought alongside the ship, and the lightest crewman was attached to the monkey rope and lowered onto the whale's body. Men stood on planks over the mass with long flensing knives.

A hooked line lowered, the light one attached the end of the strip to a hook. While the line was cranked up by the windlass, the flensing knives freed the strip's edge, rotating the body and separating it like an orange's thick rind is separated in a spiral. Gradually, a great blanket of blubber and skin was raised above the ship's bulwarks. At the twenty-foot mark, the skin was cut, leaving the blubber to be swung over the deck to the caldron on the tryworks.

Over the caldron, the workers cut portions into the iron pot until the blubber melted. When the oil separated from the skin and impurities, sieves lifted the residue into waste buckets and tossed overboard. When a portion of the blubber had been processed, the precious oil was spooned into casks and sealed. When casks were full, they were hoisted by the windlass crew and dropped into the hold.

The stink of the cooking blubber stung Chase's nose with the odors of burning meat, rotting fish, and rancid butter.

Gradually, the carcass was stripped of its blubber. The afternoon wore on into dim light when they noticed a frenzied gathering of sharks, tearing at the whale. Captain Dallman brought out his musket to kill the most aggressive to turn the frenzy on their own. Lights were brought out as dusk turned to dark.

Finally, the carcass was stripped, and flensing knives moved to decapitate head from the body. A hoist lifted the great head onto the deck. Antonio climbed into the rigging with a bucket. They lowered him into the maw of the brain cavity where he disappeared. After several minutes, the bucket was lifted up to the men and replaced with another bucket. The first bucket was lowered and gently poured into a special cask.

"The purest sperm oil," Swain explained to Chase, "Don't need no processing. Best for making spermaceti candles."

Every drop had been scraped from the whale head, the men cut away the jaw and teeth, all the scraps kicked overboard to the waiting sharks.

Finally, carcass stripped, the windlass lifted the remainder on the flensing deck for the last precious prize. The crew scraped the intestines onto the floor, letting cabin boys scurry over the stinking mass. Men brought a wide-mouth glass beaker.

"Here it is! I found it!"

A bowel cut open, something was lifted and slid into the beaker. Chase stepped forward to examine the contents held to light. Inside floated a gray amber substance.

"What have you there?"

"The ambergris, Mister Chase. Pound for pound, the most precious part," grinned the sailor.

"What's ambergris?"

"It be perfume."

"If ladies viewed this, they'd never daub perfume again."

Lamps swung and rope shadow's danced to the yawing of the ship. In officers quarters scraps were left on the plates at the mess. Chase and Dallman lingered over the grog of diluted rum. 3rd mate McLane's head rested on the polished table. Swain, in the 1st mate's quarter, was already entering the log at his desk. Thorn was fast asleep in his bunk.

"Ship's hands have a hard life, Mister Chase. Little comfort and less profit. I pity their lives, no family, no fortune, hand to mouth, ending their days dying in some foreign clinic. I try to be the good captain, believin' men will work harder for a fair man. On the other hand, the fleet still has shipmasters who flog crewmen for minor infractions. Thems be like floatin' plantations enslavin' free men, most simple fellows, knowin' no better. "

"I do understand, Captain. Really, I do. Men at saw-mills in Maine live rough lives as well. I, like you, treated them as humans entitled to fairness. Mills are no plantations, and workers no slaves. Mill hands are free wage-earners for the working day and owners possess nothing but their time in the shop. The best examples are cotton factories in Lowell which prosper by improving their workers' minds."

A faint rap was heard above the companionway.

"What is it? Come down," Dallman called out.

A boy appeared on the stairs, hat in hand.

"What is it?"

"Sorry to interrupt, Captain. The men want to speak with the Consul, sir, if he has the time and with your permission."

"Is there a problem aboard ship? Shouldn't the cap-tain know first before ye go makin' a complaint against me?" He winked at George.

"No complaint aboard the *Mary Ann*, sir. We just want to talk to him about trouble on other ships."

"Very well, then. Consul, if you have the time, the boys would be mighty grateful for your attention."

George followed the lad from the stern's officer quar-ters, up to the deck, and before the masts to the fo'c's'le companionway, the distance between officers and men.

He crawled down the narrow ladder into crew's quar-ters. The air smelled of rancid oil mixed with body odor, damp clothes, and dirty chamber pots. Scraps of food lay in a common tin bowl. The crew laid or sat on their bunks and sea trunks. A dim oil lamp lit the room to light the variety of complexions.

George Chase sat on a nearby trunk.

"Sorry, we can't offer a chair, Consul."

"This will do nicely. What's on your minds?"

One man spoke. Chase judged him the oldest at about thirty.

"The men asked me speak up, sir. I'm Edgar Wetmore, had the most schoolin' and can speak some Portugee. Do we have yer word not to blacklist anyone fer expressin' opinions here? Do ye promise ta protect all men in the fleet, not just ship masters?"

Chase looked into the eyes of the exhausted men.

"I took an oath to protect all Americans, regardless of rank, and as a lawyer, I'm pledged to make just decisions. To calm your fears, I will hold a confidence."

"Is it true that the United States Congress passed a law forbidding flogging seamen?" Wetmore asked.

"Back in 1850 that became law when Richard Henry Dana exposed the practice in *Two Years Before the Mast.*"

"We make clear we got nothin' 'gainst Captain Dallman. He's a taskmaster, but fair. Ain't none of us e'r saw him strike a man."

The room broke into nods. "Yeah, yeah. Si, si."

"But, we know of thems what does flog cruelly, Mister Chase, and ye ought to be appraised of those masters and their reputations. If crewmen file a complaint, it ain't jest idle talk. It'd be true and somethin' ought be done 'bout it."

"Would you have the courage to give me a list of such masters?"

"That we would and we will, but there's a second matter tied to the first."

"Yes?"

"Yer the American consul, serving Americans, Yer Honor, but on these here American vessels are men of other nations and colored from the United States."

"Like me, Whampanoag and other tribes." Chase saw Charley, his harpoonist slouched on a bunk.

302

"Good of the masters to employ them." Chase offered.

"Maybe not so good. Does the law apply to them as well, since they ain't citizens and can't even testify against a master, bein' a colored's word 'gainst white?"

"Wetmore, are you implying these captains employ other races to avoid the anti-flogging law?"

"Maybe or maybe not. Massachusetts farm boys with a little education can get a regular job in the Wamsutta mill, workin' their looms. Don't need no ship's contract ta make a livin'. Ship owners have ta hire crews elsewhere now, and mean ones are happier to sign on a Portugee or better still, a runaway slave, who's 'fraid to complain. Do you understand?" He gestured at Peter Mingo, ship's cook.

"Many interesting points, Wetmore, and none have been answered by case law. Precedents haven't been set, no guidelines, no code. If I may put your thoughts into lawyer language, American law ought to apply on American ships, regardless of the race of the crewmen. You want to know if a crewman were to complain of flogging and if evidence and testimony corroborated the complaint, would I prosecute the ship officer? Further, if the complainant were a man of color, would the law still apply?

Chase hesitated.

"So far, no such case has reached this consulate."

"It will, Senator, it will. Here is the list of those ship captains with reputations for flogging."

The next morning, Chase was rowed back to Lahaina. After conferring with the royal constables and Doctor Baldwin, he lifted the quarantine. The yellow flags of plague were lowered, the signal that crews were welcome once again for liberty ashore.

Chapter Fifty-Four

A warm September night in Calais and Harriet felt the first contraction. On her side, a pillow propped under one knee, she felt tightening. "Darn it!" She chastised herself for waxing the front hall floor, ignoring sisters' pleas, to accomplish one last chore. Her belly swayed when she applied tick wax to the narrow white oak.

Mother Deborah, hands on hips, had watched from behind and clucked her tongue to see her daughter's womanly rump wobble under the skirts. Her favorite daughter would not allow herself a moment of repose while other daughters fluttered, urging Harriet to sit on silk pillows until the 'confinement'."

Harriet ignored them She'd heard their catty remarks. Undignified, pregnant at 42, a husband on a distant assignment. How insensitive of him.

Harriet's mother and sisters had arrived intermittently over the summer months to witness midwife and doctor's visits. The doctor's appearance shocked the sisters – handsome, jet-black hair and wire rimmed glasses. He strode into the house with white shirt and black suit. How could their sister allow him near her? They accompanied Harriet into the bedroom. The doctor sat on the edge of the bed and exchanged pleasantries with their sister, asking about her habits, her diet, and her functions. Harriet wore a full set of clothes.

"Vell, Missus Chase, shall ve conduct da examination?"

"Of course, Doctor Benjamin."

The doctor stood and reached under her skirts. Harriet lifted her knees and tilted her hips upward. The doctor looked at Harriet's face, asking her questions. The sisters stared at the floor, embarrassed to witness a man touching their sister's privates. Finally, Doctor Benjamin pronounced the baby to be in the correct position and active.

"I zink ve vill have a healthy baby, Missus Chase."

"Oh, thank you, doctor. That makes me feel confident."

"Da lady's confidence is her own. I have fery little to do vit confidence." He smiled. "But, vy do you insist on dis Grandma Jack for a midvife? She is so primateef."

"She's an old Calais tradition, doctor. She brought all my others into the world, and you are right, she's part Passamaquoddy and brings herbs and roots to help the women. I will have little pain."

Doctor Benjamin shuttered, then shrugged and smiled. "Fery vell, I understand, she does no harm. Your time is near. Please send for me ven da contractions come."

Some days later, Deborah Norwood and her daughters worked in the kitchen when they heard a scratching noise at the door. On the porch stood a tiny crone, carrying a basket, head covered in a shawl, a dark tunnel around the face. Her features were barely discernable, except for piercing eyes, a hooked nose, and white whiskers sprouting from her chin. The shawl covered her whole upper body, exposing only hand and wrist bearing the basket. Cooper skin stretched across veined fingers gnarled with arthritis. Bare feet stuck out from a shabby hem.

"Sorry, but we're not buying today," said Deborah, dismissing the 'Indian peddler.'

The elderly woman's free hand darted from the shawl and grabbed Deborah's wrist, nails digging into the flesh. Deborah jolted from the pain, struggled to break free, but the grip was iron-fast.

"Tell the lady Grandma Jack is here," said a rasping voice.

This time, Harriet took her examination without family. Lying Harriet across the double bed, Grandma Jack sat on a chair and lifted the skirts to expose her body below the waist. Her face inches away from Harriet's vulva, she probed, stretched, lifted, laid her ear on the distended belly, thumped, sniffed, and then sat back.

"You will bring this baby next Wednesday, maybe at night" she said. "I bring the birthing chair tomorrow."

"I must warn you that Doctor Benjamin will be attending the birth."

"Why? Are you sick? It's bad medicine for a man near a birth."

"He's only here for anything unforeseen. He won't interfere with you, Grandma Jack."

"Okay, only if he stays outside the room." She said, gathering her belongings and retying her shawl. "Boil and drink these dry leaves at night before sleep. If your pee turns clear, you will deliver soon."

Indeed, Wednesday night the contractions started, and Harriet lay counting minutes between the muscle spasms. Fifteen minutes, twelve minutes, nine minutes.

"Mother," she called down the hall. "It's started."

Deborah Norwood rousted out her other daughters to alert the doctor and Grandma Jack. Harriet moved to the birthing chair, crafted from a walnut tree, back and seat carved in unity, three legs firmly imbedded beneath, built to withstand stress. The seat only provided a brief surface for the buttocks, but extended with side handles. Cloths were laid on the floor underneath to absorb fluid.

Grandma Jack kneeled on the floor between Harriet's legs. Harriet's mother and sisters gathered around her sides, holding her arms. The midwife demanded silence, glaring if a sister dared snivel. Doctor Benjamin sat in the parlor, ready if called. He had brought the latest technology for childbirth: forceps, a bottle of ether and mask, if Missus Chase chose unconsciousness.

The midwife reached into the birth canal, felt the baby's head crowning, and urged Harriet to push. Harriet strained in the birthing chair, pressing her back against the chair and her mother's arms, pulling on the handles, while pressing her abdominal muscles.

After minutes of straining, the baby slid out into Grandma Jack's waiting hands. The old woman carried the infant to the parents' bed, drying the slippery body. Pulling a tiny leather bag from her bosom, she sprinkled powder on the baby's brow and mumbled some words. Then, lifting the infant up, she smacked its back. The child screamed.

"You have fine daughter, Missus Chase. Have a name?"

"Yes, she shall be Julia Deborah Chase after my sister and my mother."

*   *   *

It was late October when Harriet departed for the Sandwich Islands. Instead of bringing any or placing them in a boarding school, Harriet had decided the older children were to remain with George's brother, Daniel Chase, in Calais. Young George started his eleventh grade at the Academy, and Hattie began her last year of the common school., both children part of the extended family in Calais.

Baby Julia Deborah would accompany her mother on the long voyage.

Chaperoned by Daniel Chase, Baby Debbie and Harriet took the packet boat to Boston, continuing to New York City. She had struggled to restrict her luggage to one chest.

She planned to purchase a ticket from the United States Mail Steam Line. The Line operated thirteen vessels from the ports of New York to New Orleans, eight of which served New York. The cost was to be one hundred and fifty dollars, and the voyage to the Isthmus of Panama would take two weeks.

The clerk at the ship's offices questioned Harriet about her travel, dismayed she was alone. He warned her most other passengers were rough prospectors and camp followers headed for the California gold fields.

"This ain't no yacht for a lady, mam. The other women could be wives of missionaries or, to the other extreme, streetwalkers, to be frank. You best find some lady's maid to help with that there baby."

Harriet listened to the clerk shielded behind metal bars, open just enough for money, tickets, and papers to pass through. Such New Yorkers had a strange accent, a nasal whine, and strange vowels. "Park" came out "pack," not the New England "paak." Their manners were abrupt.

She had to agree she needed a nursemaid willing to travel and live in Hawaii. Her brother-in-law inquired among the hotel staff and nearby offices, but was ineffective. Back in their rooms, he announced that Harriet and the baby would have to return to Calais.

"That's ridiculous. Not on your life, Daniel. George needs me. I will go on, even alone. Here, take little Julia. I'll return by night."

Harriet plunged into the slums of New York.

North from the Battery, she followed streets to the intersection of Park, Worth, and Baxter streets, the area called Five Points. Structures were dismal, decayed industrial buildings mixed with tenements and houses, and the stench of backyard privies filled the air. Streets swarmed with feral children among garbage. Idle young men, sporting hats and fancy ill-matched suits, stood on street corners, loitering. One group approached her.

"Would youse be havin' some spare change, loidy?" one said in an Irish brogue.

"Sure she would, Kevin, caan't ya tell she's orange," answered another. "Would youse lend us that cloak?"

"Whatever are you talking about? I have nothing for you," said Harriet.

A cigarette dangled from the lips of another, his face scarred. "Wou' the lady have some timber?" Then, under his breath, "filch her bag, Sean."

Suddenly, Harriet realized she was surrounded. They began to prod her belongings and her person. She screamed.

"Help me. Get these men away from me."

The gang sneered at her cries, when, suddenly, their moods changed. All eyes looked past her. She turned and saw a larger pack of young men, some carrying clubs, others knives of various lengths.

"Oh, shit, it's the friggin' Natives. Let's shove off, lads. Quickly now." Her assailants tried to saunter away, but at the sudden lurch of the opposite gang, they sprinted down the street, hurling back curses.

A young man in a fancy stovepipe hat, double-breasted jacket, brocade waistcoat, and plaid trousers approached Harriet and doffed his hat.

"Sorry to see youse molested by them pug-uglies, mam. The bastard sons of Erin, they are. My boys will see they don't bother you again. Youse have to be careful back in these districts. It's no place for a lady, especially one – I suppose – new to Manhattan." Stepping back, the youth glanced over her wardrobe.

"Thank you for saving me from that group, but I am just shocked by the lawlessness here. Who are these gangs?"

"We're the Broadway Tricksters, the real Americans, Protestants, if you like; they're the foreigners, Irish Catholics. The invading hordes of Hibernia, trying to take over New York, but we'll put a stop to 'em. It's a war. Just which sides are youse?"

"I don't live here. Don't you work somewhere?"

"It's them Micks took our jobs, lady."

"What jobs? The Pug-whatever, the Irish, don't appear to be working either."

"Well, if it ain't *them* Micks, it's *other* Micks."

"Look, young man, maybe you would do a job for me."

"What is that?"

"I need to find a young lady who would be a lady's maid on a long voyage, maybe to leave New York forever."

"Who would do that? We love New York. Ain't no girl going to leave home for no long voyage."

His attitude was wearing thin, "In that case, would you direct me to the Negro district?" she asked.

"What fer? You want to hire a black to care for a white baby?"

"Let me remind you a second ago you said no girl you know would leave this 'patch of heaven'."

"Lady, the only thing we and the Micks agree on is hatin' blacks. If they catch one in the Irish neighborhood, they lynch him. Don't expect me to find you no black girl."

"Very well, then, just point in the direction where they live."

Harriet located New York's African neighborhood. She passed people sitting on steps, standing on sidewalks, but spoke to no one. She realized she had no plan. Then, she saw a church, Ebenezer African Methodist Episcopal.

"Would the pastor be in?" she asked.

"Yes, I am Pastor Jordan," said the booming bass voice, the very image of a Hebrew prophet of African vintage.

"May I take some of your time? I need your help."

That evening, Uncle Daniel was relieved to hear his sister- in-law's steps outside the hotel room. Daniel asked if she had any luck finding a lady's maid. Harriet answered by opening the door wide to reveal a young black woman.

"Daniel, I want to introduce Miss Molly Washington. She's willing to accompany us to Hawaii."

A young black woman stood inside the room dressed in gingham, sturdy shoes, a satchel grip in her hand. She looked about eighteen with a womanly figure, breasts filling her bosom. An ebony complexion and large brown eyes, she smiled with confidence at the uncle.

Molly Washington stepped forward, nodded to the man, and walked over to the dresser drawer where little Julia Deborah slept. She looked down at the baby, a smile coming over her face, her features opening, focused on the infant.

"Oh, ma'am, this here is a nice baby. Sleeps so fine. Oh, she starts in to fuss. You mind I pick her up? No need to cry, you little darlin'"

Harriet turned to Daniel. "You may leave tomorrow for home. I think Molly, Julia, and I will have a successful voyage."

Chapter Fifty-Five

"Mister George, the Baldwin's invitation says 'proper attire' for the party. Whatever's that?"

"Missus Chase would have worn her hoop dress and ruffles on the bodice and wrists. She also would wear her hair up. Be prepared by five o'clock. I shall walk as you ride the gelding."

"I been tryin ma best ta mount that red horse like a lady, Mister George, 'ceptin not yet with a hoop skirt."

Chase held Matilda's hand as her shoes negotiated down to the last wide step. She would use its height to launch onto the sorrel animal.

Matilda faced the saddle and grabbed the pommel with her left hand, hooking her left foot into the stirrups. Meanwhile, George stood, hands around her waist, ready to lift. Her right hand gathered up her hoops as her right foot sprang off the step. In one motion, she jumped and flung the hoop skirt over the horse's haunch while crooking her right knee around the pommel.

"How's that, Mister George?" She glanced around at the display of calico, her skirts spread over saddle and horse.

"Everything correct." He laughed. "Horse looks like it's wearing a blanket."

Matilda wore a broad sun hat to protect her complexion, rouged at cheek and lips. A bright ribbon flowed down from the hat's brim to below her bare shoulders. Her open-necked dress revealed her unblemished shoulders, back, and cleavage, pushed up with the whalebone corset stays. Only a glimpse of lace from her pantalets showed at her ankle above the stirrup.

George Chase led his ward through the dusty lanes of Lahaina, avoiding rotten mangos. Each step raised puffs of volcanic dust that settled on his shoes and trousers. Other than red tarnish below the knees, his appearance was impeccable with black stovepipe trousers, matching swallowtail coat, batwing-collared white shirt, and flowing cravat. On his head, he wore a silk top hat.

The couple passed native people who watched the procession under the shelter of trees or canopies, cross-legged, men in the *malo* loincloth, and women in the *muumuu* dresses. They murmured at how the *haoles* could tolerate such clothes.

Suited Hawaiian men took the bridle from Chase at the Baldwin's yard. Reaching up, the consul lifted Matilda down from the saddle to firm ground as she managed her hoop hem.

The Reverend Doctor and Missus Baldwin greeted their guests. The Hawaiian men had dressed like Americans, clothes ordered from Boston or tailored in Honolulu. The Hawaiian women's clothes were hand cut and stitched in Lahaina, but different in color. Instead of sober dark tones, the seamstresses had chosen bright calico colors; reds, yellows and blues.

Two matronly *wahine* sisters had given their seam-stress iron barrel hoops instead of light baleen to insert in the lining. Undaunted by the sheer weight of their dresses, the ladies turned slowly to counter the centrifugal momentum. One sister attempted to sit, and the inflexible iron hoop bumped her onto the floor, lifting skirts to the ceiling to expose a myriad of petticoats and pantaloons. Gentlemen righted the lady onto her feet, and her jolly laughter turned shock into merriment.

Matilda saw Paul among a group of young Hawaiian men, bilingual core of royal advisors. His nod in her direction acknowledged her presence. She smiled in return.

"Honorable Mister Chase, where have you been keeping this lovely creature?"

Matilda realized someone was referring to her.

"Yes, thank you, Willington. You remember my ward, Matilda Thigpen. I believe you met upon our first day at Lahaina."

Matilda curtsied to Snively. The man's gaze bored into her. Upon offering her hand, the man bent and kissed her knuckles, leaving a wet patch as if his tongue sought a taste of her skin. His breath stank of gin.

Willington turned to whisper audibly into Chase's ear.

"Say what, Chase, isn't this an odd conglomeration, the dusky deacons of a minstrel show mixing with the prissy puritans. Surely a peculiar congregation."

"And your point, Willington?"

"That these are two strange branches of the human species, having nothing in common, and who will be swept away by the tide of commerce. The future of these islands belongs to business interests. Missionaries and their Hawaiian converts are an impediment to progress."

"And yet you can accept their hospitality? I see you enjoy the refreshments."

"Careful, Chase. As Consul, your interests ought to lie with business."

"Business? What is my business, Mister Willington? To represent the United States, to resolve issues among parties such as the Hawaiian government and the whaling fleet and the sailor's welfare. It's possible to be fair and just and yet care for private interests."

The clerk rolled his eyes. Chase brushed him off.

"Thank you for your frankness. Now, Miss Thigpen and I will mingle with this – how did you put it – odd conglomeration."

Matilda found a chair free in the parlor and walked over, preparing to sit. The chair had low arms and stood against a wall. She turned her back and reached behind her, lifting the skirt until she reached the bottom hoop, which she held against her buttocks. She sat upon that hoop and the skirt lay firmly down upon the floor, a skill she had practiced only that afternoon.

Seeing Matilda Thigpen seated, Charlotte Baldwin saw an opportunity. Taking the arm of young Doctor David Dow, she drew him over to the young woman. Dow's thin frame, sallow skin, and receding hairline belied his twenty-eight years.

"Miss Thigpen, I would like to introduce Doctor Dow to your acquaintance. He has been a great blessing to my husband, especially during that awful epidemic last month. Perhaps you two shall find pleasant company."

Matilda smiled up at the doctor. He looked anywhere but at her.

"Doctor, indeed, Ah heard you was an absolute hero of the epidemic. Even sailed to Molokai to treat the poor people there, a true Christian gentleman." Her Southern accent oozed with sugary charm.

Dow's cheeks reddened. His eyes darted from her eyes to her shoulders. His voice lapsed into aphasic silence. Matilda became concerned he would collapse to the floor.

"Are you quite alright? You dear man. Should you have some refreshment?"

"Maybe you are right, Miss Thigpen." Dow slunk away to the punch bowl.

Matilda found herself alone on the chair, everyone engaged in conversation. Chase stood among a group of middle-aged men, intently discussing some weighty issue. Other young women occupied themselves. The matrons had formed a group examining some textile. From across the room, she caught Paul watching her, even as he spoke to another man.

Matilda walked across the room to the hallway table where she stepped back and halted. Carefully, she looked to the shelf beneath the table, stepping back and forth, adjusting her skirts. A mirror sat on the shelf, six inches above the floor, at an angle, for ladies to examine their hems to insure their ankles were covered. Satisfied, Matilda continued walking to join a bevy of matrons, including Charlotte Baldwin.

As Matilda approached, Charlotte separated from the ladies and met her.

"I do hope you are having a good time, Miss Thigpen. I wish there were more young people in Lahaina for your company."

"As busy as I am, keeping house for the Consul, I am grateful for your invitation to this party."

"Miss Thigpen, I must discuss a concern of mine if I may take the liberty to offer some advice from an experienced woman." Charlotte drew Matilda to a private space.

"May I consider you my young friend, Matilda?"

"Ah would be flattered that you do, Miz Baldwin, lost from my family as I am."

"Every young lady needs the guidance of a mother-figure, and here in Lahaina where society is so bewildering, a young person must choose her company carefully from a confusing array of races and classes. Oh, my, I believe I am witnessing the case in point. Would you please turn around?"

From their vantage point, they saw Paul had left his conversation and crossed the room to the hallway table, the exact place where Matilda had adjusted her skirts. Paul was halted a moment over the spot before the mirror, but instead of examining the table's lower shelf, he seemed to flex his chest, face lifted.

Charlotte drew Matilda's arm aside to follow Paul's path. The man walked across the room and sat down in the chair that Matilda had just vacated. Charlotte let out a tiny gasp.

"Did you see that?"

"See what?"

"It's the palpable lust of a helpless male."

"Paul Kamehameha?"

"He seeks the faintest manifestations of your female endowments." Charlotte Baldwin's eyebrows lifted, her nostrils flared, but her lips smiled. She emitted a tiny giggle.

"But, Missus Baldwin, what is going on? What is Paul doing?"

"You saw him stop at the table. He was entering a space you had just left where you adjusted your skirt. On the

315

chance your scent still remained, he breathed in the air. Next, he sat in that chair you had so recently vacated, knowing that your body heat remained on the cushions.

"Did I not see you riding with him?"

"Ah…yes, you did," Matilda admitted.

"You know Paul is Hawaiian and you are American. Were you not seated astride the saddle?" Charlotte Baldwin fixed her hands on her hips.

"Oh, but, Missus Baldwin, there's no proper sidesaddle in all of Lahaina, they're all built for cattlemen. That's the only way a person could ride up a mountain."

"You must be aware of the danger. Although I've never tried sitting astride, there are those who say the friction of the saddle stimulates urges dormant in a woman's loins."

"Huh? Urges? I don't understand."

"My dear, what innocence for the consul to protect! Just let me suggest that we do accept our Hawaiian friends as companions for social occasions. However, marriage isn't done between races."

"Beggin' your pardon, I did meet one gentleman in Honolulu with a colored wife an' livin' in the most genteel home. In our Bible study, my eyes just happen to read the third chapter, 28th verse of Galatians where it says there is *neither Jew nor Greek, neither bond nor free, neither male nor female for you are all one in Christ Jesus*, an' I be thinkin' it means there's no separatin' people."

"A wonderful application of the Word, my dear, and an opening for one of my ideas. The ladies of the Bible Study have been discussing the love that children have for you. We have a proposal. There are many American children around Lahaina too young for school who need to learn values through organized play and release their mothers for mission work. Of course, your services would be dully compensated. Is this proposal interesting to you?"

"You mean to get paid money, Miz Baldwin? To play with kids?"

"Back in Boston some have started a new idea called Kindergarten. Would you approach Mister Chase? I will encourage Reverend Baldwin to urge Consul Chase to permit you to teach this Kindergarten."

"I don't know if Mister Chase can spare me. First get Reverend Baldwin to ask so's the consul won't think I'm too uppity."

*   *   *

Across the room, Doctor Porter had cornered Chase.

"George, this situation is intolerable. I order supplies for the seamen's hospital and fewer are delivered than ordered. Somewhere between Lahaina and New York either money or supplies disappear. Someone is profiting from others' distress, and you have already guessed who I suspect. What are you going to do?"

"A trap has been laid for the fox, Charles. Meanwhile, I personally forward your orders to the medical firms. You will be receiving full supplies with the next shipment."

"Thank you, George. I hope you will dismiss the rogue. Did you see how disgustingly he oiled his way among the unattached young ladies?"

"Some men bring strange attitudes to adulthood, maintain no attachments, and think sex to be a weapon to wage war on the women, Charles."

"Pity, maybe, but caution, certainly."

Baldwin, meanwhile, approached through the thinning partygoers.

"Consul Chase, allow me to introduce Captain Edwards of the *George Washington*. He has a concern you may wish to address." Doctor Baldwin had brought over a rotund man with a florid complexion.

"How do you do, Captain Edwards? What seems to be the problem?"

"Transshipment, Chase. It's late in the season and I must unload my oil and bone for transfer back to Massachusetts. All the storage facilities here are full. What can I do?"

"Some of the Hawaiian farmers' sheds are yet available. Might cost you, though."

"Damn the cost, Chase. Just find me the space." The crowd paused at the curse.

Chase smiled. "Since this is a continuing problem at Lahaina, there should be a long range solution. Come to the office at dawn. I will make the arrangements."

*   *   *

Alice Richards found Charlotte Baldwin passing through the hallway as guests started to leave.

"May I speak with your, dear friend?"

"Of course, Alice, you sound concerned."

"I wanted to ask you about the new young lady, Matilda Thigpen. She has the most unusual appearance and the most peculiar manner of speaking and her grammar....well, it leaves me speechless. Is that a colored accent?"

"Heavens, Alice. It's all clear to me that's she's as white as you. Mister Chase explained her origins to me. She's the orphaned daughter of an English planter and his French Creole wife, raised in Alabama among Negro servants. She must have inherited that sensual mouth and hair from her French side. That girl was carried around by a black mammy the first three years of life. No wonder she plays loose with tenses and participles."

"Very well, then, but as a proper New Englander, I would discourage my sons from mixing with Southerners."

"If they were to try, they would be too late, my dear. I do hope that Consul Chase's wife soon appears to sort out complications."

Chapter Fifty-Six

The ship was a steamer, *The Illinois*, with two decks and three masts, 266 feet long and 40 feet wide, fitted with two oscillating steam engines and five hundred berths, filled by seven hundred passengers.

Harriet found all private cabins reserved. Missionary wives shared family quarters with their husbands and children, so Harriet and Molly were assigned to the women's general quarters. They were soon to discover the character of their companions.

The bunks in the women's steerage were stacked in threes with rows along portside, starboard, and down the center of the ship, each sleeping space five feet long. Women's steerage was separated by a partition aft from the men's forward position. A narrow door separated the two compartments.

Since there was no refrigeration, passengers shared the ship with a variety of livestock – chickens, turkeys, geese, ducks, sheep, pigs and cattle, all to be slaughtered on deck daily. The crowded conditions prevented table seating so diners lined up for plates of food, eating at berths.

Overcrowding, seasickness, rodents, and discomfort were not the only problems on board. The inadequate outhouses, intermittent structures along the railing, stunk if not flushed with buckets of seawater. The offal and blood of slaughtered animals, body odors, all contributed to diminishing appetites among the more genteel.

The first night, Harriet lay awake with the baby in the bunk beneath Molly, unaccustomed to the thrump-thrump beat of the steam pistons and the splash of the side-wheel. Since childhood, she had enjoyed voyages, sleeping on sailing ships with the pitching and yawing, but the stink of steerage and the noise of the power machinery disturbed her. Harriet soon lost interest in food.

On the first night after the women's quarters had settled, Harriet heard the squeak of the intermediary door to the men's quarters, then male whispered voices, entering the room, women's giggles answered.

Next morning, Molly confided to Harriet, "Miz Chase, these women on this ship is 'hoes.' I hear them toinin' tricks all night with men come through that door. We can't 'low that near this baby." Molly stood hand on hip, pointing a finger toward the sleeping infant.

"The clerk warned me about that. Just keep quiet for now. I will report this incident to the captain. I am so sorry to bring you into this trouble, a virtuous young woman among such rabble."

"Don't worry 'bout me, Miz Chase. I know white trash when I see it and I'm used to fightin' them in New York. These fancy gals bother me none. We're going fix us a nice trip; ain't no sluts going to ruin our time."

That morning, Harriet marched up to a mate and requested an appointment with the ship's master. The mate took her to the captain, standing at the helm, where she reported the incident, saying it must be stopped at once or there would be a scandal if government officials learned a brothel was operating aboard a United States commissioned vessel. She added the information she was the wife of a United States consul. The captain stifled a smile and assured her that the carpenter would install a lock between the quarters. Harriet withdrew satisfied.

*   *   *

"Shut that damn baby up, woman," someone yelled at Harriet from across the quarters. "I ain't going to hear no baby scream all the way to Panama. You can take it up on deck and walk it to sleep."

"Miz Chase, you don't need to pay no attention. That woman rude. Little Debbie not makin' no big fuss." Molly's voice was more audible than necessary for Harriet.

"Hey, black girl, you talking' back at me?" The rude one came over – large, pockmarked, greasy hair, fists clenched. Harriet was ready to apologize for the child to make peace. Surely, she would understand, wasn't every woman born with maternal instincts?

She faced Harriet, "I ain't layin' awake nights listnin' to that kid of youse. Shut that kid up." She raised her hand to poke Harriet, but jerked it back when Molly stepped between the women, face inches away, hands on hips, elbows and shoulders bend forward.

"Look, bitch, get your ugly face back to that bunk. Ain't no ofay bitch goin' to mess with this lady and her baby." Molly's head wobbled in anger.

"Ain't no nigger goin' to sass me." The bully pushed Molly's shoulder.

"I give you a chance, bitch, now you goin' to pay."

Molly's open hand shot forward and slapped the woman's face. The smack echoed across the bulkheads, and heads bobbed up. The force knocked the woman back, reeling. She shrieked, returning with claws, grabbing at hair, clothes. Ducking the whirl of wild fists, jabbing at openings, Molly's hand repeatedly smacked her face and blood flowed from nose and lips, until the woman fell backward onto the floor. Her eyes stared up from a mass of bloody flesh and hair. Molly straddled her, hands at the ready.

"Had enough, bitch?"

The woman rolled over, crawled to her bunk, faced the wall, and drew up her legs. Molly shrugged, slowly surveying the shocked faces among the herd of whores. Satisfied, she returned to her frightened mistress.

Chapter Fifty-Seven

By November 1853, the great whaling fleet converged on the ports of Honolulu and Lahaina. In Lahaina's Roads between the islands of Maui, Lana'i and Moloka'i anchored those ships whose captains favored the better water, the better produce, and the best entertainment of the islands. The first ships began arriving October 5th, the last ships at the end of December, filling the Roads with black hulls and a forest of fir masts, planted in a tropic paradise.

That fall, Chase recorded one hundred and twenty-three ships, barks, and brigs – some full-rigged and some hermaphrodites. In the peak day of November 25th, eleven vessels registered. That season, George Chase recorded 38,539 tons of shipping, manned by 2,453 Americans and 775 "foreigners." The fleet had harvested 3,550 barrels of Sperm oil and 80,225 barrels of other whale oil. He also noted in his report to the Department of State that the fleet brought in one million eighty thousand, five hundred pounds of whalebone for the corsets and umbrellas of the world.

Each vessel would remain about two weeks to re-stock food, water, and clothing, to repair rigging or ship parts, and to off-load the casks of oil and whalebone. The ships also used the time to wash down the decks, launder clothing, and scrub men after months of dirt and grease from blubber processing.

*   *   *

Banging woke up George. Matilda called up from below.

"Mister George, some man be knockin' the door down. See what the matter is."

Chase flung open the top portion of the Dutch door to see Paul and the constables.

"Big trouble, Chase. The whale men are rioting. Busting up grog shops, beating up our people, attacking women. They only laugh at the police. Please come."

Chase threw on trousers, jacket and hat, and followed Paul and the worried constables. He first walked to the Master's Reading Room and saw ship captains on the porch overlooking Front Street. Looking up, he entreated them to join him on the street.

"It's your seamen who are rioting, gentlemen. Come down at once."

They followed the consul to the scene. A high stone stood to the side of Front Street, used to mount tall horses. Chase climbed to the stone's crest with ship captains arrayed behind.

"You men are out of order," he shouted at the mob. "This is a riot and a violation of Hawaiian law."

The crowd laughed at the odd sight of a shirtless, shoeless consul.

"The royal constables will be forced to take action."

"Let 'em try," they yelled.

"I'm warning, constables will have to fire unless you disperse."

"Then, we'll kill all the darkies," shouted a ringleader.

"Men, let me appeal to your better angels. Don't listen to bullies among you."

Most stopped to listen to their consul.

"Who among you seamen have found me a ready advocate? Which of you could say the consul's door was ever barred against him? How many of your friends now lay in hospital under my ministrations?"

"Git down off there. Forget him, boys. Let's tear up this town," a profane swab addressed his comrades.

"Constables, jail that man. Away with him to the Hale Pa'ahao."

Chase directed the Hawaiian constables, but they milled in confusion, afraid to confront the mariners until

Paul stepped out of the crowd. His bulk loomed over the skinny sailors.

"Let police do their work, men," Chase cautioned the mob.

Paul Kamehameha's ham-sized hand came down on the drunk and lifted him to the constables who marched off to be shackled to Lahaina prison's wall.

"Now, your captains want you all to return to your ships. Your fun is over. Reverend Baldwin, please set over here with me" Chase waved to the missionary.

The two conferred, watching captains herd crews toward ship tenders.

"My friend, Lahaina needs another plan for these seamen. The threat of the law isn't enough." George Chase took Baldwin to his wife, Charlotte, on their veranda as the streets emptied of seamen.

"I was thinking the same thing, Consul. Something positive, something appealing to the young sailors, something to dissuade them from grog shops and the dusky Didoes."

"It's a rare sailor boy who comes to the church, Reverend. Yours or the Maria Lanakila. Perhaps it's time for a seamen's Bethel, a chapel just for them like they have in New Bedford, Massachusetts."

"My dear Chase, I am so pleased to hear such a suggestion from a confirmed skeptic."

"Would you approach the Congregational convention on the issue of an appropriate chapel? It will take a very special clergyman to appeal to the men, one with a calling to the project. Now, please excuse me while I confer with the native police."

*   *   *

Notices posted in American seminaries from Princeton to Harvard: *Opportunity. Pastor to the seafarers. A seamen's Bethel has been established at Lahaina on Maui to minister to the whaling fleet. A special pastorate for one called for spiritual warfare. Apply to the Congregational Churches of the Sandwich Islands. Young men with bearing encouraged.*

At Andover Seminary, a hulking redhead tore off the notice and barged into the provost's office. With only passing grades in the dead languages of Latin, Greek and Hebrew, Samuel Youngblood excelled only in preaching. The provost recommended Youngblood as gifted for such a mission, and the young seminarian departed that Christmas.

*   *   *

"Chase, Chase," a familiar voice rang across Lahaina's square. Paul Kamehameha called from the store fronts. "Can we talk?"

The consul hesitated, opening his door and looked to see his assistant, Willington, missing from his desk. He invited the head of Maui's constables into his office. The men sat opposite the consul's desk.

"Would you like to know people say good things about the consul?" Paul began, a broad smile on his face.

"Which people?"

"Hawaiian people, the Kanaka Maoli, especially at court. They say he is a good *haole,* understands us." Paul answered.

"But what does their chief constable say?" Chase countered.

Paul laughed, "The chief constable has to admit he was wrong. Chase is not a liar and protects Maui, be it sickness or drunken sailors."

"Good. Then I want to talk to you about something important."

"What's that?" Paul asked.

"Have you the men to build something significant, Paul? A building of masonry and framing?"

"I think so. My crew has the experience, building the Hale Aloha after the smallpox. What is your plan?"

"There's good money to be made in a warehouse to store the casks and bone as the whalers depart for more hunting. Someone should be an agent, charging the whalers, storing the materials, paying to transship aboard passing cargo ships, and keeping the difference. As the consul, I cannot be that agent, but I can pay for the construction, make the investment, and hire someone to manage."

"Hire a manager? Not me. Perhaps a partner, if you can be an equal with a native," advised Paul.

"I've visited the coffee and sugar plantations and tasted taro. With ships dependent on the islands between America and the orient, your future is farming. Hawaii is an oasis in an ocean desert."

"Some say only more for *haoles* to exploit," Paul shot out.

"Paul, Paul, I know what other Americans say. I hear them. 'If only the Hawaiians could change. The Hawaiian language as taught up the mountain at Lahainaluna Academy has neither history nor literature. How can those people promote equality with other civilized nations unless that language is abandoned?'"

"Many nations speak unique languages, yet prosper. The Scots speak Gaelic. The Swiss speak three languages," Paul argued.

Chase nodded in agreement.

"Yes, yes. I hear them slur the island people behind your backs. 'Consider the yeoman farmers of the Connecticut Valley', they say. 'Success in a cold climate and rugged soil! The sloth among Hawaiians! Prosperity of every nation begins with its industrial classes, no one becomes wealthy who's indolent, none moral whose daughters are not the vestals of virtue'."

Paul's head shook from side to side.

"Through a thousand years, we adapted to these islands, yet whites pronounce us failures because we don't turn into New England farmers. Twenty years among New England people showed me their shortcomings. That harsh climate drives Americans into madness: constant grasping toward business schemes, warfare on nature, and church arguments," Paul taped his chest,"…and forbidden to marry Sarah Thompson."

"Sorry, old man. I could have made that work out for you. Have I noticed an attraction between you and my niece?"

"Here we have no law to forbid marriage between races, and Matilda's no child who needs permission from you." Paul stood up, his face darkened.

Chase stood. He turned to watch the harbor from his window. He slowly turned back.

"Calm down, friend. I know about your jaunts on horseback into the mountains." Chase waved Paul back into his seat. "I know you will be a gentleman with her. She's my precious child until I place her into some other man's hands."

*   *   *

Willington opened the consulate at the usual hour, wondering when Chase would appear. He awaited the morning mail, eager for correspondence from the States.

A foot scraped, he looked up to see Matilda Thigpen at the entrance.

"Sir, I stopped to tell you Mister Chase be not comin' today. He sick last night and layin' to bed. Is there anything I kin take him?"

The clerk stood from his stool and walked over to the girl. He grinned.

"Step into the Consulate. There's something I have to ask you, Miss Thigpen."

She entered the door, which the man closed. "What is it, Mister Willinton?"

"Do I detect just the slightest indication that you may not be what you say you are? Do I hear the vestige of Negro speech coming from your sweet mouth? Maybe there's a little nigger in your woodpile."

She blanched. "I don't know what you mean?" She turned, but he bared the door.

"Not so quick, sweetheart, I believe I have something you want back."

"What?" she pouted.

"Your secret." He toyed with the girl's blond ringlets.

"There is no secret. Let me out"

"You lie, little hussy. But, I'm willing to strike a bargain."

"I need no bargain. Now I must leave." She pushed against his shoulder.

"How about a little kiss?"

"No, let me go."

He pushed the girl against the office wall. Pinning her with his left hand, his right delved her breasts. "Always wanted to cut a wooly ball of yarn." He rubbed himself against her thigh and tongued her ear, knocking her bonnet back.

Matilda screamed and struck out, clawing at his eyes. He flinched as her nails pierced his cheeks. Suddenly, the door flung open and a huge figure blocked the frame.

"Heard a lady scream here. What's going on, ma'am?" A man with shocking red head and beard set in a blushed, freckled face looked Snively Willington up and down. He put a paw on the little man's shoulder. "Could he be taking advantage here?"

"Government property!" squeaked Willington. "You can't be in here."

Grabbing Willington's collar and belt, the redhead lifted and threw him out the door and onto the dust. "Now we're off government property. Tell me, ma'am, what's happening before I do some damage to him."

"No idea what Mister Willington wants from me, never not give him no encouragements. 'Fraid goin' to upset Mister George," Matilda babbled.

Her rescuer asked, "Is this Chase, the consul, I knocked down?" He stood back, surveying Willington as he lay in a heap. He started to bend down and offer help.

328

"Heavens no. That's his assistant," she adjusted her bonnet.

"Take me to Chase, little lady. Both of us have some urgent business. Report this attack, and tell him the chaplain for the Seamen's Bethel, Samuel Youngblood, just arrived."

Chapter Fifty-Eight

December 25, 1853

Dearest Momma,

Christmas Day!! How I miss home. Don't hardly seem like Christmas with the warm weather.

So many wonderful things have happened this month. Mister George sent that Willinton away. Mister George is so smart, proved that that clerk was stealing from the hospital, has letters from a doctor's supply company to prove it. Willington was sent back to America in irons.

He gave me a nice Christmas present of clothes. Now I have three dresses and lots petty coats.

December 30, 1853

Dear Momma,

I forgot to write about the KINER GARDEN.

Miz Charlotte and the church ladies asked me to take on children too young for real school. White folks used to keep their kids behind fences, teach them with tutors, like the Thigpens at home. The Hawaiians and mixed kids go to missionary school, sit together.

The white ladies want their kids learn to get along with Hawaiian kids. So, I began this month, a few ones, boys and girls, here at the consul's home.

School began. Blond boys in uniforms, shorts and jackets. Blue eyed girls in piniefores. The first children didn't know nothin' 'bout playin. I have to teach those kids to play circle games, tag games, blind games, word games, duck-duck-goose, fox-and-geese. By friday they were laughin.

Some white mens has Hawaiian wives so their children are mixed. They asked Miz Charlotte if their kids could have this KINER GARDEN, too. Miz Charlotte said yes.

The mixed children already new how to play. They needed to learn to listen when I talk. Storytime and they still want to run around. I say watch the white children, how they sit and listen. They start to be friends, now. Learn from each other.

Then, my school got a new student.

Prince Liholiho. The king wanted his boy to attend the new little people's school cause he never played with no kids. King Kow-y-kee-a-oolee says maybe his boy can attend school with other children.

Prince start before Christmas. While the mommas bring their boys and girls, the whole royal household brought the prince.

Jest to see him you know he's different. Shaved head, cept a braid on one side, tattoos all over and that all he wear on the first morning. Buck necked like a little brown monkey.

This boy has his own servants, wait hand and foot, he point and they fetch. <u>Spoiled Rotten</u> only starts to describe this boy. Take what he want and his hand never be slapped.

Servants follow him from the palace. Prince walks under a feather parasol, necked like a baby, down the middle of the road. Servants hoverin round him. Prince stop to make pee. Servants catch it in a jar, cause that's <u>royal pee.</u>

My children at school already when this parade arrived. Prince's headman say, "Prince come to school" like a big announcement. I guess my girls did never see no naked boy before, theys eyes poppin out. Boys want to know what <u>wrong</u> with this boy.

I say to that headman, finger in his face, "You jest take that boy home and dress him proper. No child here is necked. That boy come with pants and shirt. Shoes would be good too."

Those servants were afraid to give the prince the news. All timid-like they tell him no clothes, no school and he threw a fit right there, a-screamin and a-cryin. I don't know their Hawaiian yet, but he heard my American alright.

STOP THAT NOISE, now get on home and dress like a schoolboy.

You know, he stopped. I guess nobody every spoke to him like that in any lingo. Headman told him what's what and he run on home with the servants.

Prince came back in clothes, but next the servants want to join KINDER GARDEN too, but I make them stay outside the gate. That boy got to learn some sense.

Remember the Epaminandus story? How his Momma say you ain't gots the sense you was born with? Prince Liholiho ain't got the sense he was born with cause it got all spoilt out of him.

Chapter Fifty-Nine

The Illinois arrived at the Isthmus with a gaunt passenger.

"You just let me take that baby, Miz Chase." Molly Washington bathed little Debbie, dressed her in clean clothes, and brought the clean infant to Harriet for nursing.

"Wake up now, Miz Chase," Molly roused the weak mother. She clucked her tongue to see dark rings under the woman's eyes and sunken cheeks above her jaw.

While Molly had adapted to the ship's motion and routine, Harriet wasted away with vomit and diarrhea as the vessel crossed the Caribbean. Every time the baby came away from nursing angry with hunger, Molly Washington mollified the infant with a 'sugar tit' of cotton rag dipped in molasses.

Finally, in early November the *Illinois* landed at Chagres. With the help of crewmen, Molly brought a thin and feeble Harriet onto the dock among her luggage. There an Anglo gentleman dressed in white approached the women.

"Would this be the party of Missus George M. Chase?"

Harriet answered, too debilitated to stand, "Yes, it would."

"I am William Nelson, American consul to Panama City. I have come to bring you to your Pacific ship."

Consul Nelson's men carried the luggage to his carriage, strapping all to the boot. Seating the ladies in cushioned comfort, one man drove the carriage while the other rode behind. Once the carriage arrived in Panama City on the Pacific Ocean, Nelson made arrangements for Harriet and her lady's maid on the ship, *California,* bound for San Francisco. Consul Nelson reserved a first class stateroom for the Chase party on the next voyage. Meanwhile, Harriet and

Molly remained at his residence, nursed by Missus Nelson's attention. In a few days, Harriet walked into a suite of rooms on the ship, ate at a table with all the amenities of first class service. Both baby and mother gained weight.

Molly Washington, daughter of fugitive slave parents, raised in the ghetto of Manhattan, interpreted the four weeks aboard the *California* and the following month aboard the *Frances Palmer* as forerunners of a new life. She savored the clean sheets on a generous mattress, ate all courses, stroked upholstery and wood paneling, and promenaded beside Harriet at sunset. The baby accompanied the women to all activities, which excused Harriet's insistence that a black girl join her in the first class dining room, to feed and hold Baby Debbie. While it was no surprise that no other blacks were present among the first class Anglos and Latinos, she also noted that no black faces were seen in steerage, either.

"Miz Chase, maybe there's other colored people in the Sandwich Islands? Ain't none here in this ship."

"The Sandwich Islanders are a kind of colored race, Molly. But, if you ask about American Negroes, I don't know. We will inquire when we arrive."

The *Frances Palmer* approached Oahu Island on New Year's Eve, 1853. Harriet and Molly joined the other passengers on starboard, watching the island's beaches, the Diamond Head, the palm trees on the shore, then the city of Honolulu built from shore to mountainside. The ship turned into the Pearl Harbor and tied up.

That night, the ladies checked into a comfortable hotel. After supper they walked through the city, watching revelers prepare for New Year's Eve parties and dances. Allowing the girl some freedom from her responsibilities, Harriet carried five-month-old Debbie.

Dressed in light clothes, young Molly pranced along the plank sidewalk clicking her shoes on the boards, glad to be free from two months shipboard confinement. Her eyes scanned the crowds among the buildings and streets and wondered at the mix of Asians, Polynesians, and whites.

Some were dressed formally, but most in light clothes and barefoot.

Suddenly, a tall, slender gentleman cut across the street's crowds. He wore white formal clothes, white shirt, a white top hat, and in his hand a white cane. Molly couldn't see his face until he sprang on the walkway, straight at her. When he removed his hat, he revealed an African face, as dark as mahogany.

"How are you ladies tonight? Out for a walk?" He addressed them both with lavish courtesy. "Allow me to introduce myself, George Hyatt at your service." He flipped off his top hat and bounced his cane.

Molly was struck speechless. Harriet rose to the challenge and introduced them both to the man.

"Will this crowd celebrate the New Year in taverns?" she asked.

"They call taverns 'grog shops' here, madam. But the better sort of folk will dance at parties at homes and clubs. May I stroll with you; some of the men may be rude with drink."

He asked about their voyage, revealing he had arrived from New Orleans two years before, providing Honolulu with its first American musical conductor.

Finally, Molly found her voice.

"Mister, are there other colored people in this city, or are we the only ones?"

"Young lady, there are about twenty-five African men in Honolulu. How they do all depends on personal effort, there being no color bar. We live where we want to live, go where we want to go. There's just one problem."

"What's that?"

"Loneliness, caused by a definite lack of African ladies." He stopped and looked at her. She returned the gaze.

"Unfortunately, ladies, I must depart for my evening appointment. Everyone in Honolulu knows my whereabouts, if you would want to contact me." With that, he returned to the street, a ghost absorbed in the milling mob.

The next morning, Harriet packed for the last leg of the long voyage; the short trip to Maui Island. Molly prepared the baby. Harriet noticed her examining her hands.

"What's the matter, Molly Washington? Is there something you want to say?"

"Yes, ma'am. I have something important to tell you. But first you got to sit down."

Molly placed her hand on Harriet's. She looked into the older woman's eyes.

"Miz Harriet, now that the voyage is over an' we reached these Sandwich Islands, I figure you won't be needin' me anymore. Maybe you an' your mister can find someone for service on your island."

"You want to stay in Honolulu, don't you?" Harriet smiled at the young woman. "Who could blame you?"

"I figure I have a place here and folks to talk to. They'll help me get a start."

"Smart girl, Molly, build your own life. Then, when my husband and I visit this city, we'll have a friend. Here." Harriet pressed bank notes into the girl's hands. "This will keep you some months until you're established."

Molly bundled the baby one last time and accompanied Harriet to the docks for the inter-island packet boat. There, the older woman offered some maternal advice about men and their intentions. Molly chided Harriet to gain back the weight she lost.

"That husband goin' to wonder where his wife's figure gone when he see you."

Harriet sat on an inside bench, amid her luggage. The baby gurgled in a white blanket. The boat's decks were filled with people, their belongings, and farm animals, all squabbling. Women sprawled on the bulkheads, playing cards, eating fruit, and entertaining children. On the quay, Molly waved and blew kisses until the boat hove out of sight, then turned, dry-eyed, to march into her new city.

Chapter Sixty

George Chase prepared the report for the Department of State, calculations on the whaling industry from June through December of 1853. He filled in the forms and wrote summations in a florid script, about to sprinkle sand to soak up extra ink when a boy burst into the consulate.

"Mister, you got to come. Wife on packet. She sick."

George raced to the tender's dock and let rowers to take him out to the steamer from Honolulu. Alongside, uniformed officials surrounded a fallen figure, one cradling Harriet's head. Another official held a small package in his arms.

George leaped over the sides of both boats and onto the deck. He knelt down. He could hardly recognize her face, hair soaked and plastered to her skull, cheeks sunk, dark-ringed eyes. Her bonnet clung by ribbons to her neck. Harriet's figure lay limp.

"My God, Harriet! Where is the baby?" Chase knelt and lifted her into his arms.

"We were afraid to move her, mister. The passengers found her laying on the floor, the baby crying beside her. She your wife?"

"Help me carry her into the tender." They laid her body across the thwarts. Chase shielded from the sun with his right hand while holding the infant, Debbie, with his left. "Get us to shore fast, men."

Matilda saw the oxcart pull into the yard and stop at the wide steps. Mister George lifted clothes with both arms, so gentle. What has he brought home? She left Leilei to run down the veranda's stairs.

Then, she saw a woman's face buried deep in the rumpled clothing, her bonnet swallowing her head. Carrying Harriet, George rushed past her to the second floor and laid the woman in his bed. She moaned faintly when he drew out his arms.

"Is this Miz Harriet? What happen? She sleepin? She sick?"

"We won't know what happened until she awakes and talks, Matilda. Look how thin, maybe sick throughout the voyage." George's voice had the tone of hopelessness. He had never seen a normal person become so emaciated. "Right now, we should get that fever down, I suppose." He sat on the bed's edge, shoulders slumped, and stared at Harriet's face.

"Mister George, you sit there, keep her company. I'm goin' for some cold water, fresh from the pump to chill that fever."

"Check on the baby, too."

"Baby? What baby? Oh, yeah, she was bringin' a baby."

Matilda raced down the stairs and out into the yard. The Hawaiian cart driver stood at the base of the stair, holding a bundle.

"Baby?" he asked.

She snatched the bundle from the man's hands and marched to the pump.

"Your momma's goin' to be alright, child. Don't fret none."

She called over for Leilei to take the baby as water pumped in a pail. When she carried the bucket up to the bedroom, she paused for cotton rags. Leilei followed. She found Chase still seated.

"Now, Mister George, you need to leave this room cause I need to undress Miz Harriet from her travelin' clothes and bathe her. Best clean up that baby, too. What's its name?"

"That depends, is it a girl or boy?"

Matilda probed into the baby's diaper.

"It's a girl with a big mess." She stood fists on hips.

"Her name is Deborah, Debbie for short. Must be five months old and my first time to see her." He cradled the infant, one hand under its head.

Matilda turned to Chase, her hands on his arms, eyes to his. "Mister George, you want to help? Go to fetch Doctor Porter, bring them quick." She pushed him gently from the room.

Matilda unfastened the blouse and chemise, skirt and petticoats, corset, underclothes and shoes, and tossed them in a damp pile. She washed the pale body, noticing how bones protruded under her skin – shoulders, ribs, knees, points of her hips. When she saw how deflated Harriet's breasts were, she realized the baby needed nursing.

"Leilei, go fetch Paul Kamehameha. Tell him it's important."

She hurried the washing, changing the bedclothes, and covered Harriet.

Leilei returned with an excited Paul, just as Chase brought Charles Porter into the house.

"Can you find a wet nurse in Lahaina?"

"What's that, Miss Thigpen?"

"A lady with a new baby and milk to spare. She will have to stay here with her baby, live here until Missus Chase recovers."

"I will try, can her family come, too? Sleep in the cookhouse? Who would want to do such a thing as nurse a strange child?"

"What? This will be a great honor, to nurse the Consul's child. Tell them only the best woman will be chosen. Now, go."

Doctor Charles Porter examined the patient, his friend from Calais, Harriet Chase. He felt for her neck glands, looked into her throat, listened to her breathing and heart rate then stood.

"George, this may only be some kind fever, brought on by fatigue and weakness from travel. Or it could be the Panama fever. You can see she hasn't eaten well for many weeks. I don't see typhus or cholera. She needs cold compresses and plenty of clear water to bring down that temperature. As soon as she's fit to hold food, she needs good nutrition. Don't expect a fast recovery. It will take weeks to recover. You are lucky to have young Matilda. Otherwise, you'd be nursing both wife and baby."

*   *   *

Matilda entered the bedroom with toast and tea and found two eyes fixed on hers.

"Miz Harriet, shore is good to see y'all sittin' up. May I feed you this or can you manage?"

"Still too weak. I fear I shall drop the cup." A flicker of a smile crossed her face.

Matilda sat at the bed's edge and tore off bits of toast which she stuck into Harriet's mouth, alternating with sips of sugared tea.

"Debbie?" Harriet jumped at remembering her child.

"Leilei has her downstairs with the wet nurse, Miz Harriet. Y'all don't have no cause to worry 'bout that. Little Debbie doin' real fine. Want to see her?"

"Oh, please, yes. But, first, do tell me your name, dear?"

"I'm Matilda Thigpen. Mister George at the Consulate now and be home presently. Won't he be surprised to see you awake?" She gathered up remnants of the meal and called down the stairs. A Hawaiian teenager walked into the room, clad in a bright muumuu, with a pink baby.

"My baby, my baby." Harriet held out her arms. The teenager looked to Matilda who nodded consent, and Leilei laid the infant in Harriet's arms. Harriet opened her bodice, exposing her breast to the baby's mouth.

"Miz Harriet, you sure you want to try that? It's been three weeks since you left that boat, and your milk's not gonna let down. Your Paul K, he's got us a fine wet nurse with plenty of pap."

Harriet ignored Matilda, adjusting breast or child to release the precious fluid. Tears welled up in her eyes. She tried the other side.

"Baby's hungry. I can't. Poor thing," she laid back, surrendering.

"Baby Debbie is goin' well, gained weight since your illness, mam. We got a nice native woman. Brought her family. Husband, kids, dogs. Leilei, here, explains things to her. Free yourself of worry about that child. We have a whole Hawaiian village at your beck and call." She gave a hearty laugh. Leilei took the child from Harriet's feebly clinging arms.

"Is this my house…my baby? Just what is your name again?"

"Matilda Thigpen, ma'am. Yes, this is your home in Lahaina. You got a big piece of ground, a well, outside cookhouse, a veranda, three bedrooms, big downstairs, lots of windows, close to town, a short walk to the sea. You got a pretty house, Miz Harriet."

"How is Mister Chase? Is he well?"

"Mostly. Y'all's husband is a very important American, almost as much as Doctor Baldwin, the pastor. He's so busy with the whaling ships, sometimes he be late for supper. Now, jest you rest until he come home."

She returned downstairs.

Harriet contented herself by looking out the window at the strange mountains and bright birds. She listened to Matilda's orders to Leilei and the girl's to other Hawaiians. Voices and barks mixed, a village just under her window. She stirred the day's events in her mind until sleep returned like a curtain.

*   *   *

She woke to her husband's heavy treads, mounting stairs two at a time.

"Well, Missus Chase, the patient wakes and takes sustenance." He carried flowers in a vase.

"Oh, George, Thank God. I almost slipped away from you." She reached out frail hands.

"Perish the thought. You are well on the road to good health, thanks to Matilda, Paul, and the whole town."

"Paul? Will I see him soon?"

"All things in time, my dear." He sat on the bed's edge and kissed her cheek.

Harriet rose up on her elbows. Her voice gathered strength.

"Now, dear husband, tell me about this Matilda Thigpen," she examined his eyes. "She lives here, does she not? How long have you and she occupied this house? That sugary Southern accent, such a charming girl." The remark dripped sarcasm.

"I can explain, Harriet."

"She refers to you in familiar terms, *Mister George*."

"There's a clear explanation, dear."

"I remember your letter describing a colored girl as our maid. Where is this colored girl?" Her eyes bore into him.

"My dear Harriet, there has been no indiscretion. We have much to tell each other, and you will be pleased with my story."

George described that day in Washington, D.C. when he discovered the slave market before his orientation at State. The disgusting spectacle, black people sold like cattle, the pretty mulatto – he omitted the stripping of her dress. He described the secret meeting with Senator Salmon Chase, and the proposal for assisting the fugitive.

"She's colored? Matilda's the mulatto girl on the auction block? Can they be blond and blue eyed? Wait. You assisted a fugitive slave to escape?" She fell back on the pillows. "How did you get her away?"

He told of the night meeting with Tubman, the Quaker captain, slipping out of the Chesapeake ahead of the slave catchers, the discrete living quarters, discovering her raw literacy, the urgency to improve her speech, her transformation from frightened fawn to full woman, the tutorials in speech, writing, and manners, the crew's admiration, the villainous O'Malley, shopping in Ciudad Panama, the Pacific voyage, her polished entrance into society, dining on ship or at table.

"So, how do you explain her existence here? Who do we say she is, so I may continue the ruse?"

"She is a distant niece, orphaned by the death of her parents. The trick has worked. She charms the missionary families, the unattached young people, and Hawaiian society. She is at ease with peasants or princes. She even started a Kindergarten."

"A teacher, then?"

"Remarkable, eh? Her talents are many. My only concern is Paul Kamehameha's attraction to her."

"Oh, Paul...Paul is still unmarried?" Her eyes widened, and George caught an unguarded emotion at the mention of Paul.

"Yes. He remains unattached." He said cautiously. "I suppose it has taken him years to heal from the bitterness over Sarah Thompson." He looked away.

"I don't understand." Harriet turned him back to look into his eyes. "Given her mixed ancestry, why wouldn't you promote their friendship?"

He looked her full in the face.

"Paul can become hostile at times. An angry man who might seek revenge against an American official. Think of the consequences if she disclosed my role in her escape during an unguarded moment. Paul could use that information to ruin me."

He gestured, his fingers drawing a banner newspaper headline. "U.S. Consul Secrets Fugitive Slave."

"I didn't think of that," she pondered.

"Harriet, don't interfere, and, as for the *Mister George,* she grew up addressing her master by his Christian name. It's a proper Southern custom."

Harriet crossed her arms and scowled. "But she insists on calling me *Miz Harriet.*"

Chapter Sixty-One

Harriet walked downstairs to the veranda and sat on a cushioned rocker, overlooking the cookhouse to watch Matilda and Leilei. Baby Debbie sat on her lap, tearing petals from a flower. She invited Matilda to fix tea and join her in the shade.

"Mister George told me how you came to travel with him."

The girl hesitated for several minutes. As she spoke, she looked at her hands.

"Yes, ma'am. Your husband saved my life. I was raised to be a colored lady, one who read and stay in the house doin' lady's work; they were fixin' to sell me. It was God's will your husband stopped them. Mister George is no ordinary man, never once disrespectful, treat me like his daughter. It frighten me, not knowin' how to act white, but he patient and teach me proper talk."

"I understand Paul Kamehameha likes you. Do you know this?" Harriet looked for her reaction.

Matilda's brow wrinkled. "Paul court me before Christmas."

Harriet sipped from her cup.

"If you and Paul were to become close, he would want to know more about your family."

"I'd tell him our lie, that I'm your niece." Matilda suggested. She busied her hands, peeling mango.

"Mister Chase and I have no secrets from each other, dear." Harriet insisted.

"What you sayin, that if Paul wants to marry me, I haf to tell the truf?" The girl stopped cutting.

"The first truth is your feelings for this man. Do you want him?" Harriet asked.

Matilda Thigpen's eyes grew large. "Oh, Miz Harriet, is that possible for me to have a husband as nice as that?"

"The question ought to be, my dear, if Mister Kamehameha deserves a wife as nice as you. You and I shall be partners to explore this possibility. Meanwhile, mums the word to Mister Chase. He will be apprised of this at some other time."

"But, I thought you two have no secrets."

Harriet put her finger to pursed lips. "Shhh."

*   *   *

Paul entered the compound from the dusty street behind Lahaina prison. Mango trees hung with heavy fruit sheltered the modest home of thatched roof with walls of adobe. Naked toddlers played with puppies in the yard. Great blossoms gave off a sweet musk. A lavish garden graced the far side of the property in full sunlight next to a stream running from the mountain.

A man sat next to the stream, alone. Paul joined him.

"Teacher, it is good to see you up and about," Paul said in Hawaiian.

"Oh, my best student, you take time for an old man. You are important man now, Pele." His voice rasped Paul's birth name.

"Never important as the Great David Malo – teacher, author, *kahuna*. Hawaiian people owe you much."

"No *kahuna*, Pele. I have discarded the pagan for new faith and await my time in Paradise. I ask only to be buried above the school on Mount Ball, beyond the tide of foreign invasion. May I offer you something to slake your thirst?" The blind Malo gestured to his home.

"No, Teacher. I come to ask your advice."

"Advice to the young should be offered only if solicited."

"I am troubled, *kamaaina*. I am in love."

"Is she beautiful, Pele? Does your heart leap to the sound of her voice? Is she delicate and sensual? Does she have intelligence?" The old man smiled.

347

"She is all I ever wanted. Beautiful face, a body made for love, children adore her, a person of character. I could not expect more." Paul's toe kicked the dust.

"But, why troubled, then?"

"She is *haole*."

"Her parents forbid the match?" Malo scowled.

"Her guardian is the consul, Chase, who taught me how to live in America."

"He stands in your way?"

"In America, he enforced the strange *kapu* against white women, but now he's shattered the *kapu,* but there is something that makes him uncomfortable. "

"Maybe or maybe not," answered the blind teacher. "You don't know his secret thoughts. What did your *mana* tell you?" Malo's fingers played with clicking pebbles.

"My powers felt fear come from him," answered Paul.

"Have you an intermediary? Perhaps Doctor Baldwin can reason with him."

"Thank you, teacher, for the suggestion. But I must speak directly with this American *wahine.* "

*   *   *

Harriet recovered after four weeks under Matilda's care. One morning, she saw off Matilda riding with Paul to the mountains. Later, she walked to the canal, meeting farmers and tradesmen, establishing loyalty to certain ones and walking home with a full basket of exotic food for dinner. It would be her first attempt at cooking since arrival on Maui.

"Help carry?"

It was Matilda, trotting up from behind.

"Didn't expect you until sunset. Is everything all right?" she looked up into the girl's face, but the glare of the sun blinded her.

Matilda laughed, throwing herself off the saddle. The girl rode astride, another odd habit.

"I told him all about me, Miz Harriet. I should have trusted you."

"How did it happen?" Harriet pulled wisps of hair behind her ear.

"We sat high on the slopes looking down on little Lahaina's fringe of town, so pretty. He talk about Hawaiian history, his family, all the marriages. He told me *kahuna* priests, the old ones, chant family lines, all the way back. All along the way, the Ali'i kept separate from commoners, marryin' only other Ali'i, sometimes brother and sister.

"Well, that let me to talk about my family. It just seemed the right time to spill my story. I said my family was complicated, too. My mother was the second wife of her master, my father, and my grandmother was the second wife of my grandfather, and so on back to when the first pretty colored girl come from Africa. So's all my Thigpen side were powerful landowners just like Paul's people and all my colored side was their slave wives."

"Let me try to understand. Your father was your master, and your mother's father was her mother's master," Harriet recalled.

"Momma was my master's weddin' present cause her daddy was also daddy to my master's wife," Matilda further explained.

"That makes…" Harriet couldn't bring herself to speak.

"Yep! My Momma an Miss Betty is sisters."

"So wicked a practice, so unfair to your mother, grandmother and those white wives, too" Harriet interjected.

"A person's a slave to what masters her or he says the Good Book, and a man's lust is a woman's power, says my Momma. That's just the way things is between men and women." She crossed her arms.

Harriet put her hand on the girl's arm. "Tell me what Paul said to all this."

"He smiles, sayin he, too, had a secret, same as mine. His parents were half-brother and sister, too. Grandfather,

King Kamehameha, had many wives, the father of both his parents. Now we both have a secret to keep from the *haoles*."

"Good. And what else?"

"Oh, I forgot. He asked me to marry him in June. Is that rushin' things?"

"Just time enough to plan a wedding. Let's get started."

Chapter Sixty-Two

Low tide at dawn, the golden wide swath of beach opened north of town. Clear green shallows on the left and groves of palms on the right with the island of Molokai in the distance. What could be better to release the horse up the beach, to let her run full speed?

Harriet had ridden through the town properly, side-saddle, hat, and shoes. Beyond the white settlements, these clothes felt restrictive on the sand. She dismounted and looked around. No town, houses, huts, not even farmers in fields. Who's to know?

Loosening ribbons, she flung the sunhat into the grass above the beach, kicked off shoes, and pulled the dress over her head. There. No one will disturb such a pile, looks too much like a *haole* woman lying in the grass. She felt strange standing in white underclothes, bareheaded and unshod, looking down at the empty clothes. She laughed, maybe the phantom spirit of proper womanhood lay discarded here, and true womanhood had emerged free to reach for new excitement.

She led the mare to the water so that warm surf covered her legs over the pantaloons. Why not ride sitting astride like Matilda? It's much more practical. Who's to know? She led the mare up to the level beach and stood facing the saddle; fitting her left foot into the stirrup, she swung her leg across the saddle's back and wiggled the right foot into the other stirrup. The mare whinnied and stamped, ready to go.

"Gitty up, girl," Harriet dug her heels into the horse's sides. The horse leaped forward, cantering in the soft sand. She guided the animal to the surf's edge. The hooves splashed in the foam, and canter turned into a gallop. She looked down at the water's surface to see all four hooves working in tandem, rising and falling together, to float horse and rider over golden grains. Wind lifted the mane and Harriet's hair fell loose.

All at once she saw another rider up the strand.

"Oh, no, I can't be caught like this. I'd be so embarrassed."

The rider came closer, and Harriet saw it was a Hawaiian woman, young, riding bareback. Her *holoku* skirts were lifted to her hips, her legs dangling to bare toes. Her black hair hung loose to her waist. She stopped beside Harriet, white smile set in tan face.

"Aloha. You ride?"

"Yes, I ride. Where do you ride to?" Harriet spoke each word deliberately.

The *wahine* shrugged and tossed her hair. Too much English, she seemed to say.

"We ride?" She turned her pony back up the beach.

The Hawaiian's horse took off as she slapped its rump. She screamed cries at the wind, yipping and yodeling, gaining speed. Harriet dug heels into her mare.

"Get up, yip, yip." The horse needed no encouragement, racing to catch the other. Harriet tried to pass, both horses splashing in the narrow track where water met sand, but the *wahine* wouldn't let her, instead looking back and laughing. A race.

Bareback, the Hawaiian girl clung to the horse's neck, one hand clutching the mane where her face lay. She stretched out, her feet grasping the narrow behind the ribs. Harriet bent low over the saddle. She felt the heat and smelled the animal's sweat.

The racing pair reached a rocky protrusion where the beach ended in a black coral escarpment, hanging into the water. The horses stopped, heaving with heavy breaths. The younger woman tossed herself into the soft sand to let the sand cake on her sweat-soaked skin. Harriet dismounted, letting the reins fall.

Then, the girl rose and gestured for Harriet to follow. She ran into the waves, diving into deep water and emerging otter-like, sleek and wet. She called out something. Harriet, standing in water up to her pantaloons, cupped her hands, splashed her face, and let water trickle down her clothes. She stepped farther, dipping knees tentatively. Minnows played around her feet. Deeper to her waist. How deep should she go? She knelt, crouching, water to her shoulders. Her hands played on the surface.

Looked like fun, the Hawaiian girl swimming. She couldn't swim. Who did in Maine? Certainly, not girls. So envious of her companion who cavorted around her, laughing.

The Hawaiian swam over to Harriet and took her hands. She chirped directions and moved her arms in a swimming rhythm. Why not try? Even at my age I can learn to swim. She paddled like a dog, cupping her hands, kicking her feet, keeping face above the surface. The other nodded, saying "yes, yes." Then, "good," and waved her back to the beach.

Both women remounted. The *wahine* pointed to the ground and made a statement. Then, she waved "Aloha" and rode off inland.

Was that an invitation to return to this spot tomorrow? How would she know except to ride here again? Harriet rode back to her outer clothing, dressed over the wet underclothes, and rode back to home. "Women should have fun, too," she thought.

The next morning, she found her friend waiting beside the black coral cliff.

*   *   *

Afternoon hazy with humidity, sun moving toward hard horizon, George and Harriet walked along the beach, baby toddling and falling to everyone's delight, until they came to the village. An activity was happening in the open space under the trees. They wandered up the slope and slipped between the grass huts.

A matriarch, dressed in sarong, sat to the plaza's side. To her left, six boy drummers, to her front a score of girls.

Before the woman's legs, a long hollow log lay on two rocks, two slits cut the length, a strip of wood on top. The boys had other kinds of wooden articles. Drum sticks beat rhythmic time.

The floor of the plaza swept of debris, no stone, no grass, no sticks, only hard surface, and dust dampened down. The girls lined in groups of six, forming four rows on the clearing's edge. The solemn troupe listened to the matriarch's instructions given among short drum bursts.

She held the attention of the youths without effort, the boys eager, sticks raised, girls posed in uniform stance. Appearance spoke her authority, long hair streaked gray, full-bodied, ponderous breasts hanging over skirt waist and a generous rump spread over sides of her stool. Flesh under her arms swayed and rippled as she struck the log drum.

Grandmother.

Honored *wahine*.

George and Harriet walked all the way up to the edge of the plaza before the woman noticed their arrival. Turning, she gestured to a log bench, "*Aloha, haole*." Harriet pulled the baby onto her lap.

After a long set of instructions, the woman began to beat the log drum, accompanied by the boy band. The first girl in each line stepped forward, left, left, left legs ahead of right, then switching back to right, right, right. As each leg jutted forward, the hip flipped upward. No, something was wrong. Grandmother scolded and the girls' line returned to the edge.

The girls were young, none at puberty; breasts only promising buds. Each wore a brief skirt, rolled at the hips to give them womanly rumps. The skirt material shook with every hip thrust, shimmering in the fading light of afternoon.

Again the music, again the lines moving forward, better this time. The girls raised their arms above their heads, then down, parallel to their shoulders, hands and arms rising and lowering like swells at sea. The hips, exaggerated to buxom proportion by the rolled skirts, swayed side to side, then following directions, pelvises undulated forward, and then stomachs rippled. Three abdominal motions done in sequence to command.

Suddenly all stopped, another scolding. Music began again, and this time the girl's little feet slapped on the hard wet surface of the red clay. Another component, accepted in solemn grace, serious tan faces on motionless heads over writhing bodies. Grandmother was pleased, smiling as she beat the rhythm. Hands, arms, hips, and feet all moving in syncopation, successful; music flowed without interruption.

Class had mastered rudiments of the *hula*.

*   *   *

Matilda and Paul married in June in the Waiola Church, Doctor Baldwin presiding, with a cloud of witnesses wishing the popular couple a happy marriage. The Chases rushed home to greet the crowd at the reception. A crowd of cooks had worked for days preparing the lavish *luau,* digging pits for baking the pigs, potatoes, vegetables, and fish. The matron who taught secret classes for *hula* brought a retinue of girls who were allowed to present a modest version wearing muumuu. The name of the Lord was invoked in English and Hawaiian in extended graces. Baby Debbie was handed from guest to guest and ended by throwing a tantrum, until her mother consented to lie down until she slept.

Paul had a new house built for them up the slope of the mountain. They traveled to the palace in Honolulu for a honeymoon, escorted by the Chases and other Americans.

The packet boat loaded that morning with the wedding party and their belongings for the trip to Honolulu. Ladies, dressed in lavish costume, prepared for their arrival at the capitol city. The Chases brought baby Debbie and Leilei as the nanny, amid a retinue of friends. Valises, hatboxes, and assorted gear filled the companionways on the steamer.

Children ran about the ship, playing on the decks, and climbing the rails. Harriet felt peeved that the missionary families, so strict on morals, were so lax on safety with children. The tension rose as a stiffness in her neck watching little ones gambol about.

"You must relax, Harriet," George counseled. "They aren't our children. Ours would be seated as long as the vessel was in motion."

"My father's spirit prompts me of danger. Yet, I know I would be out of order scolding them. I just hope the ship's officers take charge."

Harriet sat, trying to focus on the passing scene, looking over starboard. Beautiful water, passing islands, and dolphins following the ship's wake. The crowd pressed against the railing.

A child climbed up the rail to Harriet's right. About three-years-old, she was dressed in a white pinafore, bloomers, and shiny black shoes, light hair tied with a blue ribbon. Adults behind her were distracted by conversation.

Suddenly, the boat lurched from a starboard swell. The child disappeared from view. Harriet jumped to her feet in time to see a white dress enter the water six feet below the ship's deck. A woman screamed and pointed, the crowd rushed forward gesturing. The pilot cut engines, but no one moved. The ship had no flotation devices.

"Move over," Harriet's voice cut through the passengers against the rail.

The crowd parted to see a woman in her underclothes leap onto the top rail and dive into the green water. She disappeared under the surface, reappearing yards back of the stern, stroking toward the spot the child had dropped. Again, she disappeared under the waves to emerge holding a tiny form; the toddler. A rope thrown, Harriet latched on with her left hand, winding it around her arm. Men pulled in woman and child, lifting the girl from Harriet's arms. Women brought blankets to hide her body from view and brought her to George. Other women found the pile of clothing.

"My darling wife, how did you do that? Was that a spontaneous miracle we saw or have you always known to swim?"

"Hawaii has brought on many surprises, dear husband. Our native friends have much to teach us."

"You never cease to astound me."

Chapter Sixty-Three

The whaler *Saratoga* lay at anchor off Lahaina. The harbor master, in the shade of the trees, watched from the ruins of the old fort. Adjusting his telescope, he waited for a whaleboat to row the ship's captain to Lahaina.

"Almost noon. We best send out the tender to check her. 'Could be plague aboard," he said absently to his Hawaiian assistant. "Take the boat, ask the master his intentions."

The Hawaiian rowers bent to their task as the light tender swiftly skimmed the surface of the sea. No movement could be detected half-way to the ship except crewmen sitting on the railing, lounging against lines.

"Hallo, *Saratoga,* is the master there?"

"Aye, he's here, who's askin'?" came the reply.

"Harbor master's query."

Along the railing smokers slumped, slouched in slumber.

"Who goes there?" a bearded man in black jacket peered over.

"Harbor master wants to know your intent. Why has no one come ashore?"

"Tell your master that this captain needs the consul. Tell him I'm not leaving my ship."

"What reason should I say to come?"

"Work stoppage."

*   *   *

A black suited George Chase stepped onto the *Saratoga*'s deck and sensed tension. Missing was the ordinary bustle. Crew lounged about the deck neither hauling nor scrubbing, but every pair of eyes fed upon the sight of the United States consul.

Captain Ephraim Harding greeted him amid a bevy of ship's officers. The group asked him to accompany him to the officers' mess. There, they laid out their problem while Chase remained standing.

"This voyage commenced December 14 of '52 from New Bedford with crew signing on for 50 months duty. If the voyage stretches to the full 50 months, New Bedford won't see the *Saratoga* until February of '57."

"Is the stoppage because they want to sail home?"

"Yes. We have a full cargo of sperm, whale, and bone. We either unload and transship the cargo or we sail home, two years short, a waste of the owner's investment."

Chase wrote notes in his binder.

"Captain Harding, were I to inquire among the crew, would there be other complaints? I refer to the 1850 law against flogging and other abuses."

"Upon the Lord's holy scripture, I have never laid a hand against any man on this ship and, further, I have commanded all officers to do likewise." He examined surrounding faces and continued, "I captain a clean vessel. All Americans so there's no need for a rule against speaking another tongue. But, to maintain discipline against disrespect, insolence, or insubordination I must take measures – irons or double-irons, confining on deck or in the run below decks, and short rations."

"Are men dissatisfied with provisions?" Chase asked.

"At this point, we wait to load fresh provisions at Lahaina. At this standstill, the men refuse to unload the bone and casks, and I refuse to bring fresh provisions on board until they do. That's the long and short of it. Will you help us?"

"I shall speak with the men." Chase offered.

"Something we can arrange. I will hold an inquiry. My mates will select crew members to testify. Sit here in the officers' mess, we'll bring them to you."

"How much will I hear, Captain Harding? The men will be intimidated from speaking their minds. To solve your problem, I need access to the men, best if I find my way to the forecastle."

"It violates my rights as the master. A captain must be able to control the ship."

"Control? Do you not see already that you have lost control of your ship? I assume you want my authority as consul to change the situation. For the purposes of justice, a judge controls his court. Otherwise, one party will consider the proceedings prejudicial. Let me do my work, Ephraim. Hand me the ship's articles first."

Consul Chase crossed the invisible line before the foremast, separating officers from ordinary seamen, and approached a sailor.

"Is there a spokesman among you?" he was taken down into the forecastle of the *Saratoga,* a hole, stinking with the effluent of dirty bodies and damp clothes. The crew arrayed themselves among their bunks.

"Consul, I'm William Brown, ordinary seaman. Crew's asked me to make the plea."

"Good, I'm consul here at Lahaina. I've heard captain, now its time to hear you."

"Our complaint is simple, Mister Chase. The *Saratoga* has a full hold; oil and bone we've worked to collect. Here we are, two years into the voyage, with only one liberty ashore, and now captain wants to unload this cargo. Once that cargo leaves this ship, we're out both pay for the off-loading and our lay."

The men mumbled in agreement. They feared, once Harding off-loaded, pay earned over the past 24 months would be lost. It had happened to other crews.

"So, there are three points of difference: only one liberty ashore, no off-loading pay, and losing your lays for this cargo of oil and bone. Are your fed well enough? Has there been harsh treatment? The truth, men, don't exaggerate," Chase demanded.

"Well, sir. We're short rations here and now. Sea biscuits all wormy. Salt beef hard. Captain won't stand for a smart answer, claps 'em in irons or assigns hard tasks like scraping out trypots."

"Hear, hear," a chorus of agreement from the gathering.

"Gentlemen," Chase brought the meeting to order, "I have here the ship's articles to which your names are attached." The men nodded.

Knowing one-fourth of most whaling crews were illiterate, he read a portion.

"I quote, '*Master has liberty to ship oil or bone home from all places he shall think proper*'," he offered the document all around. "Refusing to continue the voyage means you are being insubordinate. I can have your ringleaders confined to the Lahaina prison for a term of months, and that side of Lahaina is no paradise."

The men grumbled.

"Further," Chase continued, "the articles show you agreed to 50 months duty. How many so far?"

"Twenty-four, about," they agreed.

"There is no evidence of flogging or striking. Meanwhile, fresh rations await you on the docks of Lahaina. Only this strike separates you from fresh food."

He lowered his voice, "Now, gentlemen, if a consul could persuade a captain to pay the crew longshoremen's wages to off-load and if a consul could persuade a captain to guarantee a seaman's lay for transshipped oil and if a consul could persuade a captain to grant shore leave, would a crew cease and desist from their work stoppage?"

William Brown looked around. All nodded.

"Much obliged, Mister Chase. We warn you Captain is a hard man."

Consul Chase re-crossed the deck. Officers looked up as the consul entered their quarters.

"Captain Harding, would you be willing to relent on some minor items?"

"I'll not barter away my powers, Chase."

"A ship's not a plantation, Ephraim. The men are not slaves. They're free Americans. Think of the *Saratoga* as a

360

floating factory where men will work hard for incentive rather than to avoid punishment."

"I have no choice. Order the tender to start the off-loading."

Chapter Sixty-Four

George and Harriet walked through the red dusty lanes to the Seaman's Bethel. The unadorned one-storey building bore no cross, no stained glass windows, no symbols of faith. Inside, rugged benches served as pews, set on a brick floor. The ceiling arched to a center girder, exposed rafters bowed like a ship's timbers. The front had no altar, instead, the ship carpenters, who built the chapel, created a centered pulpit shaped like a ship prow jutting over the first pews. Ropes led from the boom to the ceiling like fore skysail stays.

A piano tucked into a corner played the opening hymn:

I sing the mighty power of God that made the mountains rise
That spread the flowing seas abroad, and built the lofty skies
I sing the Wisdom that ordained, the sun to rule the day
The moon shines full at His command, and all the stars obey.

Reverend Youngblood trod through the threshold dressed in a black suit and a black sailor's hat. All eyes followed his rolling gait up the aisle. Tall, barrel-chested, broad-shouldered, he gave off the appearance of a prize-fighter in the heavy-weight division rather than one to turn 'the other cheek.'

The pastor strode to the front, under the ship prow pulpit and pulled a hawser. Down came a rope ladder from the side of the bulwark. Youngblood scrambled to grip a rung and heave over the rail, to emerge above the congregation, hand on the bowsprit. When he hung his hat on a handspike, he revealed close-cropped red hair, balanced by a short flaming beard.

"Ahoy, mates. He with ears, let him hear....Today's Bible lesson is from Isaiah, Chapter 58. Behold the Word of the Lord:

They seek me daily, and delight to know my ways, as a nation that did righteousness, and forsook not the ordinance of their God: they ask of me the ordinances of justice....

Youngblood read more Isaiah:

...To loose the bands of wickedness, to undo heavy burdens, and to let the oppressed go free, and that ye break every yoke... then shall thy light rise in obscurity, and thy darkness be as the noonday...for then the glory of the Lord shall be thy reward.. thou shalt be like a watered garden, and like a spring of water, whose waters fail not...thou shalt raise up the foundations of many generations; and thou shalt be called the repairer of the breach, the restorer of paths.

"My mates, what should this passage mean to us? For me, it speaks to every man jack aboard this earthy vessel, be he the lowest greenhand in the fo'c's'le or the highest officer at the helm. Jehovah's purposes are clear.... Justice. Give justice and expect to receive justice."

Chase distracted himself, his mind released to dwell on Sabbath pleasures. He and Harriet had resumed habits of Sunday afternoon intimacies. He marveled how life on Maui had released inhibitions. Feeling guilty of letting his fantasies wander, he snapped back to the moment.

But, what was Youngblood's point? Was this subversive talk a mutinous suggestion? Or was this aimed at him? He opened the scriptures. Phrases sprang forth:

Loose the bands of wickedness... undo heavy burdens... let the oppressed go free...the glory of the Lord shall be thy reward...thou shalt raise up the foundations of many generations...thou shall be called the repairer of the breach.

Quaint language. He shrugged. Good of Youngblood to bring religion to the masses aboard the fleet. Gives them hope. What was that Gibbon said in *The Decline*? In Rome, all religions were considered by the people as equally true;

by the philosopher as equally false, and by the magistrate as equally useful.

*   *   *

George looked at the digits. He held the paper at arm's length. He couldn't make out his own writing. Eyes getting bad must check into glasses when next in Honolulu. Fiftieth birthday was next month, March 14th. Age. He shrugged.

Through the window, he saw a man approach the office; the youthful Reverend Samuel Youngblood from Seamen's Bethel. He entered to greet Chase.

"Good morning, Consul. I wanted to stop by to thank you for your attendance Sunday and pass along a compliment."

"For whom?" Chase gestured toward a chair.

"For you, as the United States Consul here. Some of the men at chapel were singing your praises for reconciliation of crew and captain on the *Saratoga*. I believe the term used was 'a fair man'."

Youngblood eased his huge frame into the chair.

"It can't always go their way, Samuel. I hope you understand. They did sign a contract; the law holds them to that."

"Understood. They only want what's just and fair."

The outer door opened and a group of seamen entered, young and unsure. All doffed their hats, the group a mixture of races. One pushed forward to offer Chase a piece of paper.

"Would you like me to leave, Mister Chase?" asked Samuel Youngblood.

"I don't think that's necessary, Pastor. What is your concern, men?"

A white sailor stepped forward to hand him the paper.

"We're a delegation from the crew of the *Tamerlane*, sir, and we have a petition from the men, all signed, explainin' our complaints."

"What's your name, young man?"

"George Bartlett, I am, and this…" he introduced the others.

"Good, now let me read your petition."

This pretition is wrote to the consil at La-haina by the men what sign below or fix their mark.

We the crew of the Tamerlane wish to be dismissed from this ship on akont of the cruelty of the captain, Mister Joshua Winslow, and his mate, Valentine Lewis. Many hands flogged, rations short, belaying pins used on heads, and seizing. Our mate Manuel Silvia was murdered.

We pretition the United States consul for these greevences and ask redress – released from our contract & permission to enlist on other vessels.

The Crew of the Tamerlane
February 25, 1856

Chase noted the captain's name, Winslow. Wasn't Winslow his mother-in-law's maiden name?

"This is quite a list of allegations, son. Murder?"

"Yes, sir?"

"How do you say that happened?"

"This captain, sir, is special cruel to the dark ones. He rode our Manuel terrible hard, floggin' him. Last blow was when he 'seized' Manuel in the rigging by this thumbs so as his feet could just touch the deck. The boy screamed.

"That night after Manuel was cut down, the boy threw himself overboard. Just couldn't take it no more."

Bartlett continued, shoving a young Hawaiian sailor forward.

"Now, Winslow's newest target is Eddie Looker, sir. He won't say much, talks little American. He's in danger."

"What's your Hawaiian name, son?" Chase looked into the boy's eyes.

"Keipapa"

"Is this true, Keipapa?"

"Yes." He looked down, afraid of the white authority.

Chase turned back to the delegation and said, "I can't send this group back to the ship. Winslow might sail off. I'm boarding you at the seaman's hostel until the matter is settled. Sam, would you please accompany the boys to their quarters?"

Chase wrote out a message to Captain Winslow:

George M. Chase
United States Consul
Lahaina

Dear Captain Winslow,

I am writing in my capacity as Consul to request your presence at the consulate this afternoon to discuss a matter of complaint against your captaincy, lodged by several crew. The petition also includes allegations of a capital nature.

I shall expect you at my office by the third hour o'clock.

Respectfully,
Geo. M. Chase.

He brought the note, sealed, to the harbor master for delivery to the *Tamerlane*.

Chapter Sixty-Five

Harriet and George ate the noon meal on the veranda. Leilei hovered, serving food. Debbie played on the floor rolling pebbles.

"How horrible, those men confined on a ship with a madman," Harriet doled meat and vegetables.

"If it is true, Harriet. I will go aboard and interview the crewmen like the *Saratoga*."

"Please go into the fo'c's'le again. Consul or captain, the poor things have little reason to trust you. If you can stop outrages on the *Tamerlane*, maybe outrages will stop across the whole fleet. What is that rogue captain's name?"

"Winslow, Joshua Winslow. Any relation?"

"Could he be from the Marshfield Winslows?" Harriet noted George's temples, white hairs salted among the black.

George rushed to the office after the meal. As he approached, a figure stepped into the sunlight. Standing before the consulate was a man in blue cap and suit, holding a piece of paper.

"Captain Winslow?"

"You sent me this damned note." As the words shot from his mouth, a purple hue rose in the man's face.

"Yes. We have allegations to discuss."

Winslow ignored the issue. "Where are those men who stole my boat? I demand their return."

"In my custody and will not leave this jurisdiction. Were you planning to depart with the *Tamerlane*?"

"Yes, but without a full crew we are stranded."

"By my authority, the *Tamerlane* is not discharged from Lahaina until I am satisfied no crimes have been committed aboard."

"Do you dare investigate my ship?" Captain Winslow's voice rose, and he came inches from Chase's face. His hands clenched into fists as he waved the paper.

"We will begin reading the ship's log, Captain," George turned to enter the office door, signaling the close of the conversation.

"Stand where you are, Chase," Winslow pushed him against the wall, "I'm going to settle this matter between us like men. No one's interfering with the *Tamerlane*."

"Belay there! Take your hands off Mister Chase."

Reverend Samuel Youngblood's great hand grabbed the back of Winslow's neck, paralyzing nerves and tendons. The captain's hands dropped to his sides. His eyes bulged from their sockets as the pastor lifted him off his feet.

"Let him go, Samuel."

Youngblood released the man who found his feet and stumbled, sputtering.

"I will be rowing to your ship within the hour. I expect full cooperation. Have a table and chairs set up middeck, logbook set on the table. We will interview officers and men. Come to your senses, man, and act like an officer."

The captain walked away.

"Samuel, find us Paul Kamehameha and Father Demonts at Maria Lanakila Church. We will need translators at the *Tamerlane* inquest."

*   *   *

The ship sat at anchor a mile out from the reef. As Paul and a constable rowed the delegation to the ship, Chase could see the vessel's shabby condition. Copper sheathing above the waterline pealed away from the wood, replaced by barnacles and green slime. Scraps of sail hung from upper spars, torn in gales, left to rot.

The table and chairs were arranged on deck behind the mizzenmast where seamen are prohibited unless on special duty. Chase ordered the furniture brought forward, midline of the ship, within bounds of the sailors.

The delegation consisted of the consul, Paul Kamehameha, Father DeMonts fluent with Portuguese, Reverend Youngblood, and a Hawaiian constable, bearing the only sidearm. As he requested, the logbook was set onto the table. Chase swept it into his leather case as he took a chair. Sam Youngblood sat to his right, taking notes.

"May I see the ship's manifest and register?" They were produced, and Chase scanned the writing while sailors stood nearby forward on the ship and officers congregated aft. Captain Joshua Winslow took a chair near the table.

"Samuel, have you a fair hand?"

"Only fair, nothing pretty, Mister Chase."

"I need you to record every jot and tittle of this proceeding." In a loud voice Chase announced the start of the inquest.

"As United States Consul at Lahaina, I am conducting an inquest into the death of one Manuel Silvia, sailor on the *Tamerlane*. I call first John Allen, blacksmith."

A large black man stepped from the crowd.

"State your full name and your home town, sailor."

"I be John Allen from New Bedford, sir."

"Mister Allen, have you seen flogging on this ship?"

"Well, sir, it's like this. I seen whippin' and sometimes kickin' and strikin'. But, floggin'?" His voice trailed off as he looked back at his mates.

"Don't be afraid to testify, Mister Allen. If justice is to be served, the truth must come out. Let me help you with the right words, Mister Allen. What happened to Manual Silva on board this ship?"

"Manuel Silvia. He be treated like a dog. He was drove to his death. Captain, he crazy."

"Hold on there. You take the word of a nigger against me?" Winslow interrupted. "In the United States, no black can witness against a citizen. I protest."

Chase turned to the captain.

"You disturb the proceedings of an official United States inquiry, Mister Winslow. As to your protest, I agree that the laws of the United States do pertain aboard a vessel

370

bearing the stars and stripes, but, looking around, viewing this lovely location, you will see we are two-thousand miles from the United States; and the complexion of this crew compels me to confer upon every one of them the privileges and responsibilities of citizenship. Otherwise, how is a consul to conduct his duty?"

"But, this can't be..." Winslow stood and shook a finger.

"Sit down, captain, or you shall be confined to quarters." Winslow backed off.

Next, Chase called other seamen: Whites, Indians, Polynesians. Hawaiian harpoonist, Peter Good, testified through Paul, confirming the allegations that Manual Silva was tied to the rigging by his thumbs, tearing his muscles away from bone, making his hand useless. Peter Good described Winslow laughing at Silvia's condition.

"Write that down, Youngblood. Evidence of aggravation," George whispered.

The harpoonist blurted out a stream of words. Paul listened intently. When the man finished, Paul reported, "Consul Chase, this ship may be unseaworthy, in need of much repair. Rats bite the men, and provisions are inadequate. Their food is rotten. Look at their festering mouths; they're ripe with scurvy."

Father DeMonts interpreted for Portuguese sailors, translating their testimony to Sam in a heavy French accent. Finally, it was the officers' turns to rebut the allegations.

Third mate, Pardon Simmons, was called to stand before the table. His discomfort was palpable, shifting from foot to foot, twisting his hat.

"Mister Simmons, you've heard the allegations. What is your experience on the *Tamerlane*?" Chase looked up to see a young man, cap held in two hands, a posture of supplication.

"If I were to speak my mind, sir, would the Consul find it in his heart to remove me to another vessel?"

"You have my protection, son, and it's perjury to bear false witness. Samuel, note he speaks under duress."

"The captain serves corporal discipline upon everyone 'cept white crewmen. Them, he abuses verbally, with overwork, and withholding provisions. He is aided by first mate, Lewis. He's the ship's mole, doin' captain's dirty work. Would ya like ta see the cat?"

"You mean there's a cat o'nine tails aboard?" Chase examined the man's face.

"Swear by my mother's grave, sir. Cap'n keeps her hid in his cabin." Pardon Simmons looked him square in the eyes.

"Duly noted. We shall move forward to Captain Joshua Winslow's testimony."

Winslow slouched back into his chair.

"Will you stand to give your rebuttal?" asked Chase.

"No. First, Consul Chase, I regret to say I do not recognize the authority of this hearing. You are no court judge in Hawaii and have no power here. Therefore, whatever you decide, I shall ignore.

"Second, only citizens of the United States are covered by its laws. The ordinance against flogging on American ships does not apply to non-citizens. No captain would be able to manage a crew without the power of fear and intimidation. Without a captain's power, there is no whaling fleet. Without a fleet, no consul's job.

"Third, George Chase should not be sitting here judging me. I looked into your family, and it would appear that your wife and I are cousins, distantly, but enough for your recusation from any case respecting the *Tamerlane*.

"Finally, Manuel Silvia having thrown himself into the sea makes me innocent for his death."

Winslow waved his hand as if to chase off a fly. Chase smiled, waited for Sam Youngblood's scratching to catch up with the words, and then answered.

"First, as to the power of this hearing, the laws of the United States give extraordinary powers to all consuls in foreign ports. We control all ships registered in the United States and their personnel. You may come to be amazed at my jurisdiction, sir.

"Second, whereas no case has yet reached the courts of the United States regarding the justice of applying anti-flogging laws to foreign nationals, Negroes, and Indians, American officials may choose to enforce the law for all persons on American ships, *as if they, too, were citizens.* Try me, captain. I would like this to be the first such case. Make me famous for applying the *ordinances of justice*," Chase leaned back, glaring at the captain.

"This case may be the *foundations of many generations.*

"My light shall *rise from obscurity.*

"I shall be *the repairer of the breach.*

"The Lord will cause me *to ride upon the high places of the earth.*

"The glory of the Lord shall be my *reward."* His voice stopped.

Reverend Youngblood dropped his pen and looked up. Tears wet the consul's eyes. The crew looked at each other. Captain Winslow thought the consul mad.

Chase swallowed and continued.

"Third, the alleged shame you may have brought on the Winslow name would scandalize pilgrim forbearers you share with my wife, connections too distant to influence my decision.

"Finally, the injury you inflicted on the young sailor, Manuel Silvia, resulted in his death. Such cause would suggest the impeachable offense of manslaughter."

Captain Winslow stood his ground. "What is your next action, Chase?"

"This inquest is concluded. We shall depart to shore, except for constables, who shall stand guard on rotation, monitoring the health of the crew. Cash will be garnished from the ship's treasury to pay for food, water, and other provisions. The ship is forbidden to leave port, meanwhile, pending a decision by the United States Commissioner, Luther Severance, at Honolulu. He will receive my recommendations forthwith."

"And the escaped crew and my boat?" asked Winslow.

"In my custody. They are the lucky ones," answered Chase.

Chapter Sixty-Six

Sunday afternoon, March 16, 1856, Harriet and George returned from services to find a cart next to the veranda and Paul and Matilda inside the house.

"Surprise, Mister George. Happy birthday." Matilda rushed down the steps and enveloped him.

"How did you know?" George beamed at her florid face.

"Miz Harriet invited us, and I brought that special dish you always asked for when we was first in Hawaii." She swept aside the cloth to reveal several calabashes of food. Paul beamed with pride at his wife's gifts.

"'Were', 'were in Hawaii.'" George persisted.

"Yes, we was just here. You remember?"

George noticed her figure. Had she gained weight under that muumuu?

The couples unloaded the cart, carrying the dishes to the dining room. Leilei fussed about with dishes, cups, and saucers. Debbie played on the floor amid an array of wooden toys.

"Leilei, do take care of that china."

"What do you have there, Miz Harriet?" Matilda's eyes sparkled to see the colorful ware. "Look at this, Paul. Maybe when you build those shelves up high we could have such dishes. I don't think it proper to eat from old calabashes, and we need a real table, too."

"Wong ordered this set from China. George brought me to approve the design. See, Paul, it's different from my mother's blue willow."

Paul stopped to look. Eating at the Norwoods in Camden, the plates had Chinese scenes in blue. The new plates showed multicolored monarch butterflies, dragonflies, moths, and swallow-tailed birds of paradise cavorting among flowers. It could be a scene on Maui. The set contained large dinner plates, smaller salad or desert plates, and generous cups and saucers.

"This cost much, Missus Chase. Maybe we wait, sweetie, afterwards."

They sat, said the blessing, and food began to circulate. They talked news from America. Cousin Salmon P. Chase had been elected governor of Ohio. Everybody knew he wanted to be president; the first Republican. The crisis over slavery got worse. In an effort to halt the slide toward war between North and South, Ralph Waldo Emerson proposed the British method to end slavery, purchase and freeing of every one at an estimate of $2 billion.

Matilda hated political talk. "Don't say you didn't notice, Mister George. Look at me." She stood and stretched the thin cotton material over a bulging abdomen. Thick breasts protruded over the bodice.

George laughed. Not satisfied, she turned to show her profile. Matilda always missed the proper message about prudery.

"Paul says I'm eating for two." She sipped her drink.

"Perhaps George shouldn't pour the rum in your punch, my dear," Harriet grasped for another topic.

"Oh, a little won't hurt the child, Harriet. Didn't Doctor Benjamin recommend an occasional wine for you?"

"Heavens, now we're talking about my pregnancy," Harriet blurted, the conversation quite out of control. Harriet looked to Paul. Her eyes pleaded.

Paul asked, "When do you expect a response from that Honolulu commissioner?"

"In a few days. I'm concerned Severance will take the case away from me, and Winslow will be released. It's politics. What must the royal Hawaiian government think?"

"The chiefs are angry. The new king, Alexander Liholiho, Kamehameha the Fourth, is suspicious of Americans since the time he was a prince traveling on a railroad in the United States and a conductor put him off for being colored. If Severance lets Winslow go, the government will withdraw all Hawaiian sailors from the fleet and consider restricting whalers from liberty on Hawaiian Islands. It's a crisis, to be sure."

"Paul, darling, can't we discuss a more pleasant subject? It's Mister George's birthday, and I baked a cake. Who cares about that silly old government, anyway? Look at little Miz Debbie. She goin' to have a new friend, soon."

*   *   *

The party released George from his cares, hard burdens he did not enjoy. Weeks of tension caused him to lose sleep. He felt relieved to be under orders to enjoy himself, pouring more punch than usual.

As darkness fell, they lit the whale oil lamps. A yellow glow filled the rooms. Mountain breezes drifted through the windows, bringing down scents of flowers and crops.

Matilda fatiguing early, Paul took her home. Debbie fell into a deep sleep, lying against Leilei. The Chases remained outside on the veranda, together in rattan chairs. Harriet's hand wandered across the chairs' gap and stroked George's.

"Let's walk down to the beach, George, and listen to the waves."

They walked south across the town, past humble homes, grass, and stick houses, to the beaches. George picked his way stumbling over the rubble of logs and coral to the smooth sand, walking in his high-topped shoes. Harriet lifted each foot in turn, pulling off her shoes to skip over the high tide debris until her toes dug into the cool sand.

She laughed and kicked at the surf lapping in the shallows, letting her skirt fringe dampen. George stood back, watching her.

She skipped up to him.

"Take off your shoes, George Chase, or they'll get wet." He sat in the sand and pulled them off. Straddling him, she reached and pulled him up by his cravat.

"Now you come into the water, sweet Georgie Porgie, and get those pasty white feet wet."

He permitted her to tug his cravat until they both stood in knee-deep water. He felt a letting go, a release from care. The world went away and only he and Harriet existed. He embraced her and found her mouth in the darkness. They kissed and kissed, hungry for the taste. Wisps of her hair tangled their mouths.

She broke the embrace.

"When you were a boy in Vermont, you and your friends played in a creek?"

"We were young, then."

"Did you wear clothes?"

"No. Buck naked, my dear."

"What do you think?" she leaned back to see an expression on his face, but the dark obscured him.

"No one can see us," his voice whispered.

They emerged to the upper strand and removed their clothes, she tossing, he folding. Nude as Eden, they took hands and walked into the surf.

*   *   *

The letter lay on his desk. An official envelope with a return address:

The Honorable Luther Severance
United States Commissioner
Honolulu
The Sandwich Islands

Chase sat looking at it, guessing the message. It was thin, not the package of documents he expected. Orders to arrest the captain, send him under guard to prison in Honolulu? Orders to send those poor sailors back to the ship and possible death? He hated to be the instrument of other men and, yet he feared to bear the responsibility. Let Severance take control, please, God.

Using a penknife, he cut through the envelope.

Honorable Geo. M. Chase
United States Consul
Lahaina
Maui Island
Sandwich Islands
April 15, 1856

Sir: In the matter pertaining to the alleged incidents on the ship, Tamerlane, I have full confidence you will use your best judgment in any decision you reach, as the consul is vested with the responsibility.

My regards to Missus Chase and the family.

Your humble servant,

Honorable Luther Severance, United States Commissioner

"Damn him! The little bureaucratic bastard kicked it back. Refused to take the risk and make the decision," Chase threw the letter back on his desk. "Severance hopes for a nice sinecure with the royal government and a pension from State. 'Alleged incidents'! As if I invented the evidence."

Chase took out the set of statutes; black bound books to guide a consul, and leafed through chapters on criminal law. Opening his binder, he copied notes on lined paper. After several hours of thought and writing, he called for the royal constables.

*　　　　　　*　　　　　　*

The afternoon sun spared no portion of the open Lahaina Roads, arching toward the far islands. The whaling fleet baked at anchor. Crews gathered to watch an unfolding drama. On this windless day, the harbor's surface lay like blue glass.

Under the shade of palms, a crowd formed along the town's beach. Customers and vendors stopped trade in the market while traffic along the shore road halted.

As the native rowers pulled out to the ship, center thwarts bristled with constables, rifles at the ready. The police chief wore a Colt revolver, six cartridges in the magazine. Chase stood at the stern, eyes upon his goal, a document in his jacket's breast pocket. Silk hat pressed down to his ears, the consul felt both American and Hawaiian eyes.

"Throw down the ropes," the chief ordered.

The company of constables clambered aboard and stood in formation. Finally, George emerged on deck. He called ship's company to attention. Captain Joshua Winslow strutted from his quarters.

Chase reached inside the pocket and drew out the document.

He read: "Whereupon the condition of the vessel, the Tamerlane, is found to be unseaworthy, whereupon the crew of the Tamerlane charge abject abuse by Captain Joshua Winslow and first mate Lewis, whereupon the said captain is suspect of flogging on a United States vessel, whereupon Captain Joshua Winslow is indicted for manslaughter in the death of a seaman, it is incumbent upon the American consul here resident to take action. By the power vested in me as United States Consul at Lahaina, I now take possession of the vessel, *Tamerlane*, of New Bedford, Massachusetts, forthwith for the purpose of disposing of her cargo and supplies. I take the crew into custody, room and board at the ship's expense. Each man will also receive compensation for the value of the oil and bone according to his original lay. I arrest Captain Joshua Winslow and First Mate Valentine Lewis..."

"Impossible. What American court has jurisdiction, Chase?" Winslow blurted. The constables surrounded him, one large Hawaiian grabbing the captain's arms from behind.

"…on the charge of manslaughter to be tried in accordance with Hawaiian law. Both accused, meanwhile, will be incarcerated at Lahaina's prison, the Hale Pa'ahao. This vessel shall be sold at auction, and proceeds awarded to the Seamen's Bethel for its ministry."

Chase's voice stopped for the crowd to absorb the order's audacity. No one spoke until Winslow struggled against his captor and wined, "Be reasonable, man. Think what you're doing to take on the whole whaling industry. The U.S. government, too. Besides, how can you hand a white man over to savages for barbaric justice? My god, the Hale Pa'ahao's a hellhole."

"Look, Consul Chase, the cat!" A young constable emerged from officers' quarters holding the short whip. "Crew says he flogs 'em with this."

Chase examined the black leather handle. The cat-o'-nine-tails. He counted the cords. Yes, nine. Each rawhide strand had intermittent knots along the length, flecks of blood and skin glued to the surface.

Chase intoned, "Chief, do your duty." The Hawaiian police collected Winslow and Lewis and forced them into the boat. Chase turned to the crew.

"All seamen, listen well. The seaman's hostel expects you this evening, but hear a warning. Police will take measures toward drunkenness, rioting, wenching, fast horse riding, and Sabbath breaking. Be sober tomorrow. You will be paid longshoremen's wages to transport this cargo ashore. Those who cooperate will ship out with real money."

While crew bustled to load for shore leave, Chase stood at the stern, eyes fixed on Maui's mountains. His hands folded and refolded the notes, reading portions over.

Five sailors swung off the last boat free from davits and dangled her over smooth water.

"Looks like consul's still aboard. Musta' missed his tender," one pointed aft to the lone Chase.

"Ya best bring our consul back to his senses, Toby, an' call him down here. I kin tell he's bit more off than he kin chew this time."

Chapter Sixty-Seven

The steam frigate *U. S. S. Susquehanna* cleared Cape Charles and plunged north into Chesapeake Bay. Placid waters welcomed the vessel on the September afternoon as fishing craft and crabbers darted out from lush coves to ply the waters. Flocks of ducks, thick enough to block out the western sun, passed overhead, looking for easy marshes along the shores. At this speed, the navy ship would dock in Washington by morning.

George Chase let the breeze rustle his hair as he stood hatless on the bow. Acrid smoke poured from stacks over the ship's rear, and he needed a clear head for thinking. At the forward railing he could also avoid contact with naval officers from whom he'd maintained distance on the voyage.

He had expected some repercussions after the arrest of the *Tamerlane's* officers and confiscation of the whaler, but George knew he had no choice. Ah, well, events had a way of playing out in unintended consequences. He smiled at the memory, back in his consulate, when the navy boy attempted to arrest him.

       *   *   *

The white-clad officer stood before him that morning. His stern manner belied his youthfully high voice, perhaps a newly minted lieutenant from Annapolis. A leather holster poked out from his tunic.

"Sir, I'm under orders to escort you to the *Mississippi* where you are to be transported to Washington." The young man delivered this message at full attention.

"Oh, dear. Well, son. How much time have I to prepare for this journey?"

"My orders are to escort you aboard immediately, sir," he said looking at the wall.

"Am I under arrest,..." Chase eyed the insignia, "...lieutenant?"

"Ensign," he corrected. "I am ordered to escort you aboard, sir."

"And who's to serve as consul in my absence?" Chase asked.

"Commissioner Severance is sending his assistant for now, I am told, sir," the young officer stared ahead, reciting his directive.

"Very well, just a moment while I gather my papers." George Chase assembled files and slipped them haphazardly into the leather case. Outside, he toyed, lowering the flag in order to close the consulate properly. A small crowd began to notice the activity. A boy scurried off down Lahaina's shore road toward the royal compound.

The ensign and the consul picked a path across the square and through vendors' stands toward the water. A United States navy boat sat docked at the market's canal. Upon the pair's appearance, sailors hoisted oars at the ready. The closer the ensign and consul came, the louder the crowd muttered. Soon, natives crushed against their path.

"Let me through, let me through, official United States naval business here," the ensign's voice cracked.

"Chase, what's happening?" Paul emerged above the crowd.

"It seems my government calls me back to our capital. I hope for consultation." Chase looked small among so many people.

"Looks bad to me. No time to pack, say good-bye? Missus Chase know this?" Paul shouted above the noise as his hand grabbed the naval white tunic.

The officer jerked away. "You are interfering with official American business," his hand unsnapped the pistol strap.

Paul ignored him.

"Come with us, Chase. We take you home," Paul reached out for Chase's hand.

The officer drew and fired a round into the air.

"Back away," he ordered, but as he spoke, others shoved him hard into the market canal. His whites disappeared under the scum until he emerged sputtering, uniform covered in sewage, pistol dropped in muck.

The crowd carried Chase to his gate. Inside, he mounted the veranda stairs to find Harriet looking over the Dutch door. Paul sent for Matilda while staying to argue from the stairs.

"They can't make you leave, Chase. Quit this consul job and be like your friend, Elisha Allen; work for Hawaii government. The Kanaka Maoli need a smart American lawyer to protect the kingdom. You understand both America and Hawaiian people."

"Don't stop him, Paul," Harriet spoke from the shadows. Little Debbie clung to her skirts, watching the adults. "He has to do this."

"Do what?" Paul demanded. "They'll punish him for disturbing their business and handing over Winslow to Hawaiian justice."

"Paul, Paul," Chase's hand swept in a calming motion. "If I take a position with the royal government, they'll say I'm just another one gone native. Maybe I would help fortify Hawaii against foreign powers, but if I allow myself to be taken to Washington, I have the opportunity to do something far greater; something to help my people overcome this flaw that excludes colored from protection under the law."

The gate opened and Matilda ran up to the house.

"What's this 'bout they takin' my Mister George?" she wept. Tears marred her face as her feet plodded up the steps. "How could they reach all the way out here after so many years?"

"My dear sweet girl," George hugged her. "It's got nothing to do with your escape. It's all about this dreadful business with flogging and colored men's rights aboard. If I go back, I might straighten out the problem and stop the mistreatment. I promise to return as soon as I'm finished. Now, if you'll excuse me..."

He opened the door and stepped into the house. "I have to pack quickly before that silly ensign makes any more trouble."

But, instead, Chase collapsed into a dining room chair and removed the hat, setting it gently on the tablecloth. He gestured for her to join him.

"Second thoughts?" she asked, pulling out the chair and sweeping her skirt smooth. Debbie leaned on her mother's lap.

"Brave talk, this business of rights. The reality is I could be charged with impeding lawful commerce and false arrest. That's only the worst. The least is what I expect to happen." Chase looked at his wife.

"And that is...?" she prompted.

"Dismissal from the consular service and ruin. Even if we return to Calais, who would do business with a man who deserted party principles? I'll be branded an...abolitionist." He looked away.

"Don't slump into melancholy, George. That's just what they hope you'll do," Harriet whispered. "If you lose heart, for sure you'll loose the fight. The man I married made a career out of standing up for the downtrodden. Mill workers, school teachers, petty rumrunners, slave girls. Providence keeps placing you in special circumstances. Every time you're faced with a decision, you've chosen what's right over what's convenient, and now you've reached an especially hard one. Providence must have fixed this just for you. Look forward to what awaits you in Washington and trust in what's right, darling."

She rose and embraced the seated George, pressing his face into her bosom. She stroked back her husband's full hair and noticed how white strands had spread evenly through his pompadour.

Chapter Sixty-Eight

This time, he didn't offer a tip to the black bellboy. Instead, Chase dropped coins onto the bed as they entered his room at the Willard. He said thanks while looking out the window, and, when the door closed, he smiled to see they disappeared from the spread. He opened the sash to admit fresh air. Below, slave women laughed as they shook out dry bedlinen, folding sheets and pillowcases in pairs like girls skipping rope. Hair covered in bright bandanas, they wore uniforms of white linen, starched stiff. Deft hands turned the stark white bedding into neat packages, tucked into a laundry basket.

"OO! Hear wha' she say? Girl, betta not sass like that, gonna catch hell."

"I ain't takin' that man's shit no mo' Him runnin' his mouf at me."

"Gonna catch a beatin', chile..."

Chase closed the window and sat in the dark.

*   *   *

Consul Chase waited in the Secretary's anteroom, hat on his knee. Clerks scurried in and out of Marcy's office, bearing files. The appointment to have been at ten o'clock, his fob watch read twelve already. Another way to generate anxiety, he thought. Make 'em sweat.

"The Secretary will see you now." A clerk ushered Chase into the presence of William Marcy and another man.

"Sit down, Chase," Marcy directed. He shuffled papers on his desk. "My legal advisor, Biddle Cadwallader, here joins us down from Philadelphia." The soft-eyed Cadwallader gave no sign of recognition.

Marcy continued, "Seems you've caused us a bit of a scrape here at State."

"If I may explain..." Chase began.

"Let me lay out the problem, first." Marcy read from a scribbled list. "Confiscation of a private American vessel by a consul at a foreign port. Sale of cargo and distribution of proceeds to a crew. Sale of vessel and contribution of funds to church. Finally, conveying an American captain into the hands of a foreign government for trial and punishment on a charge, possibly a capital one. Have I missed any point, Chase?" The Secretary crumpled the list and dropped it into a waste basket.

"All actions within the purview of an American consul, sir." Chase answered.

"Narrowly interpreted," Cadwallader interjected. "Precedent does exist. There was the case in Santiago, Chile..."

"Damn, damn, damn." Marcy shook his white mane. "No tangents, please, Cadwallader. Explain to Mister Chase the ramifications of this pile of wreckage." He waved his hand at the waste basket. George Chase fingered his hat rim and picked a piece of lint off the felt. Marcy noted his distraction.

"You won't show such a flippant attitude once you've heard these repercussions, my boy. Tell him, Cadwallader."

The Philadelphian turned to look at Chase. As he spoke, elbows at rest on the chair's arms, pale finger tips patted together like hands in prayer.

"The *Tamerlane*'s owners have brought pressure on the Department for compensation for ship and cargo, but, worse still, their string of friends from captains association to ship owners to whale oil processors scream for your head. Then, there's the issue of turning over an American officer to a foreign government. If this were to become common, who would travel without the protection of consuls to shield them from arbitrary arrest? Finally, the most dire issue is this attempt to apply the anti-flogging laws to colored crewmen."

Cadwallader stopped for emphasis.

"I have no doubt you meant well, Mister Chase, but that's a can of worms we can't afford to open."

"I beg to differ. It's enlightened self-interest to solve this controversy, gentlemen," Chase argued. "As more young white men take factory jobs, they're being replaced on American ships by Negroes, Indians, Portuguese, and Hawaiians. Are the whaling fleet and merchant marine fleet to become a floating chain of plantations, white officers over colored sailors, working under the lash? The worms already crawl from your can."

Marcy exploded.

"What's he saying? Worms? Ships as plantations? Colored with rights? Hogwash...horsefeathers..." He floundered for the right expression. "Bullshit! I won't have it. You will back down, Chase, or I'll feed you to the lions. You will meet with Biddle Cadwallader and write apologies to all factions of the ship and whale industries, and then you will persuade that barbaric Hawaiian government to retract charges against poor Winslow. What's got into you? Rights for colored men on shipboard would split the country because it wouldn't stop on that slippery slope. Next, it would be colored testifying in court, and soon after they'd be demanding the vote. Why, even white women don't vote!" Marcy slammed his fist on the desk, scattering papers.

The Philadelphia lawyer leaned forward and whispered, "Please, Chase. No more discussion. When can we meet privately?"

"Tomorrow morning. Room 312 at the Willard."

*   *   *

From Pennsylvania Avenue, something drew Chase south, walking through long barrack office rows toward the river. The market hadn't changed in three years. Stalls still sold produce from Maryland and Virginia farms, and the horse auction continued to exchange animals.

Chase bought a rum punch from a tent saloon and wandered further into the labyrinth of passageways until he located the slave auction. Business was lively with staccato calls of the sale.

A parcel of kids stood in attention's glare on the platform. Barefoot, ragged clothes, nappy hair, and a patina of red dust on ebony skin. Like flotsam from a wreck, they had floated among a wash of black flesh, passing from owner to owner, until, lorn of all, no one recollected their origin. The children stood hand in hand and prayed to be sold together.

The auctioneer made his pitch. Willing workers, easy to train and manage, years of service. Customers vied for ownership until one bid topped the others. Sale employees were bustling the kids off stage, when one called out, pointing at Chase.

"Abolitionist. Stole a mulatto girl. Grab him." A mob blocked Chase's escape.

Chase stood silent until police escorted him away. In a station, he explained his business in Washington, hardly a typical Underground Railroad type, a United States consul. He denied any involvement in the abolition movement. A little man in suit and bowler hat interrogated him, jotting notes under the watchful stare of constables. After an hour, Cadwallader entered the room. Displaying State Department stationary, he shooed police from their presence.

"Been busy today, Mister Chase?" He took a chair nearby. "I assume this is all a misunderstanding." His elbows leaned on the table, fingertips patted under his chin.

"Quite, no association with any radicals. Nevertheless, just how much trouble can police make for me?" Chase sat, wearing the stovepipe hat.

"A lot, if Justice wants to. You're an item on front pages now, not just a controversial abstraction for editorials. Slaveholders dominate the Justice Department, busy chasing fugitives from the Mason-Dixon Line to Canada and indicting Underground Railroad agents. Your case could blow sky high," Cadwallader's hands sprung out, fingers splayed.

"Should I seek my own lawyer in that case?" Chase's voice flattened.

"Certainly not. That would be seen as distrustful of State. You're in our consular service. You are ours to protect."

Chase looked at the doe-eyed Philadelphian.

"And yours to dispose. May I return to my hotel room until this is resolved?"

"Already arranged, consul. Meanwhile, we have our appointment tomorrow at ten. We'll iron everything smooth then. Let me walk you out." Cadwallader took his elbow and chaperoned him to the street where the consul sped off.

Chase walked into the Willard's telegraph office, tucked into an annex off the lobby. A young man sat on a stool amid a web of wires, jotting notes as his machine clattered a message.

"Would you send one for me?" He handed over a note.

"Got it. Okay." His finger tapped out the dots and dashes.

G-O-V-E-R-N-O-R S-A-L-M-O-N C-H-A-S-E stop
C_O_L_U_M_B_U_S O-H-I-O stop
C-O-N-S-U-L N-E-E-D-S C-O-U-N-S-E-L stop
W-I-L-L-A-R-D H-O-T-E-L stop
C-O-U-S-I-N G-E-O-R-G-E stop

Returning to his room, he sat in darkness until a tap sounded on the door.

Chapter Sixty-Nine

Two men walked up the Capitol building's granite steps, each clutching leather cases against black wool coats. Congressional staff parted to step back in awe, recognizing one, guessing at the other. Around them, aides clustered, shoes scraping the marble treads.

Upon reaching the entrance plaza, the colossal size of the Capitol made one man stop. He turned and looked out over the city where rude buildings squatted between wide boulevards. In the distance, a white oversized chimney jutted above the landscape, the half-completed Washington monument. To its right, the White House sat amid a park of naked wintry trees.

The taller one waited, gloved hands clasped on his satchel handle. Throats cleared among the young lawyers who stamped against the December chill, eager to proceed, but the friend frowned them into patience. Satisfied, the man nodded and entered the door.

The delegation's feet echoed down marble stairs through a confusion of hallways until they arrived in the Capitol's basement. There, outside a set of brass doors, guards directed them to sit in a waiting area, warning all to speak in whispers. A huddle of lawyers argued in the far corner, among them sat a well-dressed black man.

George turned to his attorney, "My God, Salmon, is that the case from Missouri we've read about? Dred Scott, himself?" The black man listened intently to a lawyer.

"Poor fellow. The Court's dragged its feet, demanding yet another appearance today, December 15th. The justices know how much is at stake. One man's freedom would tear this country apart or worse," explained Salmon, removing his hat. He smoothed back wisps of hair from his bald crown, fringed by a tonsure.

"War between North and South?" George finished the thought.

"Whichever way the Supreme Court rules. The threat of war is imminent. Violence has already started."

George shook his head, "I can't believe just this May Senator Sumner was beaten half to death upstairs at his Senate desk, and by a Congressman, no less."

"Amid pitched battles in Kansas," added Salmon.

"Every lunatic in the country's been unchained," George declared.

"That's why the Court's delayed a decision on *Scott v. Sandford.* Buchanan's win of the Presidency last month gave them breathing room."

"Who's Dred Scott's lawyer?" George asked.

"Montgomery Blair, former mayor of St. Louis and a U.S. solicitor. Ambition drives him to represent Scott. It's so high profile."

"Not to be ungracious, cousin, but they say you have aspirations beyond being a governor," confided George. "I'm counting on that fervor. If this case earns you the Presidency in 1860, well, then, so be it."

As George removed his hat, his fingers combed back a high sweep of hair. Salmon noticed gray flecks spread from his temples to salt the pompadour.

Salmon shrugged, "I like a good fight, George, especially if I have an edge. The chief justice has a liberal history, freeing his own slaves. With four justices from northern states, he's the pivotal vote who could swing the court to you. They know, if colored crewmen have protection under law, the constitution may apply to all free men of color. It's incremental progress, but *Winslow v. Chase* could appease the abolitionist cause without making southern states bolt the Union. Your case may be an attractive alternative to Dred Scott's."

George felt his stomach churn. Was it the Willard's breakfast or stress?

Aching shoulders reminded him he'd been in Washington's climate for three months, and rheumatism returned

392

to attack his joints. His body longed for Lahaina's dry heat, the veranda of the plantation home, and Harriet.

The fleet would now be arrayed off Maui's shore in their winter lay-over. On whaling ships, crewmen slept in cramped fo'c's'le berths and hammocks. Whites, Blacks, Indians, Latins, Hawaiians. Slumbering citizens of the seas.

Brass doors swung open and a guard waved in George Chase, his attorney; Salmon Chase, Governor of Ohio, and their aides. Dimly lit by a chandelier, nine black-robed justices sat along their bench, facing spectators and attorneys. Voices and chair scrapes echoed against the boxy room's marble walls. The two Chases took chairs at the defendant's table, spreading papers over the oak surface. Opposite, other lawyers sat at the plaintiff's table, hired by the oil industry to represent Joshua Winslow's interests.

High at the center of the judge's bench, the ancient chief justice's robes swallowed his shrunken form. The chair back towered over the venerable head where disheveled gray hair fell long over his high collar.

"The Supreme Court of the United States is now in session," barked a clerk. "in the case of *Winslow v. Chase.* All rise for Chief Justice, the Honorable Roger B. Taney."

George Chase reached into the bottom of his case and pulled out a cloth package. He unwrapped the *Tamerlane's* cat-o'-nine-tails and stretched the whip's knotted cords across the table's length.

Chapter Seventy

The train lurched through the Maine forest, dense woods alternated with clear-cut land. Sparks flew along the rails only to be snuffed out by surrounding snow. New houses had sprung up outside Bangor and Machias, old town centers appearing prosperous. He looked forward to seeing Calais and his children again.

The ache in his shoulders had worsened in the damp cold, sitting up in a stream of poorly heated train carriage cars. George Chase had to pay to have his luggage carried, but on the last leg, he sprawled on the seat and distracted himself by recalling his brief appearance at the Supreme Court two days before. Had Salmon pleaded *Winslow v. Chase* well enough?

*   *   *

That day, oil industry lawyers stuck to the material substance of monetary compensation, avoiding the issue of rights. To them, the consul had exceeded his authority by confiscating the cargo of whale oil, bone, and baleen. The *Tamerlane* had been the rightful property of its owners, and any proceeds from its sale belonged to them.

Behind the plaintiff's table sat the owners, a gaggle of Quakers in similar plain costume from New Bedford whose sect required they remove hats only for God. Unfamiliar with their divine ordinance, Justice John Catron scowled when they refused to doff their black headgear and threatened to have them expelled for impertinence.

Winslow's attorneys pictured their client a victim of government run amuck. A ship's master must maintain order among an unruly crew of mixed races and languages in order for the fleet to bring vital whale oil back to the United States. Why, if every jacktar were equal to his captain, the fleet would collapse and lights all across America would flicker out and cast the nation into darkness. With that dramatic close, the attorney sat down.

Salmon P. Chase rose for the defense.

"If the court would indulge me, the argument for the defense rests not on the issue of compensation but on the issue of the protection of the law," he began.

"Who's speaking for Chase?" Justice Catron interrupted, holding up the court's printed schedule as he adjusted his glasses in a pretense of myopia. "Oh, it's Chase himself."

Chief Justice Roger Taney rapped on the bench. "John, you very well know who's speaking. Salmon Chase. The defendant is George Chase, the consul. Please proceed, governor."

"Governor?" Catron continued. "Is Salmon Chase a governor today or is he re-assuming his earlier incarnation as 'attorney-general to the fugitive slaves'?" Catron guffawed, glancing up the bench at his colleagues.

"Justice Catron, please," Justice John Mclean of Ohio pleaded. "This outburst ruins the court's decorum. Allow Governor Chase to advance his argument."

Catron retreated into his robes.

The governor held that Consul Chase acted within his authority and that precedent existed of other consuls acting in other cases to confiscate ships and cargo. The case had jumped through circuit courts at the behest of all parties, as important as it was, but Salmon Chase saved his greatest zeal for the issue of the anti-flogging laws protecting all crew members, not just the white sailors.

Was a ship more like a factory or like a plantation where sailors surrendered their rights upon signing on as crewmen?

"A reading of that statute reminds honorable justices that the law contains no mention applying the law only to whites, but that flogging is simply outlawed on American ships." Salmon held up the statute. "Allow me the honor. When President Fillmore signed the 1851 naval appropriations bill on 28 September 1850, the law read 'Provided, That flogging in the navy, and on board vessels of commerce, be, and the same time is hereby, abolished from and after the passage of this act.'

"Finally, gentlemen, I enter into evidence our only exhibit, the *Tamerlane*'s cat-o'-nine-tails." Salmon held up the short whip, cords dangling. "The blood and skin attached attests to Captain Winslow's disregard for the 1850 law that banned the punishment aboard American ships."

He stepped forward to offer the whip to the bailiff who carried it down along the bench for each justice to examine, until it reached Catron.

"Oh, my," he mocked. "These flecks of skin appear rather dark, not much different from my own overseer's bullwhip."

A scrape of a chair and Justice Ben Curtis jumped up and walked across the platform to Catron.

"You are a disgrace to the law. Stand up!"

Catron sneered, "Name the place and your choice of weapons."

"Gentlemen of the law, take your seats." Taney bleated above the fray. "My apologies, counselor. Please continue." He gestured to Salmon Chase.

"I close only with a humble entreaty to the Court. As you ponder to untie the Gordian knot of America's constitutional crisis, consider *Winslow v. Chase* an opportunity to soothe the wounds of sectional conflict. Find for my client, the Honorable George M. Chase, and you will have appeased the national discord between brothers."

Fine words, but the Supreme Court's justices would offer no decision, of course, that day. Salmon said the Court wouldn't announce a ruling until early 1857, so each man headed home for the Christmas holiday until telegrams called them back to Washington. George had only exchanged letters with his two teenage children over the past three years. How would they have changed in that time?

The carriage doors opened and George stepped onto the Calais station platform. A pretty young woman flew into his arms, and a young man extended his hand in greeting. Home again with Hattie and George Junior.

Chapter Seventy-One

Young George blew on the flames in the parlor stove while Hattie pumped water in the kitchen. Chase watched his big children take over the house; their home until he and Harriet had left in '53.

"Once we've got fires in all stoves, it'll be just like home again. Hattie, shake the dust off the bedspreads."

"Already done, father," she called from the kitchen. Her aunts had seen to her learning the domestic arts while she excelled in academic subjects at Calais Academy.

His son kneeled before the stove. Big hands, deep voice. The house already groaned with warmth from his rapid work. Soon, Hattie called the men into the dining room to a full meal. George poured himself a neat glass of rum.

"Make that two, father," his boy said, glancing up.

"When did you start to drink?" George Chase asked, hand poised above the glass.

"You needn't be so forward, Georgie," Hattie leaned across the table. Her eyes looked to her father for approval.

"How much do you drink, son?" George examined the boy.

"Uncle Dan and he fight about it," Hattie revealed.

"I can see my absence has brought a detrimental effect," said George, sitting down.

Young George put down his fork, stood, and walked over to the liquor cabinet. He poured a short drink and returned to his chair.

"You are going to let him get away with that?" Hattie chided her father.

George Chase stopped eating. "Hattie, I think you still have some clothes over with Uncle Dan and Aunt Minerva. Young George and I will clean up after the meal."

They finished eating in silence. Hattie excused herself and left the house.

"Father, how much trouble are you in? I try to read about the case, but I want to hear about it from you," young George opened the conversation.

"I have the best representation available in the United States. If the case goes as Salmon wants, it could resolve a major crisis in the country and keep the Union together."

"Who cares if the Union stays together?" his son asked. "I'm tired hearing about the South. If war's to happen, let it start now. We'll whip 'em in a week. All the papers say so." He laughed, pushing back his empty plate.

"I care if the Union stays together. You're nineteen, son. I'd hate to lose you and a whole generation of boys to fix a problem that old men should be able to resolve. Didn't the British just buy all the slaves in their empire and set them free? Emerson figures that could be done with the sale of public land," Chase reasoned.

"But that only says they had a right to own slaves in the first place. That's cheating! Why should they get paid for something they stole anyway, kidnapping them from Africa?" The boy tipped his chair back.

"Well, my case isn't about freeing slaves anyway. Dred Scott's about all that. All I want is protection for colored sailors. Our cousin, Salmon, thinks it's bigger than just sailors. He thinks…"

"Why can't I come to Hawaii with you, father? I hate it here in Calais, working with the mills and Uncle Dan. Let me come along when you go back. I'm so bored, and Hattie starts Mount Holyoke next fall. Hawaii could be my college."

"If…I go back. Not happy with your situation in Maine? You could always follow my trail later."

"I'll do anything to get to go, father," he pleaded.

George Chase smiled. "Pour that drink away and don't take another until you reach Hawaii."

*   *   *

398

A boy in cap and uniform knocked on the Chase's door and handed George a telegraph message:

"DECISION ANNOUNCED SOON stop
COME BACK stop
SALMON stop"

Chapter Seventy-Two

The huge Salmon P Chase fought through the crowd, following a court official, with George in the wake.

"Make way, defendant and attorney!" The guard plowed through ladies and gentlemen in the Capitol's basement.

"Why the crush? Can't be just our case, can it, Salmon?" George called over the din.

"Simultaneous rulings," Salmon called back. "We're to sit among spectators until our case is called."

The two shouldered into the small Supreme Court room next to the front rail. George recognized Montgomery Blair and his client, Dred Scott at the plaintiffs' table.

Salmon whispered into George's ear, "President Buchanan hinted at the Dred Scott decision in his inaugural two days ago, a flagrant breach of ethics. Damned Taney and Buchanan have been in cahoots all along."

All stood when the justices entered and a clerk called the room to order. "All rise for the United States Supreme Court in session this day, March 6th, 1857."

As soon as Chief Justice Roger B. Taney sat, he began to read in a shaky rasp. Chief Justice since President Jackson, the elderly judge bent over the pages, voice almost inaudible. George caught only a few faint words: "...more than a century...regarded as beings of an inferior order...unfit to associate with the white race...in social or political relations...no rights which the white man was bound to respect...the right of property in a slave is distinctly...affirmed in the Constitution" Spectators gasped. Dred Scott slumped as he realized he lost his suit for freedom.

George's and Salmon's eyes met and their faces fell. If the justices could find so severely against Dred Scott, what hope did George Chase have?

"Now the gauntlet is thrown at the feet of the North," Salmon confided.

The clerk polled the nine. Only Mclean from Ohio and Curtis from Massachusetts had voted to free Scott, a 7-2 decision. The bailiff clamped handcuffs on the black man, lifted him from his seat, and pulled him, shuffling over to his owner. The case disposed, the court moved to other business. Outside the court's doors, voices shouted in protest that the seated spectators wouldn't leave. Everyone wanted to hear the fate of the Chase decision.

"Next case, *Winslow v. Chase*," called the clerk, handing up a file to the 80-year-old Taney.

Knees buckling, George ached to sit down. His skin crawled with fear, but oil company lawyers on the other side grinned expectantly.

The rasping voice rose from a whisper to a mono-tone: "The inviolability of property being the keystone of the United States Constitution, the court finds that Consul Chase did exceed his authority under State Department guidelines in confiscation of said vessel at Lahaina, Maui Island in the Sandwich Islands, and in confiscation of said vessel's cargo, and the State Department is to compensate the owners for their property. As to the charge that Consul Chase committed unlawful arrest of Captain Joshua Winslow, the court finds that Chase…"

George blinked his eyes and flexed his shoulders to keep from blacking out. Salmon's hand squeezed his arm.

"…acted within his authority as an officer of the United States, correctly interpreting the statute against cruelty on board vessels registered to the United States, regardless the nationality or race of the punished crewman. While the protection of this statute extends to colored crew members, in no way is this ruling to be interpreted to extend them full citizenship."

George heard a soft "damn it" from Salmon.

"As to George M. Chase's position as consul for the State Department, said consul is to be reinstated with full authority and escorted back to his post. As to Captain Joshua

Winslow, the court requests Consul Chase intervene with Hawaiian authorities for the captain's release, pending local procedures, so he may be returned to the United States in Naval custody, stripped of his ship master papers, never to command another vessel in international waters."

*   *   *

The two talked at the foot of the gangway. George's luggage had already been loaded onto the Navy's steam frigate. Salmon swayed from foot to foot, distressed at the floating dock's motion.

"Never could stand open water. My roots are too deep in Midwest soil. I don't envy your voyage out," he said.

"If you seek a move from state house to White House, you'll get used to occasional ocean trips as commander-in-chief." George looked toward the noise of bustle on deck.

"Glad to leave all this?" Salmon gestured at the city.

"I'll never get used to the sting of newspaper attacks. Leave me to my little corner of the world, be it Maine or Hawaii." George nodded.

"Like headlines reading 'Chase: Sop Tossed To Forces For Abolition After Dred Scott Defeat'? Be happy, cousin, you have a victory to celebrate at home. The case might have stretched to offer free blacks citizenship, and that would have mollified the North, but Taney clearly closed off that door. Now there's hell to pay."

"It seems to me the glass is half-full. Taney's not long for this world, and other cases will arise. A new Chief Justice perhaps..."

The frigate's horn blew a long note. George took Salmon Chase's hand.

"I expect to read about your rise to high office in the Honolulu Friend and the San Francisco papers, but I can't say when we'll meet again."

Salmon looked into George's eyes.

"On the other hand, I need no paper to tell me what George Chase is doing. Wherever there's the heavy hand against the weak, wherever there's an underdog, wherever there's a struggle for fair treatment, I can expect to find the name of George Chase."